SHELBY FOOTE

Follow Me Down

Although he now makes his home in Memphis, Tennessee, Shelby Foote comes from a long line of Mississippians. He was born in Greenville, Mississippi, and attended school there until he entered the University of North Carolina. During World War II he served in the European theater as a captain of field artillery. He has written six novels: *Tournament, Follow Me Down, Love in a Dry Season, Shiloh, Jordan County,* and *September September.* He was awarded three Guggenheim fellowships during the course of writing his monumental three-volume history, *The Civil War: A Narrative.*

ALSO BY SHELBY FOOTE

Tournament

Love in a Dry Season

Shiloh

Jordan County

September September

The Civil War: A Narrative

VOLUME I.
  Fort Sumter to Perryville

VOLUME II.
  Fredericksburg to Meridian

VOLUME III.
  Red River to Appomattox

FOLLOW
ME
DOWN

FOLLOW ME DOWN

Shelby Foote

VINTAGE BOOKS

A DIVISION OF RANDOM HOUSE, INC.

NEW YORK

FIRST VINTAGE BOOKS EDITION, AUGUST 1993

Library of Congress Cataloging-in-Publication Data
Foote, Shelby.
Follow me down / by Shelby Foote.—1st Vintage Books ed.
p.   cm.
ISBN 0-679-73617-4 (pbk.)
I. Title.
PS3511.0348F6 1993
813´.54—dc20   92-50648
CIP

Manufactured in the United States of America

10 9 8 7 6 5 4 3 2 1

Enter a Doctor.

MALCOLM. *Comes the King forth I pray you?*

DOCTOR.

    I Sir: there are a crew of wretched Soules
    That stay his Cure: their malady convinces
    The great assay of Art. But at his touch,
    Such sanctity hath Heaven given his hand,
    They presently amend.   Exit.

MALCOLM.   *I thanke you Doctor.*

MACDUFF.

    What's the Disease he meanes?

MALCOLM.   *Tis call'd the Evill.*
           —MACBETH: IV, iii.

Contents

ONE

1. Circuit Clerk

Generally the first week in September brings the hottest weather of the year, and this was no exception. Overhead the fans turned slow, their paddle blades stirring the air up close to the ceiling but nowheres else; they made a steady squeaking sound, monotonous (—you heard it for maybe the first ten minutes and then didnt hear it at all, unless you remembered and tried) above the rows of town and country men and women in shirtsleeves and calico and above the smattering of Negroes in the balcony with their high boiled collars and watch chains. The country women, friends and relatives of Eustis and old man Lundy, held cardboard fans, Cardui and Tube Rose snuff, gone limp by now and mostly frayed at the edges, for this was the fourth day: it was over now, all but the verdict. Judge Holiman was instructing the jury—an old man with wattles like a turkey cock, ten years older than anyone else in the courtroom, talking around the stem of a bulldog pipe youd think he got at Yale in '96 except he never went to any college, let alone up East; he used a box of kitchen matches a day to keep it lighted, hawking and spitting into the chamber pot that sat beside and just to the rear of his chair in a litter of broken match stems matting thicker and thicker all morning, so that by afternoon if you came upon him from the rear, the soles of your shoes wouldnt touch the floor. I never saw him strike one without breaking it; the whole right half of the bench was scored and criss-crossed with scratches that probably had a phosphor gleam at night. He

3

always took aim at the pot but Ive yet to see one go in, even by accident, though he never missed it spitting. Once somebody asked him, "Why dont you retire?" and he looked back at them, glaring down from the height of all those bachelor years: "Retire?" he says, "I am retired. I'm clean away from this world and sitting in judgment on it"—hawk: spit. Frank James died in his arms out West, he told me once. He—(the Judge, not Jesse's brother, though maybe there is something in that too) he liked to watch their faces when he gave it to them. I think the man he hated most in all this world was Parker Nowell, who had robbed him of so many. But wait; I'll get to Eustis. As for Eustis:

He put you in mind of an owl from the minute you saw him—hornrim glasses, sharp little beak of a nose, a tuft of hair on each side of his forehead; you more or less expected him to turn his head on the top of his neck and blink his eyes and say whoo. Point of fact, he never said anything at all, except maybe a word or two behind his hand to Nowell while somebody was running him down on the stand, Beulah the dead girl's mother for instance; he sat removed, showing the jury how crazy he was or how crafty. Nobody blamed him, considering what hung in the balance was a seat in the old shocking chair and a trip to the big beyond, where every imp in hell had polished the tines of his pitchfork shiny bright and old Satan himself was planning to handle the damper. He played it just right: not too much, not too little: just right, the way Parker Nowell had coached him. You almost had to respect him, except then youd remember that girl and the three days she spent in the lake, food for the shrimps and gars, and he was the one who put her there and had planned it in advance.

I swore him in. I have sworn in a many a one in my time, being circuit clerk these past six years. Ive seen them all kinds, tall and short, jumpy and confident: "You swear the testimony you are about to give in this case will be the truth the whole truth and nothing but the truth so help you

God?" and some were sheepish, reaching out for the Book the way a man would reach out to touch a stove lid to see if it's hot, while others blustered, clapping their hands on it like they were glad of a chance to show how forthright and upstanding they were, glad of a chance to speak their piece in the sight of God and everybody—these were the most outlandish liars of all. But Eustis: he stood blinking and listening while I rattled it off, just his fingertips touching the leather, and when I finished he bent forward all of a sudden, like there was a spring in his backbone, and kissed it. I had an impulse to jerk back on the Bible, but almost before I knew what had happened, he was standing up straight and blinking at me again. Parker Nowell hadnt moved a muscle in his face; I could see him out of the tail of my eye and I wondered if he had coached him. Eustis stood there. "Do you?" I said, but he just stood there; "*Do* you?" I said again. "Do I what?" he says. So I had to run through it again, keeping a firm grip on the Book, ready to jerk it back in case he tried a repeat on the kissing act. "I do," he says, real solemn. His voice was low.

The first I heard of all this was a Friday morning late in June, more than two months before. The sheriff's office got a call from Miz Pitts, a fisherwoman who lives over on the island with her deaf-and-dumb son and makes a living, if you can call it that, running trotlines in the lake and the river and tending a vegetable patch; she was rowing to town, she says over the phone, and she came upon this body. So the sheriff and Willy Roebuck got in a car and drove out north of town where she had called from. That was middle-morning: they got back just at noon. I went with Roebuck up to the Greek's for dinner and he told me what they had seen. It wasnt the kind of thing youd normally want to hear over a meal, especially not at the Greek's.

Miz Pitts was waiting for them at the side of the road, Roebuck says, a big hard-looking woman with a mustache, in rubber boots and corduroys and a man's double-breasted coat with the buttons gone. She took them over the levee and down to the lake and there it was, up in the shallows already, nudging the bank. Pretty soon there was quite a crowd around her: Doc McVey the coroner, Light-Hearse Harry Barnes the undertaker, Russell Stevenson from the paper, and some others. They had to use a blanket to lift her out; she was coming apart, and Roebuck says it was an awful thing to see—three days in the water, bream and minnows holding old home week and sending word out to the channel cats to come get in on the fun, and two of those concrete revetment blocks had been wired to her throat to keep her down. Then Mr Barnes got to poking around and found this fine gold chain sunk in the meat of her ankle. A little golden heart was fastened to it, winking in the sunlight, and Miz Pitts took one look and knew. "It's Sue," she says, "She got what was coming to her, sure enough." Roebuck says it made his blood run cold, the way she said it.

Then she told the sheriff how she knew. Three weeks ago this couple came up to her on the wharf and asked to ride back to the island in her boat. It was getting on for dark, no time for fishing, and they didnt have any tackle anyhow; all they had was the clothes they stood in, a bundle tied up in a scarf the girl was holding, and a cigar box and a Bible the man had under one arm. He looked about fifty, she says, under-sized and a trifle humped in the back, the way a man gets from plowing. The girl was considerably younger. They were down from Missouri, man and wife, he told her, hunting a place to live cheap till cotton-picking. It seemed like a crazy thing to Miz Pitts, what with the season a good two months away, but the man talked like he knew what he was doing. Besides, it was government land: if she didnt row them over, somebody would. So she said all right, get in, and they got. But Roebuck says Miz Pitts said she knew from the start. They hadnt any more than pushed away from bank before she knew they werent married; it was like she could smell it—smell sin. Women can do that, some women.

6

Their name was Gowan, so they said: Luke and Sue, from up near Port St Joe. They slept in her cabin that night and next morning set to work clearing briers and creepers out of the tumble-down shack the voodoo man had lived and died in. Miz Pitts didnt tell much about their life there; that came later. She just said they were there two weeks, living as man and wife or a little more so, and then one morning they were gone, shack empty, no scrap of anything left to show they had been there at all except for the weeds being cleared and the crawdad houses raked out and the bateau missing. Next morning she found the bateau on the other side of the lake, and two days later, crossing to Bristol with a couple of gunny sacks of potatoes her boy had dug out of the garden, she came upon the body. At first she thought it was a channel cat, a big one dead of the bloat, but then she saw the feet, the nibbled toes. So then she knew, and she rowed on to bank and walked up the road a piece and called the sheriff. She said she had a notion from the start but it wasnt till Mr Barnes held up the ankle chain with the little golden heart that she knew for sure it was the girl and said the thing that made Roebuck's blood run cold.

He ate while he talked. The Greek leaned toward us, elbows on the counter, taking it in. I said, "What was that you said he called himself?" "Gowan," Roebuck says, "Luke Gowan. From up near Port St Joe." We matched for the meal. I lost. "One thing's sure," I said; I paid the check; "Whatever he calls himself, he's gone for good. This neck of the woods has seen its last of him." "Och, poor girl," the Greek says, and gave me my change.

That was Friday. That evening the story came out in the paper: GARROTED BODY FOUND IN LAKE, and went on to tell about a search being instigated. "About fifty years of age," it says, describing Gowan more or less the way Miz Pitts had done: "Light brown hair, five feet seven, khaki trousers, black felt hat" and so forth, with a few extra flourishes the Stevenson boy threw in for good measure. The description wouldnt have fit more than two-three hundred men walking around right here in Jordan County. Next morning the sheriff told me he had notified the authorities up at Port St Joe and had sent out a general alarm. "I'm not too hopeful," he said. I reckon not, I thought to myself.

That was Saturday. Next morning the wife and I went up to Indemnity for Sunday dinner with her folks. We got back late that night, and the following morning when I came to the courthouse (this was Monday) Roebuck was waiting with a big grin on his face. "Come on, Ben," he says, "Lets take a stroll out back." The grin was too broad for it to be something ordinary; I think I knew already, but I went along with the joke. "Well now," I said, grinning too, "It was time you boys were bringing in another still. What kind of a bead has this batch got?" But he was too pleased with himself to hold back; he even stopped grinning. "It's the fellow that put the girl in the lake," he says, "We caught him yesterday. He's back there now, in a cell. We got a signed confession and everything."

It was true, every word of it—except he leaned pretty hard on the We. Miz Pitts' boy, the dummy, came over from the island Sunday morning and handed the sheriff a note telling who the man was because he had seen it on the flyleaf of the Bible: Luther Eustis, Solitaire Plantation: and the sheriff called Roebuck and they rode down to Lake Jordan and picked him up. Just like that. He had gone back to his wife and daughters and was all settled down to live out a peaceful life, thinking those concrete blocks would keep her down forever. "God's will be done," he says when they put the cuffs on him. He was so surprised he admitted everything, right off the reel, and signed a statement telling how he did it. The two of them, he and the girl, had gone down for a twilight bath, and he wrapped a low-hanging willow around her throat and held her under till the bubbles stopped. Ach, poor girl, I thought, like the Greek three days ago.

There was a little knot of people in front of the jail, hoping to catch a glimpse of him; Captain Billy Lillard was among them, phony medals tinkling on his chest. Just as we reached the stoop the door came open. It was Stevenson, from the paper; he had been in for an interview, but I could see from the look on his face he hadnt done much good. Roscoe was seeing him out. He started to close the door, but when he saw Roebuck and me he stood aside and waved us in. Roscoe is the turnkey, a talkative fellow. All the time he was taking us back to the cell block he was talking. "Aint said a word, wont eat," Roscoe says, clanking his keyring ahead of us, up the stairs, shaking his head from side to side and mumbling: "Maybe it's one of them hunger strikes like they have in the papers every now and then. But I dont know," he says, "It's hard to tell with one of these here sex fiends." "If theres anything you want to know, just ask me," Roebuck says, "I'm a sort of a sex fiend myself, on occasion."

We passed the cell where old man Lundy was standing, head cocked sideways, looking between his fists clenched loose on the bars. He didnt say anything, just watched us on the chance we'd brought a letter from the governor, pardoning him before he'd even come to trial. I didnt pay him any mind, for by then we could see in the cell where Eustis was. He sat on the cot with his feet planted flat on the floor, hunched over with his jaw on the heels of his hands, like the last scene in a movie called *Crime Doesnt Pay*. We stood and looked at him for maybe a full two minutes. He must have known we were there, but he never even so much as raised his eyes—I guess he was like Judge Holiman says, clean away from this world. Seeing him like that, through the bars, youd never have thought he could entice a girl into a soda shop, much less off on a wild abandoned island to live in a voodoo shack. I sort of felt shamed of myself, to be standing there like that and looking all that misery in the face.

Then we turned and came back down the cell block, past old man Lundy face-down on his cot. He lifted his head and watched us going by. Just as we reached the door again, there came a rapping, a polite but sort of determined sound, like whoever was making it had every right and knew it, and when Roscoe unbarred the door and swung it back, there was Parker Nowell in his linen suit, looking cool and neat as always; he might have stepped out of a bandbox. Oh-Oh, I thought. A country woman was with him, tall and stringy, eyes sunk back in her head like a person after a long bout with the fever.

"Luther Eustis," Nowell says, standing in the sunlight, crisp and cool. The woman held her hands across her stomach, clasping her wrists the way they do. Nowell says, "This is Mrs Eustis, Mr Jeffcoat. We have come to see her husband, if you please." He said it the way he says everything: pleasant yet not friendly either, so that you wanted to take exception without being able to say just why. Roscoe stood there goggle-eyed, but when Roebuck and I stepped aside Nowell and the woman came in. She looked scared and nervous, the way those people always look when they get around the Law.

Roebuck and I went out. "Well now," he says, "Well now. That sort of changes things, dont it?" Because Nowell never took a case unless it was hopeless, and it was a long way from hopeless once he had hold of the reins. "Wait till the sheriff hears about this," Roebuck says, "Just wait till he hears about this, after all the pride he took in that arrest." "I dont know," I said, "Maybe not. Maybe this is one time Parker Nowell bit off more than he can chew."

It certainly looked that way, and in the two months before the trial, it looked more-so all the time. Stevenson ran a series in the paper, quoting the confession about how Eustis said he watched the bubbles, then drug her across the island and pitched her in the river, all trussed with wire and revetment blocks, and went home to his wife as if nothing had happened. Gradually some of the background came out: how he first saw her at an Easter revival and had been running after her ever since, forgetting his wife and children, forgetting farming, until finally he persuaded her to take off for the island with him, and then had a change of heart or something ("I wanted to go back to my home and family," he says in the confession) and drowned her.

All through what was left of the summer, while he sat in the cell getting paler and paler like something damp hid under a log, people talked about it. They said the verdict was foregone. "I hope they put *me* on the jury," some of them said. Then it was the end of August; court convened. When old man Lundy got the chair for shooting the night marshal down in Glenmora, the first Jordan County white man to draw the death penalty in more than forty years, everybody says "Oh-Oh. Oh-Oh," they said, "It's going to be a double-header."

We had a time empaneling a jury: people who could honestly say they hadnt formed an opinion were few and far between. Tolliver, the district attorney, was short on experience—two years out of law school, not counting the war—but he knew enough to be opposed to anybody the other side would accept. Nowell had his notebook with him, the loose-leaf kind with a limp leather cover. In it he had listed alphabetically every man who had served on a jury in circuit court since he first began reading law in his father's office thirty years ago; under each name he had a record of the cases the man had sat on, what the verdict was, and (whenever possible, which was usually) what his vote had been on the first ballot. They say that in any given case Nowell can take that notebook and go up one side of Marshall Avenue and pick a jury that will convict, then down the other side and pick one that will acquit. Then, they say, he can turn around and do the same thing over again, vice versa.

He is the best example I ever saw of a man gone sour. Ten years ago he was on the way toward everything all this country's big men ever had, a leader already in the legislature and not far from the governorship, perhaps. After that, it was anybody's guess. Then his wife, the best-looking woman in the Delta, hightailed it off with another man and left him stranded.

He sent a note resigning from the legislature, stopped going down to his office, and when anyone called wasnt home. Then he left town. Someone said they saw him in New Orleans, bending his elbow in one of those French Quarter bars. After a while he gave it up; his stomach wasnt built for that. He came back home. Youd pass the house at night—the big old house on Lamar Street that his grandfather built, Judge Nowell: the social center of Bristol in its day—and the curtains would be drawn and all youd hear would be highbrow music booming out of the thousand dollar phonograph he ordered from New York City, New York.

Then he began to take a case every now and again, all of them criminal. "He's keeping his hand in," we said, "He's about to come back." The first was a gambler: shot a man across the dice table because the man wouldnt recognize a pass, a cold-blooded killing if ever there was one, and Nowell got him off on self-defense because the dead man had been cleaning his nails at the time with one of those little knives that you wear on the end of your watch chain. By the time Nowell got through hocuspocusing the jury, that knife was two feet long, with a saw-tooth blade. His next was more-less like the first. A nigger drew a ten-year sentence for running amuck with a razor at one of these sanctifyings down by the river (—cut the head slap off one woman, carved three others so their own mothers wouldnt know them when they came from under the bandages) because by the time Nowell wound up his closing argument, the jury was blaming the Holy Ghost for getting the nigger wrought up. Manslaughter, they called it, and managed to keep a straight face.

After four or five like that, people began to realize what he was doing. It wasnt for money (which they could have understood and even sympathized with); he already had money, and theres no money in criminal law anyhow, compared to what he could have been making out of civil cases he wouldnt even touch. What it was, he was sour on the world—the woman had done it, leaving him for another man the way she did, putting his manhood in question—and he was getting back at the world by keeping the outlaws in circulation. Everybody knew what he was doing: it was the talk of Bristol. But it was one thing to condemn him when court had adjourned and you looked back on what he had done, and it was another different thing entirely when you were sitting on the jury with a man's life in your hands and Nowell was walking up and down in front of the rail in that crisp white linen suit, stopping every now and then and leaning forward to speak in a voice that was barely above a whisper, the courtroom so quiet you could hear your neighbor holding his breath and every time Judge Holiman raked one of those matches across the bench it was like the crack of doom, Nowell throwing law at you with one hand and logic with the other, until finally you got to thinking you were all that was left in this big wide ugly world to save a poor victim of malice and circumstance from being lynched by the State of Mississippi.

This time, though, he was working a different tack. Every juror he didnt reject offhand had the same question put to him: How did he feel about insanity and legal responsibility? So that was how he was going to build his case. But when the news got round, people said "What of it? They shoot mad dogs, dont they?" Insanity is something we never put much stock in, not when it comes to making it an excuse for doing all the things a sane man would do if he was just crazy enough: such as getting rid of a girl because his fancy had played out and he wanted to go home to the wife he never should have run off from in the first place, coming into the house, fully dressed and in his right mind again, saying "Here I am with my sins like driven snow. Let all be forgiven. I just went crazy for a while," or words to that effect. Nowell pled him not guilty.

But Tolliver was ready. His first witness was Dr E. P. Goodnight, from the crazy-house in Jackson. I swore him in, a stumpy little fellow getting bald on top and wearing steel-rim glasses. Everybody leaned forward to get a good look at a man who of his own accord spent a lifetime tending loonies. He sat down, folded his hands in his lap, playing This-is-the-Church This-is-the-Steeple all the time he was on the stand—except when Nowell had him going: that came later. After identifying himself and Eustis he testified that he had interviewed the accused in his cell the day before, had given him the tests they give with hammer taps and ink blots. "And your opinion, doctor?" Tolliver says. The room got quiet. The doctor made a little hocking sound to clear his throat: "In my opinion"—he made the sound again, "In my opinion, this man is as sane as you or I or anyone in this court room." Ahhh, we thought; it was almost a sigh; you could almost hear us thinking. "Your witness," Tolliver says.

Nowell was very respectful toward the doctor—not at all sarcastic about it, either—asking him again what schools he had been to, what degrees he held, and so forth. They made quite a list, impressive. "So, doctor, if any man is competent to judge of a fellow being's sanity, that man is you," Nowell says, "Isnt it?" The doctor nodded. "Well, Dr Goodnight," Nowell says, "Suppose"—he paused as if to get it straight in his mind, "Suppose a man spent half his waking hours reading the Bible, made a habit of stopping his plow in midfurrow to read the Bible under a broiling sun, and went around preaching the end of the world was at hand—" "That man would be a fanatic." "Thank you," Nowell says, and began again: "Suppose this man tried to give away all his worldly goods in hopes of purifying his soul, and—" "A fanatic is an overzealous, not a crazy person." "Thank you," Nowell says, and went on with it as if the doctor hadnt spoken. He told about this supposed man having an aunt already in the loony bin in Jackson and an idiot daughter at home, about how he tried to slit his throat with a razor one night because he was obsessed with sin—and a whole lot more. By the time he got through, he had described what practically amounted to a raving maniac. "What would you say as to the sanity of such a man?" Nowell says, winding up. The doctor looked at him over the rims of his glasses: "Assuming all those things, I would say such a man was insane, but—" "Thank you, doctor," Nowell says, and walked away.

Tolliver was already on his feet. "Dr Goodnight," he says, "I'll ask you again—and never mind the supposed lunatic Mr Nowell has conjured up for the entertainment of the court: That man right there," he says, pointing at Eustis, "Do you judge him sane or insane?" Everyone looked at Eustis: flick: then back at the doctor. "When I examined him he was sane," the doctor says. Tolliver was about to press him, but then thought better of it. "Thank you, doctor," he says. "No further questions," Nowell says, busy with some papers. Dr Goodnight came down off the stand.

Next up was Beulah's mother. Her name was Joyner: plump, flashy-looking, with a glint to her hair like brass; you wouldnt have thought she was old enough to have a girl eighteen. Judge Holiman was giving her the eye around his pipe, and the jury commenced to cross and uncross their legs and clear their throats. Tolliver got her to tell what a home-body her daughter had been—"A sweet fine girl," she says— until Eustis lured her off. She would have stopped it before it got started, she said, but he had the girl bewitched before she knew what was happening. When Tolliver held up the ankle chain for her to identify, she couldnt speak for crying into her handkerchief, and when she finally got hold of her-self and took the handkerchief down, it was full of red and her face looked considerably paler—older, too. "That was a present from her fi-ance," she says, "From the boy she was going to marry till *he* came along," and she nodded toward Eustis, who sat there with his head down, not paying her any more mind than he'd paid the Whitfield doctor. By the time Tolliver finished leading her through a picture of her happy home, the way it was before this fifty-year-old jelly-bean stepped in and wrecked it, the women in the courtroom were wagging their heads and the men had their mouths pulled down in hard straight lines. You could almost hear the hum of the electric chair, see the little blue crackle of fire, the spiral of smoke that corkscrews up when everything is over. "Thank you, Mrs Joyner," Tolliver says, and his voice was soft and gentle.

But here came Nowell, already out of his chair: stood with his arms crossed, looking at her with a mean kind of sneer on his face, like an old-time actor. It was enough to make you think he was some sort of a fiend, because here was this poor woman, weeping over a daughter killed and flung in the lake by a man that was sitting not fifteen feet away, and Nowell came at her with a sneer already fixed on his face. She cringed. "This man you say your daughter was going to marry," he says, "Can you tell us his name?"—"Objection," Tolliver says. He didnt know what was coming but he knew it wouldnt be good. "Overruled," Judge Holiman says. He wanted to hear about it.—"Sergeant George Scalco," she says, talking into the handkerchief. "Of the U.S. Army? Formerly of Detroit, Michigan?" "Yes sir," she says, her voice getting smaller still. Nowell put out his hand and wagged a finger close to her face, stabbing in time with the words: "Is that the same George Scalco you haled into court down in Issawamba County a year and a half ago on a bastardy charge but couldnt make it stick because three other men, likewise U.S. Army, testified that they also had had relations with your daughter and, what was more, could call on you to sustain their testimony because in each case you had been a witness to your daughter's shame?" First everything got still as still; you could have heard an ant crawl. Then a sigh went up, then a babble of voices. "Order! Order!" the Judge was shouting, banging the gavel while the courtroom buzzed and hummed and ohd and ahd.

That was only the beginning. Nowell kept at her for better than half an hour, making her corroborate things he told the court (Isnt it true you did this? Isnt it true she did that? Isnt it true you both did the other?) and making her tell things even he hadnt known about, until finally he had wrangled the whole ugly business out of her, how she'd had the girl in juke joints before she was thirteen, using her as a stalking horse for men, how she'd coached and primped her, shaped her into just what she wanted. His language got stronger and stronger; his finger wagged faster and faster—Tolliver meanwhile bouncing up and down so fast youd think he had a spring in the seat of his pants, hollering "Objection! Objection!" every two minutes, and Judge Holiman rapping the gavel and booming "Overruled!" right back at him—until it got to the point where the Judge had to warn Nowell that Mrs Joyner was not the one on trial. "I cant help thinking she ought to be," Nowell says, "Because she's the one who killed that girl, as sure as if she'd put her in the lake." "Objection!" Tolliver hollers, springing up. "Sustained," Judge Holiman says at last.

Nowell stood there, facing the jury with his arms akimbo, then shrugged and took his seat as if to say he was glad to be done with her. Tolliver came back and had her run through it again, about what a happy home they had before Eustis came along. It didnt carry much conviction now, though. "Thank you, Mrs Joyner," Tolliver says, respectful. "No further questions," Nowell says, as if to say he wouldnt touch her again with a ten-foot pole. He had got what he wanted from this one too, the same as he had from the doctor. By now there was considerable doubt in most people's minds, including my own, as to just who had lured who off onto that island in the first place.

So much for Wednesday. Thursday was much the same, so far as breaking down witnesses was concerned, except for Miz Pitts' boy, the dummy. He was about seventeen, bigheaded, with a bushy thatch of hair and small round ears. This was the first time a deaf-and-dumb person ever took the stand in these parts. Tolliver had a clip board and a batch of paper handy. I wrote at the top of the first sheet: *Do you solemnly* and so forth, and the dummy wrote beneath it, in the handsomest script I ever saw: *I do*. I held it up for the

Judge to see and he nodded his head: "Proceed." So Tolliver took the board and wrote questions and Dummy wrote the answers in that smooth-flowing script you only see in copy books and old-time documents, telling how Beulah and Eustis lived together on the island, how she cooked and washed for Eustis, looking after him, doing everything she could to make him happy, and how she told him once (Dummy, I mean) that something was going to happen to her, she knew, and sure enough two days later they were gone, the voodoo shack standing empty, no sign to show theyd been there, and three days after that his mother told him she'd found Beulah (Sue, he called her) floating in the lake, done up with baling wire and concrete blocks, and he knew right then and there that Eustis had done it.

When he reached the part about the girl predicting that something was going to happen to her, Nowell objected on grounds that lip-reading was inadmissible. But the Judge tested Dummy—one of the few times I ever saw him without that bulldog pipe swooping out of his face—and ruled the evidence was admissible. Nowell let it pass, much as to say it wasnt important anyhow, and on cross-examination he only asked two questions. The first was: *Were you in love with that girl?* Dummy took one look at the board and turned red to the rims of his ears, then took the pencil and wrote: *I never told her so.* "I see," Nowell says, writing some more while he spoke, "We'll let that pass. Now how about this?" and passed him the board with the second question on it: *More than anything, you want to see the man charged with her death get punished—dont you?* And Dummy snatched the pencil and wrote, not in script now but in printed capitals: YES, with a line slashed under it. "Thats all," Nowell says, handing the board across the jury rail.

Tolliver's final witnesses were Lonzo Mercer, a part-time window dresser who took a photo of Beulah laid out on the blanket by the lake, Roebuck, Doc McVey, and Miz Pitts. Nowell didnt bother with Lonzo or Roebuck, but when

McVey got through (his testimony had been pretty wild; he claimed the girl had been strangled with superhuman strength, for instance) Nowell asked him if he had been drinking on the day the body was found. A ripple of laughter went across the courtroom and the Judge hit a couple of halfhearted licks with the gavel, sort of smiling himself, because anybody who ever saw Doc on one of his rips, which all of us had, knew what a sight he was. McVey bristled up (he was wearing his teeth at the time) and said he hadnt touched a drop in over six months. Nowell let his eyebrows rise in pure amazement. "Are you referring to whiskey, Sir?" he says, eyebrows still jerked up. That started them laughing again. "I am," Doc says when it quieted down at last. So then Nowell asked him how often he'd been off for the Keeley cure, but withdrew the question before Tolliver was half out of his chair to object. "I just thought it might be of general sociological interest," he says.

Miz Pitts wore a dress for the trial, something nobody remembered her doing before; it made her mustache seem more noticeable. Tolliver had called her, but by the time she got through he was wishing he had left her on the island. She told about Beulah and Eustis and their life (calling her "Sue—I mean Beulah") but it was a different picture from the one her son had painted. To hear her tell it, Eustis was the one who did the cooking, the washing, the looking-after, while Sue—"I mean Beulah"—had Dummy off to one side, making sheep eyes at him till he didnt know coming from going. Then Tolliver shifted his ground: began treating her like a hostile witness, taking a leaf from Nowell's book to do it. He made her admit she'd cooked a sweet potato pie and brought it to the jail a week ago. "In fact youre fond of him, arent you?" Tolliver says. "I am," she says, and before he could stop her she went on: "I think he's a good man that got pulled into something by a bad girl because he's a little crazy."

Tolliver went off like a rocket, having her say a thing like that. Then he quieted down and had her words struck from

19

the record; the Judge instructed the jury to forget them. He was about to go on questioning her but he took one look at her sitting there with her eyes ablaze, all set to launch off another tirade, and changed his mind. "Your witness," he says to Nowell. But Nowell passed her up: says, "Miz Pitts has already told us what we wanted to hear," and added in an undertone: "Even if it has been expunged and forgotten." Judge Holiman gave him a hard look, like he was considering throwing the gavel at him, or maybe the bulldog pipe or the chamber pot. "I'm warning you, Mr Nowell," he says, pointing the pipe at him stem first, and Nowell bowed to the bench for apology.

That was Thursday. Nowell began introducing witnesses Friday morning. They were from down in the lower part of the county, the Lake Jordan district: Eustis' wife and oldest daughter, a jackleg preacher named Jimson, and half a dozen others who had known him most of his life. One by one they testified he had done the things Nowell told about at the beginning of the trial, back when he was supposing to Dr Goodnight. Then Saturday morning Eustis took the stand. That came as a surprise. "What can he gain by that?" people wanted to know, until somebody also asked: "What can he lose?" When all the testimony was in, Nowell had his cross-examination of the psychiatrist read back by the court stenographer. "Assuming all those things," Dr Goodnight had wound up, "I would say such a man was insane." Nowell closed his case on that.

In his closing argument Tolliver told the jury not to let their minds get fogged with all the irrelevants the defense had stirred up to screen the central fact that a girl had been murdered—"Most foully murdered," Tolliver says, mouthing it—and for no reason except that Eustis, grown tired of her, had murder in his heart. He reminded them of the confession Eustis had made—"Made and signed of his own free will and accord," Tolliver says, "—back in June when the blood still smoked on his hands, when he was thinking of saving his soul instead of his neck." He tore it to tatters, like an actor on the stage. And you could see it was taking effect. The jurors began to shift on their hams and look kind of hangdog about it—as if, being members of the same human race, they had a share in the crime. He had them, right then and there, if he'd been willing to stop. But no: he had to go on with it (he was young and fond of the sound of his voice; his main fear was he might leave something unsaid) until they began to come out of their uneasiness and finally just sat watching him with hard unblinking eyes, the words like so much wind and himself an actor.

Nowell didnt give any such performance. He leaned on the jury rail and talked in a voice so low that those in the back of the room bent forward, cupping their ears, and the Stevenson boy from the paper, who was right down front with a note pad on his knee, had to write fast and listen close to catch a sentence every now and again. He was through before we knew he had started good, and everybody sat back feeling cheated; theyd expected a raree show. Nowell's point was that the facts were in and there was no use mouthing at them, which was a kind of backhand lick at Tolliver and Tolliver knew it.

Then Judge Holiman instructed the jury, fans going cree, cree, cree out of the overhead dimness and Eustis just sitting there watching his hands in his lap, the same as he had done for the past four days, except what time he was on the stand and Tolliver tried to mix him up but couldnt. The jury rose, filing out, and Roscoe and Roebuck brought in the prisoners for sentencing. By the time the last juror went through the door, old man Lundy was standing in front of the bench, craning his plucked chicken's neck to look up at the Judge and working his jaw that was all caved in where he'd broken his lower plate.

2. Reporter

This began like any other morning, ad men and others hurrying round while the teletype clattered and bucked and whirred and the linotypes made a tinkling in the background, myself getting wire copy untangled, Lonzo clipping features from the canned release sheet, Benny giving his machine old two-fingered hell about how the Cats made baseball history in Sportsman Park last night, and Gladys steamed up because of a printer's error in yesterday's paper.

"I certainly marked it on the proof," she said. She was dressed for a garden club luncheon, with one of those hats. "I marked it plain as plain, for I just knew theyd miss it; something told me. I drew a little ring around the *i* and a line going out to the *a* in the margin, the way you showed me."

"On the galley proof?"

"As plain as plain."

"Did you check it on the rebound?"

"It didnt come back. There was just that one error was all."

A collar of white lice. "Then thats why," I said. "Anyhow, you should have caught it on the page proof."

Lonzo hid a smile behind the paste pot.

"It was smudged," she said.

"You could have called for a re-do."

"Why—you know perfectly well how they yowl every time I ask them to do a little something extra. Ye gods." She sighed and made a flipper gesture with one hand. "Anyhow it's done. Theyve laughed at me over every supper table in

Bristol, and now theyre laughing at me in every store down-town."

"Dont fret, Gladys," Lonzo said, solicitous. "Sometimes it's a good thing to bring a smile to people's faces. Besides, the comic muse is the greatest of them all, according to Meredith."

"Keep your two cents to yourself!" she said, flaring up. He should have known. "Spare me your cracker barrel philosophy, Mister Mercer, and your quotes out of Meredith, too."

He retired behind the paste pot, licking his wounds.

After the reception, the bride and groom departed by rail for a honeymoon in New Orleans. The bride wore a tailored Palm Beach suit, suntan and beige with matching accessories, and an eyelet blouse with a collar of white lice. "It's just my luck," Gladys said. "As often as theyve dropped the ends of my stories in the hellbox, youd think they could do it just once when it was needed."

There she went with that jargon. We never even knew it was called a hellbox till that book of O'Hara stories came out a couple of years ago. Thats Gladys for you. Or any woman, for that matter.

"I can see them now," Benny said, rolling a new sheet into his machine. "Ive got a mental picture of them in the Pullman berth, fighting the lice while they consummate their union."

"And you too, Benny Peets!" She flared up again. "Who pulled your chain?"

That was when the phone rang.

I figured it would be one of her friends, calling to commiser-ate with her over the way the boys in back had bitched her page again. She said in her bright Society voice: *"Clarion:* Miss Triplett speaking." Then she frowned, said "Just a minute" in her normal voice, and shoved the phone toward me. "For you, Russell," she said. "It's Dr McVey."

Doc is the coroner; he used to be a dentist, before the whiskey got him. I often wonder which is hardest to under-stand him, when his teeth are in his pocket or in his mouth.

"Say, Steve."

They were in his pocket now.

"Yair, Doc."

"Lonzo there?"

"Right here by my warm side."

"Then bring him out here with his kodak. We found a woman drownded in the lake. Foul play victim, looks like."

"Hey! Where are you?"

"Bachelor Bend, three miles above town. You know the old logging road, runs over the levee?"

"Check. Say, Doc."

"Yair?"

"Thanks."

He said "Humph," and hung up.

"Lonzo," I said. He looked up from pasting one of the canned features onto a sheet of copy paper, doing it neat. "Get your box. McVey's got something for us."

"Dear God," he said. "Dear God. Does it mean what I think?"

He was a window dresser by trade, though only as a sort of part-time job. For nearly a year now he had been working at the desk two days a week as Feature Editor because the chief decided the paper lacked refinement. If refinement was what he wanted, he certainly hired the right boy.

Lonzo was nearing fifty but didnt look within fifteen years of it until you really examined him up close. Then you saw his face was a network of wrinkles. He affected baggy tweeds and a horse-blanket coat, thick-soled shoes and a Windsor knot between wide-spread collar points. At first sight a stranger might think himself confronted by a somewhat shriveled reincarnation of a college boy just roused from a thirty-year trance.

Besides handling most of the feature stories, he wrote a column called *Side Lights (On the Arts)*, a chatty sort of rigmarole—it wasnt bad, in its way—with a poem a week, one for the first robin, one for the last red leaf, and so forth, along with a bunch of drawn-out chitchat on local personalities and occasional excursions into Jordan County's charming past. Whenever he put pen to paper, lace tumbled over his wrist. His favorite color was green, which Havelock Ellis says is characteristic, and he had a prissy way of walking, short steps with the knees held close together like a woman in fear of assault. There is a musical term that describes him perfectly, if you pronounce it the way it looks, disregard its true meaning, and take it to mean what it sounds like: homophony.

On the way out to Bachelor Bend, bouncing and jiggling over the corduroy road, Lonzo held the camera on his knees. He had taken up photography as a hobby, mainly for nature studies, but now every time there was a cutting scrape down in Lick Skillet, Doc McVey would call for him to come take some snaps for the record. If he had known it was going to be like this, he said, he never would have offered his services in the first place. Sometimes for three nights afterwards, he couldnt sleep for seeing it in his dreams.

"It's bad enough when I shoot it," he said. "But it's even worse in the darkroom afterwards, smelling the hypo, when it comes out on the print right under my eyes. The blood is always black and shows up first."

"Why dont you tell McVey and give it up?"

"Well—it's just like finding seven-fifty every time. Besides, I wouldnt hurt his feelings for the world. He's been so nice."

That was Lonzo's way. Whenever he wanted to do a thing, he always found a reason, though generally he called it an obligation; Obligation was one of his favorite words. Anyhow, I had a life-size picture of McVey feeling hurt or being nice in the first place. Then I remembered: Lonzo had persuaded Doc to come into the AA, and now he didnt want to alienate him for fear he'd drop out, come tumbling off the wagon. Alcoholics Unanimous, somebody called them.

Mainly, though, the reason was the money, the seven-fifty. Lonzo was a close one with a dollar, saving up for those twice-a-year trips to New Orleans. He had a connection with one of those special cat-houses where he could rent himself a couple of boys and chase them around the room. That kind of fun comes high, or so Ive heard.

Short of the levee we caught up with Roebuck walking along the side of the road—a typical chief deputy: brick red in the face, khaki shirt, a wide sand-colored hat, and walks with a lean to the left to balance the weight of the pistol. He got in the back seat, fanning himself with the hat.

"This sure aint the weather for walking," he said. He had been out to the highway to phone for Harry Barnes, the undertaker. "I cant understand why he wasnt here before us. He must be getting old."

That was why they called him Light-Hearse Harry. He could smell a mishap fifty miles away and sometimes farther. Usually he was the first man on the scene, standing there figuring costs when the others arrived.

We hit the rise and I shifted into second. The engine began to tremble and whine and I dropped into first. Soon as we topped the levee I could see them. The road ran down, curved left, then back to the right, and disappeared into the lake like a warped plank tilted under the edge of a rug—a dirty rug, for the river was on the boom and flecked with foam. I stopped the car.

A little more than halfway down the slope, between the first curve and the water, I saw what I thought at first were three men standing in a group about twenty yards from a sort of bundle on the ground, something huddled under an army blanket. I knew what that would be and I wondered how long she'd been down before they found her.

They were maybe two hundred yards away but I recognized the sheriff and Doc McVey. When they looked up, watching us come toward them, I saw that the third was not a man at all, in spite of the mustache. It was Miz Pitts, a fisherwoman from over on the island, dressed in boots and trousers, a double-breasted coat and frayed straw hat.

"Dear God," Lonzo said, trotting alongside, hugging his camera. "It's just like always."

First I went to the sheriff.

"Ask her," he said. "She found her."

Miz Pitts said, "It was like I told the sheriff. I was rowing across and I saw her in the water, floating belly up with her head drug back by the weights, in close to bank. Then I walked out to the road and phoned the law."

"What time was that?"

"Was what?"

"When you found her."

"About an hour ago. Maybe less."

That would have made it nine oclock. I put down 8:45 to make it sound more accurate. These river people have no conception of time.

"And what did you think, Miz Pitts?"

I was looking for human interest, something seen from an angle. Thats what readers want to know: What does a person think when he comes upon a dead woman floating in the lake?

"Think?" she said. She stared at me for a moment. Her eyes were yellow, like a goat's, and hard as agates. "I didnt think nothing except here was somebody drowned."

While I was scrawling what should have been her answer, we heard a roaring on the opposite side of the levee. I looked up and saw the ambulance top the rise, slewing mud. The assistant was driving and Mr Barnes was on his right, hunched forward over the dashboard with his bright little hot brown eyes already fixed on the bulge in the blanket.

"Morning, gentlemen," he said, coming out spry before it had even stopped rolling. "What we got here?"

He hadnt taken his eyes off the blanket. He was rubbing his hands together the way a fly does when it lights.

"Drownded woman," McVey said. "Looks to me like she's been in the water a week. You want to take a look-see?"

But Mr Barnes had already started toward the blanket—one of the lucky ones of this earth, in love with his work.

"Come on, Wilbur," he said, passing the ambulance, and

the assistant got out, a beefy young man with pale blue eyes the color of early violets, but glassy, depthless.

I went over with them, and so did Roebuck and McVey. Miz Pitts and the sheriff and Lonzo stayed where they were, Lonzo nursing the camera against his chest, looking mournful. Just as I came up, Mr Barnes leaned down, took hold of one corner of the blanket, and with a motion of his wrist, as if he were turning down the covers to climb into bed, flipped it back.

"Whew," he said. "Now aint that something?"

It was something, all right. I took one look and thought of the way our Gladys would write it up:

Miss Whatever Blank comma *debutante daughter of Mr and Mrs Nemo Blank of this city* comma *attended a swimming party on Lake Bristol last Sunday evening* Stop. *Miss Blank wore an appropriate ensemble consisting of eight or nine yards of baling wire and a pair of matching pyramidal concrete blocks pendant one beneath each ear* Stop. Paragraph. *Today Miss Blank received a select gathering at Bachelor Bend and was the cynosure of all eyes* dash *what was left of her after her week end with her kinsmen west of Bristol* comma *the Shrimps and the Gars* and so on for three galleys, down to the 30 she puts at the end to prove she's a newspaperman.

"Can we handle her, Mr Barnes?" the assistant asked, his cornflower eyes expressionless.

"I handled worse in my time," Mr Barnes said. "Wait till youve been in this business a while, youll see. And you are wrong, Doc. She's been down four days at the outside."

All this time McVey was watching her too. Even in the days before whiskey got him, he must not have been much of a dentist. He never even managed to fit him*self* with a decent plate: carried the misfitting one in his pocket except when he got a craving for something he couldnt gum, or felt a special need for dignity. He said:

"You know more along those lines than me, Mr Barnes,

but I know one thing sure. Whoever put her in there meant for her to stay."

Mr Barnes chuckled. It made his chest sound hollow.

"Then he just should have known better. Few years ago we had a woman brought up a Model T engine and most of the differential. Theyll do it every time. All it takes is a little thunder. Up they come. Sometimes it dont even take that."

He had squatted beside her, examining while he talked. I saw him pause and look hard at a place above one ankle where a crease ran all the way round it, like a scar.

"Snips," he said, reaching over his shoulder without looking back, imitating a surgeon in the movies.

The assistant took a pair of long-nosed pliers from his pocket and passed them forward. Mr Barnes gouged in the crease, then steadied and squeezed—"Ah," he said, squeezing—and there was a little *click*: not loud, but with a quality of awe and even terror out of all proportion to the volume of sound.

"Ha!" he said, raising the pliers. "Here's what you call a clue."

He looked at Doc, feeling proud of himself, as if he expected his name to be changed from Light-Hearse to Sherlock, and his mouth was all set to say 'Elementry, my dear McVey.'

A fine gold chain hung from the jaws of the snips, the kind women wear on their ankles—some women. Two-thirds down from where he had clipped it, there was a little golden heart hooked to one of the links. It turned slowly, glinting in the sunlight like a spark, and when I leaned closer I saw a word engraved on the heart.

Love it said, turning and glinting, engraved in a loopy script across one side. The other side was blank. It revolved, strophe and antistrophe—Love: blank: Love: blank: Love—as if it were alternately shouting and pausing for breath, until at last the spinning stopped and the heart just hung there with the blank side toward me, silent. I remembered Rosalind saying *Men have died* and so forth *But not for love,* and I thought: It's

29

a good thing she didnt say Women, because here's at least one case would prove her wrong.

It was as if I knew the whole story already, for I had no sooner thought it than I heard Miz Pitts coming toward us, boot soles pounding the sun-dried mud a little too fast for walking. Her breath was wheezing by the time she reached us and bent forward to look at the chain and the heart—not because she needed to (she had recognized it already, from back where she stood with Lonzo and the sheriff) but just to make sure. Then she looked down at the pale, swollen, pulpy mass on the blanket, and a glint came into her eyes.

"It's Sue," she said, her mouth drawn in a line below the mustache. "She got what was coming to her and no mistake."

All the time she was telling the sheriff about it, how the dead girl and the man who said his name was Gowan had lived together on the island, posing as man and wife though anyone with half an eye (Miz Pitts said) could see they were no such thing, I was taking notes and thinking what a thing Fate is—that will let you get up in the morning believing this is going to be a day like any other, Gladys fuming over the latest printer's error and Benny ragging her, all as usual, and then the phone will ring and it's for you and you answer it, still thinking this means nothing special, and a voice without teeth comes over the wire and drops the whole thing plump in your lap:

"Come on out to Bachelor Bend. We found a woman drownded in the lake."

And you go and there she is, all right, laid out like a side of beef gone bad, only more so, and nobody knows her; it's a mystery and you think it's going to stay a mystery. Then the undertaker gets to poking round and comes up with a little gold heart on a chain that says *Love* blank *Love* blank *Love* and somebody that knew her takes a look and comes running: "It's Sue," she says, and the thing begins to unfold, fact by fact, like a draw poker hand when a gambler cracks it card by card to find if he's holding a bust or a winner or something in between.

"What was his first name?" the sheriff asked her.

"Luke."

"How do you spell it?"

"Like in the Bible," she said.

He put that down and so did I.

"What did he look like, exactly?"

"He wasnt much to look at."

She guessed at his weight and height, the color of his eyes and hair, the clothes he wore, and so forth. One word would have covered him: nondescript.

"Anything else?"

"Not as I remember. He wore glasses, spent lots of time reading the Bible." She paused. "But that was toward the end," she said. "That was only just before they left."

I made notes on the pad: *bespectacled, Bible-reading,* doing it *Time* style. I'd have liked to question her right then, while she was going good, but the sheriff wasnt through and it wouldnt do to interrupt him. I'd tried it before, on other cases.

You could see he was thinking he might as well turn the body over to Mr Barnes and forget about it, for all the good an investigation was going to do. There werent even any clothes for laundry marks. Whoever she was, Jane or Doris or Billie or just plain Sue, nothing could help her now. And as for Gowan, whatever he called himself, if he had gone to all the trouble to truss her up in wire and hang those concrete tetrahedrons around her neck, he wasnt likely to be waiting around to see how long it would take before she bobbed to the surface again, if ever.

They lived in a vacant shack, Miz Pitts said. I thought: Shack? Something was trying to rise to the surface of my mind, nudging, nudging—then it came to me: the voodoo shack. I remembered it from when I was a boy. An old man with a filthy tangled beard had lived in it, selling mojoes, grisgris charms and passion philters to Negroes who rowed across by the dark of the moon. He had the evil eye. There was talk about buried money, the quarters and fifty-cent pieces his customers exchanged for the voodoo stuff, though no one was ever reckless enough to investigate. And when he died nobody knew about it for weeks until some hunters happened over and found him. The Negroes had known, those who had come to make their purchases since he died, but they wouldnt tell, afraid of the evil eye. Then for a time white men were crossing with picks and spades, honeycombing the ground in a search for treasure. At last, however, they gave it up, stopped digging, and the land went back to jungle. Nobody lived on the island at all. Then one day a few years later we heard there was a fisherwoman building a cabin, she and her deaf-and-dumb son.

It was almost too good to be true. Black magic, the lurid element: everything any story ever needed. I was making notes as fast as the pencil would move across the pad. Then the sheriff closed his notebook, put it into his pocket as a sign that he was through. Now it was my turn to see what I could pump her for.

While I asked her questions, mostly getting her to enlarge on things she had already told, the others leaned forward, listening and glancing down from time to time at the mess on the blanket. We were all there now except Lonzo, who stood off to one side, hugging his camera, looking miserable over what he knew he had to do when Doc McVey called for him to step up and earn his seven-fifty.

They turned their heads from one to another of us while I questioned her—'Wait and read about it in this evening's paper,' I felt like telling them—getting an earful about how these two people, a man crowding middle age and a girl fairly young, came out of nowhere and set up light house-keeping in an abandoned shack on an island, living a wild outlandish life that shocked every fiber of Miz Pitts' Baptist soul (they did things by moonlight, she said: pagan rites, something; she wouldnt give me the details. But that was all right: I couldnt have printed them anyhow)—until one morning she walked over to the shack and found them gone back into the nowhere they came out of. 'Thats the end of that,' she thought. 'Good riddance, too.' But three days later she came upon this body in the lake and it was dragged out on bank but she didnt know for sure, and then the undertaker bent down, googed around, and brought up something shiny and she knew.

That was all I could pump her for. Most of it was like pulling eyeteeth, but when I got through I knew I had the makings of something that would jerk them back in their chairs when they flipped the paper open after supper. *By Russell Stevenson* (bfc).

I said, "Thank you maam."

"Humph," she said, much as McVey had said it over the phone, except with teeth.

So then it was Lonzo's turn to do his stuff. All this time he had been hanging back, looking the other way and nursing the camera like a babe in arms, probably screwing up his courage by imagining the fun he was going to get from the seven-fifty he hated so much to earn.

"Hey: Lonzo."

When Doc called him he came slowly across to where we stood. His face was drained white and he moved like a man on the way to the chair, keeping his eyes away from the direction of the blanket.

"I have to have something to stand on," he said. "It's supposed to be shot from above."

One thing you had to give him credit for: Much as he hated to do it, he wanted to do it right.

Roebuck went to a nearby clump of bushes where he had spotted a barrel. It had been there since the high water, two years ago. Anyhow it looked it. Some of the staves were missing and the head was gone from one end. I was glad *I* wasnt the one who would climb it.

33

"Dont worry," Roebuck told him, rolling it out. "If it dont hold, we'll be right there to catch you."

Lonzo looked at it doubtfully while Roebuck was shifting it into position. He shook his head from side to side; he didnt like it. But then he turned his attention to the camera, adjusting the various gadgets around the lens and opening the flaps on top to expose the view finder. Meanwhile Roebuck up-ended the barrel at the feet of the corpse and he and I got on opposite sides. When we helped Lonzo up, it creaked and groaned. We figured it would probably hold—at least long enough for him to get a focus and snap the shutter, and that was all that mattered.

While we were busy doing this, Doc walked back to the sheriff's car and rooted around in the trunk till he found a rag. Then he came back to the blanket, where the body lay in the position of labor—knees drawn up, thighs spread—and placed the rag across what was left of her crotch.

"Keep it decent," he said.

The innocent-eyed assistant sort of snickered but no one else did. Doc was right, of course, but there was something nasty about the way he said it.

I had hold of Lonzo's right knee and I could feel it tremble, partly because he was scared of the rickety barrel, partly because he was scared of what he knew he was going to see on the ground-glass plate. Then the trembling got worse and I knew he was seeing it. He steadied for an instant and there was a *cluck!*—a sound that somehow managed to be at once both vivid and dead, loud against the silence: the shutter had tripped—and Lonzo was hissing and spitting like a cat, holding the camera against his chest with one hand and slapping alternately right and left with the other, clawing at our wrists across his knees.

He wanted to get down and he wanted to get down in a hurry. But before we could turn him loose to take hold of his arms and help him down, there was a splintering crash:

the barrelhead cracked and the staves gave way. He came down in a hurry, all right.

On the way down, nursing the camera with one hand, he was still slapping and clawing at Roebuck and me, flailing at our heads and shoulders now. At first I thought he was mad because we hadnt held him well enough, but finally I realized I had it exactly wrong. What he really wanted was for us to turn him loose. So I let go, yelling for Roebuck to do the same, and Lonzo landed in the wreckage of the barrel, already running head-down for the bushes, straddle-legged.

He made it to the clump the barrel came from, still holding tight to the camera, and went down on one hand and both knees. We heard him vomiting, a series of gagging sounds that continued long after there was nothing left to heave. We just stood there, not looking at him and not looking at each other. We felt ashamed.

After a while, when the gagging finally stopped, I went over to see if there was anything I could do to help. I felt a little responsible, because after all I was the one who brought him out here and I was the one who would be taking him back.

He sat hunched down on the soft damp ground that had been beneath the barrel before Roebuck rolled it out for him to stand on. He was still hugging the camera with one hand (give him credit for that) while with the other he held a handkerchief over his mouth, breathing with short, feeble groans and drawn-out sighs.

"Can I help you, Lonz?"

When he looked up and saw me, he made a weak motion with one hand, the fingers boneless.

"Dear God," he said, speaking through the handkerchief. "I nearly, I nearly threw up in my Graflex."

I waited, watching him. In a minute he said:

"Dont look at me in this condition, Russell."

A moment before, I had heard Doc McVey say, "Well, gents, I reckon thats the ticket. That winds it up." Then Lonzo

35

asked me to look the other way and I saw Mr Barnes nod at Wilbur, the blue-eyed assistant, and Wilbur walked over to the ambulance, opened the rear door, and began to ease out a long brown wicker basket. It was almost seven feet long and only a bit over two feet wide and high, the size and shape of a barnyard watering trough. He walked with it balanced on his shoulder, rejoining the group still clustered about the blanket. Miz Pitts stood apart, hands in her coat pockets, looking out over the lake.

"Ready to go?" I asked Lonzo.

He didnt answer, just lurched up and started toward the car, camera under his arm. His face was grayer. He was showing his age. He got into the car and sat waiting, handkerchief over his mouth, shoulders slumped, while I said good-bye to the others, not forgetting to thank McVey again for having called me.

When we pulled onto the hump of the levee the engine stalled. While it hummed and coughed with a dry tubercular sound, I glanced up at the rear-vision mirror and caught a glimpse of them lifting her into the basket. Her legs were so high, they couldnt close the lid. The last I saw, Mr Barnes put his hands on her knees and was leaning forward. Then the engine sputtered alive; the scene slid off the mirror and the knife-blade crest of the levee rose like a curtain in reverse (it went down to open the scene; now it went up to close it) and we were back on the flat, riding east along the corduroy road.

Pellets of dried mud made a steady tinkling under the fenders and the camera bounced on Lonzo's knees with a sound like hollow drumtaps. I thought about death as I had seen it over the levee. Nothing could have been much uglier. But then (I thought) it's always ugly, always. No matter how they dress it up with rouge and a sewed-in smile and highflown words, the final scene of any life is always an indignity, a return to matter, slime. It has almost no connection with that bill of goods the preachers and poets and undertakers hand us. *In feces et urinas* . . .

Nothing in that kind of thinking, I told myself, and turned my attention to Lonzo.

"Feeling better?"

He sat facing the front, his face still gray.

Then I turned right, onto the highway. The camera stopped bouncing. There was only the long smooth whispering sound of rubber on asphalt.

"I'd rather not talk just now, please," Lonzo said.

That was all right with me. I went back to the dead girl's story, what little I knew of it, turning it this way and that in my mind, getting all the angles squared away. There were plenty of them. Black magic: Love—Bible-reading: Pagan rites. It would take some doing.

I dropped Lonzo at his house; he had his dark-room there. By the time I got back to the office I had the story so well organized I didnt even need to use my notes. I went straight to my desk and typed through three sheets without stopping. It shaped up good, with plenty of room for expansion to-morrow.

Press time was a good two hours away, so I stacked the sheets to let them cool before reading copy on them. While I was sitting there wondering which to tackle first, the wire stuff or a bunch of locals Benny had left on the spike, I suddenly remembered something the excitement had made me forget. I knew then the drowning story must be really some-thing, to make me forget a shot at ten sweet bucks.

There was no need to be careful who was watching. Gladys had gone to her garden club luncheon and Benny was cover-ing Kiwanis. I had the place to myself.

I took the Society page out of yesterday's paper, clipped the paragraph about the bride with the white lice collar, and pasted it to a sheet of copy paper. Beneath the clipping I wrote that I was submitting the above to the "Slips that Pass in the Night" department, typing my name and address at the bottom—my home address so nobody here at the office would see the reply. Then I got a stamped envelope out of the chief's desk and addressed it to the *Digest*.

Gladys would fling a fit if they took it. I could hear her already, yelling about the nation-wide ridicule. But I figured they would give me ten dollars for it, and at ten bucks each I'll take all the tantrums she can spare. She wasnt likely to know who sent it, anyhow. Probably she would think it was Benny—he's the one who rags her most. And besides, even if she somehow discovered that I was the one who mailed it in, she'd never suspect that yesterday I'd pulled the corrected galley proof off the hook and ditched it in the waste basket.

So much for that. I cleared up the wire copy and Benny's locals. Then I was ready to put the final touches on my story. First I wrote a three-deck 36-point Caslon head, two-column: Garroted Body/Found in Lake;/Suspect Sought. "Suspect Sought" was pretty tame. I let it go, however. It balanced nicely and I like alliteration.

It would have been first lead, at the upper right—we play up local stuff—but that had to be the day the Democratic whip predicted Congress would pass the housing bill, Truman sicked the FBI on the Alabama Kluxers, Hiss himself was on the stand, and Roosevelt Junior made his maiden speech. Which was just my luck. I could get an exclusive interview with the ghost of FDR, telling what he really thought of Stalin, and the day of its release would be the day the Russians dropped the bomb.

The story read even better than I'd thought. I touched it up a bit, wrote *Garroted P-I* across the top, and was just about to hook it when an impulse made me pause. I had forgotten something, and almost immediately I knew what it was. I put the sheets back on the desk and wrote:

by Russell Stevenson (bfc)

above the first typed line. I must have gone soft in the head to forget a thing like that, my own by-line.

Then, since it was lying right there on the desk and deadline was a good half-hour away, I thought I might as well read it through again. This time was even better. I touched it up a bit, dab here, dab there, and put it on the hook.

"Copy!"

Sol came up from the back, dumped an armload of proof. He took the story off the hook and walked back toward the composing room, looking it over. Then he stopped in the doorway, the sheets stark white against his apron and inky fingers.

"What kind of looking girl was she?"

"We couldnt tell," I said.

Then he reached the part where I had Miz Pitts declare what a looker she'd been.

"Says here, a beautiful blonde."

"They all are, once theyre murdered. Besides, maybe she was. Anyhow she was a blonde. Natural, too."

He left.

I sat there, linotypes tinkling in the background, and thought what a shame it was, not to be able to follow it up tomorrow with something equally gutty. If there was a chance in a million of catching the man, what a series I could do on it. But all I had to do was put myself in his place to realize just how far away he was by now. Bristol, Jordan County, Mississippi, had had its final look at him, Gowan or Go-on or Gone, whatever his name was.

2. (Continued)

That was Friday and I was never wronger.

Saturday I wrote a follow-up, leading off with her burial in the pauper lot at the back of the cemetery, then going into a rehash of yesterday's story on the finding of the body. I wound it up by saying that the manhunt was still under way though the Missouri authorities had wired back that they never heard of any Luke Gowan. Calling it a manhunt was a prime example of journalistic courtesy in the first place. I should have called it hopeless wondering, for that was all the sheriff was doing—or anyone else for that matter, myself included.

The follow-up came out Sunday morning. The *Clarion* is an evening sheet except for Sunday, which is really the Saturday paper held up for the sake of the extra advertising drawn into a Sunday edition featuring such stuff as Gladys' layouts for brides and so-called debutantes, Lonzo's *Side Lights*, and a special farm page I rig together out of releases from the County Agent and canned junk off the clip sheet—I'm an expert farmer with a pair of scissors. So, anyhow, Sunday is really a holiday, in spite of the fact we have a Sunday paper. It's not nearly as complicated as it sounds.

Usually I spend it on the links. I play eighteen in the morning and another eighteen after lunch, Watt Mosby and I. Poor Watt the hare: I spot him three strokes on the nine, and today I had him two down on the morning rounds. When we came in on the final nine, just at sundown, I gave him a little extra-pressure talk and he flubbed his putt. That made it five, at a dollar each, and I was feeling good. Nothing warms the cockles of my heart like the chink of cash.

I was back in the locker room, changing my shoes and drinking a coke, when I heard these three men talking. Watt had left, swearing he'd never play with me again. But I knew better. He'd be back next Sunday morning, arguing I ought to give him another stroke.

"He was right there all the time," I heard the first man say. "Sitting and waiting to see what was going to happen."

"Who is he anyhow?" the second asked.

"Small farmer from down on Lake Jordan. You know the type."

"It's a wonder he didnt take off," the second said.

"Not really it's not," the first one told him. "He thought she was down to stay. Remember those concrete blocks and all that wire. Besides, you know how that class of people are: barely the sense to come in out of the rain. You or me, now, we'd have been long gone, cooling our heels down Mexico way or some such place at the far edge of the map. But not his kind. Not him. He went home and waited to see what was going to happen."

"Dont they beat all?" the third said.

Soon as I had my street shoes on, I went to the phone. Roscoe must have been sitting beside it, he answered so quick.

"County jail. Jeffcoat speaking."

Youd have thought he was the head of Standard Oil.

"Roscoe: Steve. Whats all this talk?"

"Whatever theyre saying, it's true. . . ."

He sounded as proud of himself as if he'd been the one who made the capture, braving gunfire.

"I got him right here in a cell. He signed a full confession and everything, telling us how he done it. Come take a gander at him. He's a funny-looking coot."

"Funny ha-ha or funny peculiar?"

"Funny anything. Come see for yourself."

But there was no point in that. Roscoe isnt the type you have to humor, and deadline was a good twenty hours away. Besides, I was on my own time until tomorrow morning. Even a mule gets to stay in his stall on a Sunday.

"He'll keep," I said. "Right now all I want is just enough information to keep the press from looking ignorant."

"Well, I'll tell you how it was . . ."

A heavy hum came over the wire: Roscoe was getting his thoughts together. It was as if I could hear his brain gathering itself, like a muscle. Then he told me the whole thing, so far as he knew it.

Miz Pitts had a son, a deaf-and-dumb boy about seventeen or eighteen, maybe younger. He had a real name, I suppose—even the mule they let stay in the stall of a Sunday has that much—but I never heard it. They called him Dummy; that was all; nobody could speak to him anyhow. I'd seen him a couple of times when he came to town with his mother (if she *was* his mother), walking a little behind her with a croaker sack over his shoulder full of potatoes, or whatever else was in season, out of the little patch of a garden beside their cabin. Mostly he stayed on the island.

He was the one who tipped the sheriff, Roscoe said. Somehow he found out the man's true name and address while they were on the island. During Sunday dinner, two days after the body was found, he showed up at the sheriff's house and handed him a slip of paper. *Luther Eustis* was written on it: *Solitaire Plantation.* Everybody knows Solitaire; it's written up in the books. That was where General Jameson's father, old Isaac, first settled in 1820 before there was any such thing as Jordan County. It's one of the best-known places for miles around, whats left of it.

So the sheriff called Roebuck and they piled into a car and rode down there, taking Dummy along to make certain. And sure enough, the man came to the door and Dummy put the finger on him, prancing up and down on the porch the minute he saw him. He was the one and no mistake, and he knew they had him cold. He told them everything they wanted to know, from the very beginning.

He was the one who called himself Luke Gowan, took the girl to the voodoo shack where they lived together, and killed her. They were taking a bath in the lake, he said—in close to bank where the willow trees hung down—and he wrapped a switch around her throat and held her under till the bubbles stopped.

'Why did you do such a thing?'

'I wanted to come home to my wife and daughters and she wouldnt let me.'

Just like that, Roscoe said. Just that and no more.

'All right,' they told him. 'Go on.'

Then he tied the blocks around her neck and let her sink. She went down fast: for keeps, he thought. The first he knew of her bobbing up was five days later, Sunday, when he looked out of the window and saw Roebuck and the sheriff and Dummy coming through the gate. The sheriff and Roebuck could have been coming for almost anything, electioneering maybe, but when he saw Dummy he knew she was up and he knew why theyd come. Right off, he told them everything.

So he said good-bye to the wife and daughters, took the Bible under his arm, and rode the thirty miles to Bristol without saying another word, sitting with the handcuffs on his wrists. When they got to the jail he told it all again, in more detail this time, talking slowly so Roscoe could hunt-and-peck it on the typewriter. Anytime Roscoe couldnt keep up, he'd stop and repeat what he'd said. Then he signed it and went to sleep in his cell without waiting for supper. He was up there now, asleep, Roscoe told me.

"Who is he?" I said. "Where is he really from?"

"He's just one of them peckerwoods, Steve, like the others you see crowding the sidewalks of a Saturday, with a sack of store-bought candy in his fist and a passel of towheaded kids hanging onto the slack in the seat of his pants, in town with the old woman to look in the Marshall Avenue windows and show off the mail-order dress she bought for Easter, saving her egg money. Youve seen ten thousand like him. He's a farmer on Solitaire, down on the lake. Been there man and boy for fifty years."

"How about the girl, then? Who was she?"

"She was from down in Issawamba County. Nobody knows much yet. Her folks are being notified."

"Hadnt they missed her till now?"

"If they had, they didnt say so. Not so we know of, anyhow."

"O.K. Roscoe. Thanks.—Say!"

"Yair?"

I thought I'd lost him.

"What was her real name?"

"Ross: Beulah Ross."

"Right.—Hey, Roscoe!"

"Yair?"

"How old was she?"

"Eighteen, he says."

"Thanks. I'll see you in the morning."

"Sure, Steve. Glad to. Any time," and hung up.

He meant it, too. I'd hate to try to think of something Roscoe wouldnt do for the sake of getting his name in the paper.

Whatever was coming my way, I figured I was ready for it. I felt my luck was running strong. Wanting to press it, I took a chair in the poker game that sits every Sunday night at the club. When the game broke up, around three, I had lost the five I won from Watt and another four went with it. Talk about heartbreak—

A couple of the players had brought bottles. I drank my share, to keep the night from being a total loss. But next morning I had not only dropped nine bucks, I went to work with a head three times its size. Within an hour I had things organized: well enough organized, at least, to leave. Benny said he would take the desk and if anything came up he'd call the jail. God knows I hoped nothing did. All my aching head could think of was those nine dropped dollars.

The jail, behind the courthouse, is of concrete: one of those recent structures with hard uncompromising lines, strictly utilitarian, a product of this modernistic craze—or so youd think. Actually it was built in '73, the oldest standing thing in Bristol except Judge Holiman, Captain Billy Lillard, and the trees. I remember it from when I was a boy, in the days when it had a beauty only Time can bring. Its bricks were handmade, smooth with age, cool in the hottest weather, soft as satin to the touch. Then Bristol began to suffer growing pains. Shameful, people began to say of the jail. An eyesore, they said. So the Board of Supervisers pacified them: had it slabbed with concrete, dirty white and graying with the years —no curves, no useless ornaments: only the harsh flat concrete streaked with rain as if by tears—like an old lady in pancake make-up, weeping. I'd see it and think of the brick building crouched inside, the Old South under the garish façade of the New.

I thought of it now, crossing the courthouse lawn toward where a small crowd had collected in front of the stoop, waiting on the chance they might catch a glimpse of Eustis through the bars, or at least a chance to question someone who had. Most likely they knew more about it already than I would learn in a week of work on the story.

Captain Billy Lillard was among them, nearest the door. He spends his time sitting on the base of the Confederate monument, whittling and waiting for jury duty, revolving clockwise around it to stay in the shade.

"Young feller . . ."

He leaned on his cane and turned his head from side to side like a sparrow. He had had his ribbons drycleaned and had polished his medals, which meant that he considered the occasion something special.

"I witnessed the paper he told how he done it in. And yestiddy I was the one that pinted the way to the sheriff's

45

house for the deef-and-dumb boy that tipped them off. What do you think of that?"

Human vanity and curiosity beat all. Always before I condemn them, however, I remind myself that they created my job and keep it going.

"Good for you, Captain Billy," I said. "Maybe theyll strike you another medal or something."

They moved in closer when I knocked at the door. Roscoe opened it and they craned over my shoulders, looking past him into the damp cool dimness of the hallway. I stepped in and he closed the door behind us. For a moment we stood in the gloom. It faded from almost black to dusky gray. Then he moved past me, leading the way to the office. His keys clinked faintly.

Following him, I moved again among the mingled odors of creosote and urine and sweating iron, which in time I had learned to identify one by one, but which at the beginning, in their mingled anonymity—first when I was on the high school paper, the *Jackdaw*, and later when I was a cub on the *Clarion*—I had thought of as the particular odor of sin itself coming from the convicts, the converse of that odor of sanctity said to emanate from the holy martyrs of old.

The office seemed bright and airy, if only because of the contrast. One wall was plastered with circulars that reproduced the heads of a thousand nonconformists, full face and profile, with numbers beneath their chins and ears, hatred and fear in their eyes—except the Negroes, whose faces showed nothing at all. WANTED the circulars said, usually with an exclamation point: $200 REWARD (or more or less) and then a description that would fit almost anyone except for the incidental scars and tattooings. Roscoe spent his spare time memorizing them, faces and texts, in hopes of collecting rewards. He had yet to spot his first.

In the far corner the pot-bellied stove, kept cherry red in winter by one of the trusties, wore a faint coat of rust, as if someone had blown a handful of rouge in that direction. A naked light bulb hung like a plumb bob from the center of the ceiling. Three rifles and a brace of single-action .45s were racked and locked in a glass-front case on the opposite wall. A progressive public might slab the outer walls with concrete, but nothing in here ever changed.

Roscoe opened a drawer of the roll-top desk beside the door and brought out two sheets of legal foolscap, both packed close with single-space typing. At the foot of the second page, the signature *Luther D. Eustis* was shaky above the puckered place where sweat from his wrist had dried. To the left of this, Roscoe and Captain Billy had signed as witnesses.

"Here you are," Roscoe said. "The whole kit and caboodle, that tells how he done it and all. You should have seen him, sitting there cool as a cucumber, telling it slow enough for me to type while he talked. He was willing; he was anxious, even. Once he'd told it, though, he changed: clammed up. And now wont eat. Just sits up there on the cot with the Bible by him."

He went on but I stopped listening: I was into the confession by then. It was as if I could see them the whole time I was reading; the thing came alive in my hands. If I could write like that, I told myself, I'd be at the top of the ladder by now. The trouble is, you have to have lived it first. No thanks: it isnt worth it.

First he told how he saw her at a church picnic this past Easter, some kind of shindig over across Lake Jordan. For a while they met on the sly but it wasn't enough; he wanted to get her away from everything she'd ever known. I had to keep reminding myself he was up in his fifties, because from the way he told it, even looking back over all that happened, youd have thought he was sixteen, off on his first rutting spree. He knew about the island opposite Bristol (anyhow what used to be the island before the engineers put the cut-off through in '35) and they went there, a jungle paradise.

Then conscience or something began to gnaw at him. Or so he said. Probably it was because he was really into his fifties after all; he had about caught up on being young. In his sleep

he began to see his wife and daughters holding out their arms
to him, especially the youngest, a sort of dimwit. So he told
her it was no go; they had to go back.

But she said "No we dont," or words to that effect. "I'll
follow; I'll tell," she said—according to him.

He looked at her hard when she said it. There wasnt any
doubt about what the look meant. She understood, all right.
But she still said no, and wouldnt let him leave.

Two nights later they walked down to the lake for a twilight bath and he told her again: "I have to go back." But she
still said no, looking right back at him and understanding. So
he used a willow switch and put her down, watching the
bubbles. She didnt fight it, he said, until the very last. Then
he pulled her out on bank and trussed her up with some of
the blocks and wire the government engineers had left there
fifteen years before, when they built the cut-off.

This time he didnt need to push. She went down fast. For
keeps—he thought.

He went back to the shack and got their things. There
wasnt much; they hadnt needed much for what they had in
mind when they set out. He wired her clothes to another
block and sank them, then rowed across the lake in a bateau
that belonged to Miz Pitts.

For a couple of days he wandered around. That part was
hazy; he wasnt clear on what he'd done in all that time.
Maybe he didnt know. Anyhow he finally rode back down to
Lake Jordan on the train. This was Friday, the day we found
the body. When he came walking through the front door into
the house where his wife and daughters were waiting, it was
as if he'd stepped out for a bucket of water or something.

"Now praise the Lord," he said, walking in. "Ive been
through the valley of shadow, but now I'm home." Or words
to that effect.

It was like old home week, everybody happy, especially
the dimwit. Then two days later, Sunday afternoon, brakes
squeaked on a car out front, and he looked through the window

and saw three men climb out, first the first, then the second, then the third; the third was Dummy and he knew. He knew she had come back up and had been identified. But how? How had even Dummy known his true name?

They told him how. From the Bible, they said. And he confessed in full, once at home and again in the county jail, where Roscoe took it down at his dictation. He signed and the witnesses signed, and now it was in my hands, two typewritten sheets, and I had finished reading it: from *I, Luther Dade Eustis, being of sound mind*, down through Captain Billy Lillard's signature.

"Aint that something?" Roscoe said.

It occurred to me then that probably his voice hadnt stopped once in all the time I was reading. He leaned over my shoulder and tapped at the upper sheet. The rim of his nail was a crescent of black.

"Right here's the part I like," he said, breathing against my cheek. "Here, where he tells how he done it. . . ."

He slid his finger down and tapped again.

"Here too: where he tells what-all he done with her afterwards. Aint that something?"

It was something, all right. For a minute I'd even forgotten my aching head.

I made notes, a quote here and there from the parts Roscoe and ten thousand like him wanted to read, avid after the vicarious thrill, a party to murder. When I handed the sheets back, he seemed disappointed that I hadnt made a full transcript to run in a 10-point double-column box down the center of the front page with an ornamental border, including his signature as a witness.

"You get all you want?"

"Save something for the follow-up," I said.

He shrugged, put the sheets regretfully into the drawer, and turned to the door.

"Then lets go take a look at him," he said, brightening at the prospect.

When we entered the central hall again I saw Mrs Jeffcoat watching us through the door that leads back to their quarters. She had a towel around her throat to hide the goiter, head craned sideways, making certain I wasnt a woman out here with Roscoe. She watches every move he makes.

He turned left, leading the way, and we climbed the metal staircase, mounting in two tight spirals around a pole up toward the cell block. I followed the clink of his keys down the corridor that runs between the cages. Last night's whiskey was so much acid in my stomach, laving; the odor was stronger here—pungent, faintly ammoniac, as in a menagerie. The bullpen convicts watched us, their skulls like fuzzy cannonballs, dark faces with assorted razor scars, eyeballs looming and rolling as we came past.

Eustis was in the far cell on the right. I knew it well. That was the one where I interviewed the Negro cornet player, nine years ago, on the night before they burnt him, the first in Jordan County to get the chair; all the ones before him had been hung.

"St! St!" came suddenly from the left.

I turned, startled, one arm already raised to shield my face. But it was only old man Lundy, looking out from between his fists where they clasped the bars. I had forgotten him, though I had done a series on him the month before, right after he shot the marshal down in Glenmora. No jail could hold him, he said then. He was old news now.

"Is it come?" he said. "Has the governor wrote in yet?"

He meant his pardon. He was expecting to be pardoned before he ever came to trial. He had been saying all along they couldnt keep him in jail, not with *his* political connections. Now I could see he was starting to doubt.

"Not yet, Mr Lundy."

"To hell with you," he said; "God damn you all," and turned away.

Roscoe meantime had stopped in front of the last cell. He unhooked the keyring from his belt and selected one of the keys. When he turned it in the big iron lock, the tumblers clanked like a broken crankshaft making one last revolution. He swung the door ajar and stood aside, and I saw Eustis sitting on the cot.

One look and I knew I'd done just as well when I decided not to call Lonzo to come along for pictures. Anyone seeing the cut wouldnt bother to read the story, unless it would be for the sake of finding out how a squirt like that, past fifty, could get himself mixed up in such a fracas. That was my first thought.

He sat sideways, hunkered between the upper and lower bunks, both feet planted flat and side by side like army shoes in a barracks when the men are out for drill. His elbows were on his knees, his chin on his hands. They were the hands of a workman, splayed and callous, with thumbnails thick as little oyster shells. His back was humped a bit—they get it plowing —and his shirt was faded paler over the hump.

When the door swung open he lifted his head, turning it slowly sideways, not moving otherwise except to drop his hands in his lap. His hair stood in tufts on both sides of his forehead, a little like horns (they reminded you of horns) and there was a scuffed leather Bible on the cot beside him. He looked at us—I say he did; it's possible he didnt. Possibly his eyes were closed, for highlight from the window overhead made his spectacles gleam with a bright quicksilver sheen, the lenses opaque and perfectly round, like mirrors.

I stood in the doorway, watching him. And all of a sudden, out of nowhere, I remembered Milton's fallen angel. I had forgotten him since high school English.

> *Round he throws his baleful eyes*
> *That witness'd huge affliction and dismay*
> *Mix'd with* something something *stedfast hate.*

Now that was a strange thing, to look at Eustis and remember poetry I hadnt thought of since the first time I heard it on a fly-buzzed October afternoon in a classroom a dozen years ago. For he resembled nothing less than he resembled an angel, fallen or no, and he'd never known a paradise, much less lost one—unless he was playing Adam to Beulah's Eve on the island opposite Bristol. If so, he certainly jumped the script on the final scene.

And as for the interview, I might as well not have bothered to climb the stairs. All he did was quote the Bible at me: mostly from Revelations, I think. The black horse, the red horse, the white horse, a man with a pair of balances—I couldnt follow. Besides, if I'd wanted to read the Bible I could have stayed at the office and done it. The chief keeps one on his desk, part of the standard equipment an editor is supposed to display, stacked between the *World Almanac* and *Business Trends*, the least-used one of the three.

Every time I'd try to pull him back to the subject at hand, he'd say "I already told the sheriff yesterday." Then he'd quote something at me. "In my poor sinful way," he'd say every now and again. He wasnt so much excited as he was disconnected. Thats what he was: disconnected. One thing I'll say for him, though: He knew the Bible. From time to time he'd reach out his hand and touch it, the way Ive heard old people used to do when they were dying.

I wasnt getting anywhere and I knew it. The confession gave me everything I needed, as far as it went; he was right about that. So finally I told Roscoe I had enough and we left. Eyes glistered from behind the bars as we came down the corridor in the opposite direction. Old man Lundy didnt speak and I didnt bother to notice if he was awake.

We descended the spiral staircase, myself in front this time, then through the gloomy hallway to the door. When Roscoe lifted the bar and swung it open, daylight struck me a slap across the eyes.

Then I could see again: a knot of faces uptilted toward where I stood on the stoop looking down.

"How is he this morning?" Captain Billy Lillard asked, batting his eyes.

Roebuck with his brick-red face, like a man in apoplexy, and Ben Rand the circuit clerk, tall and skeleton thin, with a head like a skull, were coming through from the rear. Rand has been around the courthouse since he was a boy: announced for office the day he turned twenty-one, and has been on the county payroll ever since. They came past me and Roscoe let them in. The door slammed shut.

"Fine, Captain Billy," I said. "He's doing fine."

I went on through, around the side of the courthouse, across the lawn dappled with midmorning shade, and past the Confederate soldier high on his shaft, both hands gripping the muzzle of his musket. *Duty: the sublimest word in the language* was carved on the base, quoting General Lee who never said it. I used to plan to climb that shaft someday, just to whisper in his ear he'd lost the war.

A block from the courthouse, who should I meet walking toward me but Parker Nowell, neat as ever in his panama and linen suit, coming down the sidewalk with a country woman and carrying an undersized cardboard suitcase. He leaned toward her, talking.

"Good morning, Mr Nowell."

He looked around and saw me.

"Morning," he said, and turned back to the country woman, talking.

Her eyes were red at the rims. She was tall and rawboned. I wondered what kind of legal hullabaloo he was fixing to stir up now. There was sure to be a story in it somewhere, if I only had time to get in on the know.

That was when it first occurred to me what a thing it would be if he took the Eustis case. We'd see some fireworks then, I thought. Now that I came to think about it, I saw that it was just his kind of thing. I even considered going back and asking him, on a hunch, but he looked busy with whatever it was the woman was fretting about. Besides, I had already used up half the morning on the story. Back at the office there was sure to be a ream of wire copy waiting for me, long as a sideshow snake.

I went by city hall for the building reports and suchlike, which killed another half-hour. Then I went to the post office for the mail. To cap the climax, as I was coming down the steps Will Cato tagged me. He was hatching a special program for the Rotary luncheon Thursday, a new plan to make the world safe for hypocrisy or something.

"Here's the set-up," he said, hooking one finger inside my shirt pocket, the way he always does, breathing a reek of peppermint in my face.

Beyond his shoulder I saw Parker Nowell crossing the street toward the Mannheim Building, where his office is. The brim of his hat was absolutely level. He walked with his arms held slightly away from his sides, the palms turned backward like an old-time gunman. Whatever it was he went to the courthouse for, he hadnt wasted much time.

Finally I shook Cato. When I got back to the office it was almost noon and my desk looked as if a snowstorm had hit it. Benny certainly hadnt strained himself. He had gone to lunch already. The others were leaving too. I rolled up my sleeves and pitched in. Within forty-five minutes I had it cleared at least enough to be able to see the desk top in spots here and there.

I had the place to myself by then: I could settle down to my story uninterrupted. (Gladys was the worst about that; she couldnt or wouldnt use the dictionary, and had the habit of asking me how to spell every third word she wrote.) All the time I'd been doing the others, I had been turning the Eustis story over and over in my mind. So it ran as smooth as silk runs off a loom, or maybe smoother. All I had to do was wiggle my fingers above the keyboard, hands limp at the wrists, and the words came clacking onto the platen. I was what you might call inspired.

But it wasnt until I was reading copy on it, having caught up with the teletype in the meantime, that the idea really hit me. There was a good fifty, maybe sixty bucks in this thing, if I handled it right. All it would take was a little extra asking around, mainly into their backgrounds, and I'd have it: duck soup. I got to feeling perky, just with the notion. As soon as I'd written the head and hooked the copy, I started to organize it, A to izzard, rolling a fresh sheet into the machine.

I figured it for six sections, something shy of a thousand words a section. Like this:

1. Backgrounds of E and B.
2. They meet, sneak off to island.
3. He kills her, then goes home.
4. Body found, E arrested.
5. Trial and sentence.
6. Electrocution.

The main thing was to keep the story simple, pour on action action action so fast the reader wouldnt have time to look up for a sip of coffee, and keep it short, short, short. Five thousand words would do it easy, I was telling myself, and there was someone breathing down my neck.

"What you cooking, Steve?" It was Benny Peets.

Benny is all right, in his way, but he'd steal the pennies off a dead man's eyes if he thought he'd find a story underneath them. Before I came to work on the *Clarion* he did everything —news, sports, features, all of it. He had been around for ages and this Eustis thing was just his brand of stuff.

I got the paper out of the machine as fast as I could without seeming to be in too big a hurry. I folded it and slid it into my pocket, trying to look as if I was thinking of something else all the while.

"Man," Benny said, watching. He held an unlighted cigar in one hand, a match in the other. "This case has kind of got you going, aint it?"

"I was just getting it squared away in my mind," I said. "I'll have to do some follow-ups. And anyhow I want to be ready when it comes up for trial in September."

Something told me I was protesting too much.

"Sure you do," Benny said.

He finished licking a loose flap on the cigar, then raised one knee and raked the match across the back of his thigh. He held the tip of the cigar in the flame until it was drawing to suit him.

"I was thinking," he said. He let smoke leak from one corner of his mouth. "I might take a fling at it myself." He coughed a jet. "For the magazines, I mean. *True Detective* or one of those with a babe on the cover's got half her dress ripped open and a knife in her hand dripping blood."

It's no easy job to tell whether Benny is serious or joking when he looks at you around one of those cigars. That glint in his eye might be humor, and then again it might be just pure shrewdness. He looks more like a horse-trader than a sports reporter anyhow.

"Why not?" I said, hoping it sounded unconcerned.

It didnt.

I went over to the teletype, ripped off a couple of yards of copy, and made myself busy, watching him out of the tail of my eye every now and then. He stood looking at me for a while, smoking slowly, then ambled over to his machine, flopped down lazylike, the way he does, and began to pound out one of his columns on our chances for the pennant.

Your correspondent, he calls himself, a great one for the editorial We, and screams like a ruptured walrus every time I try to straighten out his syntax. I watched him typing. It was something to see. He keeps his index fingers stiff, thumbs and wrists lifted high for every stroke, like Rubinstein playing the *Fire Dance* in the movies.

One thing sure: I'd have to get it in under the wire ahead of him. Maybe he was just guying me. Then again, maybe he wasnt. There was no use taking chances, anyhow, because Memphis was loaded with smart birds pecking around for just such a chance as this. They wouldnt have my sources, not the best ones at least, but if I wasnt careful theyd knock something together and have it in the mail before I got organized and sat down to write.

The best thing, I decided, was to get it in quick: have it accepted and paid for before the others—Benny's included, in case he meant what he said—came plumping onto the editor's desk for comparison.

So that knocked Section 6 in the head. The electrocution scene would touch it up, but it was far from necessary. It certainly wasnt worth waiting around for. Besides, leaving it off would give me more room to spread out in the earlier scenes. The minute old Judge Holiman leaned across the bench and gave Eustis that hard-eyed look before hoping God had mercy on his soul, I'd wind it up and slap it in the mail, self-addressed stamped envelope inclosed, and bide my time till the check came.

I didn't know what they were paying nowadays but I figured I ought to get sixty dollars for it. Maybe seventy.

3. Dummy

Mother crossed the lake on the Friday morning after the Wednesday the bateau was missing and I walked over to the shack and found them gone: Gone, the shack said, whispering it to me: Gone. I stood listening to the emptiness (this on the Wednesday) and I know it was true, they were gone, and would never come back. Then two days, it was Friday and Mother went down the rows where I had spaded the potatoes out of their hills the evening before: put them in two sacks, carried them down to the skiff, one on each shoulder: then got in and motioned good-bye. I watched her go, oars lifting and winking in the sunlight, like a bug across a sheet of chocolate paper. Midmorning: I was alone for the first time since three weeks ago when she brought them here from town. So I went back to the shack (this on the Friday, the first time since the Wednesday) and it was the same: Will never come back, the emptiness told me, whispering. I went to the far corner, under the sashless window where I used to stand outside, looking through, and see them sprawled in the moonlight, hunching, hunching: Her arms and legs ran pale in four directions. I lay on the dirt where the pallet had been. The warmth was from the sunlight falling on it, I knew that, but a part of my mind kept saying it was some of her warmth that had not cooled through those two long days and three nights. And lying there with it warm against the side of my face, wallowing, nuzzling, remembering, I felt the hot salt taste of tears on the base of my tongue. It will drive you crazy, Mother said.

That afternoon I looked up from spading and saw the skiff coming back across the water, oars lifting slow and steady but not winking now because the shadows were thrown the other way. You go through life like that, in a rowboat facing rear, not seeing where you are going, just where you have been. Her hat took shape, round, gold-colored, fuzzy at the edges like a nimbus; then her back, as broad as any man's; and finally I watched her tie the painter. She was late. I could see trouble in her face across the distance. But she would not tell me: She avoided my eyes all the rest of the day, and all that night, and all the following day. Whenever her face turned toward me, I looked her right in the mouth: Tell me, Tell me, I said with my eyes: But she looked aside, she looked aside every time. I would ask with my eyes, Is it something to do with Sue? (I called her that) but she looked aside, she kept it to herself; I found out by a headline in the water.

I was bailing the skiff out (Saturday—afternoon) and a pleasure boat came twinkling with polished brass, swerved close to shore: four men in yachting caps, three women in sleeveless dresses and painted faces. The man at the wheel reached down and brought up a package wrapped in newspaper, tore off a strip around the top to expose the neck of the bottle, tilted it once, then once again, and passed it back to the others, throwing the strip of paper over the rail. They drank, all seven, once around; the boat swung on, was gone. All that was left was the strip of paper, undulant, riding the waves of the wake. It came toward bank like a swimming snake, big headlines on the left and right and small ones in between: DEMOCRATIC WHIP the right one said, floating wavy on the water: But I went no further with it, for by then I had seen the headline on the left: GARROTED BODY FOUND IN LAKE; SUSPECT SOU and the rest was torn. It's Sue, I said: It's Sue.

That night, before bedtime, we were sitting on opposite sides of the table, the lamp between: she was putting a seat in a pair of my wornout jeans and I was reading the dictionary; **gar-rote** it said (gă-rōt'; gă-rŏt') *v.t., to execute by strangling,* *seize by the throat*: when all of the sudden she reached across, pulled the lamp toward her, turned up the wick to a point just short of smoking, and folded her hands. That was the sign: She had made up her mind at last: She was going to tell me. The light fell full on her face, making the mustache stand out dark and exact. Now I am going to know, I said. But at the final minute, before she spoke, I wished she would go on keeping it a secret: Because though I almost knew already, so long as I did not know for sure, it was as if she was still alive. Mother's lips moved carefully, telling me, and I sat there, out of the lamplight, keeping still.

I saw Sue, she said: Drowned in the lake. I knew by the heart chained on her ankle. The Law is looking for Luke. They think he did it.

Then she went back and told about it, how she came on the body and called the sheriff. Sue had wire around her throat and two of those four-sided concrete blocks they put into the river bank to keep it from washing away. She stayed down three days, wearing the blocks, until her rising time, and then she broke the surface and Mother found her. The undertaker came: He took her away. Today they buried her.

I asked with my hands, holding them into the lamplight: Do they think they will catch him?

She said: They think he is far away and gone for good. Back to Missouri, if that was where he came from, if Gowan was his name.

Lamplight showed the worry in her face beginning to clear. She had held off telling me because she knew the way I felt: She hated Sue. She never would have told me at all, except she decided I was sure to discover it sooner or later anyhow, from a newspaper dropped in the water, the way it really was, or some such way. But now that she had told me, she felt better and the worry in her face began to clear.

Except for asking if the Law expected to catch him, I did not question her about it: I did not show a thing in my face. When she finished I pulled the lamp back to the center of the table, turned the wick down to where it was before, and went back to my reading. There was no need to ask, there was no need to worry about it. From the minute I saw her mouth shape Sue-is-dead I knew already what I was going to do and exactly how I was going to do it, too.

I did not even have to stop and consider. I could see that Bible flyleaf in my mind, as clear as if it was written on my forehead in reverse so that all my brain had to do was look through the front of my skull and read it plain, with every loop and curlicue and the precise position of every dot over every i. But there was no hurry, I kept telling myself there was no hurry: I bided my time through another two columns, gar-ter to gas-tro-pod, and finally she gave the table a nudge to signal good night. I nodded without looking up; she went to bed. There was no hurry: I gave her plenty of time, gas-tru-la to gauz-y, then got up carefully and went to the door of our room, peeping through. She had turned her head the other way but I could see her chest rising and falling regularly and her two fists, knotty and hard from working, clenched on her chest like two pieces of rock somebody had scrubbed at for a while to get them clean but gave it up. Vibrations from her snoring came through the soles of my shoes and up my legs: She has slept like that ever since the doctors turned her into a man.

grief the dictionary says: *sorrow on account of present or past trouble*. Obs., *physical pain*. There was nothing obsolete about what I felt. The trouble with the dictionary is it tries to explain with words, and there is a limit to what can be said with words: No one can know what a word means till he feels it. I knew that, now. Grief, for instance.

Back at the table I got out the India ink and the pens and the box of good rag paper she gave me for Christmas. The light was wrong, too much yellow, so I trimmed and adjusted the wick, set the lamp where the shadows would fall away from the penpoint, took a deep breath down far in my lungs to steady my hand, and went to work. I had only seen the flyleaf once, a glimpse, but that was enough: It was as if I had the Bible at my elbow, and I did a careful job.

> *To Luther Dade Eustis on his twelfth birthday.*
> *From his Aunt Mamie, at Solitaire Plantation,*
> *1910—& may he read it dayly. Matthew 633.*

Three times I wrote it, breathing between the words, and the third time was just right: No one could have told it from the original except for the different paper, the strong black ink. I burned the first two in the grate, taking a chance on the smell of burning waking her, and started in on the second note. I printed that one in small capitals, finished it in a hurry. It looked good too, in a different way.

> WAS ON FLYLEAF OF BIBLE HE HAD. NAME WAS
> NOT GOWAN THE WAY HE SAID. HE KILLED SUE.

I folded them separately, careful to keep the folds from creasing a line of writing, and put them in separate pockets.

I was ready: I could have left right then. But there was no use rushing, I told myself: If he was going to run he would have run long since, and if he had gone home, that was where he would be tomorrow when they went after him, wherever it was. The only thing that really bothered me was that his conscience might save him: This might be the very night it would lead him to give himself up to the Law, and that way it might go easier for him in court.

Wait, I said—not so much that I minded crossing the lake at night: I had to be gone before day anyhow so Mother would not have a chancě to stop me: but I wanted dawn to be breaking when I reached the other shore, because I would be likely to miss the road and have to beat my way through a cypress brake to strike the highway. I got in bed with my clothes on and lay sprawled for sleep. But sleep would not come: I kept thinking of Sue, the way she died. I had thought something awful was going to happen to her (she had said so, she had told me to expect it): and after she was gone without saying good-bye, I even knew it. But getting a hint from the snaky-looking headline in the water and having Mother tell me she had found her like that, wrapped in wire with blocks to hold her down, made it worse by far. I was afraid: afraid that if I went to sleep I would see her in the water, halfway down, between the ooze and the surface, hair flowing back and wire squeezed into her throat. If one of her arms trailed out in a beckoning motion (Come to me) I would join her in the water, dead or no; I knew. That was the way she made me feel from the first, two weeks ago when Mother rowed them over. Luke stepped out first, Bible and cigar box under his arm. She came out behind him, carrying the bundle. I said, Who would live here that had any choice, any sayso? It seemed all wrong. And then I saw her. The sun was going down through the trees behind me; it threw a blood-red light on her face, soft-looking, and she looked at me (the light was more shadow than light: a blood-red shadow: and I could see she was thinking, What kind of creature is that? Her eyes got wider): I knew from the start.

That was a strange time, four of us living where two had lived before, and one of us being a girl and I had never known a girl before. The only woman I had ever been around was Mother, and Mother was mostly man. Sue was like the wicked ones the Prophets roared against: wore her clothes the way they did, and had that little gold chain on her ankle: walked the way they must have done, hip bones loose in their sockets, the bottom part of her stomach held well forward: talked the way they talked, too, I suppose, biting the words off sharp with her lips and using the tip of her tongue to give them shape. I could smell her, a female smell I never smelled before: faint yet clean like fresh-cut meat, and also like a melon past the ripe. I wanted to tell her the first time I saw her, You could teach me, if you would: You could make me understand. What is it keeps me awake at night, lying wide-eyed in the dark, feeling the vibration of Mother's snoring while summer's hot breath moves over my flesh and makes it creep? I wanted her to tell me all those things: I knew she could. Then later, when I had seen her like a statue in a garden the sun never reaches, with hair like moss in all the secret places: If you just would, I said.

As for Luke, whatever other things he told us that were lies, he spoke the truth when he said he was a farmer. After two days of fixing the empty shack he came and worked alongside me in the garden. He would work straight through without stopping until he had up a sweat, the blue of his denim shirt getting darker and darker across the back, a sweatstain shaped like a bib upon his chest; he was a farmer, all right. But then he would stamp the shovel upright in the earth at the end of a row (or sometimes before the end: in the middle) and take off for the shack at a stumbling run. He had short legs, long arms, and a sharp little nose, green eyes (so pale!) and reddish hair the shade of new-cut cypress planks, except he mostly wore his hat pulled down. He was good with a hoe, too, chopping steady and sure, making every lick count: I could see by his hands he had used one all his life, calluses shiny on the insides of his thumbs. He did better than a row and a half to my one, and Mother always told me I was fast. Something was driving him: Something was in behind him.

That was at first. Later he worked with me less: began to take long walks, alone, all over the island, staying gone so long that sometimes he only got back just at sundown: Whatever was driving him was letting up. Not long before they went away I was walking across to the Arkansas side, to check on the trotlines there, and I nearly stumbled over him down on his knees in a clearing. He was praying: had his hands joined at the front of his throat, tips of his fingers touching the point of his chin: and did not even open his eyes or notice me in any way, though he was sure to have heard me coming because I could feel the cane shoots popping against my boots. I kept going. Seeing him praying like that, I felt the way a person would feel if he walked in through the wrong door by mistake and caught somebody doing something nasty.

He never had anything to do with me at first, except for working alongside me in the garden (and that did not count: I might as well not have been there, where he was concerned): But later, after I began going over to the shack while he was off exploring the island and praying, I would look up from my work and find him giving me glances between chops. His face had a speculative expression, pale eyes narrowed to slits with the light peeping through in glints, and I would turn my head, feeling a quaver of fear creep up my backbone: because I knew it was wrong to feel the way I felt, even if she was not his wife, and I knew too what Jesus said about it being as much of a sin in your secret heart. I had the feeling that when he looked at me with those narrowed eyes he was reading the words right off my heart: and I was afraid. Because all I had to do was imagine what I would be likely to do if she was mine and I had her off on an island, ready at hand, and then read words like those off the heart of another man, even if he was nothing but a dumb one and would not know how to go about sinning unless she showed him: I would know he was wanting, and that would be enough.

I was afraid: I was really afraid, my heart knocking in my throat most of the time. But I was not afraid enough to stop. I would watch through the clearing leading down to the shack, where maybe a finger of smoke came lazy and thin from the crazy-angled stovepipe, and as soon as I saw him come out of the door and head off into the woods and swamps, I would put down the spade or hoe and go to see her. She would be standing at the stove, making a ruination of the vegetables Mother sold them out of the garden because he would not take them as a gift, or sitting on the up-ended nail keg that was their only piece of furniture, looking out of the window where I had stood looking *in* the night before. Her hair was the color of cornsilk when the ears begin to tassel, and she wore pennies under the flaps of her shoes. I stood in the doorway and she would look at me and smile and motion hello, friendly but secret too. At least I thought it was a secret.

After the first time, I began to learn the shape of her mouth and we could talk: or she could. And after the first few times, all we needed was our eyes. I would squat on the packed dirt floor, looking up at her like a dog and almost panting, and she would sit on the nail keg, looking down. Our eyes did the talking: like this.

Hers: I know and I would if I could but I cant.

Why? Why cant you?

He says No.

Mine: Did you ask?

Yes. He says No.

I wouldnt tell.

And hers: He would know.

How would he? How?

He just would.

And mine: Please. Please?

No. He says No.

And when she crossed or uncrossed her legs I would think if I could just hear that little silky sliding sound of meat against meat, maybe that would be enough; maybe I could go and never come back. Or if I could touch her, really touch her, I thought. And I would screw up my courage (lean slowly? lunge?) to touch her once and run: but I never could. I would stay as long as I dared, and finally go back to the cabin, hangdog, shamed. Mother would be waiting for me, hands on hips, eyes blazing.

When Luke began coming to work in the garden less and less, spending more and more time off to himself in the cane brakes, it came to me all of the sudden: Maybe, I thought, Maybe he will go away for good, leave just the three of us together here on the island. But I knew it would never work out: Sue would go after him, even if she never found him, and Mother would not have her here in the first place except for Luke. Then finally, Sunday, two days before they left,

I went to the shack and she was by herself, cooking dinner on the rusty cast-iron stove. She turned, stirring the pot, and nodded hello. I noticed two things: One, she had been crying, for the tears were still bright on her lashes; and Two, she was not wearing her ankle chain. She kept her back to me, stirring mustard greens, and I took a seat on the nail keg. That was when I saw the Bible.

It was lying on the pallet, one scuffed corner showing from under the blanket. That meant he would be back before long, I told myself, because he took it with him everywhere he went: Chances were, he would walk lop-sided without the weight of it under his arm. She kept her back to me to hide the tears. I ought to go, I told myself. I felt ashamed. Then, for no reason at all, I leaned forward and lifted the Bible off the pallet. It fell open at the flyleaf (Look at me!) and I saw the writing: *Luther Dade Eustis, Solitaire* and the rest, written by a hand more accustomed to churns and mops than holding a pen. After the once when she nodded hello, Sue never looked back: She was hiding the tears. I leaned forward again and put it back on the pallet with the same scuffed corner peeping from under the blanket. I said to myself: What kind of a man is this, would steal a Bible?

I had barely straightened up from laying it down when she turned from the stove, holding the long-handled spoon, and I saw it all in her face, written plain as plain in every line and angle: *Something is going to happen to me!* And I knew then, already, as well as I knew later when everything was over and done: He did not steal it; Eustis is his name, the name he was born with. He is using the other name to hide behind, so that when he has done what he knows he is going to do, he can go away, go back to where he came from, and no one will ever know, will ever be able to follow and point him out and say, There: There is the one who was with her on the island when she was alive. And I knew too, as well as I knew my name—James Elmo Pitts—why he was always going off by himself to pray. He was praying for strength to do evil, and when he had prayed up strength enough *something was going to happen to her!* and she knew it.

It was no good trying to sleep, and never would be as long as I knew now what I had known for sure ever since Mother sat across the table from me and told it with the lamplight on her face. I sat up in bed. The cadence of her snoring was slower now, the way it always is between 2 and 3, so I knew what time it was, within an hour. It was still too early but I could not wait any longer: I felt my way, took the lantern off the nail above the door, being careful not to knock something over and wake her, and went down to the landing. Dew had not fallen yet; the weeds were dry and harsh against my legs. The moon was down but all the stars were out, spangling the vault of heaven, rim to rim. I got into the skiff and poled away from bank as long as I could touch bottom. Then I sat and rowed, for by that time I was in the clear: If she heard the oarlocks squealing now, she might wake up but she could never catch me in the dark.

Once I saw in a book that people who lack some one or two of the senses, sight or touch or smell or hearing, make up for it by being stronger in the others: Compensatory perception, the book said. And it is true, to an extent, as far as it goes. For example I think my sense of touch is heightened: I can feel all kinds of vibrations Mother never notices; I can feel a steamboat round the bend. But what the book failed to mention was that sometimes the senses are hooked together, interdependent: If you lose one, another goes with it. With me it was balance and sense of direction. Once I fell into the water, out where it was over my head, and I beat on the muddy bottom, trying to find the surface, until finally I gave out and floated, more dead than alive. I had that to worry about now. I knew Bristol was to the east, about two miles south, so I kept Polaris (off the outer lip of the Dipper) straight down the starboard oar and let it drift a bit toward the stern a little every now and then. The trouble was, How much?

It was not until I reached the other bank that I knew I had done wrong. If I had kept Polaris straight to starboard all the way across, not letting it drift, I could have floated down the left bank until I came to the concrete wharf: But the way I had done, letting the star drift toward the stern every now and then so as to make a diagonal crossing, I did not know for sure if I was above or below town. For a moment I had a terrible notion that I might have gone around the foot of the island and hit the Arkansas bank. But then I put it out of my mind: impossible. At first I was fairly sure I was north of Bristol, because otherwise (I told myself) I would have seen the reflection of the street lights. But then I got to thinking how high the levee was in front of town and what a late hour it was for the lights to be burning, and I did not know: Once you start doubting, you go whole hog. I had never left the island alone before, not even by daylight: Up to two weeks ago, when Luke and Sue came, I had never been out after dark in my life, except along the path that runs to the privy. I was lost: Lost. I knew where North was, I knew where South was: I knew where East was, I knew where West was. But where was I?

I got calm and thought. A north-south highway runs through Bristol: good. If I head east (if I am not in Arkansas) I will strike it above or below: good, for there will be time to wonder which way to turn after I reach it. So I lighted the lantern and tied the skiff to a sapling. But when I turned to take my bearings by the stars, there were no stars; there was only that double-thick blackness that comes before dawn. I was alone in a globe of golden light whose center was the hand that held the lantern. Where the light met the darkness was like a wall: It seemed I could stretch out my other hand and feel it solid against my fingertips, except it was just beyond reach and would stay beyond reach until I set the lantern down. Then suddenly, out of nowhere, the golden globe was

filled with wings and needles. Every moth and gnat and
mosquito in this end of Jordan County had seen the light at
once; I was breathing and tasting them before I realized my
mouth was hanging open. I blew out the lantern; the dark
walls rushed together like pressure into an abolished vacuum
(I almost believed I heard the resulting clap) and I was nowhere.

The stars that had burned hot and bright were gone; the
night was shaped to my body, glove to hand. Darkness was
so much like two thumbs against my eyeballs, I began to
believe I could feel the whorls of thumbprints. It must be
almost dawn, I said. All I could do was wait for daylight:
Without the stars to guide by, I was as likely to strike the
river as the road. That meant I had to light the lantern to find
a place to sit down. I did, and for a moment I was alone again
in the golden globe: then *flick!* it was filled with wings and
needles, fluttering, stabbing, stabbing. I stumbled through
briers and creepers, half blinded by gnats and mosquitoes,
beating at them with my free arm (like boxing a flurry of
snow) until I came to a stump with a little clearing at its
base. I kicked at it a couple of times to see if a moccasin had
got there before me, hoping it was no female with her young.
I set the lantern on the stump and blew it out, then sat with
my back against the stump, and waited.

I went to sleep: I went to sleep twice and I had two dreams.
In the first I go down to the shack and everything is the way
it used to be: Sue is sitting on the nail keg and Luke is off
somewhere in the canebrakes praying, and she says: I decided
it will be all right, no matter what he says. She holds out her
hands to me, palms up, with a bit of rag tied round one finger
where she burned it on the stove, a soda poultice. This is just
at the end of day, the sun going down like blood on her face,
all soft. I go toward her: Sue, I say: You will have to show
me, Sue. I will, she says: I will: Come on. She motions with
her hands for me to hurry (Hurry, she says: Hurry, before
you wake up and it's just a dream: Ah, hurry! Hurry!)

wriggling her fingers: The rag makes a blur: But a cold wind blows between us, blowing darkness. I woke up.

It was all so real I could not believe it was only a dream and she was drowned and buried. I put my hand above my head, fumbling along the top of the stump until I touched the lantern. It was still warm, almost hot. I could not believe so little time had passed. Away off in the distance I thought I saw a pale pale glimmer of dawn, dove-gray in one direction. That would be East, beyond the levee: I was between the levee and the lake. I will wait for it to grow, I said. I watched it, waiting. The glimmer seemed to spread, away off in the distance: or perhaps I imagined it did. The stump was rotted soft as any cushion. I will wait, I said. But then, without how or why, I am walking along a beach or sandbar: It goes on and on, out of sight. The water alongside, clear as clear, has an amber light, a queer sort of sourceless glow, almost a radiance, and all at once (I have been walking forever) I see her the way I was afraid I would see her when I lay in bed back at the cabin, unable to sleep because of the fear of seeing her exactly as I see her now.

Halfway between the bottom and the surface, she rocks, rocks gently, turned on her side, pale hair trailing back in whorls like smoke. Far overhead the sky is blue, the perfect cobalt of a summer day: but seen thus, through the amber undersea light, the surface has a greenish tinge. Her head floats lower than her feet, and that is strange, I think, considering the mammary fat on her chest: But then I see why. She wears concrete blocks, like truncated boxes, suspended from her throat for ballast; they keep her down. I remember that a while ago I lay awake for fear she would beckon: Then I realize something even stranger. I am not looking down at her, I am looking up; I have walked into the water without knowing it; I am walking on the golden sandy bottom; I breathe water like air and it is sweet to my lungs, though faintly salt. A current rocks her gently on her side, hair writhing; one arm snakes out, limber as an eel, the hand performing that beckoning gesture I feared so much. Come here: Come here. But as I move forward, toward her, the water grows warmer, warmer; she radiates a fiery glow—the water is filled with invisible sparks; they strike my skin like the points of pins. She is guarded by pain! I came awake with a great jump, falling backward. The sun was like polished brass, high above the treetops, full on my face. I had fallen backward, into the rotted stump.

I lay there, knowing it had been a dream but thinking I was still on fire from the undersea sparks (thinking: Thus we bring the pain we feel in dreams out into the conscious world with us. For they were as real awake as they had been asleep) until, looking down, I saw that I was covered with small red ants, the kind that hurt, hundreds of them, thousands, and each one biting me for all he was worth. I was wrong: I had not brought the pain out of my dream: It had seeped into my dream from the conscious world.

It took me a while to get the ants off, another while to guess at my bearings and start. I walked with the sun in my face, East, and after perhaps an hour (I cannot tell) I struck the old logging road: That was luck, for it leads out to the highway. The sun was almost overhead when I struck the highway, turning right, and walked along the shoulder. Cars came past me, going fast: I would feel the vibration mount to a climax, then *zip!* the inward suck of the vacuum would tug at the front of my shirt. At last one slowed to a stop fifty yards down the road, pulled halfway off the concrete. A man and his wife were in it, dressed in style. But when I drew close the woman turned and looked at me and all of the sudden her eyes were full of fear. She rolled up the glass in the door and shoved at the man with her other hand: I could see her mouth twisting with fear as she spoke: Go on, go on, Fool! clawing at him with one hand and holding onto the inside door-handle with the other: Drive on! The car bucked off, slewing gravel, translated almost instantaneously from a standstill to full speed ahead, back onto the concrete and down it, getting smaller, and was gone. I noticed then, for the first time, what the night in the swamp had done to me: My clothes and hair were caked with mud and pieces of rotted stump, and my face was swollen out of shape by the ant bites and mosquito welts. No wonder she was scared, I thought: No wonder.

I had noticed they were dressed in style but it meant nothing to me until I got to town and saw others like them, walking lazylike in groups, all of them wearing their finery: It did not come to me what it meant until I was almost at the courthouse. I felt a sort of trembling in the air, vibration, and when I chanced to look up at a steeple I saw churchbells ringing. Today is Sunday! came to me in a flash. I stopped dead still in my tracks. That meant I would have to go to his house, wherever it was.

An old man sat on the base of the monument out on the courthouse lawn. Both hands were on the knob of the walking-stick planted between his feet, and his chin was on his hands. Watching me come toward him, he took one hand from under his chin and smoothed the ribbons and medals on his chest. I made signs but it was no good. Hey? he kept saying: How was that? Finally I thought to draw a star on my chest, and he understood. Sheriff, he said: What you want with the sheriff, boy? His lips were loose because of his teeth being gone, but I could read them. He pointed the way with his cane and signified with his fingers, first how many blocks: 3, then how many houses: 2, on the left-hand side.

When I got there they were at dinner: I could see them through the screen. I rapped and at last a Negro in a white jacket and cross-barred trousers came to the door. What you want? he said, looking at the mud and the welts. I made the star on my chest again. What ails you you cant talk? he said. I could see them past his shoulder; those on this side of the table had turned half around in their chairs. There was a telephone on a stand inside the door. Then the one at the head of the table rose, a pot-bellied man with a dinner napkin in his hand: He came toward me and I saw a little six-pointed star pinned to the pocket of his shirt: SHERIFF it said, bent in a bow. All right, he said: What is it? The Negro in the jacket and convict pants went back to the dining room.

I gave him the first note first. When he had read it he looked at me with a curious expression on his face, holding the note in one hand, the napkin in the other. Then I gave him the second note. He read it fast, eyes going narrow, then gave me a quick little positive nod: Wait there. He took up the telephone but the mouthpiece hid what he said.

TWO

4. Eustis

All the wild time afterward looking back, up till almost the end, I was able to point to one thing sure in all the swirl: It was God's will I was led to her, for it was God's work I was attending when I saw her that first time at the pavilion on the other side Lake Jordan. Brother Jimson planned for the service back in the dead of winter, an Easter picnic with prayer meeting to follow, held in the open air so that whoso would be saved could be saved in the sight of all. The women laid out cloths and hampers on the slope leading down from the road to the lake; it was grassy there. "We'll fight old Satan on his own ground," Brother Jimson said.

He was talking about the pavilion. It stood empty through the winter months but any day now the man that owned it would hang up the paper lanterns again and plug in the music machine and the nights would be filled with tumult. They built it early in the war, to draw the soldiers from up at the Bristol air base, a dance hall open on all four sides where they came through spring and summer and fall, planting time through picking, to do a heathen dance with girls in short silk dresses and paint on their faces and legs; the soldiers would throw them out, holding onto their fingers, and they would come prancing back, pigeon-toed with little mincing steps, shimmying their shoulders and bouncing their bosoms and making a display of the inside of their thighs. That was what Brother Jimson meant by the devil's own ground. People came from miles around to watch and be corrupted, then went home and lay in bed remembering. Dissatisfaction came into their minds. Next morning they looked at their wives, comparing them to the pigeon-toed prancers back on the lake, and the dissatisfaction got worse.

Satan's own ground, he said. But it was cold right up through Easter this crazy year; the man hadnt even strung the lanterns yet, much less plugged in the music. After the women cleared away the picnic things, Brother Jimson stood on the seat of a folding chair down by the water's edge. You might think he was limiting himself, preaching off a chair, but it was his prideful claim that he could save more souls without moving out of his tracks than most preachers could do by turning the rostrum into a circus ring. Some did just that, but not Brother Jimson. First he stood like a calendar Indian, staring from under the flat of his hand, first right, then left, then center. Everyone got quiet, watching him; there wasnt a breath, until after a while he spoke.

"I look out," he said. "I look out from the heights of salvation, and what do I see?"

From all directions, right and left and center, voices rose in a quaver. "Tell us, Brother, tell us. What is it you see?" Then a pause.

"Unrighteousness," he said, making a sweeping motion with both arms; he screwed up his eyes; "Unrighteousness on every side," and went directly into it without any more to-do. "Lo! I knelt down in the darkness alone with my Lord (for He was beside me you can be sure, as ever He is): 'What must I do, Lord? What must I do?' Thats what I asked, cried out. And lo again, a still small voice like unto that which spake unto Samuel (for I was as a little child again) sayeth, 'Go forth; go forth, Brother Jimson, and let the sweetness of My salvation rain like the dew.' 'I hear you, Lord,' I made reply— and felt a squirming down deep in the depths of my bowels (Do you know that feeling, Brother? Do *you* know it, Sister?"

"Oh yes!" from all sides. "Indeed, indeed we do!"

"Fine," he said; "Thats fine," talking with his normal speaking voice and even smiling; "Youre Christians all: or almost all," and then boomed out with his pulpit voice again; the smile was gone:) "—right down to the depths of my bowels, a-squirming, while my heart swole big with the strength of God. Enormous. 'Yes, Lord, yes,' I made reply; 'I hear you, Oh my Lord; I'm on my way.'"

I never knew him to go into it so sudden. Most times he starts out low, letting it build up stronger and stronger till finally a man three fields away can hear him plain as the ones on the moaners' bench. Maybe that was because today was Easter and there was a greater need for salvation because the world was wickeder than it had been at any time since that first Easter, nineteen hundred and some-odd years ago, when the Roman soldiers hunted the martyrs with swords. At the start, when he first began, I told myself: If he keeps on like this for long, he'll be so wore out we'll have to take him home draped over the tailgate. In my poor sinful way I overlooked the very thing he was preaching about: the strength of the Lord. He was counting on that to see him through. And it did—up to the point where trouble started—though truth to tell, his voice got gravelly long before the close.

He was bull-necked, bench-legged and thickset, gristly without an ounce of fat on his body. Preaching, he mopped at his face with a blue bandanna. His forehead was pocked with smallpox scars and his nose was broad and flat at the bridge where it got broken when he was a sinner in his youth. My sinful youth, he often said. Today he wore his preaching clothes, a full-skirted broadcloth coat and a narrow string tie bunched at his throat, a boiled shirtfront with one brass stud and trousers so long they crumpled down over his shoes. Every now and again he would beat at the air with his hands, waving the bandanna like a flag. He had a way of standing that showed off the bulge of his crotch, but nobody took it amiss; they knew that was part of what he meant when he spoke of the strength of the Lord.

We sat in rows on the slope, heads tipped back to watch,

the men with their hats on the grass beside them, brim up
to let the sweat dry, napes showing a bone-white line between
the shaven rims of the Easter haircuts and the brick-colored
leathery necks with pale creases, and the women with their
faces hid from the side-view by bonnets tied under their
chins. Men who were eldest sons and heads of families wore
vests with watch chains that had belonged to their daddies
and granddaddies looped across them, each with his children
ranged to right and left according to age. At the beginning
most of us leaned back on the heels of our hands, moving a
bit from time to time to pluck a blade of grass to munch,
but when Brother Jimson got going good, we all leaned forward, lacing our fingers in front of our knees, and rocked
back and forth to the rise and fall of his voice.

Kate was on my left, with Luty Pearl between us, and
Myrtle was on my right. Rosaleen, our oldest, was in the rear
with her husband, Cary Poteat; I could hear her cries coming
shrill above the others: "Yes, Lord, yes! Oh yes, indeed!"
Once when the preaching got louder all of a sudden (it was
husky already by then: "I'm asking you now, you sinners; I'm
asking you now. Are you saved in the sight of God?") Luty
Pearl began to whimper, fingering at her harness belt, and
Kate had to break off listening to comfort her.

Uncle Denny Poteat, Cary's daddy, a thin little man about
seventy, was the first to come through. That was as usual.
Some of the others had barely begun to twitch, shifting their
legs around because they felt the edge of the Spirit beginning
to enter, when all of a sudden Uncle Denny jumped up and
began to kick and hit.

"It's *on* me!" he hollered, flinging about, the way he always
does. "It's *on* me! I feel the Power!"

Women sitting near him dodged and bobbed, keeping out
of the reach of his fists and feet, and three of the men (they
had known it was coming) jumped him and held him down.
He thrashed around for a minute and then lay still. Uncle
Denny was always the first and the final, taking a sort of pride

in being so, but it never lasted for long at a time. Sometimes I misdoubted him, the way it went like clockwork.

"You can turn me aloose now," he told the men, his voice just barely getting heard because of the way they had his face pushed in the grass; "I'm done subdued."

So they let him up and he dusted off his clothes and took his seat, sitting proper and prim as if nothing had happened. Everyone within reach kept an eye on him, though. They knew he was due to come through at least twice again before Brother Jimson was done.

But the preaching had hardly got resumed before it happened to another one: a woman this time, a big full-bodied woman with a snuff-colored face from down in Issawamba County, south of the lake; she had come up to visit relations. Nobody had noticed her much before, but now they did. She went over backwards without any warning, hollered Whooey! just once as she flopped (it shook the ground) and stretched out straight with her arms held stiff as pokers at her sides. She lay there a minute, rigid; nothing moved. Then her body began to rise and fall in the middle, her bottom thumping, and every time it hit she would move down the slope six inches or so, like a measuring-worm.

People drew aside to let her by, not interfering, and when she had passed through three rows she lay still, right in front of the preacher's chair and almost under it. Her snuff-colored face had gone so white, the freckles stood out like liver spots, dark brown almost to blackness. We watched her lying there and nobody moved. Her under lip was sucked between her teeth and a little dribble of spit ran down from the corner of her mouth. She lay with her underdrawers on display until one of the nearest-by women leaned forward and pulled her skirt down over her knees. She didnt even twitch.

Brother Jimson looked down from up high on his folding chair and his face was aglow with joy and pride at the sight. This was his doing, a proof of his power. "Oh Brothers," he cried; "Oh Sisters," he cried: "We are going to save some souls for God this glorious Easter day!"

Inside the next half-hour three others were taken likewise, a man and two more women, but the real descent of the Spirit was yet to be. They were only the regular ones, like Uncle Denny: Brother Jimson was after the sinners today. I had the feeling that by sundown the whole mass of us would be sanctified, talking in the tongues, for that was what Brother Jimson was working toward; that was why he never came down off his chair to comfort a one of the early ones with the balm of his touch. From time to time a car would ease past on the road above, gravel creaking under the tires until they pulled to a stop (town folks, mockers, out for a Sunday ride in their Easter clothes) and sat there watching us down by the lakeshore, shaking their heads at the sight, and smiling at one another behind their hands.

We paid them no mind until finally one came along with the engine snarling, whining in low gear, tires making a sound like tearing canvas while gravel slewed and tinkled against the rims and under the fenders. A cloud of dust boiled up at the rear, banking and floating down the slope toward where we sat, and the car was gone. By the time we got the dust snorted out of our noses and Brother Jimson finished wiping it out of his eyes and mouth with the blue bandanna, we heard them coming back.

The horn was blowing this time: Aoooga! Aoooooga! two long hoots, and I looked up through the rolling dust and saw them: three men in khaki soldier suits, two girls in short-sleeve dresses. All five were turned sideways on the seats to watch us, laughing. She was up front with the driver, mouth lipsticked red. So far as I know for sure, that was the first I ever saw of her in my life. They came by twice again, going south, then north. When they passed the fourth time, the driver had thought up the notion of turning the ignition off and on to make the engine backfire. The dust rolled down. By the time it settled again they were gone for good.

But Brother Jimson had lost the fever pitch. He had to build it up again, from scratch. Down front, the Issawamba woman was still stretched out in her faint; she was dead to the world. Dust had settled an eighth-inch thick, turning her face snuff-colored again, and the nearby woman that had pulled down her skirt leaned forward once more and flicked at her with a handkerchief, knocking some of it off but not much; she slept on. Brother Jimson pounded and swayed. In the course of time he got it back toward a high plane again; he strove mightily and he did some good, but it never came anywhere near the pitch he was heading for when the car came along, went A*ooo*ga! and slewed all that dust in his face. Before it was over, four had given testimonials and another half dozen came through, not counting Uncle Denny his second time, but the sun went down and flared and died, blood-red in the western sky, without seeing the mass sanctification Brother Jimson had aimed at back in the dead of winter when he planned it. We broke up at dusk-dark.

The moon came up between the mules, in line with the wagon tongue. It rose big and golden, swelling toward the full, while we followed the road that winds around the head of the lake and down the eastern shore past Solitaire. Brother Jimson sat up front with me. Kate sat on a canebottom chair in back. Luty Pearl was asleep on a quilt in the bed, and Myrtle dangled both legs over the tailgate. We were the final wagon, for Brother Jimson had had to wait to shake hands around.

He kept his head down, letting it bob with the jounce of the wheels. Grieved as he was over the way the meeting hadnt come up to what he planned, he hardly said a word. The mules clopped on, ears at four crazy angles against the moon. Then we saw the campfire, like an eye in the night, and soon we came to the car parked half in the ditch.

"Pull up," Brother Jimson said when he saw it. "Pull up, Brother Eustis; pull up."

Before I had time to so much as twitch on the reins he was over the wheel, and by the time I got the mules to haw, he was crossing the ditch. His hat went down, then up, and he was standing at the rim of the circle of firelight, looking down at two of the soldiers and one of the girls. They raised up on their elbows, looking at him.

"What is it?" Kate said, coming out of her sleep when the wagon stopped. Then she saw them. I was wrapping the reins around the handbrake. "Mr Eustis," she said. "Mr Eustis, stay way from them people."

"Wait here," I said, and I thought to myself: Far be it from me to commiserate with a man that gets his comfort on a direct line from God, but this time for sure he is going to need more than the help of the spirit.

In my poor sinful way I thought he meant to fight them. He had provocation enough, the Lord knows, after the way they had spoiled what had been his heart's desire since back in the dead of winter: I couldnt have blamed him. All this time I was wondering where the other soldier was, and the other girl. I climbed down over the wheel, hurrying fast as I could without breaking my neck by tripping over the vines that matted the floor of the ditch, but before I could get across he was already talking.

"Brothers and sisters in Christ," he said, booming it out of him the way he does, "I come in the guise of the Spirit that tempereth the wind for the shorn lamb. I ask you to rise up out of your sin and iniquity, to go down on your knees and pray forgiveness for the wrong you done the shepherd and his flock. I ask it in the name of the Lord, Who sustaineth me in the asking. Let us pray."

They had a little radio shaped like an undersized suitcase, with even a carrying handle. It had been going all along but Brother Jimson drowned it out. Soon as he stopped speaking, it blared back up again, playing dance music, and a fellow's voice came out of it, singing with a whine about how he used to walk in the shade with a bluebird parade but now he had crossed over to the sunny side and was happy. It didnt make much sense to me, or maybe I heard it wrong.

"Take it easy, podner," a soldier said—except he didnt say podner; he said podry.

If he had waited, or if Brother Jimson had, maybe I could have got it straight what the whiny voice said next time it came around. But as it turned out, I never knew. Brother Jimson walked straight across one corner of the blanket to where the little radio was sitting, and without even stopping to draw back his foot, kicked it in a high slow looping arc, outside the circle of firelight and into the bushes. It hit with a clunk. I had half expected the singing fellow to give a squawk, like the kick had landed square in the pit of his stomach, but he didnt; he just quit cold, in the middle of a word, and things got quiet. I heard the katydids choiring off in the night.

One of the soldiers sat up in a hurry. "Hey," he said; he sputtered. "Whats the idea doing a thing like that?" He didnt rightly know what he was saying, he was so surprised.

"Sounding brass!" Brother Jimson shouted at them. "Sounding brass and tinkling cymbals! Hell is deep and yawns for such as you!"

That was when the other soldier, the one that was driving, came up. He was tall and thin and he stood just clear of the screen of bushes, holding a car seat under his arm. The stripes on his sleeve came up to a point and he wore his cap tucked under his trousers belt.

"Whats coming off here?" he said.

"Crazy son bitch of a preacher," the first one said. "Busted the radio."

"Broke it?"

"Broke it," the second said. "Walked up out of nowhere. Kicked it in the bushes. Blip! Like that." When he said Blip, he gave a little kick to show what he meant.

Brother Jimson stood watching them, holding his arms a bit away from his sides. "I ask you again," he said, "I ask you for fair: Kneel down with me and pray the Lord's forgiveness."

"I'm damned," the tall one said.

Then she came out of the bushes behind him, twisting at

her skirt to get it straight. Just as she came out, the fight began.

When it was over—two, maybe three minutes later—all Brother Jimson had to show for it was a rip in the tail of his broadcloth coat and a line of red above one eye where a fingernail had scraped. I say two-three minutes but there was no telling, really; it happened so fast. She came out of the bushes; the tall one dropped the car seat, started forward across the blanket, the other two soldiers coming too; and for a time the air was filled with khaki flags.

One by one Brother Jimson lifted them over his head and threw them into the darkness, first the tall one, then the other two, fast as they came within reach. They clawed and kicked at the air, sailing up and out in slow motion. Two landed in the bushes with a crash, the third against a tree trunk. Being the lightest the third one sailed the furthest; I heard the hasp of his back as it broke, a great loud crack like a stick of kindling snapped across your knee.

The girls ran out of the firelight, dresses fluttering bright against the darkness for a moment, and were gone. Brother Jimson stood alone in the center of the blanket. He was breathing a bit shallower than usual and just a little faster, holding his arms away from his sides the way he had done at the start when he first saw they were going to lunge.

"Lo, the wrath of a righteous God," he said, standing with the firelight flickering round him. There wasnt a sound from out in the bushes where the soldiers and girls were hiding and watching. "Lo, the wrath of a righteous God!" he bellered, standing straddle-legged.

A thing like that begins. Then something grows out of it and you look back. Chances are, you tell yourself it was all foretold in the seeds of that first beginning, if you could only have read them. But that was not the way it was with us. I took no more part in the fight than she did, just as earlier at the lakeside she had not done the driving nor I the preaching. We were caught up in events concerning others, like a man

out for a holiday swim that paddles full tilt into a whirlpool, never suspecting it was there until he begins to spin and hears it gurgle. I'd seen her twice, once in the car while it hooted along at the tip of a funnel of dust, once by firelight when she came out of the bushes with the soldier carrying the car seat they had sinned on, and both times I told myself if I stood a little closer I would smell the reek of sin coming off her like brimstone off the devil. But that was all she was to me. That was all on earth she was to me, just yet.

The mules had gone to sleep in the traces, standing with their heads down near their knees and hardly breathing. Brother Jimson and I climbed over the wheel, back onto the wagon seat. Kate just sat there: wouldnt talk or look at us. "Willikers, Brother Jimson," Myrtle said; "You sure pitched them." Luty Pearl hadnt stirred, curled up on the quilt. I unwrapped the reins from the brake and clucked the mules. They stumbled into motion, still asleep. Beside me, Brother Jimson was praying under his breath, asking the Lord's forgiveness in case He objected to what he had done. Overhead the stars were spattered bright and thick.

I wasnt praying. I was remembering her face, the way it looked when she came out of the darkness with the flush of sin still on it, and I told myself: It's because a godly man feels drawn to sin every time. Ungodliness needs salvation like a magnet needs iron. Like to unlike: thats why, I told myself, remembering her face, the fullness of thighs under the twisted skirt.

We drew up at the church and Brother Jimson climbed down over the wheel again. He lives alone, a widower, in a cabin just behind it. The scratch above his eye looked darker and broader now, almost black in the starlight. "Good night with God's blessing," he said.

"God's blessing," Kate said, like an echo.

"Good night with God's blessing," I said, and clucked the mules.

When we stopped on the road in front of the house, Luty

Pearl sat up in the bed of the wagon, turning her head from side to side, and began to moan and whimper. The stars looked almost close enough to touch. "There, there," Kate said, patting her shoulder. "There, there."

"Just listen at her," Myrtle said. "For shame. Going on twenty-two years old, carrying on like that."

In the end I had to tie the reins, climb down off the seat and lift her, quilt and all, and carry her into the house. She stopped moaning soon as I picked her up, but her head rolled loose on her shoulders and her mouth sobbed hot and wet against my throat.

"If that aint something," Myrtle said. "I ask you. Going on twenty-two years old and still being toted from place to place like a baby."

"You hush," Kate said. They were walking behind me, single file, the stars spattered thick and yellow above like drops flung onto a ceiling off a paintbrush.

"Whynt you tell *her* to hush? She's the one's been making all the racket."

"Am I going to have to tell you again?"

"Noam," Myrtle said, pouting.

Going up the three steps to the porch, I had a moment's vision of myself climbing the staircase to eternity with a whimpering in my ear and a hot wet sobbing mouth against my throat, carrying her past my fifty-first birthday, two months off, then ten years later my sixty-first, then ten years later my seventy-first, until at last—at the top—I'd stop and set her down, a little old wrinkled woman by then, and someone in the heavenly choir would ask me, 'How did you spend your time on earth?' and I would point to Luty Pearl: 'Carrying her,' I would say.

I went through the hall, and when I put her on the bed she was already asleep, fingering at the harness belt in a dream. Coming back from the lot after baiting the mules, I thought about being fifty-one years old, my life one long straight road without bends or hills so I could stand at any point and see clear to the end. Past fifty you can do that; all men can. For me, though, it was a road that began on a night over forty years ago, when a hand on my shoulder shook me, woke me up, and when I opened my eyes it was my father, bending over me; "Run down the road," he said; his face was pale, and I got out of bed and ran, my feet making puffs in the dust, and when we got back, Granddaddy and I, the flames made a roaring, curving over the eaves, all red and yellow with greens and blues mixed in, a striped swirl. When the roof caved in, the sparks made a tall round tower, a pillar of fire roaring up and up; it hung for a minute, then faded. They saw him through a window and he was praying, on his knees in the heart of the fire.

I undressed in the dark, hearing Kate begin to wheeze through her nose, asleep, bulging the covers no more than a plank would do, and then I remembered the girl again, the way I saw her through the dust and again by firelight, young and rounded and rosy with sin, in a twisted skirt. Her life was no straight road, not by a long shot. I knelt by the bed in my nightshirt and prayed for strength and guidance to see me through the burdened years down the long salvation road to my reward.

It began like that, with a sort of fretful unrest. There were two people inside my head, and both of them were me. 'Go to Brother Jimson,' I said to myself. And the answer came back: *What will he do but pray over you? Your ailment's in a spot no prayer can touch. You were ever sinful, Luther Eustis.* And I said to myself, my other self: 'I know it. But what must I do?' And the answer: *Wait and see. Just wait and see.*

And sure enough, after two weeks (it was as if something gave me two weeks to wonder) I began to see her everywhere I looked. That happens. One day you look into a crowd of faces and for some reason one of them jumps at you, fixes itself in your mind, and from then on, wherever you look you see that face. During the one month of May I saw her four different times, three of them only fleeting. The first of the four was May Day, a Sunday. We had just finished planting, for this was a late year because of the rains.

I was on the gallery, waiting for supper, and a car clanked up, an old one, wearing a plume of steam on the radiator. Fellow hollered at me, calling me Pops: "Hey, Pops. Got any water you can lend us the loan of?" He sat with both hands on the wheel. I had recognized her, sitting beside him, before the car stopped rolling.

He got out and came to the gate, a dude, wearing two-tone shoes and a hard straw hat with a candy-striped band. His coat was a split-tail model with pads in the shoulders and a belt sewed onto the back. He chewed gum and his jaw moved sideways, chewing.

Myrtle brought him a lard bucket full of water from the kitchen pump. "Check-o," he said, grinning at Myrtle, chewing with a sidewise thrust, and Myrtle turned her head to hide her face. He poured slow while the radiator gurgled and spat, and she sat with the car door open for coolness, skirt laid back over her knees. She turned and saw me looking but her eyes just paused in passing, then flicked on, like I was a bug or at best a rag.

"Thanks, Pops," the fellow said. He set the bucket upside-down on the gate post. The starter hummed and then the engine sputtered. He raised one hand: "Ta-ta," and they pulled off. She hadnt even looked around again.

One week later, to the day, we were coming out of church and she went past in the same car she was riding in three weeks ago, at Easter, across the lake. There was no moon; I might not have seen her. But just as they came abreast of us they met another car coming from the opposite direction. The headlights flashed through the windshield, full on her face. I saw her plain for an instant. The tall soldier was driving, the same as before, and she was on the seat beside him, also the same as before. She raised one arm to shade her eyes and turned her head toward the side of the road where I was standing. It was as if I saw her by the glare of lightning: flick, then lost in blackness. After the fading sound of gravel slewing, tinkling, there was silence again. The dust began to settle.

"Who said you were?" Kate said.

"Were what?" I said.

"A bug or a rag," she said.

The third time was in Ithaca, two days later; I hitched and rode into town to get a clevis bolt for the harrow. When I came out of Ledbetter's and was walking back toward where I parked the wagon, I passed the drugstore and saw her sitting at one of the marble-topped tables, drinking a soda. I stopped in my tracks, right there on the sidewalk, looking at her through the open door.

She had the glass tilted back, shaking the ice to get the last few drops with the tip of her tongue; it was pink, like a cat's. And maybe as rough, I thought, standing there watching her. When she brought the glass down she saw me over the rim, standing still and looking at her. We were maybe four feet apart, and then she smiled. Her voice had sounded and stopped before I realized she was speaking to me.

"I know you," she said. Like that. "Youre the little man was at the picnic." She smiled. One hand was lifted, holding the soda. "How's your preacher friend these days?" Her eyes had the bold, glassy look that all their eyes have, plotting a downfall.

I dont know if I ran or not: I got away in a hurry. I was halfway back to the house before I could collect myself, take stock. 'Go to Brother Jimson,' half my mind was telling me. But the other half was saying, *What will he do but pray over you?* the same as before.

Somewhere once I heard that in the olden days they punished certain crimes by tying ropes to a man's two wrists, hitched horses to the ropes on opposite sides, then gave the horses a cut with whips so they bolted and tore the man in two. Riding home in the wagon under the heat of the noon-day sun, it seemed to me that God and Satan were doing the same with my soul; they were tearing it in two between them. But was it for a certain sin? Or was it for sport, the way they did with Job?

Between that third time and the fourth, nearly another pair of weeks went by. I could feel it building up inside me, the two-way pull. I knew already; it was like I had a voice inside my head: Something is going to *happen* to you! *Something* is going to *happen* to you! Rain fell, kept falling, the ground getting wetter and wetter, the cotton seed rotting, and the nearer it got to the end of the month, the louder the voice spoke to me: *Something is going to happen to you!* until finally here came the end of May and the rain let up and stopped and the ground dried fast, and sure enough, it happened.

This was just at sundown. I was raking out the cottonhouse down at the southwest corner, the one by the road, when I heard a clatter, a sputter drawing nearer, like somebody running with a metal washtub partly full of nuts and bolts and scrap iron. Maybe I knew already, remembering the sound. The blind wall of the cottonhouse was toward the west, and when I went to the door and looked out, I was just in time to see the car pull up. It coughed and wheezed and died: the same car as before, the one from May Day, overheated again. The same little puff of steam, like a feather balanced on its point, stood on the radiator cap.

"Hi," she said.

She was driving and at first I thought she was alone. Then I looked in the back and saw the fellow that was with her the first time, the one in the split-tail coat and two-tone shoes. He was sprawled on the seat, belly up, like in the old days when they brought them home on a shutter. His hands were clasped on his chest in a pose of peace, the hat with the candy-striped band placed over them. Somebody must have done it for a joke. "Looks peaceful, dont he?" she said, the point of her chin against the point of her shoulder.

He did. There was even a smile on his face, the kind the

undertaker makes with little hidden stitches inside the corners. Then I saw the drool, a shiny thread dropped straight as a plumb-bob line to a puddle of vomit on the floorboard, and I began to smell it.

"Is he all right?" I said, to be saying something. I was still holding the rake, the head of it inside the door, myself on the outside in the slanting sunrays.

"Aint he a sight?" she said, still smiling, and her eyes had that glassy look—glassier than before. We were like any two people making smalltalk in the sunlight. "We was on the way to the pavilion," she said. "Decided it was early yet, and stopped and had a few. And look at what happens. Aint he a sight?" Her face was sort of limber, loose. "I'm drunk too," she said. "I'm drunk as *can* be. Will you give the car a drink of water? It got hot. Woo."

She said it that way: "Woo": and then leaned sideways toward me, all of a sudden. "You not fooling me one teensy bit; no sir. Youre the little man was with the preacher. *I* know you, and youve been watching me. I know. And I know what youre *af*ter, too. But youre not going to get it, no sir." She took a breath. "Unless you got three dollars. Have you got three dollars, honey? My name is Beulah."

We were like any two people anywhere, standing in broad open daylight. Seeing her without hearing the words, anyone would have thought she was talking about something ordinary —the weather, say—and as I stood there, facing her, it came to me how easy some people take to sin. It fits them like the clothes they wear, all loose and flowing; they breathe it like air. But a man with sanctity wears armor; he breathes sin like fire. Every time he moves he clanks, and every breath he draws is a breath of pain.

I dropped the rake and crossed to the car, opened the door and took her by the wrist, and all this time a voice was like a roaring in my ears: *Teach her what it means to be a Christian; teach her in the only way she knows. Bow down to the flesh and I will give you strength: depend on Me.* In that final half minute before the two of us were joined so close together that nothing could part us, saving death, I believed that what had drawn me, what had had me in a stir since Easter, was an ache to save her soul.

"Woo," she said, looking up from the cottonhouse floor where I had raked it smooth ten minutes ago, as if I knew already she was coming, like a groom turning down a bride-bed; "Woo," with her head thrown back, eyes glassy, knees drawn up, waiting for me the same as she had waited for all the others: "You smell like a billy goat, honey."

Outside, the sun was gone but the light still held. Here inside, night had almost come. The whites of her eyes glittered and I couldnt hear her breathing; the whiskey had died in her, for God had exalted me above all his creatures. "I been so miserable all my life," she said, and while she talked, telling me about it from the start, I began to hear a high thin sound going zzz zzzzz in the gathering dusk outside. It was the dude on the back seat of the car, three feet beyond the blind wall, snoring. "All my life," she said.

4. (Continued)

It surprised me how little the island had changed in all those long forty-two years since the spring of Oh Seven when Granddaddy took me with him to Bristol for the barbecue the veterans gave every year across the river. I remember we stood on the Texas deck going over; I was nine and I held on tight to his hand except what times he used it to point with or to take his turn when the demijohn came round. All the veterans were officers by then. They were old beyond time, and seemed bigger than life in their gray full-skirted coats and wideawake hats with plumes. Their buttons winked in the sunlight and their sleeves were laced from wrist to elbow with the yellow braid that they called chicken guts. Granddaddy's other sleeve flapped loose. It had been that way since Shiloh, his first battle, when he was seventeen. I remember he used to tell about it, how the bonesaw sang when they took off his arm and how they put him in the bed of a springless wagon to ride from the battlefield back to Corinth, twenty miles, alongside a man that had his bottom jaw shot away so that his tongue lolled down on his throat like a bright red four-in-hand tie; hail came down the size of partridge eggs; the boneless stump swung from his shoulder, a little sack of bloody meat. He told about it on winter evenings when he could feel snow in the air. I'd ask him, "Did it hurt much?" and he would look down at me with his eyes bulged out of his face, and: "Hurt?" he'd say: "Like nothing *you*ll ever know." I thought about it while we rode the steamboat, and I re-

member I held onto his hand because I'd never been so far
from home before. Every now and again one of the veterans
would sneak a hand up to his mouth, take out his store teeth,
and cut loose with that squalling screech they called the rebel
yell: *Eeaaaaay!* and my blood would run cold at the sound,
though I knew that pretty soon afterwards one of them was
bound to tell how Stonewall Jackson used to say it was the
sweetest music known to man.

Twenty years later they were all dead, down to the final
home-guard drummer boy (only they never said *died*; they
said 'went up') but now they were young again, off on their
yearly spree. The steamboat warped in, backing water. Soon
as the stageplank went down they trooped ashore, formed
ranks at the edge of the woods and were assigned to details
by an old man with a shovel beard that grew high on his
cheekbones, almost up to his eyes, and even more braid than
the rest; they called him General but Granddaddy told
me later he'd only been a provost guard lieutenant during
the war; the only powder he ever smelled was burnt by a
hemmed-in deserter—"Not that there wasnt some danger in
that," Granddaddy said. They brought along half a dozen
niggers to do the work, all named Orderly, so pretty soon the
barbecue pits were going and everything settled down to a
regular hum. After they were full of sidemeat and whiskey,
they sat back in the shade while first one and then another
got up on a barrelhead and told about the boys in gray and
the fair ones left behind. When one got through theyd all
wake up and give him a cheer, and then another would climb
up on the barrel, flanked by a couple of Orderlies to keep him
from pitching off when he reached the part about States'
Rights and got excited, flailing his arms around. Far as I could
tell, they all made the same speech. But that didnt matter;
that seemed to be the way they wanted it.

After the second speaker, when the third was getting
started, I saw they were all going to be the same and I stopped
listening; I began to look around. I'd never been away from

home before but I knew that even if I had been everywhere, I would never have seen anything like this island. A man alone here, it seemed to me, would be like the only person left alive on earth. Except for the barbecue pits and the old men in uniforms lying asleep in the shade, it might have been the world the way it was before God made creatures to walk it.

The gathering broke up at sundown. We went back aboard the steamboat and then across the river to town, and all the way home on the train, with Granddaddy asleep on the dusty plush beside me, tuckered out from the yelling and drinking, head bobbing in time with the clack of the wheels, I thought about the island, about going back for the barbecue next year. But Granddaddy died that winter, of chills and fever—it was right after Christmas; some of the veterans came down for the burying, and one of them blew a foxhorn over the grave —so I never went back again in all those years. I kept it in mind, though, and the more time went by, the more beautiful it seemed. I used to dream about it, green and peaceful, shining in the sunlight: a promised land. Later, reading of Adam and Eve when the world was new, I understood what the Garden was like before the Serpent snaked in and corrupted it.

So in June when it came time for us to leave, to get away, I thought of the island. Now, I said: Now. I was like a man that dreams a thing for forty years and all of a sudden sees it about to come true. "You be Sue and I'll be Luke," I told her. "Sue and Luke Gowan," I said. I told her about the island, how it would be—no more meeting in cottonhouses or on creekbanks by the dark of the moon: just the two of us standing alone, out of sight of the world and all it stood for. "I know the place for us," I told her.

"All right," she said. Like that.

We went to Bristol by separate trains, myself one day and she the next, so no one could guess and follow. I had fifty dollars in bills and change, carried in a cigar box with my razor and two extra pairs of socks. Excepting my Bible, that was all I took. I spent the night in a workingmen's boarding house and went up to the wharf next morning; I asked around. There was a fisherwoman living on the island now, they said. It wasnt what I was hoping for, but it could have been worse. I kept telling myself it could have been worse, to keep from having time to be disappointed.

Miz Pitts, they said her name was: "She comes over on Friday mornings." This was a Friday, and sure enough after a while here she came, rowing across the water: a big woman dressed like a man (at first I thought she *was* a man) with a mustache and hard yellow eyes. She tied the skiff and set out for town with two big sacks bulging over her shoulders.

I waited for Beulah around by the side of the post office, the way I'd told her I would do, and when I saw her coming toward me with the bundle under her arm, it was like we were off alone already, far from the world. We went to the wharf and waited by the skiff. It was late afternoon by then, and after a while Miz Pitts came back. The sacks were empty now, dangling limp from one of her hands, like flags.

She looked at me hard while I told about being from Missouri, down for the picking season and wanting a place to live cheap in the meantime. She looked away once, at Beulah beyond my shoulder when I said Man and Wife, then back at me. Her eyes were hard and yellow. They shifted fast, but when they stopped they looked directly at you. She knows, I thought. She is going to say No. But she didnt. She just shrugged. "If I dont, theres others will," she said. "It's government land, open to all. Get in."

We got in. She pushed off. The minute the skiff cleared bank a heavy weight slid off my heart. I sat facing Beulah. We were at opposite ends of the boat, Miz Pitts between us, rowing, and I had to lean sideways to see around the big straw hat. Beulah watched the water sliding past. I realized then that up to the minute I saw her walking toward me, around by the side of the post office, I had been afraid she wouldnt come. I was still trembling from it, and I knew then how really far gone I was.

98

All through May, up into June, I had been two people, one of them standing outside myself, watching what I was doing, accusing me. At night in bed with Kate I would feel a trembling in my legs, a fever flush all over my body, wanting the other one. 'Is this really me?' I kept asking. And I told myself it wasnt sin. Sin was something done for its own sake; this was for her sake and my sake, not sin's sake. I told myself that. Then this other voice outside myself would come through, accusing me. *Thats just talk*, the voice would say. *Youre doing this because youre fifty-one; youre fifty-one this month and you are scared. Youre scared youll wake up dead in the by-and-by to find there aint any heaven, or hell either, and you wont have a thing to regret, much less to hope for.* That was the outside voice. And I would answer, still trying to explain: 'It's not for sin's sake,' I would say. *Ah no; thats only talk,* the voice would say. *Youve lost your faith. Maybe you never had it.*

I could have put up with that, the voice coming at me out of the night while I lay there trembling, feverish. The real trouble was, every inch I pulled her away from evil, I slid an inch closer myself. And I knew it; I knew it. It was like I once heard Brother Jimson say in church. There had to be a balance in the world, so much corruption to so much sanctity, or everything would come undone. People were little wheels in one big clockwork, so when one wheel turned in one direction, the one alongside it, meshing, had to turn too, in the other direction: for if once a wheel turned so much as a tiny fraction of an inch and the meshing one stood still, the strain would be too much; the clock would fly apart, explode. We would be at Armageddon.

'Then all right,' I said; 'so be it. My fate be in Thy hands.' And on the appointed night, when everyone in the house was fast asleep, even Luty Pearl, I put on my low-quarter shoes, took the cigar box with the fifty dollars, the socks and razor in it, and left by the back door. At first day-dawn the train pulled into the Ithaca station, its firebox shining red against the tracks, and I got aboard. The wheels turned slow, then faster, faster still.

"I know the place for us," I'd told her.

"All right," she'd said.

But all the way to Bristol I was worried, and even after we were in the boat, getting nearer and nearer with every stroke of the oars, I thought how much might have been done to it in forty-two years. It looked the same from across the water but I was worried. Then we were there. Miz Pitts went over the side, wearing boots, and pulled the front of the skiff up onto bank.

Her boy was waiting; they told me back at the wharf that morning he would be there: Dummy, they called him; it was all the name he had. He was about sixteen, with a head as round as a cannonball, a snub nose, and round little ears that hugged in close to the sides of his head, almost hidden by the hair curling long around them. When Beulah stepped out of the boat, he stood with his mouth hanging open and damp. Miz Pitts looked sideways at him, frowning. The sun was just going down.

I stood and looked at the island, thinking how much it had changed, how different it was from the way I remembered it, as if it had been sprinkled with a magic powder that made everything smaller. The sand was dirtier, too; I remembered it clean and white, like diamond dust. The trees that I remembered tall and leafy, shining green, looked bleached and stunted. I wanted to go back.

Then all of a sudden I realized it hadnt changed at all. *I* was the one that had changed: I was remembering through a little boy's eyes. Forty-two years is no long time in the life of an island, no more than the tick of a clock; but strap them onto the back of a boy and see what happens.

Miz Pitts led the way. "Youll have to bunk with us tonight," she said. "I'll take you down to the shack tomorrow morning and you can start to getting it cleared out. Nobody's lived there in ten or fifteen years, before my time."

Beulah and I had been apart two days. That was no longer than average. The point was I had spent them looking forward to this first night on the island, away from everything. And here we were already mixed up with two people, fixing to sleep in the same house with them. The world had got more crowded instead of less so.

I woke up before day, and at first I couldnt remember where I was. All I heard was a buzzing, a great loud rasping sound like a dozen ripsaws going at once, cutting pine. Then I remembered. Miz Pitts was in the next room, snoring; that was the buzzing sound; and Beulah and I were on a pallet in the other room. When dawn glimmered through I saw her sleeping beside me, hair swirled loose on the blanket above her head, clothes thrown over a chair beside the pallet, one hand on my chest, one knee between my legs. In the night she had kicked the blanket down. She was sleeping in silk pants and that was all.

After a while the snoring stopped dead still. It cut off all of a sudden, in the middle of a breath, and when I looked back toward the door of their room, wondering what had caused it, I saw Dummy standing in the doorway looking at me and Beulah on the pallet. I wondered how long he had been there, and while I was wondering—before I even thought to draw the blanket up—a long brown muscled sunburnt arm came round the jamb; it took him by the shoulder and snatched him back into the bedroom. I pulled the cover up to Beulah's throat, in case he came peeking again. She went on sleeping.

By then the sun was about to come up. It did, and I heard Miz Pitts stomping into her boots. I was tying my shoes, turned sideways on the pallet and being careful not to waken Beulah, when she began yawning and stretching. "What time is it, honey?" she said between yawns, sleepy voiced. I never could get up the nerve to ask her not call me that.

"Late," I said. I turned to watch her over my shoulder.

She made a little squealing sound: "Ooee," half yawn, holding the edge of the blanket under her chin and squirming so

that it rippled. "Come on back for a while. . . ." She rocked
on her hips, smiling at me over the edge of the blanket.

"There aint time. Miz Pitts—"

"*Take* time."

It wasnt the words so much as the way she said them, the
way she looked: not to mention the ripples in the blanket,
the little animal yawn, "Ooee"; I was fixing to climb back
in, shoes and all. But then Miz Pitts came out of the other
room, dressed the same as the day before, in corduroy pants,
blue jumper, and boots; the wrinkles were in the selfsame
places, even. I would have thought she hadnt undressed at
all, except I'd heard her stomping into the boots and I'd seen
the long brown naked arm come snaking round the doorjamb
after Dummy. "Morning," she said. Dummy came out behind
her.

"Morning," I said.

We had corncakes for breakfast, with blackstrap and coffee,
but Miz Pitts didnt do the cooking: Dummy did. That was his
job, along with tending the garden. I hadnt thought anybody
but Kate could make coffee as good as that, boiled in a bucket
with a spurt of cold water to settle the grounds. I began to
see him with different eyes, even if he was peculiar looking,
deaf-and-dumb, and had a habit of peeking around doors at
people before they got up in the morning. Anybody that can
make coffee gets respected.

That was a Saturday; we moved into the shack that evening.
Miz Pitts was right when she said it would take some fixing.
Weeds and creepers had taken it, inside and out. The roof
sagged at two crazy angles and the hand-hewed shingles had
curled so the sun made a checkerboard pattern, sliding gradually down the walls and across the packed dirt floor. But that
was all right; rain wasnt apt to fall this time of year, and if
the wind was going to blow it down, that would have happened long ago. Working all morning with a kaiser blade and
a hoe, I had the weeds hacked out by dinnertime. A rusty
cast-iron stove in one corner was the only piece of furniture,

but Miz Pitts lent us two sawhorses and some planks to make a table, a nail keg for a chair, and two blankets that I spread close to the window for a bed, packing sassafras leaves under the bottom one to make it soft and sweet. By night we had a home. Miz Pitts' cabin was nearly half a mile away, screened by trees. If I sat facing the opposite direction, so as not to see the smoke from her chimney rising, things were just the way I wanted them, almost.

For two days I was raking and straightening, getting it squared away. Tuesday there was nothing left to do. All morning I sat with my face in the sun, except what times I shifted around to the shade and drowsed. Inside the shack, Beulah was clattering pot lids, learning to cook. By dinnertime I was jumpy. I got up from the table and went outside. But I couldnt sit still; I got more and more jumpy—until finally I couldnt stand it any longer; I walked over to the garden patch where Dummy was working. For a while I watched him turn potatoes. Then I took up a spade that was leaning against a post, ran my hand along the handle to get the feel of it, and went to work alongside him. It felt good.

The sun was a little past the overhead, coming down strong and hot, and after a while I began to sweat. In two hours I sweated enough to make up for the morning's idleness. Dummy was a right good hand, spading steady and smooth. I held back, staying alongside him. Then I had to let go; I moved ahead. When I made the turn at the end of a row and met him face to face coming back, he kept his eyes down, spading steady.

Friday made a week we'd been there, a week and a day since I stole away in the dead of night and caught the north-bound train at the Ithaca station. I had fifty dollars in the cigar box when I left, but now it was down to thirty-eight. At that rate we wouldnt last another four weeks. Even allowing for the first week costing more because of the train fare and the one-night board bill and such, we wouldnt have more than five or six at the most. What then?—I'll worry about that later, I told myself. I'll worry about that when the time comes.

Miz Pitts was going to town. I went over early to give her the list of things we needed for the coming week. Dummy was out in the garden but he had already sacked the potatoes and corn for her to take to market; they leaned against the front steps. She looked at the list: short ribs, side meat, flour, molasses, sugar: then nodded and put the list in her pocket, throwing one hip out of joint to get her hand in, the way a man will do when he is wearing tight trousers with slash pockets.

We each took a sack on our shoulder, walking down to the skiff. She took the potatoes and left me the corn, which was lighter, though I could see she was having an easier time with the heavy sack than I was with the light one. When we had stowed them, she took her seat, hands on the oars, and I bent forward, bracing my legs to push the boat away from bank. There was something about her face, watching me over the knotty pair of fists that held the oars. She looked like an Indian, some kind of foreigner, or maybe her skin was like that from washing in muddy water all these years.

"How long will you be here?" she said.

She said it all of a sudden, but I could tell she had been thinking the words a long time and had just made up her mind to bring them out. I was bent over, ready to push, and it took me so by surprise I couldnt answer. She watched me and my legs went slack, unstrung. "A week?" she said. "A month?" Her eyes didnt flicker, watching me. "Or just till you get tired of it?" she said.

I braced and pushed; she went away backward, already beginning the stroke. But even the strain of rowing didnt change the look on her face, the steady yellow eyes. She watched me till we were blurred by distance. I stood looking after her, and I wondered just how much she really knew.

At sundown I watched her coming back across the water. The groceries were stacked in the front of the skiff, but I waited till after supper to go for them. We lit the lamp and cleared the table and I told Beulah, "I'm going over to pick up the things from town." She nodded, up to her wrists in suds, rinsing the bucket lids we used for plates.

It was not quite dark outside; I could follow the path already beginning to be worn between the shack and the garden where I went every morning to work. That way I came upon the cabin from the rear. Through the window I saw Miz Pitts and Dummy in the sitting room. They had finished supper; Dummy was washing the dishes. Miz Pitts sat at the table, hands moving fast in the lamplight, mending a minnow seine a gar had torn. Overhead the stars were winking through. I went around to the front and up the steps.

"Evening."

She looked up. "Good evening," she said. Her hands got still. Dummy turned and looked at me; he must have felt it through the floor boards.

"I came for the stuff. . . ."

She motioned with her head, both hands tangled in the net, and I saw the packages stacked against the wall. The store receipt was on top, with change from the five dollar bill. I was leaning down to pick them up and I heard her say, "Luke . . ." She'd never called me by name before. "I didnt mean to be prying," she said.

"Maam?"

"Because I know what prying is," she said, as if I hadnt spoken. She used the seine like a muff to hide her hands. "Sit down," she said, nodding at the empty chair drawn up to the table. I sat and she hitched her chair around sideways out of the light, her face toward me and the back of her head toward Dummy. "I wouldnt pry in anybody's life," she said. "I had too much prying in my own." She was quiet, collecting her thoughts. Then she looked over her shoulder to where Dummy was washing the dishes, making sure he couldnt read her lips. "I'll tell you," she said. It was sudden, the way she said it, but

I could see she had been deciding for some time, going over the words in her mind.

She came here from Alabama a dozen years ago: traveled west until she struck the river, and settled down. Dummy was still in short pants; the two of them lived in a leaky tent while she built the cabin. "I wanted to get away from people," she said. She had been a country school teacher, thirty years old, almost beyond the marrying age, when this insurance salesman came along. His name was Pitts, James Elmo Pitts. He sold burial insurance, a new thing in those days: went from door to door collecting, fifty cents here, seventy there, depending on what style coffin a customer wanted. She married him and quit teaching school. They rented a house of their own: frilled curtains, primrose china—everything. He went out in the morning, making the rounds, and came home every night. "It was a good life," she said. Her hands, folded half in the minnow seine with the lamplight falling on them, looked like they had been in river water for months and then had been taken out and scrubbed, but the mud got soaked too deep in the skin to wash out. "In its way," she said.

For three years, almost four, things went like that; they lived like any two people anywhere. Then one day, out of a clear blue sky, she told him they were going to have a baby.

Pitts was forty-five, beginning to go to fat, with a little paunch to button his vest across. He had blue eyes, pale blue, and wore his hair brushed straight across his forehead. All these years he'd been a bachelor. When they were first married he used to speak of having a son to carry his name on down. But time wore on and nothing came of it; he put it out of his mind, so that by the end of three years it was like something he had never considered, much less counted on. Then she told him: 'We are going to have a baby,' and everything changed. "You wouldnt have known him," she said. From that day he began to walk with a strut, like a Bantam rooster or maybe a Shetland stud. He was sure it was going to be a boy. Months went by; he was selling policies hand over fist. It made people happy just to be near him; they bought everything he offered. Finally the time was up. She went to the bathroom late one night and while she was in there it started. She came back and told him, 'The water broke.' He was on his way to phone the plumber; she had to stop him and explain what it meant, and then he got excited. She had a hard delivery. It came feet first and the doctor got rattled, but finally on the second day the baby was born, and sure enough the husband was right. It was a son. "He was fit to be tied," she said meaning Pitts.

She was quiet for almost a full minute, keeping her head down, her face in shadow, her hands twisted into the net. Behind her, Dummy was finished with the dishes. He leaned against the sink, watching us though he couldnt tell what she was saying because her back was to him and her face was in the shadow. All the time she talked I wondered why she wanted to tell *me* all this. She came all the way from Alabama, getting away from people that knew and pried, yet here she was telling me about it, the very first person to live near her in all these years. It made me wonder—Is that the way it is? I thought. When you carry something locked in your secret heart, do you feel obliged to tell it to everyone comes near you? And why is it beginning to sound so much like *my* life? Is she making it up? *And how much does she know?*

The only one that could have told her was Beulah, yet I knew for certain they hadnt exchanged a dozen words in all the time we had been on the island. For a minute I thought she might have heard something in town; maybe they were looking for us already. Then I remembered she began it even before she set out for Bristol that morning. So thats not it, I thought. And I thought some more, watching her: Wait, I thought; wait—beginning to understand. It's because two people, any two, can tell when they share the same sorrow. It shows in their eyes; they recognize it in one another's eyes. Wait; wait—I was beginning to understand, but she started talking again.

"He was fit to be tied," she said. He pranced and strutted

worse than ever, wanting to hold the baby before it was even handed to its mother: made a fool of himself the usual way, in fact. For instance, he made a to-do about the baby's eyes ('As blue as my own!') until the nurse told him all their eyes were blue. That took some of the wind out of his sails, but not for long; he bounced right back. "You ought to seen him," Miz Pitts said: close to fifty, inclined to fat, and making a display. All that month he came home loaded with toys. He was forever bragging about how good the baby was, how it didnt cry or beg to be rocked. But Miz Pitts knew already what was wrong; she was with it twenty-four hours a day, and she knew. Its face would wrinkle and go red; the mouth would shape for squalling, fists clench and legs draw up: but no sound came, only the whisper of wind in its throat. She knew but she couldnt bring herself to tell him. On top of everything else, she began to get an ache at the pit of her stomach. Finally she told him; the baby was one month old; 'You better call the doctor,' she said. And sure enough, the doctor came and looked down the baby's throat and it was true, what she suspected. There wasnt any voice-box: no strings for it, anyhow. The baby was dumb.

Dummy came across the room from the sink. When he got near the table Miz Pitts stopped talking. She turned in her chair and watched him take up a book and sit with his back to the lamp, beginning to read. The book was limp and black, with thumb tabs down the edge; I thought it was a Bible until I saw it open beyond his shoulder in the lamplight: a dictionary. She watched him, making sure he wasnt trying to find out what she was saying, then turned and went on talking.

Pitts couldnt believe it; he seemed to think nothing that bad could happen to him. "He'd never known real trouble before," she said. She would wake up in the night and hear him praying for a miracle. Then later she'd wake up again and find him bending over the crib with a pocket flashlight, looking to see if the miracle had come true. "He kept hoping against hope," she said. All this time the ache at the bottom of her stomach was getting worse. It was really a pain now, sharp, and it never let up. Finally she told Pitts and he went and got the doctor. 'Female trouble,' the doctor said, and told her to come to his office for a check. She went and he told her to come back two days later, and when she came he said he would have to operate—history-rectum, something like that. 'All right,' she told him; 'Whatever you say.' So much had happened already, she figured anything else would be down-hill. But when the doctor got her on the table, laid open, he took one look and then began cutting and taking out. By the time he got through, all she had left was stomach and bowels. She came from under the ether knowing something awful had happened to her; she felt empty inside, the emptiness of pain, like something washed up on a beach. Three weeks later she went home, where Pitts had been nursing the baby all this time, and it was right after this that the change began. First her voice got deeper. Then hair began to sprout on her arms and face. Before long she had a fine, downy mustache, like a boy in his middle teens.

After that, things came apart in a hurry. The neighbors were talking about it, how a woman down the street was changing into a man right under your very eyes. They made special trips to see her, coming in twos and threes for safety, claiming it was out of the goodness of their hearts, commiserating and bringing her bowls of fruit. Then they would go home and tell their friends about it ('She's got a mustache and a bullfrog voice and everything.' '*Every*thing?' 'Almost everything. Aint it spooky?') until finally when they called, nobody answered the bell. Pitts took it hardest. People questioned him so much, he stopped going out: gave up peddling policies and sat at home, just the three of them in the house, not answering the bell. When the money ran out (— it wasnt long; the doctor took all but a little) Pitts got a job on the WPA, pushing a shovel for eighteen-twenty a week rather than go from door to door collecting on burial policies from people that asked him questions about his wife. Then one evening he didnt come home. "I never saw him again," she said.

She kept her face down, out of the light, both hands wrapped to the wrists in the net. "But I never blamed him," she said. "He'd already paid the doctor and hospital bills and a month's rent in advance. Most men wouldnt have done even that much." Next morning she found a twenty-dollar bill in the sugar bowl, left where he knew she'd find it. "I wondered how he'd managed to get it," she said. "Then later I realized he must have saved it out of the money he had before. He had been planning all that time to get away. But I never blamed him; I never blamed him. He had every cause."

Before the month was up and the rent came due, she took a job on the WPA, like her husband. They put her to renovating mattresses. "Theres many an Alabama couple sleeping soft tonight because of me," she said. She worked at it six years, looking more like a man all the time, and then the last thing happened. The boy got sick. It began with a fever that went on for two days. He lay there with his head pulled back, pointing his chin in the air. 'Meningitis,' the doctor said. They thought he was going to die but they were wrong. He didnt die; he lived. But he lost his hearing: seven years old, the age when you first really start paying attention to all the different sounds in the world around you, and he was stone cold deaf. The meningitis wrecked those little bones inside his eardrums, the ones you hear with. If a cannon went off behind him now, he wouldnt hear it. "That was the last," Miz Pitts said. "I had enough."

'It's a curse on the land,' she told herself. All the neighbors came back in twos and threes, commiserating, prying. She stayed out the month till the rent was due, then sold the furniture second-hand, knowing she was being robbed—'Take it or leave it,' the man said, and she took it—bought bus tickets for herself and the boy, and headed west to get away from people. At Bristol she struck the river and she stopped. "I wanted to get my bearings," she said. Then she heard about the island. It sounded like just what she was looking for. She spent what was left of the furniture money, buying equipment, and moved onto the island. She started a new life, away from people. Except for the weekly trips to town, selling vegetables and fish in season, she kept to herself. Soon as Dummy was old enough to be left alone on the island by himself, she stopped taking him with her except for a special treat. Her old experience teaching school came in handy. She taught him how to read and write: first a little at a time, and then a lot. Once he got started he learned fast—sign language, print language, lip language, all together—until now he spent his spare time reading the dictionary and practicing penmanship.

Miz Pitts was quiet. Then she raised her head, leaned forward with both hands on her corduroy thighs. Her face came into the lamplight. 'Thats my life up to now,' she seemed to be saying; 'Whats yours?' Her nose thrust forward, nostrils lined with dark fur above the dark mustache.

I looked at her for a minute, then got up. I didnt rightly know what to say: whether to tell her I admired the way she left the world (I'd done it too) or sympathize with her for all the trouble she'd seen. "I have to be getting back," I said. She sat there, watching me; I felt foolish. I got up, crossed the room, and took the bundles under my arms. "Good night," I said. I stood in the doorway. She just sat there. I went out.

The one I felt sorriest for was the husband, Pitts. I thought of all the bad-luck things that came his way, first a son born dumb (he had wanted a son) and then a wife changed into a man right in front of his eyes. Where is he now? I wondered. Like me, most likely, I thought: Gone off with another woman. The moon had come out, swelling toward the full. The stars were paler. The milky way arched right across the sky. Then all of a sudden it came to me why Miz Pitts had told me all that. She told it because she thought I might leave Beulah. But it didnt work the way she meant. It made me think of Kate, and Luty Pearl.

Then I saw Beulah through the window of the shack, like in a picture frame, sitting on the keg with her chin in her hands. Her eyes were open but she was looking at nothing. When she heard my footsteps she looked up.

"What took you so long?"

"Miz Pitts," I said. I put the bundles on the sawhorse table. "She got to talking about her trip to town." I knew it was a mistake as soon as I said it. Always before this, I managed not to mention town at all.

"Whats playing at the picture shows?"

"She didnt say. . . ."

We sat a while. It was too late for the twilight bath we usually took, by the edge of the lake in a covy pool. We'd gone there every night except this and the first one. Then I got out the Bible and began to read it—the first time I'd done that since I left home. I read in the Book of Job how he scraped at his boils with a potsherd and sat in the ashes, and when his wife advised him to curse God and die, Job thought: Theres woman for you; aint that just like a woman?

Beulah sat for a long time watching me. Then she undressed and got in bed. Whenever I glanced sideways from the Book, I saw her watching me with reproach in her eyes. Curse God and die, they were saying. So it seemed to me. Finally I blew out the lamp, undressed, and got in beside her. I stayed flat on my back, trying not to breathe out of time with her breathing. It wasnt easy. I could feel the strain of her waiting: Touch me! Touch me! but I didnt touch her; I went to sleep, and almost as soon as I dropped off I began to hear Luty Pearl whimpering. I was half from under the blanket, on the way to comfort her, before I woke up and remembered. Moonlight spilled through the window. "I'm off on an island," I said aloud, and didnt know I'd spoken till I heard the sound of my voice. I was dreaming, I thought. But soon as I went back to sleep, I dreamed it again. I could hear her whimpering, plain as plain.

Night after night, for five more nights, I lay there hearing her. Soon I got so I knew it was a dream; even inside the dream I'd say to myself, Youre dreaming; it's a dream. I'd wake up and lie there, the echo of her sobs still sounding out of sleep, and I wouldnt so much as stir; I knew I was dreaming and she was thirty miles away. A man can get used to anything, almost. In the daytime, for six days, I prayed. I stopped working in the garden. I went into the canebrakes, off to myself, and fell down on my knees and prayed for guidance. 'What must I do, Lord? What must I do? Tell me what to do: I'll do it,' I prayed: 'I'll do it gladly, whatever.' But there was never an answer, nothing; I was praying to deafness and I was alone. The sun came down and the steam went up from the marshes; I could hear the snakes and tiny creatures stirring. Once Dummy walked up on me, down on my knees. Still I prayed: 'Tell me what to do, my Lord.' But the Lord had forsaken me. I was alone.

All this time Beulah was watching me, waiting. There was something in her eyes. 'Youre trying but youll never make it,' they seemed to be saying. 'Salvation's not for you. Curse God and die.'

Finally at the end of six days of praying, six nights of dreaming, I made up my mind. I could trace back to what caused it, what began it. Miz Pitts' story, that tallied so close with my own at so many points, was the beginning. If she hadnt told me her life, all this wouldnt have happened, this dreaming, this praying. Or anyhow it would have been delayed till there was no turning back, which was just as good.

When the six days were up, it was Friday again. I saw Miz Pitts that morning, and when she asked me what we wanted from town, I told her: "Nothing, I thank you." She looked at me from under her hand, shading her eyes from the sun. I walked away, feeling the eye beams meet at the center of my back like spears.

Next night the time was up; I had made my decision. All that was left was telling Beulah. She cleared away the supper things and lit the lamp. We sat on opposite sides of the table, looking at each other. It went through my mind like a streak of light: *She knows! She knows what youre going to say before you say it! But what will she do?* I watched her across the table, shaping the words to my tongue, and then I told her.

4. (Continued)

"I have to go back," I said.

By then there was more behind it than just the misery Miz Pitts had started me to thinking on. Beulah had showed me she was already past saving, past my poor sinful power to raise her up. This was the Wednesday before; we were lying in bed; it was late. She began talking of Dummy, how he'd come and sit and look at her, honing, while I was off at the other end of the island. "I swear, honey," she said, "I feel so sorry for him I could cry."

She was leading up to something, some kind of notion. But I was so busy wondering, I missed what it was. All I caught was the tail end of her words. "Let me," she said. "I wont unless you say I can, but let me. One more wont hurt, and that will be all; I promise. We can make believe it was before—before we met. Because if I dont, maybe nobody will, not ever. You want him to go through life like that, not knowing?"

—Depraved, I thought. She's all the way depraved.

"Do you?" she said. When I didnt answer, she rolled over and leaned on her elbows, one hand on my shoulder, looking down. Above us, stars were twinkling through the roof. Her hair hung forward, down both sides of her face. She was in earnest. "Please, honey, just this once and then no more. It's not for myself I'm asking. Youre all the man I want; you know that, honey. It's just I feel so downright sorry for him, being the way he is. Will you let me? Will you?"

"Turn loose," I said.

She saw how mad I was. "All right," she said, and took her hand away. "But you have to admit I was honest to ask." She leaned forward and her hair fell on my face.

Thursday I was coming back just before supper, Bible under my arm, and I saw the back of Dummy's shirt; he was running up the path I had worn on the way to the garden every morning. For a minute I thought, She did it anyhow, no matter what I said. But when I got to the shack she was standing at the stove, the same as always; I knew I was wrong. She didnt mention it again until that evening at twilight. We were down at the lake for our bath.

The shoreline makes a dip there, forms sort of a cove, an inlet, waist deep, surrounded by willows; they screen it on all four sides. Late in the day, sunlight has a golden color, strained through the pale green branches. But at night, if the moon comes up early, the air is silver and stars are reflected on the water like a double handful of dimes and quarters flung on a marble floor. Frogs boom and crickets chirp; they get louder and louder as daylight fades and night comes down. It was like what I thought the island would be when I first left Solitaire: paradise before Eve and the snake corrupted it.

There was still a little daylight left when we got there, the moon standing white like a scrap of paper above the trees. We undressed and waded in. She's going to start about Dummy, I thought, and all of a sudden it came to me: *I lived through this before!* And sure enough, that was the first thing she said. She bent down with her forehead touching the water, washing her hair. Only the tips of her bosoms broke the surface.

"He was over again today. He's really bad-off."

I stood and watched her, my arms hanging just past wrist-deep in the water. Her hair spread out like a fan beyond her head, the suds dissolving, winking away. She waited for me to say something, kneading her pale gold hair. The moon was beginning to gather some light but the trees were still black. When she had the soap out, she put the flat of her hands across her eyes, still bending forward, and raised up out of the water, bringing her hands straight back across her head. The weight of her hair swung heavy over her wrists, streaming back, and she was standing in the moonlight. Her hair fit like a helmet, gold, and made her face look sharp. The water streamed and trickled and stopped.

"Are you mad at me?" she said, standing with her arms wrist-deep, like me except for the helmet of hair, the bosoms, the flare of hips. "How are we ever going to live in the world if you start out being jealous of a dummy?" I couldnt tell if she was smiling or not.

"We're not going to live in the world," I said.

She waded toward me, coming so slow that the water moved around her without a ripple. The moon was brighter now, collecting light; it turned the willows silver and gold, the gold of her hair, and she was standing directly in front, the two of us a little less than waist-deep. She touched me underwater. "Honey," she said, "I told you before, I'll tell you again; need be, I'll tell you every day of my life. Youre all there ever was and ever will be. No matter where we go or what we do, I'm always with you. *Al*ways."

My flesh crept underwater, more from the sound of her voice than the touch of her hand. I towed her by the wrist toward bank and the water hugged at my knees to hold me back. It was my last sin, and I knew it at the time; I even thought it. My last sin, I thought in the act of sinning.

Afterwards, sitting on bank, I watched her in the water, bent forward the same as before, washing the twigs and leaves out of her hair, and hate was like a knot drawn tight in my chest. We were drowning in the cold pale glare of moonlight. I could have done it then: I had the impulse. But it passed; it left me empty, like Miz Pitts when the doctor got through snipping and removing, cutting and dropping her entrails in a bucket; it left me like something washed up on a beach. I breathed shallow in my throat. She came out, spreading her hair across her shoulders, and we walked back to the shack with our clothes in our arms: old Adam and Eve.

I thought it was then but it wasnt. There is no one point a man can point to and say, There: there was where my love first turned to hate. Nothing is ever that simple or that quick. It grows and grows until all of a sudden it's there; you know it's there; but theres no one point you can point to and say, There.

That night I had the dream again. It came to me as real as real; I dont know how long I'd been asleep. I heard the whimpering down the hall, and woke up stroking Beulah on the shoulder. "What is it?" she said in a whisper. "Whats the matter?" She sounded scared. I looked at her and she drew back a little. I must have looked strange, sitting bolt upright in my sleep, breathing hoarse and stroking her shoulder like that.

"I thought you were Luty Pearl." I said it before I thought what I was saying.

"Who's Luty Pearl?"

"My daughter," I said. "My last-born, that was meant to be a son." I was still half asleep or I wouldnt have said it. Because how could I explain?

Next morning was when I told Miz Pitts we wouldnt be needing anything from town. I think from the way she looked at me, the eye beams coming into my back like spears, she knew already. And next night, after supper, I told Beulah; "I have to go back," I said.

I sat facing her across the sawhorse table. My back was to the window. Between us the lamp was smoking, turned too high. We hadnt been to the pool: her hair was dry, lamplight reaching under both sides of her jaw and glinting on each separate fine gold thread. Seeing her like that I remembered the first time, Easter night, by firelight, when she came out of the bushes behind the soldier with the car seat under his arm. Her lips were red then, salved with paint. Now they were pale and bloodless. That was nine weeks ago, and my life was divided in two: nine weeks on this side and almost fifty-one years on the other.

Her hand came out and turned the lamp wick down just short of smoking, then crept back across the table and into her lap. "Back to your wife and children?" she said. "Is that what you mean?"

"Yes."

A pause. Then:

"No."

"Yes."

"No."

"Yes!"

Fast. Like slaps.

"No," she said. "I wouldnt let you."

"I have to, Beulah."

"No."

"Yes."

"I'll follow . . . I'll follow you right to your house; I'll knock at the door."

"You wont do that," I said. "You want me to tell you why you wont do that?"

"I'll—"

She looked at me and her eyes went big. She looked down, twisting her hands in her lap. "I'll follow," she said. "I will. I'll follow you wherever. I dont want a life with you not there."

There was a rustle in the bushes beyond the window, then a crash, and something running. I thought it must be a wild hog on the prowl except I hadnt seen one on the island. By the time I got to the window and held the lamp out, whatever it was had gone. There was nothing, only the darkness beyond the lamplight; even the crickets had stopped. I turned, coming back to the table, and she hadnt moved. She sat with her eyes cast down.

"It was Dummy," she said. "Some nights he comes and stands at the window and watches."

"Watches? Watches what?"

"You and me. In the moonlight."

I stood there holding the lamp and I looked at her. Depraved, I thought. She's really depraved past help, past anything I or anyone else can do.

I put the lamp on the table in passing and went on out the door and into the night. The moon was riding high, smaller now but brighter and almost full, more silver than gold, and pocked with black. Beulah called once: "Luke!" and then no more. I could tell by the sound of her voice she was still at the table, sitting where I left her. She remembered to use my new name even then, or maybe she had forgotten the old one. Mostly it was Honey anyhow. I walked fast, not paying any mind where I was going. The dry weeds hissed and whispered against my pants legs.

No telling how long I was gone, but it was long enough, anyhow, for her to be in bed and fast asleep. So I thought. But when I headed back I saw the lamp still burning, and coming through the door I saw she was still at the table, eyes cast down. I went past her, took off my shoes, and got in bed with my clothes on. Facing the other way, I could feel her lift her eyes and look at me.

That went on for another little while. Then the lamp went down and out. There was blackness for a moment, until moonlight spilled through the window onto the pallet. Her clothes rustled coming off, the way they always did, and she got in beside me. We lay there, flank to flank, and I felt her trembling down the whole length of her body, much as children tremble just before they break out crying.

"Luke," she said. She waited. "Are you asleep?"

I closed my eyes tight shut, breathing regular and heavy. But she knew; she could tell.

"Durn you," she said. "Sst—Luke. Sst, sst."

But I lay there, eyes tight shut. She was afraid to touch me with her hands, and she whispered just short of loud enough to make me mad.

"Youre not asleep," she said. "I know youre not."

I felt her warmth coming through my clothes, all down my flank, so warm she burned.

"You hear me?" she said, leaning closer. Her breath came into the hair at the back of my neck. "I meant what I said. I'll follow, Luke; I'll knock at the door, I'm telling you. I dont want a life with you not in it. You hear what I'm saying? You hear?"

I realized then I was holding my breath. I let it out, breathing regular and heavy. Somehow I felt ashamed and wanted to laugh, both at once.

"Durn you," she said. "Durn you, Luke."

Next morning I was up and gone while she was still asleep. It was Sunday and the rest of the world was at church; they were singing by now, Brother Jimson beating time with his arms, striding up and down the rostrum: "Are you Washed? In the Blood? Of the Lamb?" Luty Pearl always quieted down for that one.

Off at the other end of the island, on the Arkansas side, I sat with my back against a tree and read in First Samuel, 28: how Saul called on the Lord and got no answer, so he went to the outlaw witch of En-dor: 'Bring me up Samuel,' and Samuel came and made a prophecy: 'Tomorrow shalt thou and thy sons be with me,' and Saul fell down in a faint —"straightway all along on the earth," the Book says: he was hungry—so the witch fed him fat calf and bread and he rose up and went. And sure enough the ghost spoke true; he was compassed about and fell on his sword, and that was the end of Saul and Saul's corruption.

Was it meant to apply to me?

I wondered.

Was I to go to Miz Pitts, the mustached outlaw witch, say to her: "Bring me up Samuel," then fall on a sword (or anyhow a kaiser blade) and put an end to corruption? I tried to puzzle it out, knowing the Lord moves in mysterious ways.

I was willing. But where was the David to take charge of farming the land and be a nighttime comfort to Luty Pearl?

Right then was when there came a terrible bellering screech
—OOAAAY! OOAAAH!—twice louder than any sound I ever heard;
I nearly jumped out of my skin, thinking it was God or Satan
roaring out of the whirlwind, a threat for perverting the
Scripture. But it was only a big white steamboat hugging
close to bank. I'd been so busy reading and thinking, I hadnt
heard it coming; the first I knew of it was when the whistle
cut loose in my ear. High in the cupola the captain stood with
one hand on the wheel, the other holding onto the whistle
cord. He looked down at me over his arm, not more than
twenty feet away: sort of nodded hello, the way you do to
a friend in a crowded room, and turned back to watching the
river. Theyre a proud breed of men. I saw him plain for an
instant, like a snapshot frozen in motion: bushy pepper-and-
salt mustache, eyebrows to match, and a fever blister on his
lower lip. The boat went by, a glittering wall of white. A
nigger fireman stood on the after deck, bare from the waist
up, arms crossed on his chest, and wearing a sweat-rag knotted
round his neck. Our heads were on a level; his slid by, lips
purple, eyeballs jaundiced yellow against the dark face like
a mask, and he was gone. The paddle-wheel churned thunder,
foam and mist that fell like rain. I watched the boat swing
wide into the channel, then cut left around the south end of
the island, out of sight; it was putting in for Bristol. I could
have jumped aboard when it came past: been home in time
for supper at the latest. But she said she would follow and
knock at the door, and I knew it was true; she would.

I headed back for the shack. The captain's nod, from up high
in the cupola, was my first connection with the outside world
since nine days ago. Nine days: I counted them on my fingers,
five on one hand, four on the other, and still I couldnt believe
theyd been so few. The whole second half of my life: Nine
days, I thought. Calendars wont do for measuring time. They
ought to be made of elastic, to shrink or stretch according to
how much or how little goes in them. Nine days can be half
a lifetime. They were for me.

Beulah had dinner ready, such as it was. I ate fast and was off again to the other end of the island, this time on the Mississippi side. But when I settled down to read, with my back against a tree trunk as before, my legs stretched out—I even had my chapter picked (First Kings, 1: where David gat no heat)—I found I'd left my Bible at the shack.

But that was all right: I knew the chapter by heart, or most of it anyhow. I said it over to myself and then went on to another—Jezebel: who painted her face and tired her head and looked out of a window, but the deballed men threw her down at a word from the king and the dogs ate her flesh, all but her skull and her feet and the palms of her hands, so afterwards no one could point and say, This was Jezebel.

When I got back to the shack the sun was sinking red beyond the trees. My Bible was where I left it, half under the blanket, one corner peeping out. Touching it again was like touching base in a game when I was a boy at school in Ithaca. We didnt go down to the pool. I wore my clothes for armor in bed again, but there was no need to pretend to be asleep or watch my breathing. Beulah got in without speaking, careful not to touch me even by accident. She trembled for a while but that was all. Soon I heard her breathing slow and regular. The last thing I remember, I was saying a Now I Lay Me and I slept too.

Next day was the same and so was Tuesday, up to a point. I read and prayed, off somewheres at the far end of the island. Whatever I read, I'd ask as soon as I finished: Was that some kind of a message meant for me? Was that meant for a guide on what to do? It seemed to me, out of all I'd read and thought, there had to be a message. Maybe all of it together was a message: it all tied in. Then Tuesday, late, it reached me plain what God was saying. *I'll leave it to you, Luther Eustis*, He was saying; *I'll leave it to you.* And I knew right then what He meant: I knew what I had to do.

"We'll go down to the pool," I told her. I didnt say, 'Do

you want to go?'; I didnt even say, 'Lets go': I said, "We'll go."

Beulah turned and looked at me, her back to the stove. The sun had just gone down. "All right," she said, and her voice was low.

She knows, I thought. I could tell by the sound of her voice.

We got there, night was falling, the willows black against the deepening gray. Soon now the stars would burn through; the moon would rise, turning everything silver and gold. We undressed, the first time I'd taken my clothes off since the Saturday before. She went ahead, wading so slow she hardly made a ripple on the water. It was like marble, joined at her waist. I followed.

Ten feet from the bank she stopped and turned and I stopped too. We faced each other, just within touching distance. I asked her one last time: "Did you mean what you said?" I already knew but I asked her one last time. I could barely see the shape of her face.

"I'm not scared," she said.

But she lied. She was scared. Her voice trembled.

I walked forward, she went back: like two dancers, a foot apart, when the music is slow. The surface of the pool was dim and dusky as a mirror hung in shadow. Then she was at the other bank, where the willows drooped. They made a curtain, trailing the tips of their branches in the water.

Two switches made a scarf. I wrapped them slow and leaned on my wrists, one on each side of her throat. She was still dry above the waist but an evil woman is smoother than oil. The moon came up behind me, flooding light. She looked up between my arms; I'll follow, she was saying, but no sound came; her face was like a face already drowned.

5. Beulah

The past is gone, time lost and dead, and so with the future: the future is dead. For me, this one time is the present, always sinking, always looking up. For me it's not remembering —it *is*. I watch the bubbles trailing upward, pearls on a string unwinding from my inwards in slow motion, reeling lazy toward the crinkled surface moonlight cant get through. The moon is out; I saw it. But all I know is two hands, arms like pillars rising: Die! Die!—I dont care, I want to tell him. I'm not scared, I want to say. Youll bring me up again and then I'll tell and then . . .

The child! The child!

And figures like shadows come out of the past, the dead past into the future, now the present. They stand waiting for me to recognize them; they make little fluttery Hello motions, hands limp at the wrists; they smile and the flicker of kisses curves their lips. I know them: the topless car—conversible, the sergeant said; they called him Slim and I thought he was really something until the night I saw the preacher lift and slam him—gravel chattering under the fenders, boiling dust, country people in rows on the grassy slope, the preacher down by the water, exhorting from up on a chair.

—The peckerwoods, the rednecks, Gertrude said.

She was in back with the other two, the chunky one called Joe; he was a corporal, and the third called Cholly; he wasnt anything, even p.f.c.

—Give them a sure enough dusting, Gertrude said.

—Honk! and: *Honk!*

Slim (*my* date) was blowing the horn and the dust rolled down, blanketing the people and the preacher.

Four times we did that. Then we went away, around the north end of the lake, along the road the planters built in olden days to haul their cotton across to the landing. Slim parked and found a place to camp, a clearing set back from the road. Joe brought his blankets (US) and Cholly a radio. It was nice like that, having blankets and music. When the sun went down and the air got chilly, we built a fire and that was nicer. We passed the bottle from mouth to mouth, taking swigs, and Slim was a regular fury: one hand down the front of my dress, the other up my skirt—such busy fingers. He was trembling, pretending to be calm and very solemn.

—Now? he kept saying. Now?

He said it rough, to keep me from thinking he'd beg. He was begging, all right. So finally I told him:

—All right: Now.

And he went and got the car seat.

He wasnt much. He was practically nothing, in fact. We were lying there and directly we heard a rumpus from the campfire. He sat up.

—What was that?

—How should *I* know?

I was sulking.

—Dont be like that, baby, he said. Just wait till the next go-round.

Next go-round nothing, I thought. Thats all for you.

He buttoned and picked up the car seat, scared he might not find it again in the dark.

—Lets see what gives, he said.

I followed but I dropped behind, being careful not to snag my skirt. When I came into the firelight the fight was just getting started. They went toward the preacher, one two three, and one two three came sailing back again, like the daring young man in the song on the flying trapeze. Some preacher. There was a fellow with him but he just stood there, firelight glinting on his spectacles. Gertrude and I ran off and hid in the bushes. For all we knew, we were next on the preacher's list.

—Lo, the wrath of a righteous God!

And left.

That broke up the party. Soon as the coast was clear, the boys came out of hiding and began to gather up the stuff. Slim and Joe did, that is: not Cholly. He was walking bent over, one hand on his tailbone like an old man on the stage —he had all the bad luck; the busted radio belonged to him. We thought we'd heard his back break, but it was only a branch. The other two had bruises and scratches from landing in the briers; that was all. They tried to swagger it off. Joe said something about his folks had raised him never to fight with a preacher, but Cholly said he didnt notice it kept him from wanting to dust one during a sermon. He was sour on the whole shebang, with a busted fanny, a busted radio.

Two weeks later, maybe three—anyhow in May (it was May by then)—I was out with Willy Malone (he travels in ladies' shoes: thats the way he says it. He means he sells them; he's a traveling salesman, like in all the jokes—a goodtime charley, and dresses the part) and the car got overheated. We pulled up in front of a house to get some water, and who should be sitting on the porch but the little fellow that was with the preacher the night of the fight, specs and all. I had the car door open for coolness, skirt hitched up, and he was looking— I'll say he was looking; you could have raked his eyes off with a stick. If the one that brought the water was a sample of his kind of womenfolks, I couldnt blame him. Let him look, I thought.

—Thanks, pops, Willy said. Ta Ta.

And we drove off. All right.

A couple days later, in Ithaca, I was sitting in the drugstore having a coke. I had slipped off from Mamma again and was waiting for friends; we planned a blowout. I looked over the rim of my glass and there he was again, standing on the sidewalk within touching distance. He had the same look on his face, eyes bugged out.

—How's your preacher friend these days? I asked him, watching him over the coke.

He took to his heels, really comic, like a little boy wanting something he's afraid of.

All right. Another two weeks went by; it was up into May—I had forgotten him, or anyhow he'd moved to the back of my mind—when Willy Malone came through again, dressed to the nines and out to have some fun. We set out on a drinking tour, one juke joint after another, planning to wind up at the pavilion. I just took sips but Willy was wolfing it; that man could *drink*—up to a point. We were into the second bottle when he folded: crawled into the back seat, threw up once, then threw up again, and passed out cold. Bring them back alive, I always say. I put his kady on his chest, clasped his hands on top to keep it from getting blown away, then took the wheel, figuring if I rode around for a while, letting the air blow on him, he'd come to life by the time the dance got going at the pavilion. I was pretty high myself: pol*lu*ted, in fact. The road was wiggling like a ribbon on the windshield.

I must have been going too fast, racing the motor too much with the clutch in: something: because anyhow, what happened before happened again. The radiator commenced to bubble and sputter; the heat gauge said 212, away into the red. I went on with it like that, coming up the lake road, going fast, until I happened to notice I was right in front of the house where we stopped for water before. By the time I got the brake on, though, I was half a mile beyond it, parked at the side of the road by a cottonhouse, and who should stick out his head but the same little man, dressed in overalls and holding a rake. I recognized him right away.

—Hi, I said.

He was different this time. Not a lot different, but different. His eyes bugged out, the same as before, but he didnt seem

as scared. Maybe he'd thought it over, how he'd act next time
we met. And I remembered how I'd thought what fun it
would be to rouse him, see what he'd do. Besides, it was barely
sundown, two hours before the dance, even if Willy came to
in condition to take me. I had to pass the time some way or
other. So I leaned closer; I was pretty high.

—You got three dollars, honey?

I didnt want his three dollars. I wanted to scare him, see
what he'd do.

I found out. He had me by the wrist and inside the cottonhouse before I knew what was coming off; I didnt know
whether we went in by the door or the window or down
through the roof, it happened so fast. There was the musty
smell of cottonseed when it's been stored through the winter;
it took me back to when I was a little girl and stopped in one
on the way from school with boys—we'd look at each other
and giggle.

—Woo, I said.

I had forgotten him; I had my eyes closed, not even remembering where I was. When I opened them I saw him
framed against the doorway, on his knees, unhooking a strap
from the bib of his overalls. The smell came strong and rancid
through the musty smell of cottonseed: Like a billy goat, I
told him; I was lying on my back, my knees drawn up. He
struck with a stallion lunge; my God; he even neighed and
nickered, hands like hoofs. I only realized afterwards he'd been
praying all the while: what I had thought was whinnying was
praying. I should have known.

Because something came out of somewhere to reinforce him,
whatever makes thunder and lightning, fires and floods; no one
man was ever like that in all this world, alone. The whiskey
grogginess left me like the flame will leave a candle in the
wind. All there was was Now: the swoon and surge and
swoon and surge—I swung back from somewhere off in space,
again on the floor of the cottonhouse with the seeds like
pebbles under my back, and heard my voice calling Jesus,

calling His name with a high thin eerie wail. I thought at first I was cussing, but I wasnt; I could tell by the sound. I was praying. *I* was praying too.

Darkness had come by the time I opened my eyes. The patch of sky that had been pearly through the doorway was blue now, darkened almost to purple, with a wash of moonlight silvery across it and a star hanging cold and steady in the upper right-hand corner. This was a brand new different world, and nothing in it would ever be the same—all because of a little man in overalls I'd thought to kill fifteen minutes making fun of, lying on my back with both knees drawn up, whiskey-sodden, relaxed, with time enough even to tell him he smelled like a goat: one last half-instant before the thunder clapped, the world hung still, and everything pointed to Now.

—I been so miserable all my life, I said.

I told him everything I'd been and done, things I'd never told before, not even to Mamma, and all the time I was talking we could hear Willy snoring on the back seat of the car beyond the wall. It was somehow like I was talking to my daddy, who'd been dead all those years. I told it all, from as far back as I could remember and even further; I didnt leave out anything from shame.

Mamma says my daddy was a section boss on the C & B. He died with pneumonia when I was one, from working in the rain. That was 1932, the depth of the depression, Mamma says, and she married again within the year. I dont remember that one either; he caught her with another man and left. Then there was a whole long series of them—I would lie on the couch and hear the bedsprings. The regular ones brought candy and gum and danced me horseback on their knee. They smelled of shoe polish, cigars, and hair oil: mostly drummers. One brought me a doll with eyes that opened and closed and a thing in its stomach you squeezed to make it cry; I can barely remember. We went from place to place, never any one place for long at a time. I liked it. Finally I had to go to school. It was in New Orleans, a boarding school. The teachers were

Sisters; I had trouble learning not to call them Maam. I didnt like it at first. At night I'd hear the other girls crying into their pillows, being homesick, and I'd think of Mamma lying up with a drummer and showing him snapshots: Thats my little girl, the one on the left, with the hair. I'm putting her through school, a really swell one. None of this hustling life for her if *I* can help it, and maybe he'd slip her an extra five if he was the sentimental type, which mostly they were. Even after I was ten and twelve she kept using snapshots taken when I was seven. —I graduated the summer before my fourteenth birthday. Mamma came down for the exercises, the best-looking mother of them all except for maybe a little too much rouge, and afterwards on the train she sprang a surprise. We were going to spend what was left of June in the Ozarks, at the summer place of a Memphis cotton man. His name was Iverson, Mr Iverson; he had just made close to half a million dollars on something called a Straddle. The summer place wasnt much to look at, not much more than a cabin, but it was fixed up with rugs and things, real nice. My, what a pretty girl, Mr Iverson said, patting me on the head—past sixty, bald, six and a half feet tall in a linen suit, and weighed two hundred and forty-five pounds on the bathroom scales. His teeth were even and white, like piano keys, and he smiled especially wide to show them off. He called me Pet and Baby Doll. I had a room to myself adjoining theirs. That night I woke up hearing voices. They were driving some kind of bargain, in a whisper. I couldnt hear the words they said, but I found out next afternoon. Dont be scared now, Mamma said; he's just a big overgrown boy. Overgrown two hundred and forty-five pounds, I thought. All right, I said. And when she sent me to my room right after early supper, I found my gown already laid out on the bed, the new one with lace on the collar that she gave me for graduation. He came on tiptoe, barefoot, wearing a nightshirt; the sun wasnt decently down behind the mountain. Having fun up here, pet? he said. He sat on the side of the bed, smiling and showing his teeth, and plucking at tufts on the spread—he was bashful. After a while he said, Dont you think it's a little warm for all that lace? Wait, sweetheart, let me help you. Gracious, child, how nice, how very nice. I bet nobody's ever so much as touched them, except maybe yourself at night alone in the dark. You know what you are, sweetheart? Youre a bud, a tender bud; thats what you are. He shucked off his nightshirt, groaning a little as it come over his head. His skin was smooth as paper, not one single hair on his whole body; his stomach sagged down like an apron— he had been reducing. All this time he was talking, afraid to stop, for fear I'd get up and run or fuss at him or bust out crying. There now. Aint that nicer? Here, sweetheart, sit like this. Thats right, darling: one on each side, both the arms up here. Now gently, gently; I wouldnt hurt you, not for anything. If I hurt you, make a sound to let me know. A little squeal perhaps? Thats right. Oh-oh: try again. Thats right. Now gently, gently. Gently. . . . Scared as I was, I almost had to laugh—all that enormous smoothness, all that talk about gently-gently, all that bashfulness combined with all that daring. It was quite a while before I finally understood that what he really wanted to do was hurt me but he wanted to do it gently, just enough to make him feel proud of himself without feeling ashamed. He fell back and rested a while; I thought he was dead or something, it happened so quick—I thought he was bleeding down there. Finally he sat up, spry as ever. Now, baby doll, he said, we'll try something else. And, lo, he reached up and took out his teeth. That was the greatest surprise of all, for up to then I thought they were real. Golly, Mr Iverson, I said. —Next morning at breakfast he paid Mamma four hundred dollars, cash on the table, for that one night. I watched him count the money out of his wallet, and while I watched I thought what a good thing it was I hadnt told even Mamma about the altar boys those times in the sacristy, behind the stacks of missals. All told, she got twelve hundred dollars for just the last three weeks of June, plus Pullman tickets for both of us back to New Orleans. Mamma sat facing the front and I rode backwards. We watched the scenery. Did you like Mr Iverson, Beulah? she said. Yessum, I said; he was nice. Well, she said, I thought it was best that way, knowing how gentle he'd be. Sometimes the first go can be rough and nasty; it can ruin a girl's life for years to come. That was the way it was with me, she said, looking sad. Yessum, I said; he was nice. —In New Orleans she took up with a jockey. From one extreme to another: five feet two, wore striped shirts with high tab collars, hand-painted ties, and weighed a hundred eleven in his silks. Whenever she was gone to the grocer's or something, he'd creep back and slip in bed with me—I was a little the larger, even then. I didnt like him. He was mean. Mamma always had a cut lip or black eye. You wouldnt believe how hard those little fists were, and he had a little riding crop he used. Not on me: on her. She was crazy about him. She worried about the money running out; she knew he'd leave her when it did. Whenever he was racing she'd sit by the radio and bite her nails, for fear he'd fall and a horse would step on him. Then just before the season was over he went away with what was left of the twelve hundred dollars we'd brought back from the Ozarks. Oh Beulah, she said, lying in bed with the shades pulled down and a bottle on the floor within easy reach; dont ever trust a man. The more you love and trust him, the worse he'll treat you. —Things were harder for us after that. We lived in a kind of rooming house, with a slopjar under the bed and a basin on the dresser with a stack of towels beside it, a box of bichloride tablets, coffin-shaped, and a half squeezed tube of K.Y. She'd rouse me out of bed all hours of the night and I'd wait in the hall. They were mostly soldiers and sailors and merchant mariners, or businessmen down on convention. This is one lousy life, Mamma said, but I'm doing the best I can with what Ive got. I wish I could afford to send you to some kind of business school so you could learn to type. —She never did but I never blamed her. For one thing, she only turned the nicest ones over to me, the businessmen. Lots of them only wanted to have their backs scratched, a chance to tell dirty stories to someone naked; their main kick came from thinking how they were putting one over on their wives. And I would remember the girls at school, in starched nightgowns between clean sheets, crying into their pillows, feeling sorry for themselves. Nobody's ever happy, I thought; nobody, anywhere, ever. —Then she met Mr Joyner; a taxicab driver brought him. It wasnt till afterwards, lying in bed and talking, that he realized he had known her when she was a girl. His wife had just died the month before. So he and Mamma married and we moved to his farm in Issawamba County, Mississippi, within two miles of the one she had been born on. Thirty-two years, she said, and I'm back where I started. Well, well. The darkest hour is just before the dawn. That was a favorite saying of hers. She should have known better, she'd tried it twice before; but some people never learn. I started going to school again, high school this time, but the principal wouldnt let me alone. I started it, set my cap for him because he was the head of everything, but he got out of hand. He made a regular Fool of himself: slashed his wrists with a razor blade, spit on his dead wife's picture, wanted to meet by moonlight in the graveyard where she was buried, recited poetry—you wouldnt believe how excited he got, the crazy things he did. Finally we were caught in the gym, behind the lockers. His name was Calhoun, like in the history book. He got fired and I was expelled, and afterwards he kept coming around the house, baying the moon like a dog, till Mamma's husband ran him off with a shotgun. Later they took him to Jackson and that explained it; he was crazy. Well now, Mamma said; you sure do attract all kinds. She was having troubles herself by then. Mr Joyner had played out on her; at least he couldnt keep up. Something's got to be done, she told him; I can take anything but this. All right, he said, do what you want; but be here when I need you. —So Mamma and I started going around with soldiers from the air base up at Bristol. She'd use me to snag them, then she'd grab one for herself. I was seventeen by then, the same as grown. I could look back on my life, away back. And all this time it was like I was searching for something, I didnt know what, and couldnt find it. All the fun I'd ever got was seeing them get excited, and it seemed to me there ought to be more than that. I asked Mamma. What is it? I said; whats the matter with me? You want your man, she said, the man you were born to meet. How will I know him? I said. Youll know him, she said; youll know him, all right. Just wait. All I hoped was he wouldnt be like her jockey in New Orleans, the one with the fists and the riding crop. The only really nice man I'd ever met was Mr Iverson, but we'd read in the paper two years ago he was dead: dropped dead on Main Street of a heart attack. And right in the middle of all that wondering, fretting, I turned up pregnant. I waited another couple of weeks to make sure. Then I told Mamma. I think I'm going to have a baby, I said. Who by? she said. By Scally, I think, I said. That was Sergeant Scalco, from Detroit —he had been coming down two-three nights a week. Scally was his nickname. He was the one gave me an ankle chain with a little gold heart that had Love engraved across it; his folks had money. Have you told him? Mamma said. Not yet, I said. The son of a bitch, she said; we'll fix his clock. And he came the next night and she told him. How do I know it's mine? he said. And Mamma filed a bastardy charge against him at the courthouse in Eddypool. We'll show him, she said; we'll teach the son of a bitch at least to be careful. I just wish you were two years younger, she said; we'd put him *under* the jail. But when the trial came into court, he brought three other soldiers with him from the air base—two of them I'd never seen before. They swore on the stand theyd had relations with me (thats what they called it: Relations) and the judge threw the case out of court. You call this justice? Mamma said, standing up and talking loud, and the judge had her escorted out by two policemen. All this time she was hollering over her shoulder, What kind of justice is this? You call this justice? and all the faces were turning, watching us. Bastards! Mamma

shouted; sons of bitches!—Two days later, though, she changed
her tune when a hundred dollar check came in the mail. It was
on a Detroit bank and signed Geo Scalco. Well, Mamma said,
at least he's not all bad; it shows his heart's in the right place,
anyhow. Next morning we caught the milk train down to
Vicksburg, took a taxi from the station to niggertown. We
got out in front of a cabin that was just like all the others in a
row. When Mamma raised her hand to knock, a little old
yellow woman opened the door, wearing a turban and smoking
a short clay pipe. Dont be scared now, Mamma said; theres
nothing to it worse than having a tooth out. The woman went
down to the corner to telephone and after a while the doctor
came. He was old; hair grew out of his ears and his hands were
shaky. He carried his tools in a shoebox tied with string. The
woman put a sheet of oilcloth over the bedspread. Mamma
helped me off with my clothes and I lay back. The doctor got
down on his knees and I kept raising my head, looking down
the length of my body to watch what he was doing. He used
a long shiny piece of wire with a loop at the end like a button-
hook, googing, googing, then one sharp stitch of pain and
something sliding, and he handed the woman a wad of bloody
cloth and she went toward the back; the toilet gurgled once,
then sighed, and the baby was gone. It was over in no time,
dead before it was born (you ever hear somebody wish theyd
never been born? Thats what it's like to never be born) and
all the way home on the train next day I wondered if it was
a boy or a girl and what I would have named it. I hoped for
its sake, dead or no, it wouldnt have been a girl. —For two
months after that I wouldnt let a man so much as touch me.
I hated them because they had it so easy. Theyd beg and make
fools of themselves in general, almost as bad as Mr Calhoun
in the crazy-house at Jackson; a couple even hit me. But I kept
on saying no. No more Vicksburg trips for me, I told them,
no thanks. Finally I got over it, though. It was more because
I felt sorry for them than anything else—that was always my
failing; I'd feel so sorry for them, carrying on about a thing

that meant so little to me. None of them meant a thing to me;
I might as well have been off somewhere in space; it was no
more fun than chewing gum or smoking or lying on my back
to count the stars. Somehow, though, I knew there had to be
more to it than that, or why all the excitement? I remembered
what Mamma said: You want your man, the man you were
born to meet. How will I know? I said. Youll know, she said;
youll know. But she was wrong; when the time came and I
saw him, she was wrong. He stood in the firelight back of the
preacher and I didnt know; I didnt know him from Adam's
off ox. I could have laughed at him, almost, except I was too
busy getting out of the reach of that preacher's hands for fear
he'd slam me like he did the others, Slim and Joe and Cholly,
or kick me like he did the radio. Two weeks later, in the car
in front of his house, I sat and let him take a gander, chuckling
because of the way his eyes bugged out. And later in Ithaca,
over the rim of the coke, I really did laugh, right square in his
face, and sat there laughing after he ran away. But Mamma
was right, in the end. When the time really came, I knew. I
could see it as clear as I saw the star hung in the doorway, pale
yellow against the purple sky; I could feel it as plain as I felt
the cottonseed under my back, like pebbles on a beach. I been
so miserable all my life, I said.

He had put his glasses back on, two circles of white. Beyond
the wall the snoring had stopped—Willy was really sleeping
now. He was still asleep when I parked the car and went in
the house. Mamma and Mr Joyner were sitting in the front
room.

—Where you been, Beulah, all this time? she said.

I had slipped off from her again. Mr Joyner didnt look up
from his newspaper. I went on back and got in bed, and after
a minute she came and stood in the door. I turned my head
the other way. Maybe she asked me again where I'd been, but
I was asleep by then. Next morning Willy's car was gone; I
never saw him again.

All that month she was after me to know where I was going,

what I was doing. I guess the pickings werent so good without me along to snag them for her. She kept after me, snooping around, so finally I told her:

—You been running my life for almost nineteen years. Now let *me* run it a while. And dont be surprised if you wake up some morning and find me gone.

—Why, Beulah, you know I'm only thinking of your welfare. You know that.

—Howsomever, I said.

I'd slip off. We met in all kinds of strange places: twice again in the cottonhouse, then several times on the creekbank in the woods behind the church. He told me bits about his life, his marriage, his granddaddy that fought in the Civil War and came back to Solitaire farming on shares for General Jameson, snatches of this and that. Then he began to talk about the island. The way he told it, I never could be sure if he'd really been there or just dreamed it, all peaceful and green (he said) with nobody near to tell you Yes or No or ask you questions. He made it sound like something out of a dream. Then one night:

—Lets live there.

—On the island? I said.

Crickets were singing around us.

—Yes.

—All right.

It really came that sudden, out of a clear blue sky. He made the plans. He even gave us our names.

—You be Sue and I'll be Luke, he said.

That was so no one could trace us. Our last name was Gowan. By that time we were meeting way back in the woods; it wouldnt be much different as far as the nights went, and the nights were all that mattered.

—What will we live on, honcy?

—We'll live, he said.

I left it to him and did what he said. After the trainride I came around the corner by the post office and there he was,

138

eyes bugged out the same as in the old days. Lordy, I thought, here I am on my way to live on an island. Mamma sure was right about the man youre born to meet and all the things youll do to hold him once youve found him.

But what a shock that woman was: Miz Pitts. She had a mustache and she didnt want to take us, but she did. Her son was waiting on the other bank. He was deaf and dumb, under-sized with milky eyes, a whorl of first-growth beard like peach fuzz round his mouth, and hair like feathers on a ruffled chicken. He stood and looked at me, in some kind of a trance, and his mother frowned.

Next day we moved into the shack. It wasnt exactly a young bride's dream of home but we made do; Luke cleared out the weeds and stuff and I started learning to cook with the beat-up pots and pans Miz Pitts let us have, along with some greens and things out of the garden. I got to hate that old rusty ram-shackle stove more than I'd hated anything in my life; I de-spised it with a sort of *in*timate hate, like what a man can feel for a balky mule.

That was the life we led, no bed of roses. All day I'd wrastle the stove while he was off in the garden, hoeing and spading. But the nights made it worth it, beginning after sundown. We'd go down to the pool for a bath. It was peaceful there and I could forget the day that led up to it.

One night, right after supper, he went over to Miz Pitts' cabin to get the things from town. He stayed and stayed and I waited; I waited and waited, and still he didnt come. Then finally he came, and from the minute I saw his face above the armload of bundles, I knew something had happened. I thought maybe he'd had bad news from town; they were looking for us or something. But all he said was Miz Pitts got to talking. So I tried to pass it off, to bring him round:

—Whats playing at the picture shows?

As if it mattered.

—She didnt say.

It was awkward, almost spooky, sitting there like that, nobody saying a word. I was just going to ask him how about walking down to the pool, late as it was, when he got up and went across the room and took his Bible from under the cigar box on the shelf. He went back to the table, by the lamp, and started reading.

So finally I gave up and went to bed, lying on my side and watching him. Every now and then he'd sneak a sidelong glance, but that was all. Whats this? I wondered. Whats this? And after I dont know how-long, he got up and blew out the lamp, undressed in the dark and crawled in bed, pretending he thought I was asleep. I stirred and sighed a couple of times, gave a scissor kick or two, in case he really thought I was, but he just lay there. I thought: Well? Well? but he just lay there, rigid. Maybe I ought to tell him now, I thought. But after a while I really did fall asleep and next thing I knew I was lying in bed alone, blinded by sunlight coming through the window and the chinks.

That was the very beginning. He didnt come back and he didnt come back and I sat there, wondering, until at last I noticed the Bible was gone. Then I knew. He was off in the canebrakes somewhere, reading it. I had a rival worse than any woman.

And to cap the climax here came Dummy, sidling round the doorjamb with that look in his milky eyes that I first saw when I stepped out of the boat. It was his first visit. That meant he must have been watching and waiting, because this was the first time the coast was clear; always before, Luke had been either with me in the shack or with him in the garden. I should have sent him packing, then and there, but I didnt because (one:) I was lonesome—even a dummy was better than nothing, after sitting alone all morning, nobody near me, and (two:) I felt sorry for him; he was so pitiful.

From them on, soon as Luke was gone, Dummy would come sidling round the door and sit there watching, squirming and turning to hide the bulge, crossing, uncrossing his legs—downright pitiful. When I stood at the stove with my back to him, it was as if I could feel eyeballs rolling up and down my calves and along my backbone; I could hear every breath he drew. It was an awful thing to be the object of all that ache and to realize at the same time that he didnt even know just what he was honing after.

So I thought I'd ask Luke; I thought if I could tell Luke how it was, he'd feel as sorry for him as I did—he was just a kid, after all, and a dummy to boot; I thought Luke would see it didnt have anything to do with him and me. But I'd no sooner asked than I saw I shouldnt have; he didnt understand at all. We were in bed and I had one hand on his shoulder, leaning across.

—Turn loose of me, he said.

I should have let it go at that; I should have known. But next day here came Dummy again, getting more pitiful all the time. I felt so sorry for him I wanted to cry. Well, I thought, I'll try just once again.

We were down at the pool and I asked him while I was bent over, washing my hair: I thought that would show him how little it meant, to ask at a time like that. But he didnt answer; I waited and he didnt answer. So I turned, sweeping my hair back, and there was that face again, lips drawn in a line. I asked was he mad, and when he still didnt answer I asked him how we were ever going to live in the world if he started out being jealous of a dummy.

—We're not going to live in the world, he said.

That was the first time it came into my mind that he was someone to be afraid of. He had the strangest look: mad but dreamy too, and both at once. I waded toward him, took hold under water—nothing doing. But when I told him he was all there ever was or ever would be, everything changed; it was as if I had hold of a sash weight all of a sudden. He began running for bank with me in tow, lifting his knees high out of the water. It was like the first time, back at the cottonhouse. It was also the last: but I didnt know that, then.

Some time in the night I woke up hearing his voice and felt a fumbling at my shoulder.

—There, there, he was saying. There, there.

Moonlight glittered in his eyes; they were open but he was asleep. He was asleep, sitting bolt upright, groping at my shoulder and talking out of a dream. It was scary.

—Luke!

He began to wake up. He stopped talking but the hand went on fumbling at my shoulder, clumsy, stroking it.

—What is it? I said. Whats the matter?

The fumbling slowed, then stopped. The glitter went out of his eyes as the lids came down. He said:

—I thought you were Luty Pearl.

So thats it, I thought. So thats her name.

—Who's Luty Pearl?

—My last-born, that was meant to be a son.

I should have told him then. I should have said, If it's a son you want, maybe youre going to have one. But he fell back asleep, or pretended to, and I let it pass.

And next morning the ugliness began all over again. Just when I thought his mind had come through the tunnel, it ducked back in again. All I could do was wait. When I remembered Mamma and her jockey in New Orleans, it wasnt so bad. Everyone has their own particular troubles, I told myself.

That evening when he came in I could tell by the mud on his trouser knees he'd been at it harder than ever. Something is going to happen, I thought. And sure enough we were sitting there after supper and he came straight out with it:

—I have to go back.

Plunk: like that.

But I had been expecting it; I knew just what to do. I spent some time fixing the lamp, to make him think I was considering. Then I told him No, I wouldnt let him; I'd follow and knock at the door. Because when it was over, when his mind came through the tunnel, I wanted him to be able to look back and see I had stood steadfast. Mamma always said that was the

one thing they appreciate more than anything else in the world
—standing steadfast. And truthfulness too, of course: up to a
point.

He kept saying Yes; I kept saying No. I think I was making
headway, but Dummy had to come along and queer it. I figured he was there (he usually was) but what did it matter so
long as he couldnt hear us? Besides, if Luke wouldnt let me
do anything for him, I thought the least I could do was to let
him watch. It never crossed my mind that he'd be fool enough
to make a racket, get caught.

While his feet went thudding up the path Luke grabbed the
lamp and ran to the window, but Dummy was gone by then.
Luke turned and came back. I figured he knew; if he didnt,
he'd wonder till he thought of it anyhow. Besides, here was
another chance to be truthful. So I told him.

—Watches? he said. Watches what?

—You and me, in the moonlight.

He came straight past the table, put the lamp down, and was
off again, into the night. I called but he didnt answer. I sat at
the table for a long time, wondering if I was handling it right.
That Dummy, I thought—exasperated; it's what I get for
trying to do good.

I was still sitting there when he came back. It was late. He
went past me and crawled into bed with his clothes on.
Imagine. Dont that beat all? I thought, and I put out the lamp,
undressed, and got in beside him. But when I spoke he wouldnt
answer: pretended to be asleep. It made me so mad I cussed,
which is something I never do, but he still wouldnt answer so
much as a mumbling word. Finally I gave up.

Next morning he was off again, out in the canebrakes, praying. I had three days of sitting alone, and every night he slept
with his clothes on. Imagine. Dummy came from day to day
but he didnt count; I hardly paid him any mind. If that was
the way Luke wanted it, that was the way it was going to be.
I had changed my tactics.

Sitting alone like that, I had plenty of time to think. I de-

cided if he wanted me demure, thats what I'd be: demure. I
let my hair hang straight and kept my eyes down; I even took
off my ankle chain for the first time since Scally gave it to
me, back in the bygone days. But that didnt work either.
Tuesday I tied my hair up again and put my chain back on
and started trying to think of something else to bring him
round. I had to take my chances, but now that I knew what it
was to be with someone you want all the time, I wasnt going
to lose him; I wasnt going back to things the way they were
before we met. That life was behind me. It was behind me to
stay, no matter what chances I had to take, waiting for his mind
to come out of its tunnel.

And that evening I was standing at the stove and he was
sitting at the table eating supper; I heard the plate scrape when
he pushed it back. Then:

—We'll go down to the pool, I heard him say.

I couldnt believe he'd said it. Golly, I thought; golly; it's
like Mamma always says; the darkest hour is just before the
dawn. But when I turned and looked at him I saw his face
hadnt changed at all: eyebrows still pulled down, lips set in a
line; and I was scared.

—All right, I said.

The words shook in my throat, I was so scared.

Following him down the path we'd worn to the pool, I had
plenty of time to wonder. It came to me that, scared as I was,
if I could just get through this next half hour, it might be the
very thing he'd been needing to jar him loose from whatever
it was that had been eating him. If I'd known how to pray, I
would have done it.

We undressed on bank. His face and neck and hands and
wrists were dark; the rest was pale in the starlight, paler than
ever. It was as if he had bleached whiter inside his clothes
these past four days. He stood with his back to me and I
waded in, then turned and saw him coming toward me, knee-
deep, thigh-deep, waist-deep in the water. Starlight gleamed
on the whiteness; against the dark background of trees, he

144

seemed to have no head or hands. Then he was closer: I could see his face.

—Did you mean what you said?

He wanted me to say I wouldnt follow, wouldnt knock at the door, wouldnt claim him.

—I'm not scared, I said.

But I was; I was terribly scared—I thought my knees would give way. Stand still, I told my legs; stand still. But he came forward again and they took me backward. Stand still, I told myself. Even if he puts you down, when he sees you dont fight back he'll understand; he'll bring you up again. It will be like in the cottonhouse and here on bank last Saturday night; you can start all over again, from the beginning. Then I felt the willows against my back.

I watched the dark hand and pale arm go up, rustling in the willows by my head, then coming down and around. The leaves were as soft as feathers until they tightened. He leaned forward, leaning on both arms, a hand on each side of my throat, and my knees gave way. The moon came up behind him.

The child! The child!—brings me back to this one time, the present, looking up toward the crinkled surface moonlight cant get through, watching the bubbles unwind like pearls on a string, telling myself he'll bring me up again and then I'll tell him and then . . .

—No! No!

But the pearls run out: are gone.

6. Eustis

Stars were reflected on this water too, glimmering through the sheen of moonlight that overlay the surface like a coat of golden oil: I stirred them with the paddle, folding them in, but they always rose. It was further than I thought, or maybe it just seemed so because I only had one oar and the bateau was flat on both ends and I was so tired the water felt thick as gelatin barely short of stiff. When I reached the other bank the moon was high, a sickle of polished silver riding directly overhead; the stars were fading; the false dawn was a milky haze smeared above the darkness of the eastern landline: Mississippi.

I took time to beach the boat where I knew theyd find it: then struck inland, walking. High and thin as it was, the moon was so bright the trees and bushes stood out sharp and black, clearer even than they would have done by daylight. I walked half a mile and struck the levee. On the opposite slope I lay down on the grass and went to sleep. I dreamed of Jacob wrestling with the Angel. I was Jacob and the Angel said: 'Let me go, for day is breaking' but I said: 'I wont except you bless me. Whats your name?' (it seemed to me I knew his face from somewhere) but just as he was about to bless me, tell me his name, I woke up with a terrible ache in my leg, hearing two little clacking sounds, dovetailed one into the other: clack clack, clack clack, clack clack: and sure enough, day was breaking. I was lying in the grass, all wet with dew.

Leaning far back to look over my forehead, I saw two nigger

146

women walking along the top of the levee with fishing poles over their shoulders. They were old, in mother Hubbards and straw hats frayed in the same identical places, like twins; I saw them upside-down. Clack clack, clack clack: the sinkers were knocking against the poles, two clacks to a step. They were watching me, faces turning more and more to the right as they came past. When they saw I was awake and looking at them, they snapped their heads around to the front, moving both at once like twin dolls on a string, and began to take quicker steps. Clack-clack clack-clack clack-clack: the clacking got faster. It faded, and was gone; they were out of sight down the levee. I'm back in the world, I thought; I'm back in the world again.

But when I moved I remembered the ache in my leg; it had gone to sleep where a clod was pressed against it, cutting off the flow of blood in the rear, above the knee. Like Jacob, who halted thereafter upon one thigh, I brought the ache out of a dream with me, a sign from God. And remembering the dream I remembered the Angel; looking back, I knew now why his face had been familiar. He was Beulah. She came to me in the dream that brought the dawn.

In dreams a man can be cunning and stupid both at once. Things that ought to amaze him he takes for granted, but ordinary sights will fill him with wonder. Sticks and stones move of their own accord or a mule begins to speak right in front of his eyes, and he watches without surprise; he thinks, They're not fooling me; it's some kind of trick. Maybe he even chuckles to himself, thinking how cunning he is not to let them fool him. But let the simplest everyday thing happen, a kitten come bounding across the scene or an old friend be standing in the background, and he freezes in his tracks; he's all amazed; he cant believe his eyes; How can that be? he thinks. Then he stirs: lies still for a minute while the dream-shapes whirl and fade; he's really awake. And lying there, looking back, it's all reversed. The things he took for granted in the dream (while he was *in* it) fill him with amazement now he's awake, and the things that shocked him, froze him in his tracks, seem ordinary.

We're each two different people, is why, and we live in two different worlds. Just as we carry our waking bodies and some of our waking thoughts into the world of dreams, so we bring the thoughts and happenings of the world of dreams back with us when we return to the world of daylight. They mingle, they explain each other: we look forward and backward, trying to find a reason for what is happening in this world by remembering something more or less like it that happened in the other. The mix-up comes when we stand between the two, groping in both directions.

So with me and the Angel. In the dream we stood locked hip to hip and eye to eye, his arms around my waist, mine on his shoulders; I saw him plain. He wore a golden helmet and his skin was marble-smooth, no hair on his chest, no nipples even, no ripple of ribs; his face was all straight lines—mouth, nose, and forehead. When he spoke: 'Let me go, for day is breaking,' his lower jaw moved up and down, the bottom lip coming flat against the top one with a little click (clack clack, clack clack) and his eyes were cold as glass, lidless, like agates set in the sockets. I didnt think of Beulah: that came later, in that other, daylight world. The reason I didnt know her was her face was all straight lines and flattened planes. Too, I hadnt brought any memory of her with me into the dream, and what you dont remember you dont know. I knew her now, however, in the daylight world of memory, looking back. I knew she was the angel in the dream, wearing the gold helmet and cold eyes, and I knew she would return—or anyhow *I* would; I knew she was waiting for me in that other world of dreams, and I told myself I would be ready for her; I would know her when we met.

The sun rose while I lay on the levee thinking. It came up big and red, seemed to bounce like a ball, and turned fiery as soon as it cleared the landline. The cloudbank behind it—first purple, then purple-and-scarlet, then just scarlet—paled to a faint rosy flush, then raveled off in tatters, melting, and was gone; the sky was hard bright blue from rim to rim, nothing in all that high wide flawless dome except a disk of hammered brass: the sun. A scorcher, I thought, and got to my feet and limped up the slope to the crest. Bristol was off to the left, out of sight. For a minute I stood looking, then turned right and walked north along the levee. I felt small under all that arch of empty sky, like an ant walking the sharp edge of a knife-blade.

Two hours later (but no more than two-three miles away; I'd stop and sit, rub at my leg till the ache went out) I looked down to the left, toward where the river was hid beyond the trees, and saw two yellow spots of light, both fuzzy around the edges. Even behind me, the sun was blinding: I couldnt make them out. So I shaded my eyes with both hands and looked closer. It was the two women that passed me with the fishpoles on their shoulders, back at daybreak. They sat facing the other way, at the edge of a barrow pit, fishing. The two yellow spots were their hats. Soon as I saw them I knew I was hungry. I'd never been so hungry in my life.

They didnt hear me until I was almost there. When a clod broke under my foot they looked around. Both their heads turned inward, toward each other, then toward me. They froze, the whites of their eyes as yellow as their hats, then snapped their heads back to the front again, both together, still like on one string. I took the razor out of the cigar box, watching the hats, the identical frayed brims. Except for the stiff way they held the poles, youd think they hadnt seen me. Something fluttered the water in a bucket that sat between them. That was the only sound until one of them spoke—the one on the right, without turning her head:

"Whut you wants, white man?"

The bucket fluttered again. That was all until the one on the left peeked round and saw me standing with the Bible and cigar box in one hand and the razor in the other. I held it open, blade folded back, flashing bright against my trouser leg.

149

"Lord to God," she said in a low voice.

And both at once, identical, they sprang apart; they were running, one on each side, making a circle around me. Their knees lifted the long skirts, showing legs like broom sticks stuck in rubber boots cut jagged at the ankles. They met behind me and ran up the levee, side by side and in step, still holding onto their poles. One had just hooked a baby catfish; it jumped and bounced on the grass behind them. They disappeared over the hump of the levee and everything got quiet; they might never have been there at all. Then the water in the bucket fluttered again.

Three fish were in it: two perch, one small, the other right good-sized—a pound and a half or more—and a little cat not much bigger than the one that went bouncing over the levee at the end of the fishing line. I hunted around, gathering bits of sun-dried wood to build a fire, and sharpened a green stick to use for a spit. But when I had the big perch in my hand, watching him gasp, opening and closing his gills, I couldnt do it; I couldnt bring myself to do it. And I knew why. I knew right then, from last night forward I'd never be able to kill another living thing with my hands again. I put him back in the bucket and began to build the fire.

—What kind of man is this—I heard a voice say—can drown a woman, then cant gut a fish?

"That was before," I said. "And she was evil."

—Then what were those two women running from?

"The razor," I said. "They thought I'd use it."

—Ah. And would you have used it?

"No," I said. "But I thought I would, for a minute."

—I see. What made you do such a thing?

"I dont know," I said. "I just did."

—Then I'll tell you. Want me to tell you? It's a verse out of Genesis, one you know already.

Up to then it had only asked me questions.

—*Henceforth a fugitive and a vagabond shalt thou be upon the earth.* And somewhere further along theres another, goes

150

like this: *Thy hand shall be raised against every man and every man's hand shall be raised against thee.* Thats why. Thats two good reasons. And I'll tell you something else. . . .

But I stopped listening. All this time I'd been building the fire, and now it was crackling good, already beginning to go to embers. I turned back to the bucket: kicked it over. The two perch flopped and danced, dust-colored on both sides, but the little gray cat just lay on his belly and wiggled, goggle-eyed. I turned my back and heard them flopping with little slapping sounds like when the girls were children, making mud-pies under the porch and handing them up for Luty Pearl to lay in rows on the steps; Kate had to keep an eye on her to see she didnt eat them.

After a while the flopping got fainter. Finally it stopped. I waited, giving them another little while, but when I turned and looked at them, only the smallest perch was dead. The big one was still ruffling his gills and the cat was just lying there, still on his belly, looking at me with eyes like two little blisters. I took up the dead one, scaled and gutted him with the razor, and put him on the spit. By the time I'd cooked and eaten him the other perch was dead, so I cooked and ate him too. They were good, even without salt, and I was still hungry. But when I turned the third time and looked at the little cat, he was still alive. His gunmetal whiskers drooped on both sides of his thick-lipped mouth and his fin stood up like a headless nail driven into his backbone. I kicked him back in the barrow pit. He floated for a minute on his side, bloated-looking—I thought he was dead at last—then swam off, first slow, then fast, going to tell his folks back home what a narrow scrape he'd had.

The sun was straight-up, coming down hot and casting hardly any shadow at all, but I just sat there, watching the embers turn ashy, the perch scales shining like diamonds in the dust. I thought about the voice misquoting the Bible. It wasnt 'upon' the earth; it was *in* the earth. And the other verse, the one about Ishmael, had been changed around to make it apply to me. The voice must have known I was on to him; he didnt speak again. The sun burned hotter and hotter and I just sat there. The puddle, where I had kicked the bucket over, faded from black to gray, then back to white; I could see where it had been but the dust was the same. And I just sat there, the sun coming hotter and hotter.

I didnt think about Beulah. As to that, I was like a man that gets cut or shot but doesnt begin to feel it till the flurry is over and the knife or pistol has been put away. And I didnt think about Kate or the girls; I'll think about that later, I told myself. Sitting there, I got to remembering Granddaddy, the stories he told about running cartridges down to Vicksburg during the siege. That was after he was mustered out for losing his arm at Shiloh (they kept the one-armed generals but they let the privates go); he was still a boy, seventeen and eighteen, slipping past Yankee gunboats by the dark of the moon. But no matter how hard I tried, I never could picture him without his beard; it was as much a part of him as the empty sleeve.

Maybe I napped from time to time. Theres no telling. Next thing I knew, the sun was going down in a blaze of red as if all Arkansas was up in flames. I used what was left of daylight to gather wood, and when the stars came out I built a fire, partly because of the dampness but mainly to keep me company. Later, when the mosquitoes came, I smothered it down to a smudge. Soon as the first one bit me, I was sorry I had wished for company.

I lay flat, hugging the ground to stay under the smoke, and watched the heart of the fire glowing dark red at the tip of the cone of smoke. Every now and again a wind would rise and I'd see the stars come through. Then the wind would drop and the smoke would come between. I decided I must have been napping all day after all, for I wasnt the least bit sleepy. Then all of the sudden I was; I was sleepy but I was fighting the sleep. And I knew why. I was fighting it because I was scared to meet Beulah: scared to meet her in that other world of dreams, bad dreams, where she was waiting for me, down deep in my own mind.

It turned out I didnt meet her: I didnt even dream. I'd wake up from time to time and find the fire was almost gone, and I'd reach out and put on another chunk, blowing at it till it caught and flickered up again, yellow flames dancing bright against the blackness, shadows jumping, weaving. I would lie there watching it sink to a deep red glow again, and then I'd be off to sleep once more, a deep black dreamless sleep like being lowered to the bottom of a pit. That went on and on: I'd wake and sleep and sleep and wake—how often I dont know; they were all alike. But finally when I woke the fire was dead, a star-shaped crust of ashes, and dawn was seeping through. I was wet to the skin by the dew. Yesterday's fish bones were scattered around, and when the sun came up the perch scales glittered.

I stayed there all that second day, like one of those oldtime hermits in the desert, fasting in the wilderness. They lived on locusts and honey, Brother Jimson told me once, but I didnt even have locusts, let alone honey. When the sun went down, I walked up the levee and watched it. The world got gray with twilight, bullbats flying, and I stood there looking west toward where the river was hiding behind the trees. It was like standing on the rim of all creation.

That was the end of the second day and I told myself I had to go back. Everyone has to go back, I told myself. You can take a girl off on an island, but you cant stay. You can drown her and go off alone in the wilderness, but you cant stay. You have to go back, no matter. So I turned and went down the eastern slope of the levee, carrying the cigar box and the Bible.

I thought I was heading due east, but it was guesswork. After a while I walked onto the shoulder of a road. Either I had curved to the right or left, or the road had. Anyhow I followed it and it brought me out on the highway, a strip of concrete eight feet wide with gravel on both sides. I turned right, toward the reflection of town—rose-yellow, like the fires of hell must be when you come on them from a distance. The moon was not up. A red light winking high in the air was the radio tower; on clear nights we could see it from the island. Whenever a car came toward me, humming along on the concrete with its lights like two poles thrusting at the darkness, I threw one arm across my eyes to keep from being blinded. They were almost all of them coming north, country people going home from the picture show; I knew by this it must be getting late. Yard dogs came to the far side of the ditch and barked at me as I walked along on the road. After a while the houses got closer together, huddling for protection against the sins of city life, and finally there were sidewalks running pale and arrow-straight. I was in Bristol.

It was bedtime: I could tell, for while I walked I saw the lights going off in the houses, first downstairs then up, or first in front and then in back, depending on whether the house was old or new. Sometimes the people hadnt drawn the shades and I could see them in their bedrooms, the women in nightgowns and curlpapers, lying propped on pillows reading bright-backed magazines, the men in sleeveless undershirts and trousers, smoking one last cigarette, putting their keys and loose change on the dresser. They were all alike, a series of pictures out of a printing machine. Before I reached the middle of town the houses were dark. Walking from streetlight to streetlight, I imagined the people lying limp in their beds, bellies up, breathing darkness, like batteries being charged for another tomorrow.

Then I came to the main street, running crosswise to the one I had been following. Lampposts came out of the concrete down both curbs, like iron trees, and each post held five globes of frosted glass, four in a square hanging down and one on top in the center pointing up. Only the top ones were burning now; that meant it was after eleven. The electric sign at the picture show was dark. A man stood on a ladder in front of it, putting in new letters that told what was playing tomorrow. He was almost finished. ROY ROGERS it said; IN OLD ARIZO. I stood on the opposite side of the street and watched him slide the N, the A into place, then fold up the ladder and go away. Next door, the drugstore kept a light burning in the window. It shimmered on the big cardboard head of a movie star showing her teeth; *I use Kleen Tang exclusively* she was saying in a balloon that came out of her mouth like in the funny paper. Her hair was too red to be true, and a big green-and-yellow dusty-looking moth lay astraddle the bridge of her nose, fluttering its wings slowly up and down with a trembly motion. I thought what a strange thing that was, to bring her all the way from California and put her in the window of a Mississippi drugstore, just so a moth would have a place to lay its eggs. I thought too of the mill of God, that grinds exceeding small.

Then I realized I was hearing music: *had* been hearing it since I first stopped. It came from the left, and when I looked down the block I saw a square of light on the opposite side. CAFE it said on the lighted window, black letters bent in a bow. I walked toward it and stopped in front, looking through the glass. Three men sitting on stools at a marble counter were drinking something amber out of glasses. Booths ran down one side of the room, clear to the rear wall where a music machine stood with tubes of rainbow-colored water running up and down its front. Bubbles floated through the tubes; they were square in back and rounded in front, like bullets in slow motion. A girl behind the counter was dressed in white. "Two!" she cried just then, and I began to smell the cooking. *Take me where that concrete grows*, the man in the music machine was singing; "Eggs up!" she cried; *Just a keep on a wearing those frills and flowers*,* the machine man sang, and I shifted the Bible and cigar box under the other arm, smelling the cooking, the frying meat and eggs, and took hold of the handle of the door.

* From "Buttons and Bows" by Jay Livingston and Ray Evans, copyright 1948 by Famous Music Corporation.

6. (Continued)

"Pull it!" she cried. I had been pushing.

I pulled and it opened outward. She grinned at me walking in. "Fire laws," she said.

"Here's them burgers," a nigger said from the order window. All I could see was his head and hands, sliding two saucers across the board. He had on a sailor cap.

I took a stool two down from the three men. They turned and looked, all three together, wearing high-peaked hats and cowboy boots and two-colored shirts with yokes. The one in the middle had bright red cheekbones, like a man just in out of the cold.

"What will it be?" she said, and stood with both hands pressed flat on the counter, palms down. They were pink, with purple nails chipped at the edges, long as claws.

"Sandwich," I said.

"Sandwich what kind?"

I didnt know: I hadnt thought. "Like them," I said, nodding at the two set in front of the cowboys: buns with meat in the middle, oozing sauce.

"With, without?"

But I just looked at her.

"With, without onion, cole slaw, pickle?"

"Like them," I said.

"One!" she cried, not even turning her head.

"Yayo," the nigger said from the order window. A discharge

button was screwed to the front of his cap. "Here's them sunnyside eggs."

He sounded uppity to me, talking to a white girl like that, no Maam or anything. But she didnt seem to mind.

"Roger," she said, and set the plate in front of the cowboy with the cheekbones; the other two had the sandwiches. Roger wasnt his name.

"Them's what I call eggs," he said, sharpening his knife against the tines of his fork. His voice was husky, like Brother Jimson's after a day of ranting. He was a singer, I found out later—that was why.

The music box cut off, then hummed and clicked and made a scraping sound like clearing its throat, and the singing began again, with a different song. Two of the cowboys talked against it, their voices flat below the trembly moan of the singer and the drawn-out twang of a steel guitar.

I'm gonna moo-oove . . .

"We still playing the Tuesday date?"

"In Ocaloosa, yair. Across the river."

way out on the outskirts of town.

"I'd leafer not. What a dump."

"Yair, but just look at the pay."

Dont want nobody who-oo's . . .

"I'm thinking about that girl."

"The one thats out to rope you?"

always hanging round.

"Thats the one."

"A man's got to settle down some time. What you care she's got buck teeth? Buck teeth dont matter."

"O.K. then. You take her."

They leaned forward over the counter, talking around the tall one in the middle. He held his elbows high, brought the knife and fork across and across until the eggs and bread were slashed to a runny hash, bright yellow against the dead white of the plate.

Something clicked on the marble in front of me, and I

looked and it was a sandwich like the two the cowboys had, oozing sauce. I raised my eyes still further and the waitress was standing there.

She looked like Beulah!

"What will it be to drink?"

But I just looked at her: I couldnt look away. She could have been Beulah, come back.

"Beer," the tall one said, the one with the cheekbones. He leaned forward and his knife and fork dripped egg. "Three here, one there. On me."

Then I saw she didnt really look like Beulah at all. It was just a notion I had, my mind playing tricks.

"I dont drink," I said.

The music box whirred and clicked and the song came on again, the one about take me where the concrete grows. It moved with a sort of jerky trot, horns and drums blaring and bouncing behind the singing of the words.

"Sure you do," the tall one said. "On me you do."

They were all three looking, each one leaning forward further than the other, three big sand-colored hats out over the counter, two feet wide. Bull Durham tags hung from their left shirt-pockets like pasteboard coins. I didnt say a word; I kept my head down.

She brought a bottle with a glass upside-down on its neck. I poured and it foamed white and boiled over the rim. After a while, when the foam sank down, I poured in the rest. I took a sip, and she came over and mopped with a rag where the foam had spilled. It tasted like needles in my mouth. When I swallowed, it was hot all the way down my throat and my eyes got blurred with tears. I blinked, shook my head.

"Try again," the nearest cowboy said.

So I did and it wasnt as bad, but it tasted bitter.

"Now youre coming," he said, and they all went back to eating. Their hats cast big round shadows on the marble.

I drank the rest of it, my throat so paralyzed I didnt taste. Meanwhile they were talking, and it turned out they were a three-piece band: guitar and trumpet and fiddle. The tall one was the guitar; they called him Slim and he was also the singer. The other two were Preacher and Sunny, and Sunny was the trumpet. I sat looking at my empty plate and glass.

"Miss," I said. She came over. "Beer," I said. "Three there, one here. On me."

"Thank *you*," the nearest said. He was Sunny.

"Obliged," Slim said.

Preacher just nodded and winked from down the line. He was the one that was worried about the buck-tooth girl from Arkansas wanting to rope him Tuesday night. His mouth was shaped like a kiss: From blowing the trumpet, I thought. Then I remembered Sunny was the trumpet. I was getting mixed.

The music box whirred and clicked. Its inner gears chattered like teeth in a mouth full of nails.

> *Who's been here since I been gone?*
> *Pritty little gal with a raid dress on.*
> *Pritty little gal with a raid dress on*
> *—God knows*

and the drum was pounding away in the background, faster and faster, enough to make you dizzy. Every now and again, one of the horns would let out a squeal and another would growl down deep in its throat.

Halfway through the second bottle I felt so puffy, so bloated, I couldnt drink any more. I turned to Sunny, wanting to ask him something. But the words wouldnt come. My eyes were swimming with tears. I cleared my throat, bringing up the bitter taste of beer.

"You ever live on a island?" I said. The voice didnt sound like mine.

He screwed his head around, like on a swivel.

"Island?" He thought about it. "Once I did. Okinawa: I lost my buddy there. AA fragment VJ night—the fighting was over and done with."

"*I* did," I said, not paying any mind to what he said. I

leaned toward him, whispering so the others wouldnt hear. "I had a girl with me."

"*I* didnt. All we had was the gooks, the goddam gooks. You ever see one?" I just looked at him. See one what? "Be glad you never seen one," he said. He turned the glass around and around in his hands and watched it slosh. "What did she look like? Pretty?"

"Pretty," I said.

I couldnt see him very well; I wasnt even sure if he was Sunny or Slim or the preacher—Preacher. All I could see was the Bull Durham tag, and they were all three wearing them, like coins on string with little holes drilled near the rim, the way nigger women used to do when they wore them on their ankles.

"She's dead," I said: whispered. "I put her down."

I held my breath when I said it. But his face didnt change; he didnt think anything of it.

"You mean you left her?"

"I left her," I said. "Yes: I left her drownded."

"Thats too bad. Thats tough." He shook his head and made a little clucking sound, his tongue at the roof of his mouth. "Here: drink up. Theres plenty more where she came from and dont forget it. See that girl?" He nodded toward the waitress. "She'd a been a queen on Okinawa. Them Okies: gooks . . . That lousy war: cost me three years of my life, no telling *how* much nooky—I'll never catch up. Every time I remember them goddam gooks I want to reach down and pat the good old soil of the good old U. S. of A."

I got him in focus then and he was Sunny, the trumpet, the same as at the start. For some reason I thought he might have swapped faces or something. Slim and the preacher, Preacher, were leaning out beyond him. Theyd been listening: three big high-peaked hats, one after another.

"I was supposed to meet her last night," I said.

"Meet who?" he said.

"She didnt come," I said.

"Who didnt?" he said.

"*She* didnt," I said.

"The girl off the island?" he said.

"Thought you told us she got drownded," Preacher said from down the line.

So I just sat there, knowing I couldnt make them understand. The flesh of my face felt loose.

"Drink up, pops," Slim said. Like Willy Malone.

And they sat back, pushing their hats up off their foreheads and looking at one another. Sunny made circles in front of his ear with his finger, and Slim and the preacher snickered. They said things I couldnt hear, and from time to time one of them would lean forward and look at me, then turn away and snicker, saying something to the others. Then they would snicker too, all three at once.

Next time the music machine changed, I heard somebody strumming a washboard with thimbles on his fingers, the way I'd seen them do in Ithaca, and a nigger voice began to shout:

> *I'm Petey Wheatstraw*
> *The devil's son-in-law,*
> *High sheriff of hell!*

It was all unreal, as if it wasnt happening and I was dreaming. After a while when I opened my eyes they would all be gone: cowboys, waitress, cafe, everything; I'd be back at the barrow pit, tending the fire I cooked the fish on. Two days I stayed there, not letting myself think about what had happened on the island, not even daring to dream it, and then came back into the world and blurted it out to the first person I happened to sit beside. And he laughed at it for a joke, and the others laughed too—unreal.

The music box changed and sang and after a while Sunny and Preacher and Slim got up, paid, and took their instruments from where they had been leaning against the wall. I bent forward, feeling the marble cool against my cheek. The door crashed shut behind them, and almost at once, without any gap, it opens again. A breath of cool air riffles in: makes a little shudder run up my backbone.

'Come in or go out,' the waitress says, looking sulky. 'It's cold in here.'

A tall stout man stands holding the door ajar, smiling an ivory smile. He wears a long white shirt—no trousers, and he is barefoot. Standing there, he brings a little tow-headed girl from behind him, never turning loose of her wrist, and closes the door with a slam. They take two of the stools the cowboys had. When he turns and looks at me I see he has no eyebrows. This gives his face a look of surprise; someone might have just said boo to him.

'I told you he'd be here, pet,' he says, turning to the little girl on the other side of him. She leans forward, stares at me around him.

'Hi,' she says, and smiles.

Sunny sticks his head in at the door. 'Them gooks,' he says. He's gone again.

Her hair is done in plaits, tied with ribbon at the ends. When she sees me looking, she ducks behind the barefoot man again, all the way hidden. It seems to me I know him, and when I peek around between them I see that he is stroking her leg with his other hand.

'I know you,' I say. 'Youre Mr Iverson.'

'Co-rect,' he says. 'In the flesh. I made mine on a straddle, bucking the market. But this is wrong,' he says. 'Theres something fishy. Youre not supposed to show up till she'd been well reamed and broken in.'

He is frowning, angry, and I am afraid he'll think to take out his teeth and bite me with them. Thats foolish, I think; it's a dream. But just then, on signal, the door swings open again; a blast of cold air whistles in behind a little fellow, five feet two and fox-faced, carrying a riding crop. It's the jockey, in silks, wearing boots and a long-billed cap.

'Is this him?' he says, flicking the tops of his boots with the little loop on the end of the crop. 'Is this the son of a bitch

that put her down and held her under till the bubbles stopped?'
And he begins to prod me with the crop, yelling 'Confess!
Confess!' and prodding, prodding. Youd think he was fixing
to ride me.

"Mister. Mister."

It was the waitress. She was leaning across the counter, poking at my shoulder with one of those purple fingernails. I saw
her the way she'd be through glass or from under water, with
a greenish tinge. She was Beulah again.

"You cant sleep here. It's not allowed."

Then I was awake: I could see her plain and I knew her.
I was looking down the front of her dress at two blobs of fat
hanging forward off her bony chest, the nipples dark brown.
She saw me looking and straightened up, smoothing her hair.

"Myself, I wouldnt care," she said. "But he'll be here pretty
soon and it's not allowed."

"Who will?"

I thought she meant her husband or someone like that,
because of the way I was looking down her dress.

"I told you," she said. "The cop. He's due already. Sleeping
here's against the law. He'll nab you."

I looked to the left, toward the door, expecting to see him
walk in, and there was someone I hadnt seen before. Where
first the cowboy Slim had sat, the one with the t.b. cheekbones,
and then Mr Iverson in the dream, barefoot in his nightshirt,
I saw a little stoop-backed man with five or six days' growth
of beard on his face. It was scraggly, mostly gray, and caked
with dirt, like a burnt-over field. One of his hands was curled
around a glass of beer and the other was around the ankle of
one leg lifted onto the other knee. The ankle was so skinny,
his finger and thumb almost met. I'd been looking at him a
good long time, trying to decide was he part of the dream left
over—he looked it—when finally he nodded at me, dipping
his head and bringing it up again quick, like a bird pecking at
a grain of corn and thinking maybe a cat was somewhere near.

"Howdy," he said. "A beer?"

"I dont drink," I said.

I turned back to the right, and there was something else I hadnt seen before: a full-length mirror screwed to the wall at the end of the row of stools. Except for once or twice reflected shaky on the water, this was the first time I had seen myself since I left home. I couldnt believe it was me. I opened the cigar box, took out my glasses, and put them on. Is that me? I wondered, watching myself in the mirror.

The music box changed and a drum was beating slow and alone: boom, boom, boom, boom.

It was me, all right. Dried mud was caked to my hair and clothes and I had a stubble of beard almost as long (and as gray) as the man two stools away, peeping over my shoulder, watching me watching myself. I was ten to fifteen pounds lighter, burnt by the sun, and my eyes had sunk back in my head, deep in the sockets. My cheeks were flat, or worse than flat, and furrows ran from the wings of my nose down to the far corners of my mouth. It was the first time I knew I had all that gray in my beard.

"Sure you wont change your mind?" the man said.

"I dont drink," I said.

> *Bingle—Bangle—Bungle*
> *I'm so happy in the jungle,*

the man in the music box sang.

> *Bongo—Bongo—Bongo*
> *I dont wanna leave the Congo.*

Then the door swung open behind me and the policeman came in. I watched him in the mirror. He wore two belts, one around his waist the regular way, the other one over his shoulder. For a minute I thought he had come for me, but he took a stool up at the front.

"Lo, Myrtle," he said. "Half a cup of the same."

That was her name, the same as my middle daughter.

"Coming up," she told him. She reached a cup and a saucer

off the shelf and went back to the coffee urn beside the order window. The sailor cap wasnt in sight.

"Hunting a place to flop?" the man said.

At first I didnt know he was speaking to me. Then I saw him in the mirror, bending toward me.

"To what?" I said.

CiviliZAtion! CiviliZAtion!

He moved a stool nearer, next to the one I'd set the Bible and cigar box on. I kept my eyes on the mirror, watching the policeman. When he turned and looked at me the weight of the pistol shifted and his belt gave a squeak. The pistol was an automatic; he wore it cocked and locked. He took a tooth-pick out of the jar on the counter and began to pick his teeth, looking at me over his fist and making little sucking sounds with each dig of the toothpick. He didnt know I was watching him in the mirror. When Myrtle brought the coffee he looked away, then back again.

"Reach me the sugar, bud," he said. But he didnt say thank-you when the man slid it down the marble to him.

"To sleep," the man said, turning back to me. "To spend the night, whats left of it."

I shook my head, meaning I didnt have a place.

"You can bunk with me if you want. I'm in sort of a flop-house down the street. Cost you fifty cents."

"All right."

"Right. Now how's about that beer?"

"I dont drink," I said.

"Thats what you keep saying, friend. But I dont mean for you: I mean for me. Will you stand me one? I'm stony."

"All right."

"Hi—miss." She looked and he held up one finger. She nodded. He turned to me. "Peeps is the name. Pleased to make your acquaintance."

At first I thought he said Pitts but he said Peeps. The waitress was named Myrtle. There werent enough names in the world to go round.

The music machine cut off. I waited; I waited and waited, but it didnt start again. The nickels had run out. Silence came down like a quilt, and somehow the quiet seemed louder than the noise.

"Slong, Myrtle," the policeman said, getting up. His belt squeaked. "See you next go-round."

"Sure thing," she said, smiling at him and setting the beer on the counter.

The door slammed shut.

"Anything I got no use for it's a cop," Peeps said. He didnt use the glass; he drank from the bottle, throat muscles pumping under the stubble: then wiped his mouth on the back of his hand. "What kind of guy would be a cop? I ask you." He drank and wiped. "Bastards," he said, tilting the bottle for the final swallow; "Bastards all," and brought it down empty. Then he held it up to the light. "How's about one for the road?"

"The what?"

"The road," he said. "To go home on."

"All right."

"Miss"—he held up one finger, the same as before. When she brought it and was moving away, he leaned closer and said in a low voice she couldnt hear: "I saw you in the mirror, pal. You didnt have no more use for him than I did. You on the lam or something? No offense."

"The . . ."

"Lam. Thats a movie word: I'm a great one for the movies. Means running away from something—from the law. *Are* you? No offense."

"No," I said. He leaned closer. "It's the other way around," I said. "I'm going back to something."

The cash register drawer running out rang a bell, loud against the quiet. Myrtle scooped up a handful of nickels and walked the length of the room to the music machine. I watched her. She had a way of walking a lot like Beulah—hips in front.

The machine was dark; it sat there, waiting, hungry. She began punching in nickels, one at a time, and it came on again. The lights lit up. A drum beat slow: boom, boom, boom, boom: that Bongo thing again.

CiviliZAtion! CiviliZAtion!

She kept punching in nickels, one at a time, and it took them with a sound like snapping jaws.

Peeps drank and wiped, three times, the same as before, and the bottle was empty. Then he stood up, straddle-legged, and stepped backward off the stool, a little wobbly.

Bingle—Bangle—Bungle
I'm so happy in the jungle.

"Makes twelve," he said, wiping his mouth down the whole length of his forearm, wrist, and hand. "My nightly dozen. Ah —if youll be good enough to catch that first one along with the other two, I wont obtrude on your hospitality no further. We'll get for home."

Myrtle came and stood in front of me, across the counter. She didnt look at Peeps.

"One sixty," she said, being businesslike. "Seven beers is one forty, a hamburger's twenty: one sixty. One sixty, please."

I picked up the Bible, opened the cigar box, and took out two one-dollar bills. Peeps watched over my shoulder, looking down into the box.

"Say, pal, old pal: youre heeled. Youre heeled, by Christ."

But I had given up trying to understand him. Usually it didnt mean much anyhow.

Myrtle gave me the change—a quarter, a dime, and a nickel —and I put them in the box. Peeps said:

"Aint you leaving something for the little lady?"

I just looked at him.

"A tip," he said. "Something to show you appreciate the service."

So I opened the box again and took out the nickel and put

it on the counter. She looked at it, mouth drawn in a line. Peeps laughed, standing there, holding the door ajar. As I came past he spoke in a low voice, his mouth so close to my ear I could hear him breathing:

"What was the caper, pal? You can talk to me. I'm close as the tomb, maybe closer. Dont tell me you collected all that green just reading the Bible.—To the right," he said, and took hold of my arm.

The door jarred shut behind us and the music sounded faint and far away. Peeps leaned this way and that, carrying us from side to side on the paving. When we came to a big tree halfway between street lights, he stopped and looked back.

"Cop in sight?"

He wasnt.

"Hold up."

Peeps hunched forward, one hand against the tree, and began to fumble at the front of his trousers. Somewhere off in the night a clock struck one, a mournful sound, and then I heard him pissing against the tree, giving little moans and cries of pain: "Oo! Ow! Oo!" It went on for a long time, a steady splash and trickle.

"Got arrested for this once," he said between groans. "Committing a public nuisance, they called it. (Ow!) Aint that a laugh? Call it a free country, yair, then haul a man into court for making water. (Oo!) I tell you, pal—"

He fumbled at his trousers, trying to button them, then gave it up and took hold of my arm.

"I tell you, pal, this clap is killing me."

The rooming house was two-thirds down the second block. A light came out of a pipe above the door, showing the bottom few steps of a flight that went up into darkness.

"Maybe you better pay now," Peeps said, stopping under the light. "Not that I dont trust you, pal: I trust you. It's just we might forget."

I opened the cigar box, took out the quarter and the dime left from what the waitress gave me, added another dime and a nickel, and handed them to him. He looked at them under the light. One sixty plus fifty made two ten, plus the nickel I gave the waitress made two fifteen—almost enough to live on for a week back on the island. Life in the world comes high, I thought.

"Fine," he said. "Now follow me. And shh: dont drag your feet."

The staircase creaked and trembled. I followed him up it, then along a hall with doors set jamb to jamb down both sides and a light globe burning at the other end; it came out of a pipe, like a hanging tear, the same as the one downstairs. The doors were so close together I couldnt believe they led to separate rooms. Peeps went in one on the left, near the back. When I was inside with him, he took off one of his shoes and used it to prop the door ajar a bit, so as to have some light from the hall.

"There now. Nice and cozy, hey?"

The room was so narrow I could have reached out and touched both side walls at once. High at the opposite end, a window was almost flush with the bricks of the next-door building. The air was hot and close and smelled of armpits, feet, and mildewed clothes. A canvas cot took up nearly half the space. Peeps sat sideways on it, one foot bare, the other drawn up while he tugged at the knotted shoelace. Then he stopped and looked at me with a sort of lop-sided grin. One side of his mouth went up, the other down, like an S pulled partly straight and laid on its back.

"Want to turn a trick before going to sleep?"

"Trick?"

"Have your ashes hauled, lay some pipe, get some gash. Tail. Theres a couple of blisters down the hall—three bucks. A special cutrate price for friends of mine. Not bad, either, considering the price and where you are. I'll wake them up if you want to. They wont mind."

"No." I said it quick, as soon as I knew what he was talking about.

"Dont get sore, pal. I thought you might be wanting to, thats all. I cant. And when a fellow cant, he thinks everybody else in the world is honing all the time. Specially when they can afford it," he said, looking at the cigar box and grinning his lop-sided grin.

Two blankets were wadded into a brown-and-gray ball at one end of the cot. He untangled them and handed me the gray one.

"Make yourself cozy anywheres down there."

The way he said it, youd think there was acres of room.

I folded the blanket across and across, making a pad, and spread it on the floor alongside the cot. By that time he had given up fighting the knotted shoelace. He was lying down, fully dressed except for the shoe that held the door ajar to let the band of light come through from the hall. He watched me over the side of the cot while I stacked the Bible and cigar box by my head, the Bible on top.

"All right?"

"All right," I said, stretched out.

The crack of light fell between us like a wall, and almost at once I began to hear him snoring, a heavy sound; he snored in groans. I thought to myself, Thats the quickest I ever heard anyone go to sleep.

But after a while (—I'd been lying there breathing smooth and regular, not moving for I dont know how-long; I was thinking of Beulah, how heavy she was when I carried her across the island: she weighed more dead than alive) I heard a scraping, a sort of rustling by my head, and when I looked I saw a hand poked through the wall of light; the snoring was still going strong. I thought in a flash: It's her! But I lay there watching, and then I saw what it was. The hand was working the cigar box from under the Bible, bit by bit, doing it in a careful, timid way.

I sat up and the hand jerked back; the snoring stopped short in surprise. Then it started again, almost at once, going louder than ever. So thats it, I thought. And then I thought, What kind of a man is this, would try to steal from directly under the Bible?

I picked up the box and the Book and shifted them to the other side of the blanket. Just as I was about to lie back down, I thought of something else. The snoring was going strong. I lifted the lid of the box and took out the razor, then lay with it folded open, handle and blade coming out from between the backs of my fingers, my fist thrust into the band of light. It made a V of horn and steel, the blade shining bright with little flecks of rust from scaling the fish.

The snoring stopped and I could hear him breathing in gasps, holding his breath and letting it out slow. He was wondering if I was going to use it; he was scared. It was because of the water, I thought; the water made her heavier. After a while I went to sleep like that, thinking of Beulah but remembering to give the razor a little twitch every now and again to make it glitter in case he got over being scared.

When I woke up I didnt know where I was: I didnt have a notion. I didnt even know if I'd been dreaming. It was like being lost off somewhere far in space, everything strange around you, not knowing what youd touch if you put your hand out. It seemed to me I heard music, someone singing:

CiviliZAtion! CiviliZAtion!

But that was part of something left over from sleep, some dream I'd been having, back in the other world.

Then I saw the razor glinting steely where the band of light had fallen but wasnt falling now, and I remembered. I thought at first the hall light had gone out, but then I looked back over my head and saw the window faded bluey-gray. It was that time between night and day, when the air is still too dark to see through, yet too pale to carry lamplight—what Beulah said her mamma used to call the darkest hour.

—She's dead! I thought, remembering.

I'd forgotten but now I remembered. I remembered, but before it could go any further, I quit thinking about it; I put

it out of my mind. I wont think about that, I thought; and
didnt.

Dawn filtered into the room, moving from the ceiling toward
the floor, coming down, down, like the room was a tub (it
wasnt much bigger) and the darkness was water trickling down
the drain. Close at hand I heard the snoring, not near as loud
as when it was pretended. Finally I could see him lying sideways on the cot, asleep with his face turned toward me, less
than an arm's length away. His mouth was open, a hole with
stubble around it, and he was snoring in earnest, soft and
smooth, nothing put-on about it now.

He looked different by daylight, but I knew him. I knew
him but for a while I couldnt remember his name. Pitts? That
was back on the island, I thought. Besides, he didnt have a
mustache; he had a week-old beard. I watched him and all of
a sudden, just as I gave up wondering, it came to me—Peeps:
Peeps was his name and he'd tried to steal from me. I still had
the razor open in my hand.

The way he was sleeping, head up on the side of the cot
and neck stretched long and naked, puckered under the stubble
like the neck of a half-plucked chicken, he seemed to be lying
that way on purpose to have his throat cut; he seemed to be
inviting me to do it. Evil showed in his face. After all, he'd
tried to steal from me, and stealing was as sinful as the other,
as much against the Commandments; it was as bad to break
the Eighth as it was the Seventh. I lay there, waiting on word
from the Lord, and the light grew.

I could have done it if God said do it: I was ready. But no
voice came. I watched him for a long time, lying like that,
his throat stretched back. It was almost wide open daylight in
the room, when all at once he lifted his eyelids. He didnt blink
them first; he just lifted them. We were looking at each other.

"Morning," he said.

I sat up, folded the razor shut, and put it back in the box. He
didnt move except his eyes. They followed me, every move I
made.

"Sleep good?" he said, and still he didnt move. It was as if he was paralyzed.

I folded the blanket and laid it across the foot of the cot, then took the Bible and cigar box under my arm and stood looking down at him. He rolled onto his back, one shoe off and one shoe on, and lay there looking at me over his forehead. I put out my hand and took hold of the edge of the door.

"Leaving aready?" he said.

I turned in the doorway, looking back. His eyes were blue, like glass, but the whites were crisscrossed with tiny red veins like cracks. He was so bandy-legged his feet didnt come anywhere near the end of the cot.

"Give up your sinful ways," I said. "The Lord spared you just now—you dont know how close. He might not do it again."

Peeps just lay there; the lop-sided grin was frozen on his face. When I turned again and went through the door, my foot kicked something that skidded across the hall with a scraping sound and stopped against the wall on the other side. It was the shoe he'd used to prop the door ajar. I let it lay.

"I'm damned," I heard him say as the door swung to—the same thing the tall soldier said just before Brother Jimson pitched him sprawling in the bushes.

As I was going down the hall an alarm clock began to clatter in one of the rooms: first shrill, then dull, like a hand had been cupped over the bell: and it stopped. The staircase creaked and trembled as I went down. Over the doorway at the bottom, the lightglobe still burned at the end of its pipe, the last drop hanging onto the lip of a faucet, with a little skeleton of red-hot wire inside. The sun hadnt risen yet, but I could see it reflected rosy on the upstairs windowpanes. The streets were gray.

Three niggers, one behind another, were pushing brooms in the gutter, and a white man stood beside them with a pistol on his hip. They still wore the fancy clothes theyd been arrested in, around the dice table at the barrelhouse the Saturday before, striped shirts, high-waisted pants, and pointed shoes. One was doing a shuffle behind his broom, a sort of clog, and the other two were watching him. "Come on, come on," the white man said, and they stopped laughing.

I turned left, walking in my footprints from the night before, toe to heel and heel to toe, going the opposite way. In the middle of the second block I came to the big tree where we had stopped; it wasnt even damp. Four blocks ahead, the street ran into the levee where the memorial signboard was. The grass on top was bright green, for the sun was coming up behind me.

Then I reached the cafe and stood looking in the window. Instead of Myrtle, a big dark man with two gold teeth was standing behind the counter, wearing an apron with the strings wrapped twice around. Instead of the cowboys, four men were strung out down the line of stools, drinking coffee and eating eggs. The music machine was dark and quiet, no bullet-shaped bubbles trickling up its tubes, and a smell of frying ham came through the door. No music, no cowboys, no Myrtle: the place didn't look the same. The sun broke clear and gilded the sheet of glass.

Maybe it didn't happen, I thought. Maybe they weren't real; none of them. Maybe I dreamed it all.

6. (Continued)

It was the last store on the left before the levee; I'd seen it when I was here two weeks ago, walking around at a loss and waiting for Beulah. A banner ran the width of the building: BRISTOL SALVAGE CO. CLOTHES BOUGHT & SOLD, and two others, one on each side in smaller letters, were fastened slantwise across the windows: *Prices Slashed! Last Chance Sale!* The doors were locked, a chain running through two holes with a padlock sagged in the middle. So I crossed the street and waited by the war memorial, a shiny red and white affair like a signboard, lettered in blue: "May the spirit, of our boys, who fell in battle, live for ever."

I remembered that too. Three years ago, when the soldiers were coming home, a club of Bristol businessmen decided to put up a memorial with the names of the dead veterans on it. Somebody said, "What about the niggers?" and they voted to put the white boys' names down one side and the niggers' down the other, with the American flag awave between them. It came out in the paper, what they planned, and that night the president of the club got a telephone call from a planter: "This is Orley Mitchell. I'll shoot the first man puts a nigger's name on that thing." He'd have done it, too. So they took another vote and decided it would be best (cause less trouble, that is) to just say something about the spirit of our boys. Two months after they finished it, Orley Mitchell died of cancer of the throat.

Life began to stir on the streets before long, cars coming

and going, more all the time, storekeepers cranking their awnings down, and finally I watched a tall thin man with a caved-in chest step up to the doors of the Salvage Co. He took a bunch of keys from his pocket, undid the padlock, and drew out the chain. I gave him a while, then crossed the street and walked in. At first it was so dark I couldnt see. Then I saw him coming toward me, down the aisle between tables piled with clothes. His face was lantern-jawed and he washed his hands in the air in front of his vest. They made a scaly whisper, palm crossing palm.

"*Good* morning," he said. "Could I help you?" He looked happy. Generally he stood on the sidewalk, snagged customers by the arm, and drug them sideways into the store.

"I want a dark serge suit," I said. "A white shirt. A necktie. And a pair of low-quarter shoes to match." I said it like a person reciting something, for I had memorized the words while I was waiting on the levee.

"And a hat," he said, looking above my eyes.

"And a hat," I said.

"Step this way, Sir." He held one hand out sideways. "Getting married?" When I didnt answer he took it to mean yes. "You come to the right place," he said. "We'll fix you proper." We stopped at one of the tables toward the back.

I was onto him. He called me Sir to make me feel important, to make me want to show what a spender I was. But he could have saved himself the trouble: I had thirty-one dollars and forty cents in the cigar box, twenty-five of it to spend on clothes. That was why I came to a second-hand store in the first place.

The table we stopped at was piled with shirts and a line of suits hung on a rack beside it. He looked me up and down, squinting his eyes. "A fifteen thirty-two?" he said.

"A what?"

"Is that your shirt size, fifteen thirty-two?"

"Show me," I said.

He took one from a pile in the middle, held it by the tips

of the shoulders so the sleeves hung down. "Here's a beauty. Really nice." He turned it this way and that. A piece had been cut from the tail to patch one elbow. Except for that, it looked good.

"How much?"

He seemed to think. "A dollar?"

"I'll take it."

He sighed and I saw then he had expected me to argue. He laid the shirt aside and turned to the rack of suits. "I think we've got exactly the item youre hunting. The gentleman was about your build; we bought the entire wardrobe from the widow." He ran his hand along the line of suits, the dangling sleeves, and mumbled to himself. "Now lets see—ah." He held up a dark blue serge, just what I wanted. But when he turned it there was a belt in back.

I shook my head and he hung it on the rack, looking sad. All the time he was showing me the others, I kept thinking of the first one. When he was near the end I said, "Lets see that first suit one more time," and when he held it up again: "How much?"

He seemed to think. "Twenty dollars?"

"Too much." I shook my head.

"Thats one fine suit. Feel the quality of that cloth. Prewar." I didnt say anything. He turned it this way and that. "How much were you thinking of spending?"

Now it was my turn to seem to think. "Fifteen."

"Tell you what I'll do," he said. "Seventeen-fifty, it's yours. A special offer."

I said I'd take it. We went on like that: tie twenty cents, shoes two-fifty, hat one-fifty—I didnt try them on. When he had them all together in a pile, he looked at my muddy worn-out clothes. "You want to wear them now?"

"I'll take them with me."

He opened his pad and held the pencil with the point just clear of the sales slip. "What was the name?"

"Legion," I said; I'd thought of that. I watched him, wondering was he a Bible reader.

"Spell it, please."

He wasnt.

I spelled it and he wrote it down and totted up the figures. They came to twenty-two seventy: twenty-three sixteen with the tax. I paid him out of the cigar box (leaving eight-twenty-four) and turned with the bundle under my arm. It was wrapped in thick brown paper, tied with string.

"Good day, Mr Legion. Call again."

Sunlight was bright on the streets; I blinked like a man coming out of a cave. So many people were hurrying round, I thought it was Saturday till I counted on my fingers and it was a Friday. At the corner a man sat on the sidewalk, both legs cut off almost at his trunk. A hat lay in what was left of his lap, brim up, with half a dozen pencils and some silver. I lifted the lid of the cigar box, took out a dime, and dropped it in the hat. "God bless," he said. I could tell by the sound of his voice he didnt mean it. He was about my age, already gray.

I stopped on the curb, looking both ways till I found what I wanted: a barber pole three doors down, on the opposite side; it spun under glass. When the light turned green I crossed with the others and went into the shop. The barber at the first chair looked up from shaving a customer, lifting a pinch of cheek between finger and thumb. "Everything's going to be all right," one said from down the line; "the radio said so." The barber raised his eyebrows, looking at me over the rims of his glasses.

"Bath," I said.

"Go right back." He pointed with the hand that held the razor. "The boy will tend to you."

A curtain hung across the door. I lifted it and a bright-colored boy got up from a chair. "Yassir, captain." He was holding a magazine with a near-naked white woman on the front.

"Bath," I said.

"Step rat this way." He whistled, leading me down a line of doors all painted white and as close together as the ones the night before. Then he stopped and flung one open. "Soap and towels on the rack. Hot water most plentiful." I thought what would happen to him if he went down to Ithaca and sat looking at such a magazine as that. He put the plug in the tub and turned the tap. Water thundered; steam came up. "Anything you wants, you call for Joe."

Uppity, I thought.

The door clicked shut and I could hear him whistling down the hall, going back to his chair and magazine. It was one of the songs I heard last night, the one about Petey Wheatstraw, claiming he was the devil's son-in-law.

I let the tub run three-quarters full, then ran in cold until the heat got down to where I could bear it. Steam was still rising. I undid the bundle, hung up the suit and shirt, smoothing the wrinkles left from the string being tied so tight, and took off my old clothes. When I stepped in, the water came up even with the rim of the tub. I lay there, up to my chin; I soaked and soaked. It wasnt till I tried to wash my face and hair that I found I still had on my glasses and hat. Finally I pulled the plug and my sins went gurgling down with the suds and dirt. I had cast sin like a snake can cast his skin.

Considering I'd bought them second-hand and wouldnt try them on till I was clean of the island dirt, the clothes were a right good fit. The shoes were so tight I had to use a towel corner for a shoehorn, and the trousers were three or four inches too big in the waist. But that was all right. If it came to the worst I could slit the shoes with my razor, and I figured the trousers would be almost snug by the time I got my weight back. I had trouble tying the tie: I'd almost forgotten how, and the tips of my fingers were puffed and wrinkled from being in soak so long. I left the old things on the floor, split felt hat and broken shoes on top. Then I went out—like Legion in the Bible, fully dressed and in my right mind again.

"Lord, captain, I didnt know you," the nigger said, looking up from the magazine. He pulled the curtain aside and I went through.

Men were sitting along the opposite wall, waiting their turns. I took a seat among them. Finally when the barber on the end called "Next!" and nobody moved, I got up and sat in his chair.

"Shave and haircut," I told him.

"Right," he said, and pulled a lever. The chair went backward so fast I thought I'd fallen. "Quite a growth of beard you got there, mister. Been off somewheres?"

"Mm," I said. Every once in a while he'd try again, but I kept saying Mm till he gave up.

After the hot towel came the lather, after the lather the razor, a series of little scraping sounds, whiskers crackling in front of the razor edge; then the sound of the strap, pow! pow! like pistol shots; "Yes sir, some beard," he'd say, stropping to keep the razor sharp, and he'd come back, whiskers crackling. I was nearly asleep when he pulled the lever again and the chair jerked up. I put my hand to my cheek and it felt naked, smooth as Beulah's. The scissors snicked around my ears; the clippers hummed— "Next!" I heard, and woke up face to face with myself in the mirror. My nose was sharp as a knife blade, my cheeks fishbelly white, and my eyes were like two holes burnt in a blanket. Is that me? I wondered. Hair fell an inch thick on the floor when the barber shook the cloth.

I was trembly on my legs, weak-like, and I thought at first it was because of going down and up so fast when the barber jerked the lever. Then I remembered Samson losing his hair, turning weak, and I thought for a minute that was it. Then I remembered food: I hadnt eaten. All I'd had since I left the island was those two perch by the barrow pit and a sandwich washed down with a glass and a half of beer in the cafe. My stomach had been nudging my mind all this time and my mind wouldnt listen. But now it did.

I paid the barber a dollar fifty—haircut seventy, shave thirty, bath fifty: that left six sixty-four—and went out on the street, cigar box and Bible under my arm. I stood there a minute, looking at the trashcan on the curb (*Keep the Queen City a Clean City*): then took the money and the razor out of the box, put the money in one pocket, the razor in another, and the cigar box in the can: and walked on down the street with just the Bible, stepping heel to toe and toe to heel in my old footprints till I came to the cafe again.

Eggs and bacon, toast and coffee: eighty cents, plus two cents tax left five eighty-two. I went out on the street again—heel to toe and toe to heel until I came to where I spent the night with Peeps; the lightglobe dripping out of the pipe had been turned off. The depot was at an angle across the street.

"To Ithaca?" the man said through the ticket window. "She's scheduled for 9:15, ten minutes ago, but she's forty minutes late the last I heard. Thatll be seventy cents."

I paid and he gave me a cardboard stub exactly like the one Granddaddy let me hold when we came to the reunion. I put it in my hatband, the way I remembered him telling me to do, and went outside to wait.

Opposite the depot was a drugstore, the kind that sells everything. I had half an hour to wait, so I crossed over. Soon as I stepped through the door a lady came up: "Can I help?" I just stood there, looking around. There was so much stuff, I couldnt decide. "Can I help?" she said, hands clasped.

"How much?" I said, pointing to a big ribbon-tied box of candy with *Creme Delights* printed crossways on the lid. The letters dripped.

She turned it over, looked at the price on the bottom. "Two dollars and forty cents," she said.

"I'll take it."

Another thing I liked was at the toy counter: a mamma duck with three little ducks in tow. You pulled them along by a string and they waddled and quacked. "A dollar fifty," she said. I said I'd take it.

On one side was a table with a sign saying NOTIONS. That was the first I ever heard of notions being for sale. Mostly it was perfume. I bought a ninety-cent frosted bottle done up in crinkly paper.

They came to four-ninety including tax. That left me twenty-two cents. So I bought four candy bars and kept the two pennies to jingle in my pocket: recrossed the street, and walked up and down on the gravel by the tracks, arms loaded with packages, till the train came in and I got aboard.

It might have been the same green plush from forty-two years ago. All it lacked was Granddaddy sitting beside me in his uniform, snoring into his beard. The engine hooted twice, then twice again, and a series of crashes came down the line like automobiles meeting head-on; the seat bucked; we were moving, trees and houses sliding past, people standing and looking at us through the glass. Children waved from yards and porches, jumping up and down on tiptoe. We began to go faster, faster still.

Two men with a suitcase on their knees sat face to face across the aisle, playing cards. Every now and again one would say "Gin!" and the other would say "Oh Jesus," and theyd scramble the cards and start all over again: "Gin"— "Oh Jesus." It didnt make much sense.

Then we were going through niggertown, picking up more speed. The cabins were built wall to wall and all alike, cut from one pattern; the yards were smooth and gray, the color of slate, without a grassblade, and the vacant lots were cluttered with stiff upstanding weeds and rotting car-bodies. All these ran past the window with the jerky swiftness of the little cherries and plums and lemons behind the glass on slot machines. The children here stood on their tiptoes too, watching the train go by; they even jumped up and down, their pigtails bouncing. They waved at the Jim Crow cars ahead, but they didnt wave at us. When the white car came abreast, they stopped and stood flat on their heels, arms at their sides. I couldnt decide if they were being uppity or polite.

Soon, however, it didnt matter; I forgot them. We broke into the clear: ran past the city limits, out of town, and followed the curve of the rails through dark green fields. This was the first time I had seen cotton since the night I went to bed and rose before dawn to catch the train for Bristol. It had come to a stand and the choppers were hard at work, hoes rising and falling, glinting in the sunlight. Their hats were big and golden like Miz Pitts'.

—Going home.

Both card players turned their heads and looked at me, so I knew I must have said it aloud. I kept my face toward the window, lips tight shut to keep from speaking again, and they turned back to studying their cards. The packages were stacked on the seat beside me: candy, perfume, ducks, Bible. I took up the Bible and opened it on my knees, reading it for the first time in three days. *Thou hast made me to serve with thy sins, thou hast wearied me with thy iniquities.*

25. I, even I, am he that blotteth out thy transgressions for mine own sake, and will not remember thy sins.

26. Put me in remembrance: let us plead together: declare that thou mayest be—"Gin!" one said, laying his cards face-up on the suitcase lid.

"Jesus," the other said. "Again?"

"Tickets. Tickets, please."

I turned and it was the conductor; he was coming down the aisle. He came from seat to seat, bracing stiff-legged against the buck and sway. The puncher flashed in his hand. The flagman was with him. When he came alongside he punched the players' tickets, then turned to me. All this time I was fumbling in my pockets, turning them inside-out to find my stub: I'd forgotten where I put it, and I knew two pennies wouldnt take me far. The conductor stood there a minute, smiling, an old man in rimless spectacles, with little bars of gold thread sewed to his cuff: then put out his hand and lifted the stub from under my hatband. He punched it, stuck it behind the handle on the window shade, and then moved on, still smiling. The flagman walked behind him, smiling too.

"Tickets. Tickets, please."

I went back to my Bible. But the sound of the wheels got mixed in with the words. Clickety clack, clickety clack: they seemed to be trying, trying to talk, trying to tell me something. From time to time the flagman would stick his head around the door and holler the name of a station: "Sunflower!" "Talleyrand!" "Durfee Junction!" and soon the wheels would slow and the train would lurch to a stop. We'd sit there a couple of minutes while they unloaded mail and passengers. Then the engine would hoot—twice, then twice—and the crashes would travel back, jerking us into motion again: clickety clack, clickety clack.

I thought of Beulah.

Before now, she'd come to me only in that other world of dreams—just twice in three long days, so far as I knew, and both times in disguise: once as a wrestling angel, once as a little girl being messed with by a bald man—but now she was with me in broad open daylight, or anyhow her voice was. I remembered her face the way it was at the pool, tilted back between my wrists, looking up, eyes rolling in their sockets, mouth gone slack: that would be with me wherever I went. But that was memory—that was in my mind; the voice was real, as real as the clickety-clack. I began to talk with her, in time with the wheels.

Clickety-clack, clickety-clack. Do-you-for*give*-me—clickety-clack.

And her words came back; she answered:

I-for*give*-you—clickety-clack. You-*did*-what-you-*had*-to—clickety-clack; you-*did*-what-you-*had*-to-do.

"Ithaca!"

The flagman had his head around the door, hollering with his jaws apart, and almost at once the wheels began to slow. We had passed my house three miles back and I hadnt even seen it. The blistered gray wall of the depot was sliding past.

Then I happened to glance to the left, across the aisle, and the players were holding their cards loose in their hands, looking at me round-eyed. That meant I'd been talking out loud again.

But I didnt care. I closed the Bible, took up the packages—candy, ducks, perfume—and started down the aisle. Then I stopped and faced about, looking down at the players balancing the suitcase on their knees.

"Did you hear her too?" I said.

Their faces didnt change; the cards were loose in their fists and their eyes were round. Then one scowled.

"Whats a matterth you, fellow?"

So they hadnt.

I turned, went out the door, then down the iron steps. I stood in the gravel beside the tracks, looking up and down the street, and nothing had changed. I'd expected to be like a man coming back after half a lifetime to the place where he was born. But it was no different. Mr Tilden's bank still stood on the corner across from the depot, and next to it was the drugstore that used to be the Palace Saloon, where Beulah laughed at me over the rim of a coke. Against the wall of the depot was the knife-gnawed bench where they say a gambler sat when he shot a man because the man was after him with a pistol for courting his daughter (Miss Birdy Tarfeller, principal of the Ithaca school in *my* time) and then in turn got shot by Hugh Bart who owned Solitaire at the time. All that was before I was born, almost sixty years ago, but it might have been yesterday except for the lightwires and the autos parked where the hitching-posts used to be. Nothing had really changed.

The engine hooted and chuffed; the shocks traveled back and the wheels began to turn. After the clang and groan of iron on iron, the train was gone; the track glittered empty in the sunlight. Excepting the fading smell of cinders and coalsmoke, it might never have been there. I stood alone in the silence, looking up the street and down. It might have been two weeks ago; I might never have left, might never have been on an island at all. There might never have been a Beulah.

I've heard of people aching to turn back the clock, but for me there wasnt any clock to ache to turn back: all there was was Now, and nothing that was past had ever been. Or so I thought. Or so I told myself, standing there smelling the fading smoke and juggling the packages.

I walked across the yard, gravel creaking under my shoes, turned right, and walked along the east side of the street. Mr Ledbetter was sitting in a split-bottom chair in front of his hardware store, the same as always. He is close to ninety, troubled with cataracts; his sons run the store, but he comes down every fair-weather morning and sits in the chair. I touched the brim of my hat.

"Day, Mr Henry."

"How do," he said, turning his face in my direction, eyes the color of phlegm.

The way he said it was no different from always. He hasnt changed a bit, I thought. Then I thought: There you go, expecting just because youve been on an island and done things, the world must have turned upside-down while you were gone, fire and flood, earthquake and tornado. He didnt even know youd been away. Two weeks arent even a tick on a ninety-year clock face.

From Ithaca the street runs into the highway: be*comes* the highway. I followed it north out of town, treading my late-morning shadow into the gravel. I walked slow to keep from sweating, took careful steps to keep from stirring the dust up my trouser legs. But my feet began to swell until finally I couldnt stand it any longer; I sat on the ditchbank a mile from town, got out the razor and took off my shoes, and slit them both along the outer bulge. Then I put them back on, took up the packages and set out again, and that was better. Soon, though, I began to sweat—little rivulets trickling down my ribs, as cold as icewater. It broke out on my face and collected at the bottoms of my glasses. This wasnt the weather for dark blue serge, but I kept going: kept telling myself, over and over, Youll be there soon, God willing, where you can sit and rest for the next twenty years; keep going.

I rounded the final curve and there was the house, the same as always, half a mile away. I could even see the lard bucket upside-down on the gatepost where the dude in two-tone shoes hung it when he finished watering his radiator, close to two months ago. Nothing was changed, not even that. But I asked myself was one thing after another going to keep reminding me of her all the balance of my life.

The porch was empty. From the gate I saw three of Luty Pearl's spool-toys on the stoop, but there was no telling if theyd been there an hour or a week. I wondered, Have they gone? for the house looked empty too; it had that empty look. Then, when I reached down to lift the latch, I remembered something else. I shifted the bundles under one arm, put my hand in my pocket—Nothing from that world into this world, I thought—and took out the two pennies. I pitched them over my shoulder, across the road, careful not to watch where they landed for fear I'd be tempted to come back and look for them to remember her by: then opened the gate and went through it, up the steps.

"Kate?"

Nobody answered. I waited, then called a bit louder:

"Kate . . ."

The house was empty with that special kind of silence, not as if there were people waiting, listening (something lets you know: the heartbeats, maybe)—but as if there was nobody there at all.

It was nearing noon. I stood in the doorway, stock still, ears pricked, and then I began to hear something bubbling: a faint, far sound. So I walked back to the kitchen. And sure enough, there was a fire in the range. The bubbling came from a pot of greens (collards: I always liked collards best) and there was a smell of cornbread from the oven. Sho, I thought. Theyre in the field—right where youd be too, if you hadnt gone away. It's chopping time.

187

Both pairs of overalls were washed and ironed and folded on the shelf, waiting for me the same as always except one pair was usually being washed. She knew, I thought; she knew I was coming back. And then I thought: She knows me better than I know myself.

In the bedroom I took off the suit and hung it up, and then the shirt and necktie; put the shoes side by side beneath the suit, and stood naked for a minute while the sweat dried. Nothing from that world into this, I told myself again: not even sweat. The overalls, faded sky blue, slid onto my legs as cool and soft as shade. I stomped into my work shoes, tied the laces. *Now*, I thought, smelling again that sharp clean smell of yellow soap; I'm home.

From the back porch I could see them across the field, Kate and Myrtle chopping side by side, their backs to me, and Luty Pearl in the shade of a little tree, playing with some of her spool-toys in the dust. Beyond them was the railroad track I'd come south on, an hour ago, and hadnt even thought to look out of the window. My hoe leaned against the wall of the house: all I needed to do was reach out my hand as I went down the steps. It had even been sharpened, a half-inch lip filed diamond-bright, curved to the shape of the cutting edge.

I came on them from the rear. They didnt hear me coming, their hoes going *chuck* and *chuck* and *chuck* in the sandy loam. Luty Pearl was keeping busy with her spools; neighbors brought them to her from miles around. I thought to fall in alongside, joining in the rhythm of the chopping. But I stopped and stood there, the hoe handle smooth against my palms. I tried to make a smile but my mouth wouldnt shape it.

Chuck and *chuck*—

"Hello," I said.

Myrtle spun round; "Pa!" she said. But Kate just stood there with her back to me, the hoe held level, frozen. Then she finished the downstroke: *chuck*, and faced about. "Where you been, pa?" Myrtle said. Kate just looked at me.

"I was off on a call from the Lord," I said.

Neither of them said anything to that; they just stood and looked. So I stepped past them and swung the hoe off my shoulder; I began to chop, hoeing steady: *chuck* and *chuck* and *chuck*, setting the rhythm. They stood there almost a full minute, watching, then fell in behind me. We moved up the field, myself and Kate and Myrtle, one after another. Soon we began to string out, myself, then Kate, then Myrtle. Luty Pearl hadnt looked up from her spools, making double loops and curlicues in the dust. It felt good, working my own land with my own people.

We made the turnrow twice, strung out still more. The sun went past the overhead. When I came even with the starting point the third time, I stopped and leaned on my hoe, waiting till Kate came abreast.

"Aint them greens about done, you reckon?"

"I reckon," she said. She stopped and wiped at her forehead with the back of one hand, fingers curved. That was the first time she spoke.

So when Myrtle caught up, Kate and I took Luty Pearl by the arms, one on each side, and the four of us started back across the field. It was clumsy walking for Luty Pearl, going crossways to the furrows. She couldnt tell the hills from the valleys, and every step was a stumble. She began to gurgle and moan, the way she always does when she is scared. We might as well have been carrying her. Myrtle brought up the rear, the three hoes running back across her shoulder, clanging against each other at every step.

"You lost some flesh," Kate said when we got to level ground. She was watching me over the back of Luty Pearl's neck, for Luty Pearl had let her chin loll on her chest.

But I let it pass. No use starting on that, I thought. "I brought some presents," I said.

"Presents?" Myrtle said, coming up from the rear. The hoes clanged faster. "What kind of presents? Is one of them for me?"

"Wait and see," I said, and she began to walk faster. She went up the steps at a run.

By the time we got Luty Pearl inside, Myrtle was standing beside the living room table where I had left the packages. "Which one's mine?" she said, bent forward, holding her hands behind her back.

I handed Kate the candy and Myrtle the perfume. Kate just stood there, looking at the pink silk ribbon-bow. But Myrtle already had the crinkly paper broken and was sniffing at the stopper, long deep breaths, both hands holding the bottle, her eyes tight shut. "Oh pa," she said. "It smells—it *smells* so good!"

"I better put dinner on," Kate said. She turned and walked back to the kitchen, carrying the box in front of her like a tray. She kept her head down, looking at the ribbon-bow, the slantwise writing that spelled *Creme Delights* in dripping letters.

While Myrtle went on sniffing the perfume, I opened the other package and took out the ducks. Luty Pearl was sitting on a stool against the wall, head hung forward to look at her hands lying limp in her lap. She can do that for hours at a time when the notion strikes; it's like they didnt belong to her, as if she happened to glance down and found them lying there. I put the ducks on the floor and took hold of the string, drawing them along. They waddled and quacked, the mamma and three little ones, all in a row.

"Well, say," Myrtle said. She even stopped sniffing to watch. "Aint they something? Look what *you* got, Luty Pearl: some quack-quacks." But Luty Pearl wouldnt pay them any mind. She kept studying her hands, folded sharp at the wrists, resting limp like a couple of flowers in her lap. "Look at yonder, Luty Pearl. Look what pa has brought you, Luty Pearl."

I kept pulling the string, towing them along, but she kept her head down—until finally, just as they crossed in front of the stool, she heard the quacking and lifted up her head and looked at them, waddling and quacking, one behind another. First she didnt know what to make of it. Then her eyes got big; she jerked back on the stool and began to yell, squalling and kicking, trying to throw herself backwards through the wall.

Kate came running from the kitchen, spoon in hand. She leaned across her, hiding the sight of the ducks, and stroked her hair. "There now," she said; "There now," over and over. When Luty Pearl got quieted at last, Kate looked at me over her shoulder. I was still standing there, holding the string, too surprised to do anything but watch. So was Myrtle; she held the perfume bottle, forgetting to sniff.

"For shame," Kate said. "A grown-up man, scaring the child with such a thing as that. You too," she said, turning to Myrtle. "Shame on both of you."

"I didnt do nothing," Myrtle said.

So I put the ducks back in the box, shaking my head. I thought to myself: The more you try to do right in this world, the more you do wrong.

Then we ate. I had forgotten how good cornbread could be. We rested a spell, then went back to the field and worked right through to sundown, a little past. I was so tired I almost went to sleep at the supper table with food half chewed in my mouth. Field work is something a man cant do just off and on. My arms felt so heavy I could barely lift them.

It wasnt till afterwards, sitting around the table in the living room, that I remembered the candy bars I bought in Bristol. I went and got them out of my coat (half melted) and we sat munching them—Luty Pearl too: Kate peeled the wrapper back for her, like skinning a banana. Everything was peaceful, homey, each of us munching a candy bar after a hard day's work, till Myrtle caught Luty Pearl trying to shove hers under her harness belt ("Look at what she's up to now!") and Kate had to sponge her off and put her to bed.

I went in the room and undressed and put on a nightshirt, the first one in more than two weeks. By that time Kate had Luty Pearl in bed, wrists strapped to the bars the same as always. She was whimpering, restless, so I went in to give her the goodnight kiss; that was what it always took to soothe her, the only thing. But the minute she saw me bending over, she began to kick and beller, almost as bad as when she saw the ducks, thrashing around as much as she could with both her wrists tied. So I went back and got in bed. The moon came up and I lay there thinking. Always before, the goodnight kiss had quieted her, stopped her fretting: but now she wouldnt so much as let me touch her. It's because I lost my purity, I thought. She knows; she can tell without words.

After a while the yells sank down to sobs; the sobs sank down to whimpers, and finally she was quiet. Then Kate came in. I watched her in the moonlight. The house was still. She undressed the way she always does, putting her nightgown over her head and taking off her clothes from underneath it, not showing so much as an inch of secret flesh. I thought of Beulah walking around the shack, a piece of clothes draped here, a piece draped there, bouncing her bosoms or squeezing them upwards in her hands to look at the points.

"Pretty?" she used to say, and:

"Pretty," I'd say.

Kate got in bed, being careful not to jiggle the springs. I could see her against the moonlighted window, hardly sunk down in the mattress at all, yet making no more than a shallow ridge under the sheet. There was a trembling; I could feel her wanting me to want to, and I knew I ought to (for it had been more than a month, all told) but I couldnt. I would have if I could have, but I couldnt: couldnt. This is what it's done to you, I thought. I hadnt only lost my purity; I'd lost my manhood. And all of a sudden it came to me that Luty Pearl had known it all along. That was what she was squalling about: not purity. Purity had nothing to do with it.

I went to sleep with that in my mind: *Purity had nothing to do with it*, and next morning when I woke in bed alone, the words came back: *Purity had nothing to do with it*. Sleep had been like a gap for a spark to jump: I woke up where I left off and I knew the truth. God hadnt been my guide, hearing my prayers and telling me what to do: the devil had —old Satan. And now I had to live with that, unable to blame it on God.

This was Saturday, a half-day. We chopped all morning, came in at dinnertime. But I didnt go to town; I sat around the house. After dark, in bed, it was the same as the night before: I couldnt. Next morning while Kate and Myrtle were getting dressed for church, I put on my new suit and went into the living room and sat in a chair by the window. After a while they came out, bringing Luty Pearl between them, dressed up too. I just sat there. "I'm not going," I said. I was afraid if I went God would strike me dead for bringing Satan into the house of prayer.

They went without me, walking down the road, one on each side of Luty Pearl, holding her by the arms. I sat by the window two hours or more, till finally they came back and Kate went out in the kitchen, fixing dinner. After eating I came back and sat by the window again. It seemed to me I was waiting for something: I didnt know what—unless maybe for God to tell me what to do. All I knew was I was waiting; I couldnt have said for what.

I found out soon enough. A car pulled up in front of the house, tires growling in the gravel. Three people were in it, two up front and one in back. A short pot-bellied man got out on the other side and started around. Then the driver stepped out, red-faced under the shade of a wide, pale hat; he walked with a lean to the left, balancing the weight of a big nickel-plated revolver on his opposite hip. When the pot-bellied man came into the clear, I saw a star pinned to the pocket of his shirt. It twinkled in the sunlight. I didnt pay it much mind because by then the one in back was climbing out and I saw who he was: Dummy. They walked toward the house, the three of them in single file, and I knew.

She came up, blocks and all.

THREE

7. Wife

He was born right here on Solitaire, the same as his mother and grandfather before him, and great-grandfather too so far as I know. Likely it goes back further, for his mother was a Dade and there have been Dades around these parts since back in Eighteen Twenty-something when the Government gave the Choctaws word to load up their squaws and cross the river and the white men came with chairs and beds and iron tools and called it Jordan County. This house sits on the same foundation stones as the one he was born in, that burnt down when he was eight. He stood in the yard in a bobtail nightshirt, holding onto his grandfather's hand and crying because his mother and father and baby sister (or anyhow half-sister) were still inside the house, beyond the flames. I remember I was nine at the time; we lived just down the road.

No one knew his father much: where he'd come from, why he'd left wherever he'd come from, or anything. They said he was from Kentucky, but that was hearsay: likely someone made it up to keep from admitting there was something they didnt know; people will do such things. The main thing I remember was his eyes: pale green, the color you see down deep inside a block of ice, and just as cold. I was nine at the latest, as I said, and not inclined to notice much—but I remember his eyes, pale green and cold. He was a drifter; people knew that much. Pascal was his first name: Pascal Eustis. He'd work a while, never staying any one place too long at a time ("Just shy of nine months, about," people said with a laugh, for he was one for the girls, in a quiet, somehow deadly sort of way) until he struck Ithaca, clerking in the hardware store, and saw her at a dance, a church affair. Lucy Dade was her name; her mother wasnt living. He took one look and knew right then he'd come to the end of his drifting. The itch in his heel had stopped.

She'd just turned eighteen, engaged to be married to a cousin down at the south end of the county. The date hadnt yet been set but it was settled; the wedding was to be that coming spring and they were keeping steady company. I can barely remember her from ten years later. She wasnt what youd call pretty. Her chin was too short, too round, and her nose was a little too sharp. But even as a child, seeing her after theyd spent nine years domesticating her and she'd borne him a son, I could see what it was that put an end to his drifting. She was proper, almost prim. Butter wouldnt melt in her mouth, they used to say. Yet behind the properness, the almost primness, there was something bold. It was faint; it barely glimmered through—so faint, whoever saw it thought he was the only one to see it: a promise of something un*holy* that made him want to claim her for his own, write Hands Off across her before the others found out later, what everyone found out when the fire died down and the talk flared up (—sometimes it's only after you know the answers that you understand the questions) but I think I saw it even then, when she was ten years older. Anyhow *he* did—Pascal Eustis —when she was ten years younger.

The rest is hearsay. He didnt dance with her that first night at the church affair; *no*body did but the cousin. He stood in the shadows and watched, and he saw that she knew he was watching. Somehow, though, he found a way. They met in a cornfield less than a hundred yards from the bedroom window she climbed out of after the others were asleep. Three times they met like this, and he hadnt been wrong; the boldness was there, all right, behind the primness. It was August, the end of summer. He'd hear the cornstalks rattling when she picked her way across the field to meet him and his heart would knock in his throat. All the other girls he'd courted, in that quiet and somehow deadly sort of way, had just been practice. This time he meant business. Two weeks later he rented a buggy and waited at the end of the lane and she stole out and got in, and they drove up to Bristol and were married. The child was born eight and a half months later, just like clockwork. They named him Luther, after his grandfather.

They moved into the house on Solitaire as soon as they came back from Bristol, married—into the same bedroom with the window sash she'd soaped on the sly to keep it from squeaking when she raised it those four times. He quit his job at Ledbetter's and started learning to farm. It turned out he was never much good at that; his hands werent shaped to fit a plow; fifteen minutes of hoeing gave him blisters on his palms the size of quarters. But he stayed with it and people said you had to admire him whether he made a decent farmer or not, the way he saw what he wanted and planned a campaign, stole her away from among a whole parcel of kinfolks, under their noses. "Dont that beat all?" they said, and laughed —for they love to see a fellow get what he's after, providing he does it on the sly and providing it wasnt theirs. Even the one-armed father, who didnt like him from the minute he laid eyes on him, had to admit he'd done a careful job.

The only one left really unhappy was the cousin, widowed before he'd even been a bridegroom. When he got the news, it took three men to hold him—for he had seen it too, what hid behind the primness; *he* knew what he'd missed. And now when he looked back on all the chances he'd let pass, biding his time because he figured it wouldnt be long and he wanted her to respect him for his honor, he'd smash his fists against the wall and groan. For a while he considered making an assault, one stallion lunge (it wouldnt take long, almost no time at all): then let them come with their knives and pistols, cutting, shooting—it wouldnt matter; he'd be rid of his regret.

Finally, though, he gave it up. He moved away, clean out of the county: out of the state too, far as anyone knew, for he never came back. Maybe he is somewhere even now, a widowed bachelor with a long white beard, smashing his fists against the wall and groaning.

Yet I dont know. Thats only if he never heard what happened later to the man that took his place. If by chance he heard, maybe he stopped wailing; maybe he was thankful he'd been outgeneraled, shoved aside like so much extra baggage for a better load to ride. But I dont know. Regret of that particular kind is hard—it's a negative thing. Maybe he'd have been willing to take what followed for the sake of what he had missed. He'd considered facing knives and pistols for much less.

It took about nine years. The bride and groom moved in with the father, as I said. The father was already old, a Shiloh veteran, maimed, but he could do more work with his one arm in a week than the son-in-law could do in a farming year. It wasnt easy and soon it got worse, for he couldnt keep up in the other direction either. Maybe the half-hidden wildness, that had drawn him in the first place, was too much for him when it came as a steady thing. Maybe what had been a glimmer became a glare. Anyhow, he began to be outdone all round the clock. The old man was outdoing him by daylight and the daughter was outdoing him at night. What was worse, he began to believe they were laughing at him, with the shifts reversed, the old man at night and the daughter by daylight. He had to live with that, and it made him feel inferior; he began to be bitter, morose, who had always been so proud and aloof before.

That went on; that grew. They had the child by then, the son named for the old man. He was in knee pants, starting to school—I remember him well. He was a grade below me but the school was just one room; Miss Tarfeller taught the classes turns-about. I watched him—it was as if I knew already, could look right down the years. Anyone with him five minutes could see that the main person in his life was the grandfather, the one-armed veteran with the tales of war, of the battle where he'd been hurt and seen General Johnston die from a wounded leg, and of later times when he was running cartridges downriver to Vicksburg during the siege.

So Pascal Eustis had that to live with too. Theyd taken his son, made himself seem small and drab in the shadow of the old man who gave the boy his name. And that went on. Night after night he climbed in bed, nursing his blisters, coming onto a new battlefield before the wounds of the old had even begun to heal; everything was conflict, round the clock. He gave up. Eight years had gone by when suddenly, after all this time, the wife turned up pregnant again. It came as a surprise. He counted back and had good cause to believe it wasnt his doing. So *thats* it, he said to himself.

First he suspected the father—he was really that far gone in hate. Besides, he wouldnt believe an outsider could have managed to slip past him; he told himself he couldnt have been that stupid or she that sly. (But she'd been wiser than he knew: the men she chose knew how to keep their counsel, even from one another, not willing to risk losing what theyd lucked on. The talk came later, after the fire, when there was nothing left for them to lose.) Then suddenly he faced the truth. If she'd been sly enough to fool a father, she was sly enough to fool a husband too—especially when he considered that what she'd done eight years ago was prompted by vague yearnings, but now she knew thoroughly well what she was after because he had taught her. He was hoeing when he thought this. He dropped the hoe and ran across the field, up the steps of the house, into the bedroom. And sure enough, there was soap on the window sash.

He could have done it then: marched straight across the field to where she'd been chopping beside him, picked up the hoe he'd dropped—one quick hard cut, the one-armed father standing by, and it would be over; 'This is what happens when wives are sly,' he'd say, standing over her, holding the hoe, panting, watching her bleed. He stood at the window, running his fingers up and down the soap-smoothed frame of the sash, fanning his anger by imagining her as she must have been when she went out by this same window all those nights (How many?) looking back over her shoulder and seeing him lying blistered and spent on the second battlefield with the scars from the first still showing on his hands. Maybe she chuckled as she went out, he thought. He imagined her lying with the others (How many?) telling them about him so they could join in the laughter. He could have done it then, with the hoe, as I said. But he waited. I'll wait, he told himself, fearing he might have miscounted or forgotten. He decided to wait till he saw the baby. Then I'll know for sure, he told himself.

That was in May. He went back across the field, took up the hoe in his blistered hands, and chopped. She worked beside him, already beginning to bulge with the evidence of her slyness, but he refused to look at her, wouldnt turn his head in her direction. The baby was born in September—a girl, with pale fair skin, quite different from the first. Its hair was reddish. He took one look and knew.

So much for hearsay, invention. The rest is fact.

Three days later the grandfather went to Bristol for some kind of veterans' gathering; there would be a barbecue and later a banquet; he would return on the midnight train. That night, late, Luther woke and found his father bent over him, nudging his shoulder. They both wore nightshirts. His father's hair stood in a tuft on each side of his forehead, just as his own would do later.

"Get up," he heard his father say. "Run out the house and down the road. Keep going."

He did as he was told: got out of bed, went out of the house and down the road—he had always been a little afraid of his father. Before he'd gone far, however, he looked back over his shoulder and saw a flicker of fire through a side window. He stopped and faced about, watching the flicker become a glimmer, a glow. Then he heard footsteps coming nearer on the road. It was his grandfather, back from Bristol; he had on his uniform, the cuff of the empty sleeve tucked under the sword belt. "Look there," Luther said, pointing, and just as he said it, flames gushed out from the tops of all the windows, curving up over the eaves. They made a low-pitched roaring sound, like drawing breaths with a hand held just in front of your mouth.

By the time they reached it there was a pillar of fire going straight up into the night, so bright the stars were pale. Folks came from all around; they formed a bucket brigade running down to the lake, passing the buckets hand over hand, throwing water at the flames. I stood to one side with my mother and watched. Everyone else was looking at the firemen, but I watched the boy in the bobtail shirt holding onto the hand of the old man in the Confederate uniform and crying because his mother and father and baby sister—half-sister, were inside the burning house.

It wasnt long before they had it under control. The lighter parts went fast, cypress shingles, suchlike, and when only the heavier things were burning, beams and such, the men at the near end of the bucket brigade could stand close enough to douse them. I think now it might have been best to let it burn on down to ashes. The way it turned out, there was enough of her left to tell her throat had been cut from ear to ear and the butcher knife was by the bed, its handle charred almost off. The baby was still in the skeleton of the crib, and they found the husband where he had wedged himself between the bureau and the wall. He was crouched, hands joined, in an attitude of prayer.

The talk began before the embers cooled. A man who got there early told how he'd seen Pascal Eustis looking at him through the bedroom window, behind the flames. He looked calm, the man said, and he recalled thinking how brave he was, resigning himself to being trapped with the flames all round him. Then they had it under control; they could go

inside the house. Soon as they found them so, with the knife
by the bed and all, the others began comparing notes, the
ones she had been slipping out to meet. Mainly they told the
truth that night, being awed by the fire and all, but next
morning there were more than a dozen of them dropping
hints—some of them married men, at that—about how theyd
been in on it, meeting her in the corn patch or down by the
lake. Personally I think the majority lied. They couldnt pass
up a chance to brag when there was no way of checking.

One thing, though, you had to credit them for. They
stayed out of earshot of the boy and the old man to tell it
—especially the old man: because, one-armed or no, he'd had
a share in the biggest piece of violence this country ever
staged, and they werent taking any chances on what he might
or mightnt do to anyone he overheard passing such information about his daughter. So Luther never heard, never knew
the double heritage that came down—lust from the mother,
murder from the father—for him to live with all the balance
of his days.

We watched him in school and he was quieter; that was
all. His grandfather had always been the one he was closest
to, and now they were closer than ever. The old man took
him everywhere: wrote excuses for him to bring to Miss Birdy
in the first fine days of spring when theyd go fishing around
the head of the lake, talked to him all hours of the night about
the war, and even carried him to a veterans' barbecue next
summer up near Bristol. Theyd always be together except in
school, and soon as school was out we'd see him hastening
down the road, dust spurting up behind his heels because he
was in such a hurry to join his grandfather in the field or on
the roof of the rebuilt house, nailing shingles. In school, his
face would suddenly go solemn, the corners of his mouth
draw down, his eyes glaze over. If Miss Birdy called on him
at such a time, all he could do was look shame-faced and say
"Maam?" like a bleating lamb. "He's thinking about his
mother," we told each other behind our hands. Or *they* did:

I just watched. Because, as I said, it was like I knew already, as if I could look right down the coming years.

Then the grandfather died, who'd never been sick a day in his life except the time he was laid up after Shiloh while his stump healed. It happened almost too quick to realize. He was coming home from a Christmas party, carrying a piece of cake folded in a handkerchief for Luther, picking his way across the fields—zigzagging a bit, for he'd taken his turn each time the jug came round—and stumbled into a ditch half full of water. That ruined the cake and wet him to the skin. He got home sneezing and cussing, cussing and sneezing, and crawled in bed with his clothes on. Next morning he woke up with chills and fever. The chills went into pneumonia and he died before the New Year. He was sixty-three, had lived all those years, and all of a sudden he was dead. Dead—

Old folks often go like that, in a hurry—Ive seen it happen time and time again; you get so you sort of expect it. But Luther could hardly believe it: it happened so quick. He was almost ten, and an aunt and uncle moved into the house with him. In school his face was nearly always solemn those days, and whenever Miss Birdy called his name, all he ever did was answer "Maam?"

"He's *really* an orphan now," we told each other behind our hands. Or they did.

Next year he didnt come back to school. That was as far as he went, through the fourth. I went on and finished, through the eighth. The only times I saw him now was when he came past along the road, mostly on Saturdays going to town. Or sometimes on a Sunday I'd be in the wagon with my folks; we'd ride by his house and he'd be on the porch. They werent church-goers, he or the aunt or the uncle, though I found out later she'd given him a Bible once for his birthday.

Ten years that went on, and all that time he didnt so much as look at me. His eyes would sort of slide past where I sat, whether in the wagon or on the porch. But I waited: I bided my time. It was as if I knew, and I told myself he must know it too; Thats why he wont look at me, I thought. Then the war came and I prayed: Please; please, God, dont let him go. And he didnt. He was too young to be drafted and he had to stay because the uncle went. Then the war was over and they got a telegram from the Government; the uncle was dead. So the aunt went back to her people, wherever, and he was alone in the house. Now, I thought. Now he'll come. Somebody's got to do the cooking and washing.

But he didnt. For two more years he didnt. In those two years I turned down one offer flat and discouraged another— which was pretty good, considering how thin I stayed. Then the two years were past (he'd been keeping bachelor house and I was twenty-three, close on to being an old maid) and one Saturday, late, my mother came back to the kitchen; she'd been sitting on the gallery while I cleaned up the supper things. "It's that Eustis fellow," she said. "Now you be careful."

I dried my hands and went out and there he was. He had on a pair of new brown shoes and was turning the brim of a hard straw hat in his hands. "How do?" he said, looking down inside the hat, pretending to read the label pasted there.

"Wont you sit?" I said.

We sat for more than an hour. He kept twisting and turning the hat and pulling his feet back under the chair, ashamed of the new brown shoes. Anything I'd say, he'd mumble yes or no, whichever more or less applied. Finally he got up. "Good evening," he said, and turned and fairly stumbled off the porch.

"Come again," I told him. "Youll be welcome."

He went down the road. Soon as he was out of sight, my mother came to the door. "You better watch your step," she said. "Thats a queer one, that."

We married in late October, two months later. It was Indian summer and all the trees flared red. I wore a mail-order dress, the hem midway between my knees and ankles—I felt half naked; I really did—and satin shoes belonging to an aunt.

The wedding was in the early evening, a Saturday, and we came back to my mother's house for supper. Cousins and kin on both sides were there, drinking and making jokes of the usual kind. After supper, when we went out and got in the buggy to drive to his house—our house, now—they came out in the yard and lined up along the fence and threw things at us, old shoes and such. They took a special pleasure in it because he'd always been so solemn, so stand-offish.

And that wasnt all. We hadnt any more than gotten settled, sitting in our wedding clothes, lamps lighted, when here they came—men only: it was a shivaree. They rode him twice around the house, forked on a cross-tie, two at each end and one on each side to hold his ankles, keep from bucking him off. I watched through the windows, running from room to room as they went round. He hit and kicked for a while, but finally he just held on tight and moaned. They dumped him on the porch and went away. I helped him into the house and onto the bed, and he just lay there, doubled up and groaning with the stone ache. "Can I fix you a poultice or something?" I said. But he just moaned. It was three days before we were married in more than name.

Up till then I'd always thought of him as Luther, but now that we were married I called him Mr Eustis. That was the custom; it was considered proper. My mother always called my father Mr Kyle, for instance—even in bed, so far as I knew.

Rosaleen was born in August, 1921, two months short of our first anniversary, and Myrtle on Christmas Day of the following year. Both times, when they told him it was a girl, his face fell. All men want a son, I guess, but with him it was something special. In 1924 I lost a child born dead. The doctor was there, also Aunt Em the midwife—she wasnt really anyone's aunt but everyone called her that. She wrapped the baby in a cloth and laid it on the dresser until such time as she could dispose of it. Mr Eustis came to the door where the doctor was washing his hands in a basin. They talked in low voices, the doctor telling him the baby was dead. I watched them down the flat length of my body.

"What was it?" I heard him ask. Soon as he said it I saw him shrink back as if to say 'Dont tell me! Dont tell me!'—now that he'd asked, he didnt want to know. The doctor looked over his shoulder, still washing his hands; "What was it?" he said to Aunt Em, and Aunt Em turned to the bundle, lifted a flap of the cloth (they hadnt even noticed); "It was a son," she said, and Mr Eustis went away.

He was twenty-seven the following spring. Anyone guessing would have said closer to forty; he looked so long-faced, mopy. Out in the field, plowing or chopping, youd have thought he was trying to hurt the earth, he went at it such a furious way. At night, too, he was much the same in bed as he'd been in the field, lunging, plunging, making a sound in his throat. For two years that went on: I was almost scared of him. Then I was pregnant again, and I'd no sooner told him than he quieted down at once. So thats what he was after, I thought.

The baby wasnt due till late June or July, but that was '27, the year of the flood. In early May word came that the levee was broken north of Bristol and everybody began to stir about, some going to the landing to meet the steamboat, others heading for the Indian mound two miles northeast of Ithaca. That was where we went, Mr Eustis and I and Rosaleen and Myrtle, all four in the wagon along with a month-old calf; I sat in a rocking chair. The baby was thumping, kicking, acting up—I thought it must surely be a boy. The calf was bawling. What with the excitement and all, people running this way and that, the pains came on me soon as we reached the mound. By the time the water got there, I was hard in labor.

It was a girl again, born some time after midnight on the morning of Mr Eustis' twenty-ninth birthday. All that wild flurry, being up on the mound with water lapping higher, higher and higher, the doctor taking off every once in a while to set a bone or pump out the half-drowned—it's no wonder she turned out lacking. But we didnt know that then. Then, she was just like the other two, except for being smaller and less hungry and not having fingernails or a head of hair. "It's a girl," they told him, and he sort of put his chin down on his chest. The doctor had already told us this was the last, so we gave her her father's name; we called her Luther. Afterwards folks said we'd asked for trouble from the start, for that was also the name of the one born dead.

When the water went down we went back to the house and spent the rest of the year cleaning up, raking out silt with hoes and shovels, scrubbing and polishing till things were more or less the same as always. The new baby was always so quiet, so good. Give her some little something to look at and turn in her hands, a scrap of cloth, a spool, a piece of string, and she was no worry at all. There never was a baby gave less trouble. Next year's crop was made and gathered, and all this time she was never the least bit of worry. It bothered me some, the way she took no interest in walking or talking, but I told myself it was because she came early, before her time. But when we'd planted the second year's crop and she still didnt take an interest, I told Mr Eustis it didnt seem right; "Something is wrong," I said. That was on a Friday. Next day we took her to town to see the doctor.

He strapped a looking-glass onto his forehead, with a hole in the middle to peep through. First he gave her a good going-over with that. Then he took a flashlight gadget and shined it in her eyes, lifting the lids with his thumb, one after another. Finally he took off her clothes—without so much as one remark on how well I had sewed them—and spread her on the table, tapping her here and there with the tips of his fingers; youd have thought he was looking for tender spots to carve. And she put up with it all—a little past two years old and she didnt whimper; I felt right proud. When it was over he left me to put her clothes back on, and went out of the room with Mr Eustis. By the time they came back I had her dressed again. The doctor sat at his desk without a glance in my direction. I could see by both their faces something was wrong, bad wrong, and that surprised me—I'd been so proud of the way she put up with his poking and prying, with never so much as a whimper. She's going to die, I thought.

They didnt say anything, but just as we were leaving, Mr Eustis turned in the doorway. "What was that word again?" he asked the doctor.

"Which word?"

"The long one."

"Congenital," the doctor said, and began to shuffle some papers on his desk, pretending to be busy.

Mr Eustis explained it in the wagon. "She's a natural," he said, keeping his eyes on the road ahead. He wouldnt look at me either. "The doctor says she was born that way. Thats what the long word meant, and theres no cure."

Up to then he'd never had much use for the children, no more than just to notice them now and again. But from that time on he began to pay particular attention to Luty Pearl. (Pearl was my mother's name; we gave it to Luther Pearl for a middle name. A little later, Luther was shortened to Luty: so she became Luty Pearl.) He would sit by her crib at night till she went to sleep, kept her supplied with playthings, and was careful to see that none of the others mistreated her. She didnt pay him much mind, not so youd notice: but whenever he wasnt there she'd squall, and he was the only one could calm her when she got upset.

He turned to religion, too. Before then, he spent Sunday mornings in his shirtsleeves on the porch, watching the wagons and cars full of people dressed in their best go by on the road to church; I usually went with some of my kin, taking one or two of the children with me. The trip to the doctor was in June. A July Sunday I came out dressed and found him with his coat on, the mules already hitched and at the gate. I didnt say anything, just went back and got all three of the children, and climbed up on the wagon seat. We never missed a Sunday after that.

It came on him gradual, though. The first few times he sat with his fists clenched on his knees, knowing the others were watching him and talking to one another behind their song-books. He wouldnt join in the hymns or shout back at the preacher or anything: just sat there. If somebody got up and gave a testimonial, he sat through it frozen-faced, and when the preacher sent up a call for repenters he never came for-ward: just sat there. Then Brother Jimson came among us. His first sermon was on Original Sin and Redemption, one of his best. I watched Mr Eustis out of the tail of my eye. His mouth was a little agape and his eyes were wide; he bent forward, hands clasped between his knees, not missing a word. The Lord had reached him.

But it wasnt until the following spring, up in April, that he really joined, became one of the flock. There was a sanctifying across the lake, where the man put up the dance pavilion later, and Mr Eustis was one of the candidates. Brother Jimson stood waist-deep in the water, a young man then, wearing his white baptizing robes; he had only recently received the Call. Mr Eustis was fourth in line. He took it calm the first two times going under, but the third time he came up shouting he'd seen the Hosts. The Lord had reached him in his thirty-second year.

So we settled into the life we were born to lead. Rosaleen turned out pretty, with never a lack of young men wanting to squire her. She put me in mind of Mr Eustis' mother—I worried about it; I watched her like a hawk. Young men would call and I'd sit there outstaring them, not taking any chances. She married right after her sixteenth birthday. So that was that, and I breathed a long sigh of relief. Myrtle never gave me any such problems. She was plain from the start and got plainer as the years went by, always the extra girl on hayrides and picnics. Finally she was too old for even that, and she turned bitter; her tongue got sharper and sharper. At twenty she was already an old maid.

By then we were through the worst of our troubles with

Luty Pearl. It began before she was even in her teens. No matter where we were or who was watching, in church as soon as elsewhere, I'd notice people beginning to look peculiar, hanging their heads and sneaking sidelong glances, the young ones maybe nudging each other, giggling, and I'd know right off that she was at it again. "Something's got to be done," I told Mr Eustis.

So we took her to see the doctor, the same as ten years ago, thinking maybe he could give her something to calm her, some medicine or a poultice. Mr Eustis told him the problem, talking in a whisper while I waited with Luty Pearl across the room. The doctor shook his head; he was a bachelor. "Theres no such medicine," I heard him say. "If there was, I'd have a supply for myself." He stood there a minute, shaking his head and thinking. Then he brightened and snapped his fingers, unlocked a drawer of his desk and took out a book. "Come on," he said.

He led us across the street to the harness maker's, Mr Ives, a little old dried-up man with a crooked mouth. We went to the back for privacy and the doctor took the book from under his arm. CHASTITY BELTS it said in gold on the cover: *Their Use in the Middle Ages. Complete with 100 Drawings.* He opened it and I saw on the first page a picture of a lady with long pale hair and a velvet gown, sitting by a window looking wistful. Then he turned the page and I saw another picture and looked away. He turned a few more pages. "This model here," I heard him say. "Reckon you could copy it, Mr Ives?"

"Well . . ." Mr Ives leaned over the book and scratched his head. "Cant say I ever tried such a thing before. Looks simple enough"—he glanced aside at Luty Pearl "—if somebody would give me the dimensions."

So he and Mr Eustis went to the front of the shop while the doctor and I went to work with a pencil and tape. He showed me where to measure, and when I'd say a figure he'd write it down beside that strap in the picture. Then we went up front. "I'll have it done in a couple of days," Mr Ives said.

And sure enough, when I came back two days later it was ready. He wouldnt take any payment for the work, no more than the cost of the leather, and he threw in a cake of saddle soap to keep it pliant where it buckled. So that solved that. She only wore it in the daytime anyhow. At night I tied her wrists to the sides of the bed.

Rosaleen had been married and gone two years by then. There was just the four of us in the house, all set to live our lives out, taking what came—even Myrtle, though she was bitter about it, seeing Rosaleen get the looks and Luty Pearl the attention. For ten years no new problems turned up, not to speak of anyhow. Good crops, bad crops: we took them as they came. I was fifty-one and Mr Eustis was crowding fifty-one (life goes like that; if theres no special trouble, life goes fast) when we went to the yearly sanctifying across the lake, the one that failed because the soldiers dusted us. Afterwards Brother Jimson fought them in the firelight and we came home. But something had happened; something was wrong—I could tell from the start. All through the month of May it got worse. It will pass, I thought. I kept telling myself it would pass. But it didnt. It got worse.

Then one night at the very end of May he came home late with the smell of perfume on him. So thats it, I thought: after all these years. And I waited. Time after time I'd seen it happen to other men at such an age—a change of life: they get to thinking how much theyve missed, and they get scared. Just wait, I told myself, lying alone in bed those nights (it was June by then); it will play out on him soon enough. All this time he was bringing the smell of her perfume home and I wondered who she was.

Then one morning, Thursday of the second week in June, I woke up and found him gone. All he had taken was his Bible and the money he had saved picking cotton the year before for other men after our own was ginned, two pairs of socks and his razor, and I thought: Well, he took the Bible, anyhow. I took that as a sign he was coming back. At least now I

wouldnt be smelling her perfume every night when he climbed
in bed. When he comes back, I told myself, he'll be done with
her for good.

He couldnt have chosen a better time to go: I'll say that for
him. The cotton was at a stand, laid by; all it needed was a
little chopping, nothing more than Myrtle and I could handle.
I told her he was off on a Bible trip; he'd be gone a week or
ten days, I said, thinking I was stretching it for safety. Two
weeks went by. Any day now, I told myself. The third week
wore on. Myrtle was beginning to look at me with her eyebrows raised. Something must have happened, I thought, and I
wondered more than ever who she was, to be keeping him
like this. Nobody I suspected had gone away. I even made
a trip up to Ararat to see if that new widow was at home—I'd
heard some talk. She was sitting on the gallery with two
callers. "Morning," I said, and turned around. They must have
thought I was crazy.

Then it was Friday again; that made three weeks. Around
midday we were out in the field, Myrtle and I, with Luty Pearl
rolling her spool-toys under a tree. We were chopping, when:
"Hello," I heard a voice say, a little too loud for natural, and
when I looked he was standing there with a hoe across his
shoulder. He already had his work clothes on and I could see
he'd lost some flesh.

"Where you been, pa?" Myrtle said, being spiteful.

"On a call from the Lord," he said, and commenced to
chop.

When we went back to the house for dinner he gave us the
presents he'd brought: candy for me, perfume for Myrtle (it
wasnt the same kind; I took a sniff that night to see) and ducks
on a string for Luty Pearl—they scared her half to death.
And that night when he went in to soothe her to sleep, the
same as always, she flung a conniption: wouldnt have him
near her. It hurt him, having her act like that, but I dont know
what he expected after the way he'd scared her with those
ducks. Later, lying in bed, I thought: Will he touch me? Will

he? He didnt: nor the next night either. Most any hour I'd come awake and find him lying flat on his back, staring up at the ceiling with moonlight glistening on his eyes.

Sunday morning we came out dressed for church, the three of us, and he was sitting by the front-room window, wearing the suit he'd bought wherever he'd been. "I'm not going," he said, and sat there. I knew then it was something bad, something worse than I'd thought. So I prayed for him in church, for his peace of soul, though I didnt feel that the prayer was getting through.

We came back and he was still sitting by the window. After dinner he took his seat again—it was like he was waiting for something. And sure enough it wasnt long till a car pulled up. Three men got out, two of them wearing stars, one big and red-faced, another short and squat; the third wasnt more than a boy, with an empty-looking face, a bushy head. He turned out to be deaf-and-dumb; the others did the talking.

When they had taken him away, the house seemed twice as empty as it had when he was gone two weeks ago. That was because I'd expected him back, before. In bed that night I looked back over his life, the double heritage of lust and murder, and I knew what had happened. The devil had reached him. The devil had reached him in his fiftieth year.

Myrtle called from the next room, in a whisper: "Ma . . . Ma . . . You think he really did it, ma? You think he really drownded her?"

"Hush," I said, louder than I meant, and Luty Pearl began to whimper.

"Now look what you done," Myrtle said.

I lay there hearing her whimper. For a minute I had a notion to get up and loosen one of her wrists—it's small enough pleasure she gets in this vale of tears: unless perhaps the reverse is true, and she's the only one of us all thats happy. But at last she quieted and after a time she was off to sleep again, and I was too.

Next morning I knew what I had to do, but it worried me:

I'd never left Myrtle with Luty Pearl before. I got up, dressed, and packed a bag. It was early yet, not daylight. When I was all ready, I tiptoed in and woke Myrtle. "Here," I said. I gave her a dollar and fifty cents in change. "It's housekeeping money in case something comes up. I'll be gone a day, two days, or maybe three. If I come back and find that youve been mean to her, I'll tan your hide. You hear me?" I said. "Mark my words, I'll tan your hide. You hear me?"

8. Lawyer

She was a tall thin woman, raw-boned, gaunt—about fifty I'd say, though it's hard to tell with them—sitting alone in the outer office, hands clasped in her lap; she had that curve to her back they get from chopping long hours in the field. The Mozart thing was in my mind, the one so much like an American folksong, especially on the harpsichord:

I'd been trying all morning, ever since I woke up with it going inside my head, to remember what it came from. Now I had it. Sonata in C major, Köchel 296: the one he wrote for the little Serrarius girl, his landlord's daughter. It was the main theme of the second movement, andante sostenuto, and he hooked it from one of the Bach boys. K.P.E.? No: Johann Christian.

"Mr Nowell?" the woman said.

"Yessum."

"*Lawyer* Nowell?"

"Yes," I said. "Mrs Eustis?"

"Yes sir."

"Then come right in. Ive been expecting you."

I had. I'd been expecting her ever since the day before, when I heard them talking about it on the street: how they had caught him, brought him in, and he'd confessed. It was

my kind of case, I knew, and I knew she'd come. Half the
night I lay in bed, thinking any minute the phone would ring,
and that morning when I got up, between times fretting
about the Mozart theme, I told myself she'd be waiting at
the office. And she was.

However, discounting Providence it was really accidental.
A man on the train had given her my name. "You go to him,"
the man said. "Parker Nowell is the one you want, providing
he will take it." (Providing!) She walked straight from the
station to the office and sat for more than an hour until I
came. There are a dozen other lawyers on this floor alone:
they stood in the hall, within earshot, unlocking their doors
and talking to one another, most likely about her husband's
case; but she sat there, waiting till I came. So probably it was
Providence after all.

I opened the inner door and motioned her through. As she
came past she gave me a sidelong glance, still puzzled because
I'd said I had been expecting her. "Sit here, Mrs Eustis." I held
a chair in front of the desk. She sat carefully, looking over
her shoulder as if in fear I'd pull the chair from under her.
Manners make them suspicious. As a matter of fact, I suspect
them myself. Going around the desk, I stopped and looked out
of the window. Blue Monday, yet Marshall Avenue was already
beginning to fill, a brick- and glass-walled canyon, an over-
sized trap laid by merchants (and by doctors and lawyers too)
for the Negroes and country oafs blundering in with money
clenched in their fists. Four stories below, automobiles clotted
and flowed in obedience to the peremptory wink of traffic
lights, the alternate red and green, the hesitant yellow. Today
was going to be a scorcher. I flipped the air-conditioner switch;
the motor began to purr. "Now tell me," I said. I sat. "From
the beginning."

She kept her face down while she talked, watching her
hands in her lap: a laborer's hands. I didnt make a move to
interrupt her. The air-conditioner breathed clammy against
my cheek and I sat looking down at her foreshortened face,

reminded of all the others so much like her, who came and sat where she was sitting and slid their misery across the polished walnut of the desk, here in our twentieth-century confessional. It's true we have an affinity for evil. What she told me had occurred in an atmosphere much like that of *Troilus and Cressida*, in which the faithful are betrayed and the brave are slain. I was reminded of Emerson's "Our faith comes in moments; our vice is habitual."

But I not only didnt interrupt her, I didnt ask her questions when she had finished. All that could wait. Besides, she was crying by then—soundlessly, it's true, but I saw her tears fall onto the backs of her hands. I thought, Tears: the universal solvent. They melt anything, dissolve it clean away. No wonder we respect them. I said, "All right, Mrs Eustis," rising: "Suppose we go and see him."

"There is something else you likely ought to know—" Her head was down. She hadnt looked up once. "The money. We will be a good time paying. If I . . ." She blinked and looked up, full-face now, quite bleak, and the tears were gone except for the traces left in the dust from the walk and the trainride.

I told her the time to start worrying about a lawyer's fee was after he brought it up: which was a lie. Most people didnt pay them anyhow, I said: which at least was partly true, to a degree. I took my hat from the rack and opened the door. She rose. "You can leave that here if you like," I said, meaning the suitcase.

"It's not heavy," she said. Her voice was nasal.

I closed the outer door and buzzed for the elevator. Then I saw them, leaning sideways at their desks or even standing in the doorways—insurance agents, CPAs, and lawyers. They knew who she was as well as I had done when I first saw her almost an hour ago. I could see it on their faces, as if their thoughts were printed on their foreheads: Look there. She got Parker Nowell. Now we'll see some fireworks. Look how thin. No wonder he took the other one off to an island.

The elevator hummed and stopped. The door slid back.

"Step up, please," the Negro said. I touched her elbow and she stepped in and the door slid shut behind us. We began to fall, falling through space in a cage. "Main flow," the Negro said. The door slid back. We stepped into the marble lobby, then through the clashing plate-glass doors, reflected for a moment, and onto the street.

"Here," I said. "Let me." I took hold of the suitcase.

"It's not heavy," she said, pulling back.

But I already had it. We turned left, down the sidewalk past the post office, past stores displaying drugs and shoes and women's clothes. In one of these windows a dummy stood naked, sexless, awaiting its turn to be dressed; Lonzo Mercer in his sockfeet crouched in front of another, sucking his under lip and putting the final flounces in a gown. I glanced at the sun, then automatically pulled back my cuff and looked at my wrist watch: 10:30; thinking, We've progressed so far in our mechanistic materialism that now we look at our watches to check on the sun.

The jail was four blocks from the office. As we drew near I began to tell her how it would be inside, attempting to prepare her for what she would see. That shocks them most, the first glimpse through the bars, seeing the other crouched inside like an animal in a cage. Trouble comes down on them then. They begin to realize what it means to defy the State. I was talking, telling her how it would be, when I heard a voice say, "Morning, Mr Nowell." When I looked up, it was the Stevenson boy from the paper: Russell: hard-faced already from living off the misdeeds of the people.

"Morning," I said, changing hands with the suitcase.

By then we were approaching the courthouse, an ugly brownstone building with a squat, square cupola where the steeple used to be. My father's name, along with a dozen others, was cut into the cornerstone, under the moss. The jail was at the rear, a two-storied concrete abortion, perfectly square, quite as ugly as the courthouse, but in a different way. They represented different generations. One year I went off to school and returned to find that a new jail had swallowed the old one.

We followed a path beside the marble shaft where the Confederate gazed bleakly south from under his hatbrim. The path curved right, around the northwest corner of the courthouse, then left again, leading straight to the door of the jail. Half a dozen loafers stood in a knot just clear of the steps—the regular crew. They had an appearance of being at once careless and intent, lounging but ready to leap into position in case the door came open without warning. Captain Billy Lillard was among them, up front of course, and wearing all his medals. You could judge the importance of any event by the number of medals he wore. Today he had on everything from the St Louis Exposition token down to the pawnshop Purple Heart, though it's true the only wounds he got were from sandfleas when they slept on the beach near Panama City, Florida, back in '98, awaiting embarkation orders that never came. As they gave to one side to let us through, Captain Billy looked sideways at me, leaning on his stick.

"Judge—"

"Howdy, Captain," I said. We didnt stop.

"You on this Eustis thing?"

But we were up the steps by then. I knocked, and immediately—there was no pause; he must have had his hand on the inner latch at the moment I knocked—the door swung back and we were facing Roscoe Jeffcoat the turnkey, Willy Roebuck the deputy, and Ben Rand the circuit clerk. "Luther Eustis," I said. They all three blinked in the sunlight, looking at us as if from a long ways off. "Mrs Eustis, Mr Jeffcoat"—I performed the introduction. "We've come to see her husband, if you please."

They stood aside, still blinking. Then Rand and Roebuck passed behind us, we stepped through, and Roscoe shut the door. We stood in almost total darkness, waiting for our pupils to dilate, and I could hear Roscoe replacing the bar. Gradually the calcimined walls and faintly gleaming bars came through in slow detail, like the features of a face on a photographic print under the wash of developer in a tray. Roscoe stood waiting. "This way," he said, and we followed the jingle of his keys.

I took her arm going up the metal staircase, following Roscoe's broad blue back and shifting hams. At the top we went to the right and passed down the cell block, faces turning to watch us; Negro faces, all of them, until we came to old man Lundy hanging crucified, arms extended along the bars. He wheeled away with a scowl of recognition: I had refused his case. Then we stopped in front of the cell at the northeast corner and Roscoe fumbled at his keys.

Eustis had his back to us, sitting sideways on the cot. The key clanked in the lock. He certainly heard it, but for another minute he just sat there. I suppose he'd had enough by then, friends of Roscoe—Rand and Roebuck for instance—coming to stare at him through the bars, like something rare in a zoo, talking out of the corners of their mouths and shaking their heads. At last he turned and the lenses of his glasses were like two shiny bulls-eyes. A tuft of hair stood on each side of his forehead. The three-day stubble of beard was grizzled. His back was humped worse than his wife's, though probably that was because he sat hunched forward, elbows out, palms curved upon his knees. He had crossed our human boundaries: he had murdered. With those enormous artificial eyes, those tufts like horns, he resembled something out of a nightmare such as children have after an evening spent at a horror movie.

Mrs Eustis entered first. She took the suitcase from me, set it on the cot, and stood with her hands clasped loosely at her waist: any wife confronting any husband. "Mr Eustis," she said. He watched her, looked at me, then back again: any husband confronted by any wife. "This is Lawyer Nowell," she said. "He's here to help."

But this time, when he turned his head still farther to look at me, I dropped my glance and saw on the cot beside him, within easy reach, a Bible. Are the words of Christ in red? I wondered. I have an impulse to examine almost every book I see.

Then—as if he had read my thought and wanted to protect the book, prevent its being opened—one of his hands came off his knee and rested on the Bible, fingertips moving softly on the leather. The highlight was off his glasses now. I could see his eyes: pale green, with lashes bleached almost invisible.

"Hello," I said, and nodded.

When I was a young man fresh out of school, beginning to practice, that was invariably a problem: what to say to a client when I met him first in jail. 'How do you do?' was stupid, 'Pleased to meet you' even worse. 'Hello' with a nod wasnt good, but I settled on that as being the least offensive. In this case, however, I might as well have saved my breath. He looked at me for a moment, one grave flick, then back at his wife, not giving any sign he'd heard me speak. I had an impression he hadnt even seen me. Outside, Roscoe cleared his throat with what sounded like a chuckle, almost a snigger. I turned and looked at him and he looked away.

Mrs Eustis and I watched Eustis for an awkward minute. He sat in the same pose as before, except that now he had one hand on the Bible. His nose was like Falstaff's on his deathbed, sharp as a pen (*They say he cried out of sack. Ay, that a did. And of women. Nay, that a did not . . . A said once, the devil would have him about women*); it came down short to a point between and below the double circles of his glasses, more like the beak of a bird. A sparrow, say. "Mr Eustis"—she laid the suitcase flat and undid the snaps, then raised the lid and began to take things out "—here's socks and underwear and two clean shirts. You can give me those youre wearing to take back home."

Roscoe came close to the bars and stood on tiptoe, peering over her shoulder to see that no hacksaws or firearms were among the things she took out. Eustis hadnt moved except to raise his head and look at the clothes. I went to the door. Roscoe stepped aside to let me out, still on tiptoe, looking through the bars. I saw in Mrs Eustis' face that she thought I was dropping the case because I'd been snubbed.

"Call me if there is anything you want," I told her. "Either at home or the office: I'm always at one or the other. I'll be back tomorrow," I said to Eustis, more for her benefit than his. Which was just as well, for he didnt answer. I was in the corridor by then. Roscoe swung the door shut, still leaning against it, watching for files and firearms, skeleton keys and nitroglycerin. "Dont bother," I told him. "I'll find my own way out."

"Day, Mr Nowell," he said without turning his head.

Old man Lundy was at the bars, again in the crucifixion pose. "What was it?" he said as I drew abreast. "Didnt I do it dirty enough to suit you? If I'd done it with a willow switch and a pair of concrete blocks, would that have hit your fancy? Or was it just because I killed a Man?"

I was almost past by then, and I had to check myself to keep from running. We're all cowards when we're touched in the proper spot.

"You son of a bitch, I'm on to you," he said, head turned sideways, pressed against the bars. "Son of a bitch!" he cried. "You son of a bitch!"

All the way to the head of the stairs I heard him, and farther too, his voice like a phonograph when the needle gets stuck in a groove. "Son of a bitch! You son of a bitch!" I was halfway down the metal spiral, hurrying. Then he stopped. He stopped without diminution or diminuendo, as suddenly as if someone had thrown a switch. I caught hold of the inner bar, lifted and pulled, and sunlight struck me a blow across the eyes; I stood at the top of the steps, blinded, letting the door swing to. Then details began to filter through, much as they had done when we entered, except now it was by a reverse process, pupils shrinking. I was looking down at Captain Billy Lillard. His medals clinked.

"You aint answered my question yet, young man."

I came down. "It's true, Captain Billy," I told him, told them all, passing among them, down the lane they cleared. "I'm on the case."

"Then shame on you," he said. "Shame. For shame."

Whereupon I did a thing I should never have done: I stopped and spoke to him again. "You want him to face trial without defense?" The others were watching, the loafers and courthouse touts who on an ordinary morning would have been sitting on the base of the monument, whittling and shifting their seats to stay in the shade.

"Defense—" He gave me an up-from-under look, leaning forward on his stick. Then his medals clinked as he raised one arm, pointing a finger at me. "What kind of defense did that girl have? Tell me that." The others nodded. "Do unto them as theyve *done* to, what I say."

I went on, following the curve of the path out to the sidewalk, then toward town. Soon I was passing stores again, automobiles racked fender to fender along the curb, obediently within the yellow stripes, and the little quarter-dials on the parking meters counted the minutes left before violation— *Time for sale. Step right up! Buy ten minutes of Time!* On the opposite, shady side of the street a three-sheet billboard displayed Rita Hayworth, low-bosomed in a strapless gown, being embraced about the knees by a young man with patent-leather hair who pressed the point of his chin against her stomach and looked up at her through the neat fringe of his eyebrows, at once suppliant and frozen, like the lover on Keats' urn—*yet do not grieve; She cannot fade*—except that in this case a Moslem prince had got her, whisked her clean away to l'Horizon. The store windows were full of gadgets for saving time or merely passing it, talismans of the American predicament, wherein we spend our leisure seeking amusement, so that in the end we have no leisure.

As I came off the curb of the final block, the stop light glared an angry red, peremptory; I stepped back just in time to clear the way for a charging Buick. The driver's face was reflected in the rearview mirror: he was leering, chalking up another tiny victory on the tablet of his mind. I stood among the other automatons, awaiting the wink of the mechanical eye. As I stood there, under the press of heat, I thought of that pathetic little figure from the G minor Quintet, adagio ma non troppo, descendent, giddy, arabesque, forlorn: K.516 —the light blinked, trembled yellow for a moment, then went green; we stumbled into motion off the curb, performing a lock-step. As we did, the driver of an on-coming car had to jam on brakes to keep from plowing through us. He sat there, baffled, and I saw several of my neighbors give him that same leer the driver of the Buick had given me. They too, in turn, chalked up a tiny victory.

Passing the post office, I glanced to the right and saw the Stevenson boy again, at the top of the marble steps. Will Cato had hold of his shirt pocket, faces close; he was arguing for extra promotional space, I supposed, for Stevenson looked unhappy. Every occupation has its drawbacks.

A burst of laughter came from the doorway of the drug-store as I passed, and I could see them, the usual Mannheim Building crowd—lawyers, CPAs, insurance agents, along with their secretaries and a smattering of drygoods clerks—having the usual late-morning coke. Sparky Russell was telling another joke. He stood with a glass in one hand, gesturing with the other, head thrown back, eyes closed to slits. The others watched, transfixed, their mouths agape, waiting for the punch-line. I turned into the lobby, got into the elevator. We rose like characters out of one of the more improbable stretches of Jules Verne. "Step down, please," the Negro said, who though he has been running the same machine for twenty-five years, has yet to stop on a level. Unless perhaps he does it wrong for my particular benefit.

The office was clammy after the heat of the street: I'd left the air-conditioner on. I switched it off and hung my panama on the rack. Sitting at the desk and seeing my image re-flected in outline on the polished walnut (bending forward, vaguely Mephistophelean: or so it seemed to me) I thought: Where would I be now if she hadnt left me?—*Down there in the drugstore with the others, having a coke and making smalltalk during the intervals (if any) between Sparky Russell's jokes.*—All right: yes. But can a man revenge himself on a whole society?—*He can try.*—But *can* he?—*Wait and see. Youre doing all right so far. Wait and see.*

I thought of old man Lundy behind the bars, calling me a son of a bitch, and Captain Billy Lillard misquoting Christ. And I asked: But why must every human contact, excepting those on a savior-sinner basis or across the jury rail, turn out a failure? And this time there was no answer; I was alone; the clamminess was fading; I had begun to sweat. I was back where I started, looking down at myself reflected Mephisto-phelean on the desktop, like on the surface of a pool of oil.

> —*God's in his heaven:*
> *All's wrong with the world.*

Two weeks later the grand jury met. Tolliver had the evidence assembled, the concrete tetrahedrons, the rusty baling wire, the photograph of the dead girl on the lakebank, the ankle chain with Love on its golden heart; he hadnt overlooked a trick. Witnesses—the girl's mother, the Pitts woman and her son the deaf-and-dumb boy, Roebuck, Doc McVey, and Lonzo Mercer—came in one by one and said their say, except the deaf-and-dumb boy; he wrote his in longhand. Tolliver laid his cards face-up on the table, so obviously proud he was almost arrogant.

I introduced no evidence, called no witnesses. Every now and then I'd throw in a half-hearted objection, which served more to point up his case than anything. He strode up and down, kneading his palms; he was terribly young. It was his show all the way. When it was over, the jury spent a trifle under fifteen minutes indicting Eustis for murder, binding him over to the coming term of court. I wore a long face and Tolliver beamed—so terribly young. "Airtight," I heard him say to the county attorney. He said it in a way that showed he didnt care who heard him. This was his first public office in what he foresaw as a prominent career. I felt almost embarrassed for him. Still, all in all, he had done a careful job; he'd planned it well.

But that was all right. By then I knew the whole story, or most of it: enough of it anyhow to be able to shape the case to fit almost any pattern the jury might seem to want—I mean the *real* jury, the one with the final say-so, in September. While Tolliver was slamming his cards on the table, I was nursing mine close to my vest. Eustis and I had come a long way in the two weeks since that Monday when I went to the office and found his wife waiting for me. Tuesday when I came back as I'd promised, he looked at me with something like recognition, and even replied with a nod when I said hello. But I didnt press it. I told him I'd do what I could and he said all right.

Next day I stayed away. Thursday he was almost glad to see me. Mrs Eustis had gone back down to Lake Jordan by then, fretting about the idiot daughter and how the older one was treating her, not to mention the need for tending the crop. Eustis had been sitting alone, except what times another of Roscoe's special friends would tiptoe up to the bars and peep at him. So, as I said, he was almost glad to see me. I stayed two hours.

I spent the first hour getting acquainted, leading him on, and the last hour listening: he did all the talking the second hour. He told it in a highly disorganized manner. Sometimes he'd be in the approximate present, rambling on about life on the island, how they lived, what-all they did. Then suddenly he'd be in the past, before he'd ever heard of a girl named Beulah. Other times he would be talking about events he'd had no part in save by hearsay. Miz Pitts, for instance. He seemed to think the story of her life—the way she'd borne a dummy, turned into a man, been deserted by her husband, and migrated to the island opposite Bristol—had as much to do with the case as his own life. I let him talk. Anything he wanted to say was all right with me; I sat and listened. I could winnow it later, get rid of the chaff: especially the Biblical implications—he quoted and paraphrased the Bible at every turn, squeezing, patting, twisting every story until it matched his own.

Besides, I had more to go on than what he told me. Mrs Eustis had come back twice again before the grand jury met, both of which times she came to the office and sat across the desk from me and talked. She not only filled in the gaps of his narrative, she told me the background of his life—things he didnt know himself, things that would prove interesting to the jury in September, especially in connection with what I knew already was going to be my contention. He was mad as a hatter: madder. To all intents and purposes, I mean.

Nor was that all. By then I knew more than either of them, or both of them put together. Eustis had told me the story of Beulah's life, at least so much of it as she had told him, down to the grubbiest item. Hearing it, I was reminded of what the Duke said in *Measure for Measure:*

> *. . . I have seen corruption boil and bubble*
> *Till it o'er-run the stew . . .*

So I went down to Issawamba County and asked around, with the result that by the time the grand jury met, I knew considerably more. When the Joyner woman (Beulah's mother) gave her testimony, weeping into a scrap of handkerchief and losing a good deal of make-up in the process, I kept a morose expression and tried to look as sorry for her, as sympathetic, as all the others were doing, especially Tolliver. I didnt presume to question her, to add a further burden to her grief. After all, when you came right down to it, she did deserve some sympathy; she had lost her stalking-horse. Even then, however, I was itching for the day she took the stand.

The trial was two months off. The public was primed. Hardly a day went by that the Stevenson boy didnt run something in the paper. They ate it up. They were anxious to see the show—it's their only chance to see 'live' actors. Generally speaking, they wanted to see Eustis get the chair. There is nothing unusual about that: they are bloodthirsty enough by nature. Besides, it meant another show, at least an epilog, though it's true the audience would be limited and tickets hard to get. Mainly, though—bloodthirstiness aside—their reaction was based on envy. Eustis had done things they had always wanted to do, beyond the pale, but didnt dare.

Everyone has an island he (or she: perhaps especially she—women lead such pathetically *scheduled* lives) wants to get off on, and in ninety-nine out of a hundred cases it would turn out much the same as this had done: it would wind up with one of them dead, except that in better than half the cases the woman would be the one who did the killing. Which brings me to the second item they envied him for. He had killed his mate. I think women especially envied him this: wives who only realized how much they hated their husbands after the husbands had gone to war, who lay awake in bed at night, thinking of the time-difference, perhaps one-third around the globe, attempting by telepathy to bend the trajectory of Jap or German bullets, guiding them in flight to strike the hated. (Sometimes it actually seemed to work. A few days later the telegram signed ULIO would come. And what followed? Hysterics—not without an element of triumph. Then followed remorse: not for the death but for the exultation.) Husbands, too, experienced something akin to this. Lying in frozen mud and being shot at, they thought of their wives between the warm clean sheets—with perhaps a one-armed or one-lunged or one-kidneyed stay-at-home for comfort—and hated them (to quote the Bible; I must have caught it from Eustis) with a hate that was greater than the love wherewith they had loved them.

So the people envied Eustis for what he had done, and they watched and waited and hoped he'd get the chair. Time wore on—or hurried, depending on what manner of information came my way during my prowls down at Ithaca and in Issawamba County. The year moved into August. Whatever breeze stirred, and that was little, was like a breath from an oven, the earth baked powdery, ash-gray between the rows of dusty cotton stalks whose bolls were beginning to split and spill their whiteness. Soon now the pickers would be moving across the fields, enormous insects translated out of a Biblical curse and dragging nine-foot sacks. Saturdays the Bristol streets would be filled with Negro and Mexican shoppers crowded shoulder to shoulder from curb to store-fronts, the length of Marshall Avenue. Then, agriculturally speaking, a lull would follow. The gins would hush their perpetual whine; cold weather would bring hog-killing time with a tang of wood-smoke in the air. Finally the autumn rains would lower a curtain, like the darkness after fireworks Christmas night. It was the age-old cycle of the Delta year, repetitious, immemorial, and grim. Before the latter stages were reached, however, the case would be over. Eustis would either be awaiting removal or serving time at Parchman. He might even be in his pine box, six feet down; Judge Holiman was never one for delaying what he called justice.

Whenever I rode down to Ithaca, asking around, I always stopped by Solitaire. Mrs Eustis and the older daughter, Myrtle, would be chopping. The younger one, called Luty Pearl, would be off to one side, under the shade of a tree, rolling a collection of spools in the dust; that was all I ever saw her do. I'd stop the car beside the road and wait, and they would chop on to the turnrow. Though I never had anything to tell her except that her husband was 'well,' Mrs Eustis always received it as if at an audience with the Delphic oracle. She would stand with the hoe in her hands, looking down at the blade dug half into the earth, her face foreshortened much as it had been that first time in the office back in June, though now the drops were sweat instead of tears. "Tell him I'll be there Saturday," she would say.

"I'll tell him," I'd say. Then she would turn, the hoe already lifted, and chop on down the row, the daughter Myrtle falling in behind, beginning to lag. And next day, back at the jail, when I had given him the message—which he knew already, anyhow; she hadnt missed a Saturday yet—he would nod his thanks, sitting sideways on the cot, head turned away.

He had returned to the silence of our first meetings. But that was all right; he'd told me all he had to tell, and I preferred him this way at the trial. He had changed in appearance, too. His skin was beginning to bleach and his hands were softer, two months removed from labor under the sun. Those spiky tufts were getting limp; they wilted, curving forward over the outer ends of his eyebrows. He had that dreadful final calm so many of them have, the murderers and rapists caught and jailed, awaiting trial: a calm incomprehensible to those who watch and try to imagine themselves in a like position. "How can he be so *calm*?" they want to know. They stand in the swirl, onlookers, but he is at dead center of the vortex—something like Browning's patriot bound for the scaffold: "Tis God shall repay: I am safer so."

Now when he talked (he did one day, in the midst of all this calm) he did not tell of the things he had seen and done. He went into motives. His was a Faust story, he insisted: he had sold his soul to Satan, unbeknownst. Beulah, however, changed roles with each telling. One day she was the devil's emissary— the next she was his victim. I let him talk, though none of it was of any use to me. By then the end of August was at hand. The time was near.

I had waited to shape my case, to give it its final form when all the information had been gathered. Thus I avoided revision and re-revision, which for me is a particular form of heart-break. Now in the final week of August, the end of dog days, I sat at my desk in the Mannheim Building and reviewed all I'd heard from Eustis, Mrs Eustis and the others. Three biographies lumped together made a background, a foundation on which the case was built:

1) Miz Pitts', the hearing of which had been the turning-point of his life on the island;

2) Beulah's, which she had told him when they met and which had done so much to draw him to her; and

3) Eustis' own, which I had heard mainly from his wife and which explained so much about him that could never otherwise be understood:—

three biographies, all somewhat alike because they were histories of inadequacy, the failure of Love.

Then suddenly it occurred to me that they were not only like each other, they were like my own in that respect. That gave me pause, as Hamlet says. It was late; daylight was fading, almost gone. The building was quiet, for the others—insurance agents, lawyers, CPAs (query: Are all CPAs anal neurotics?) —had left by then. The air-conditioner purred, breathed moist and cool, and I sat with my arms on the desktop that gleamed dully as if it had been polished by all the tales of wretchedness that had been slid across it, breathing the used breath of the machine.

Love has failed us. We are essentially, irrevocably alone. Anything that seems to combat that loneliness is a trap— Love is a trap: Love has failed us in this century. We left our better destiny in '65, defeated though we fought with a fury that seems to indicate foreknowledge of what would follow if we lost. Probably it happened even earlier: maybe in Jackson's time. Anyhow—whenever—we left the wellsprings, and ever since then we have been moving toward this ultimate failure of nerve. Now who has the answer? The Russians? The Catholic Church? Or are we building up to Armageddon, the day they drop the Bomb? God smiles and waits, like a man crouched over an ant-hill with a bottle of insecticide uncorked.

By the time of the arraignment I was ready, or almost ready: as ready, anyhow, as I was going to be until I discovered what Tolliver might be hiding up his sleeve if anything. On the final day of the Civil term—the final day of August too, a Wednesday—they marched in all the criminally accused, twenty some-odd Negroes and half a dozen white men. Roscoe

Jeffcoat brought up the rear, wearing a big bone-handled
pistol so long in the barrel that its front sight ran down even
with his knee. One at a time, as fast as their names were called,
the prisoners stepped forward to be arraigned, and stood face
to face with Tolliver while he read the indictments. Spectators
sat straighter in their chairs, reviving after the drone of a Civil
suit.

"Luther Eustis," Tolliver said at last.

"Here," I said.

Eustis looked up when I nudged him; he hadnt heard his
name called. As he stepped forward I saw out of the corners
of my eyes that the spectators were leaning forward, most
of them with their hands on the back of the seat ahead. Judge
Holiman, high on the bench, leaned sideways in his chair. His
pipe curved down, then sharply up, unlighted; he had frozen
in the act of striking a match. Tolliver faced Eustis, holding
the indictment and watching him over the sharp edge of the
paper: "When I have finished reading this, tell me how you
plead, Guilty or Not Guilty." Then he read it.

THE GRAND JURORS *of the State of Mississippi, taken from
the body of the good and lawful men of the County of Jordan,
duly elected, empaneled, sworn and charged, at the Term
aforesaid of the Court aforesaid, to inquire in and for the
body of the County aforesaid, in the name and by the authority of the State of Mississippi, upon their oath present: that*
LUTHER DADE EUSTIS *late of the County aforesaid, in the name
and by the authority of the State of Mississippi, on the 21st
day of June in the year of our Lord 1949 in the County and
State aforesaid, and within the jurisdiction of this Court, un-
lawfully, wilfully, feloniously, and of his malice aforethought,
did, then and there, kill and murder one*
BEULAH ROSS *a human being, against the peace and dignity
of the State of Mississippi.*

"How do you plead?"

Tolliver looked up for the first time, watching Eustis from

under his eyebrows, still holding the indictment. But Eustis just stood there with the double-barreled gleam of highlight on his glasses. The courtroom was completely silent. "Guilty or Not Guilty?" Tolliver said again, glancing nervously aside at me. I gave them another ten seconds, then nudged Eustis.

"Say Not Guilty," I said.

"Not Guilty," he said.

8. (Continued)

Trial began on Tuesday, a week from the arraignment, as soon as the Lundy case was out of the way. All but four of the Negroes compromised, which was about as usual, and those four would either be tried when this was finished or else would be bound over to the following term. Lundy got the chair. "One down, one to go," spectators said, as at a game. Youd think they were looking forward to eating him. I actually saw a number of them lick their chops when Ben Rand read the verdict: "Guilty as charged." Old man Lundy sat there grinning, looking right and left. He was partly deaf and thought they had found him Not Guilty.

That ended the morning session. We took all afternoon to get a jury, for though I challenged only three for cause, I exhausted my twelve peremptories on the chance it might be useful in appeal. At five oclock Judge Holiman recessed and the twelve survivors, looking rueful, filed back to their iron cots in the jury room.

The trial proper began the following morning. When I arrived, shortly before nine, I found the courtroom filled except for the far-back rows where almost nothing could be heard above the creaking of the fans. I knew, however, that before another hour was past, those too would be filled (by latecomers—more slothful, even, than curious) if only for the sake of watching the dumbshow gestures of witnesses under pressure and hearing the occasional ringing tones of the lawyers, strident with indignation or booming with satisfaction. The Negro balcony was crowded too. Some in work clothes, some in their Sunday best—starched collars, that is, and tie pins—they came to see the white folks argue and fume over points in the white folks' law. Beneath, racked hip to hip, shoulder to shoulder, their legal betters sat, chins lifted, faces serried like rows of eggs. The corners of their mouths downtending, they resembled tragedy masks except for teeth. The women (about half of them were women) held cardboard fans which they moved fast or slow or not at all, in inverse ratio to their interest in what was going on beyond the rail. They looked at Eustis and they looked at me, and when they looked at me their eyes went hard; the pupils seemed to shrink. Ten years ago, eighty percent of them would have voted for me no matter what ring I chose to throw my hat in.

They thought me evil. That was a result of their new Liberalism, by which nothing is really bad provided they can understand it—a tolerant attitude, youd think: except it also follows that everything they cannot understand is evil. So they feared and hated me. Likewise, as incapable of comprehending him, they feared and hated Eustis. That was my problem: to make the jurors think they understood him. But I had to do it in simple terms, which was only doubtfully possible because the facts were far from simple. Once they saw how truly complicated it was, the case was lost. So I had decided to do it the easy way. Make them believe he was insane and the scales would fall from their eyes; they would 'understand'; the fear, the hate would be gone, evaporated. "So thats it," they would say; "he's crazy. I knew it all along." They might even begin to pity and sympathize. Good old Hollywood Christianity: God's gift to the Defense.

Eustis kept his head down, looking at his hands clasped in his lap. A deputy lounged against the rail behind him, a sharpened match driven like a peg into one corner of his mouth. When I came in and put my briefcase on the table beside him, Eustis turned and looked at me, eyes vacant behind the instant flash of his glasses.

"Good morning," I said.

"Morn," he said.

His voice was low, so low I barely heard him. He had bathed and shaved, his hair plastered wet and close to his skull, so thin in places, especially back from his temples, that it appeared to have been painted on with hasty strokes of a stiff-bristled brush. The two tufts, however, had already begun to dry; they were about to spring back up—suddenly they did, both tufts at once. He wore a clean white shirt, its creases as sharp as when his wife ironed it yesterday, and the trousers of the blue serge suit he had been arrested in. Mrs Eustis sat beyond the rail with her eldest daughter, Rosaleen.

Judge Holiman rapped once, cleared his throat with a rattle of phlegm, and waited for the buzzing murmur to die. His jacket had a silky sheen that rippled like moonlight whenever he moved. It was bombazine, I think, or anyhow the same material oldtime bookkeepers used to have their sleeve-protectors cut from.

"Ready, Mr District Attorney?"

"Ready, Judge," Tolliver said promptly.

"Mr Nowell?"

I rose and gave him a careful bow. "Whenever the Court pleases," I said.

He made his usual little speech about demonstrations, hawked and spat, relit his pipe and settled back, gazing at something invisible on the ceiling. "Lets get under way," he said, and appeared to go to sleep almost at once.

Then Tolliver began his big parade: "Airtight," he'd said, and I sat back to watch. I felt pretty good, but not so good that I didnt leave room for doubt. My father once told me of a case in which the lawyer took what his client said were the facts to be the truth; he felt confident the whole charge would fall to pieces. By the time the State had launched its case, however, he saw how unquestionably guilty his client was. So when it came time for him to present his closing argument, he rose, made a formal bow to the jury, and sat back down. "Remember that one," Father told me. "Call it to mind when you find yourself believing a case is cinched before it ever comes to trial."

Dr E. P. Goodnight, psychiatrist from Whitfield, was Tolliver's first witness. I had known he was coming, else I'd have called him myself. This way was better. He made a good witness, didnt get into any arguments about whether there was any such thing as 'crazy' or 'insane,' made a generally effective attempt to appear dispassionate and scientifically detached: he had been in court before, a lot of times. But when I began to draw him out, he shifted to the offensive. I saw the jurors watching him askance. So I laid the case in his lap—I presented the whole picture: "What would you say of a man who did this and that, said this and that and the other?" He hemmed and hawed, evasive, antagonistic, but finally came up with the answer I wanted.

"Assuming all those things," he said at last, "I would say such a man was insane, but—"

"Thank you, doctor," I said, and turned away.

Tolliver's second witness, Beulah's mother, was a surprise. Not that I hadnt expected her: I had—I was looking forward to the time she took the stand. But I had thought he would save her till last, for it's a general rule among prosecutors to open with their strongest witness, swing the jury their way from the start, and save the next-to-strongest for a clincher. However, I was ready for her no matter when she came. That was why I'd spent so much time down in Issawamba County, filling in gaps in the facts I'd learned from Eustis in his cell, who told them to me much as Beulah had told them to him that evening in the cottonhouse when his prayers first were answered after the flesh.

She behaved pretty much as she had done at the hearing a month before, weeping into a handkerchief and giving the jury flashes of her thighs. Out front, the crowd wasnt missing a trick. Tolliver led her through the whole heartbreaking account. By the time she got done, the crowd was murmuring, muttering, and the jurors had narrowed their eyes, glancing aside from time to time at Eustis and me to see how we were taking it. They seemed to think we ought to sink down through the floor.

When Tolliver finally turned her over to me, I saw them frown. They were wondering how I could presume to lacerate her further, after all she'd had to suffer because of my client. Even Tolliver was surprised when I rose to question her. He had thought I'd want her off the stand and out of sight as soon as possible.

I gave her the old-style treatment, with broad gestures twitching my shoulders with distaste and pulling my eyebrows down. I even managed a sneer from time to time. Before I was through with her—"A witness to your daughter's shame"—she really had something to weep about. Russell Stevenson, inside the rail, was scribbling away like fury. I carried her over the bumps and through the mud, substantiating almost everything I'd heard from Eustis and down in Issawamba. Even the things she denied were obviously true; her constant reaction was, How did you know that? The murmur behind us mounted to a roar, Tolliver yelling "Objection! Objection!" and Judge Holiman banging for order—a rareeshow. It was crowding noon when she came off the stand and court recessed.

The afternoon session went a little faster, and Tolliver wound up his case the following day. His remaining witnesses were Dummy, Roebuck, Doc McVey, Lonzo Mercer, and Miz Pitts. He had saved Miz Pitts for last—a strong impartial witness, so he thought; he took her for granted—but she blew up in his face. When he saw it wasnt going right, he should have let her alone. But no: he had to keep picking at her, until finally: "I think he's a good man that got pulled into something because he's a little crazy." She glared at Tolliver as she said it. I did not cross-examine.

Tolliver said, "Your honor, the State rests."

Judge Holiman looked at the clock on the front of the bal-

cony, then took his watch from the side pocket of his coat—
he carried it loose like that, a big old-timy affair in a gunmetal case, a key-winder, about the size and shape and color
and weight of a worn-out sandlot baseball—opened it, and
began to compare the two. He is opposed to Progress in all
its forms, including electric clocks. Then he closed the watch,
snapping it shut with a click almost as loud as a pistol-shot
against the bated silence of the courtroom, and rapped lightly
once with the gavel. "Court's recessed till nine tomorrow
morning." It was four-fifteen. He has never been known to
stay on the bench past five.

That gave me sixteen hours and forty-five minutes for
shaping my case into its final form. Subtracting four hours
for music, eight for sleep, I still had almost five. It was more
than I needed; for though it's a general policy of mine to make
no definite plans until the State has rested, I knew already
what I was going to do, and also how.

Stevenson was waiting at the rail, pad and pencil poised.
"Mr Nowell," he said. I stopped, holding my briefcase under
my arm. "Will Eustis take the stand in his own defense?" I
could tell from the way he said it, he had worded the question
in advance.

"We'll see," I said, and moved on.

"Mr Nowell—" I stopped again, looking over my shoulder.
He held the pencil with its point barely clear of the pad. "How
would you say it's going? So far, I mean."

The crowd had gathered in a semicircle, faces sharp and
eager, nostrils quivering. "We'll see," I said.

"Thanks for nothing," I heard him mutter as I left.

Some of the watchers sniggered—not so much out of malice
as from pleasure. Having overheard an off-the-record colloquy,
they felt they had somehow been in touch with the inner
mechanics of law and journalism, two professions as darkly
mysterious in our day as alchemy was in the olden days. It
made them feel important, informed; it made them feel part
of the whole—in touch. As for Stevenson, however, I knew

what was eating him. He was sour on the world because of that story for the detective magazine.

I went to the office, spread my notes on the desk, a conglomeration scrawled on dog-eared envelopes and the backs of bills. Within an hour I had them organized, the order of witnesses and what I'd ask. I was doubtful about getting through tomorrow, but that didnt matter. Another night on those iron cots wouldnt hurt them; it might make them all the gladder to see their wives. Another two meals at the Greek's wouldnt wreck their digestions, at least no worse than theyd been wrecked already. They should have thought of the consequences when they paid their poll tax—or when they let some politician pay it.

It was getting on for six when I left the building: too early to eat, too late to go home and wait. So I paid Eustis a visit. His wife was sitting with him in the cell; she was staying in town through the trial. Roscoe had brought him supper on a tray and he was eating. He looked up when I came to the door, then quickly down, continuing. For three weeks now he had been like this toward me, ever since he'd returned to the notion that I was allied with the devil. That had been his original reaction on the Monday more than two months ago, here in this same cell, when he saw me looking at the Bible and put out his hand to protect it. After five minutes I left. I had considered telling him my plan for putting him on the stand, but now I decided he would make a better impression (for my purposes) if I called him unawares.

I had supper at the hotel—"Thats Parker Nowell," Bristolites were telling visitors, rolling their eyes and talking behind coffee cups and napkins, "the lawyer defending the man that drowned the girl across the lake"—then walked home. It was dark by now, with that special kind of breathless heat that comes when the September sun has gone. I loaded the phonograph—Ravel's left-hand concerto, the Mozart 40th, Haydn's *Horseman*—and lay on the couch. During the Allegro which follows the English horn Andante, I began to think (God knows why, unless that eerie Introduction had put it into my head) what a thing it would be if I could call up the ghost of Beulah and put her on the stand tomorrow morning. However, it wouldnt do—for more reasons than one. The trouble with the dead is not that you cant ask them questions. You can. You can ask them hundreds of questions. The trouble is they wont answer. And theres a difference, as anyone who has ever tried it knows.

But it wasnt like me to conceive a thing like that. I said to myself this was what came of associating with Eustis all these weeks. Keep on like this, I told myself, youll find yourself where he is. By that time the 40th's Minuet was in full swing; I hadnt heard a note of the first two movements. So I got up and started it over again, first Mozart and his 'demoniacal clang'—music so limpid, so pure, that after repeated hearings you begin to be frightened by it, not so much hearing the melody, the music itself, as experiencing the impulse that brought it into being—then Haydn, gemütlich, a different breed of cat. When those were through, I put on a new batch, and still another when those in turn were through. The clock struck twelve while I was on the way upstairs to bed.

Judge Holiman rapped once, the usual way, and when the babble simmered down, said abruptly: "Mr Nowell?"

"Yes, your honor."

"Mr District Attorney?"

"Yes, Judge."

"Court's convened." He rapped once with the gavel as he said it. Silence fell.

Mrs Eustis was my first witness. She made a poor impression from the start. Her head trembled with a continuous quiver, like Parkinson's disease. She steadied her chin on the back of one hand, which caused her words to be mumbled. The jurors leaned forward, trying to hear what she said. "I'll ask you to speak louder, Mrs Eustis," I told her, raising my voice in exam-

ple. "Speak up, so this last gentleman down on the end can
hear you." She did better then, but not much; the trembling
grew even worse. For the jury's benefit I repeated almost everything she said: everything I considered important, that is.
Tolliver scowled, bent forward with a hand curled round one
ear, occasionally calling for a repeat of things I let go by.

I carried her through a narrative of all she had told me that
first morning at the office and on subsequent days when she
came back. I began at the beginning, when Eustis' father
burned the house. Though much of it was inadmissible, hearsay
and opinion, I managed to bring out enough to make his
background fairly clear. Then we moved on, through the
courtship (such as it was) and the birth of the first two girls.
By that time her nervousness, though no better, was becoming
accustomed, seemed practically a natural condition for anyone
who had undergone all she described. Her voice was stronger
now, but it still trembled. The jurors leaned forward, watching, listening. This was no fable read second-hand out of a
newspaper: this was Life. We had them.

So then, without waiting, I led her through a description
of his conversion after the birth of the dead son and the idiot
daughter. I was about to take her into the other, an account
of things he'd said and done during the period that followed
the May Day sanctifying, but I saw Judge Holiman shooting
glances at the clock. It was after ten and his bladder was
giving him twinges. I requested a recess.

"Granted!" he blurted, rapping once with the gavel, already
hurrying off the bench, toward the door that leads back to
the men's room.

Ten minutes later we resumed our places, like actors at
rehearsal; even the spectators bent forward in identical atti-
tudes. "Now, Mrs Eustis," I said—she had sat in the witness
chair all through the break—"I'll remind you, if you please, to
speak loud enough for all these gentlemen to hear." She nodded
and the trembling started again. It had stopped during the
recess but now it was worse than ever, more violent and rapid.

She told about the sanctifying and what had followed, until the evening some four weeks later when he came home with the odor of perfume on him. Then he was gone; he had disappeared. Then he returned, and then the sheriff came.

"Thank you, Mrs Eustis; I know this has been difficult. However, before we close I have one more question I want you to answer." She watched me, trying to steady her head with the hand beneath her chin. "You know all your husband has done, or at any rate is accused of having done. Now I'll ask, Have you forgiven him, even assuming all they say is true?"

We looked at each other, almost as if there was no one else in the courtroom. Suddenly the trembling stopped. "No sir," she said. I made a pretense of surprise. She took her hand down, gripping the ends of the chair arms. "I never forgive him, for I never felt it was anything that called to be forgiven. I never blamed him. I knew in my heart, whatever was done, it was the other Him that did it, not the one thats here on trial."

Like something out of the *Ladies Home Whatever*. They ate it up. There wasnt a dry seat in the house, as Ive heard theater people say. I turned to Tolliver. "Your witness," I said, and resumed my place beside Eustis on the other side of the table.

Tolliver didnt handle her so well, having nothing in mind to lead her toward. After a few inconsequential questions he turned her loose. It was almost eleven oclock. "Next witness, Mr Nowell," Judge Holiman said.

That was Rosaleen Poteat, the oldest daughter. She told about her girlhood, the time of her father's conversion. One night, late, she went to the back porch for a drink from the cedar bucket and found her father on his knees in the yard, holding an open razor in one hand. His eyes were blank, showing only the whites. He was on his knees in the dust, asking God if he ought to kill himself. The razor glittered.

Q. What did you do?

A. I stayed behind the door frame, watching him.

Q. Were you frightened?

A. Frightened.

Q. Then what did you do?

A. I watched.

Q. Watched what?

A. Him.

Q. Go on, please.

A. After while, when he come up off his knees and started for the steps, I run and got in bed and pulled the sheet up. He didnt have any clothes on. I heard him come through the room, walking barefoot, and stop and put the razor on the shelf. He was nekkid; I wouldnt look. Then I heard him climb in bed in the other room with Ma, and after a while I went to sleep.

Q. Did you tell your mother about this?

A. No sir. Never told nobody till I told you and you said tell it in court, same as I told it to you, excepting with more about how the razor looked so bright and scary in the moonlight.

There was a moment's silence while the crowd wondered if it had heard aright: then a blurt of laughter. The loudest laughs came from the group of lawyers ranged along the inside of the rail. Judge Holiman was laughing too, making choking sounds around the stem of his pipe, but soon he began to rap with the gavel: "Order. Order!" When it died down, he turned to the witness chair. "Young lady: from now on, answer the questions only as asked. Never mind going into details about how counsel for defense prepares his case." There was another ripple of laughter behind this. He gave them a moment at it—it being *his* joke now—then turned and frowned. They stopped. "Go ahead, Mr Nowell," he said.

She was a stupid sort of creature at best, sitting there doe-eyed, not knowing whether to giggle or frown, but pleased that she'd been such a success with the crowd. I carried her through several such incidents, all in line with what I'd told the psychiatrist at the outset. She had spent a good part of her childhood watching; very little went on in the house that she didnt know about; she knew what she was up against. And I'll say one thing for her. As soon as she could get away, she got. She was sixteen when she married.

I turned her over to Tolliver for a while, but nothing came of it. Then I had her again, elaborating. After that remark on how I'd coached her, I almost wished she had been a hostile witness so I could really give her the business. However, her testimony was excellent for the most part. She wasnt bad-looking, in a rough-textured, country way. I could see why her mother had been worried, had chaperoned her so closely through her girlhood. She had some of the qualities of the grandmother she'd never seen, the one who soaped the window sash and who even today, perhaps, was being memorialized by a gray-haired man in a bachelor room, smashing his fists and regretting. It was noon when she came down and court recessed.

First up after lunch was Brother Jimson. He wore a broadcloth coat and cotton trousers baggy at the knees from too much praying. Beneath the coat, sweat had plastered his shirt to the muscles of his chest. His tie was knotted close to the flesh of his throat, where collar-button and buttonhole were a good two inches apart because of the size of his neck. His feet were enormous, in laceless shoes with elastic panels down both sides and loops of webbing stitched to the backs for pulling them on. He gave his name, William H. Jimson—H for Hezekiah, he said—and when I asked him his occupation: "A worker in the vineyard of the Lord," he said.

"You are a minister of the Gospel?"

"A minister. Yes. Of the Gospel."

He sat with both hands on his kneecaps, elbows out. He was formidable, one of the few men I ever saw who looked big without being either tall or fat. His eyes appeared abnormally far apart because of the broad flat bridge of broken nose between them. Remembering the account of how he had flung the soldiers out of the firelight, I didnt envy Tolliver sitting there waiting to cross-examine him.

He identified Eustis, pointing him out. How long had he known him? Nineteen years. How well? *Well.* Almost daily acquaintance? Almost daily. Tell about him. "He's a good man, one of the few really good men I ever knew, and a worker in the church." But peculiar? "Well—peculiar: any good man's peculiar. He stands out." He told about Eustis' conversion. "Afterwards God spoke to him in voices."

"He told you that?"

"Yes. Often."

"God spoke to him?"

"He did."

"Was this at night, in dreams?"

"In dreams, yes. In daylight too. He'd be plowing and God would speak to him, and he'd drop the reins and kneel down in the furrow. Afterwards he'd read some in the Bible—"

"In the field? In the broiling sun?"

(Tolliver: "Objection. Suggest he let the witness tell his story unassisted."

Judge Holiman: "Sustained. Quit leading him, Counsel."

Myself, to Brother Jimson, after a bow to the Court: "Go on, please.")

"—In the field, in the broiling sun." Laughter: but it ceased as soon as the judge took up the gavel. "Then he'd close the Book, take hold of the plow again, and go on working. That night he'd come to me and tell me about it and we'd pray."

He went on with it, elaborating, checking off items on the list I had drawn for Dr Goodnight. Finally I turned him over to Tolliver. Tolliver walked up to the witness chair and started to question him, then thought better, and went around to the other side of the table; he cross-examined him from there, and I couldnt say I blamed him. What degrees did he hold? No degrees. Had he attended a seminary? No seminary. Then how had he become a preacher? On word from the Lord. Well, well—Tolliver said—it appeared that the Lord was keeping mighty busy down at Lake Jordan, talking to people. (Laughter.) Brother Jimson said it wasnt on the lake that he got the call; it was at the State penitentiary, up at Parchman.

"What were you doing at Parchman, reverend?"

"Six years."

That came as a surprise, but not to Tolliver. He made the most of it.

"For what offense, reverend?"

"Manslaughter."

By the time Tolliver turned him back to me, Brother Jimson had told the tale of his wayward youth. So there was nothing for me to do but have him tell the story of his conversion, his upright life. It took more time than I'd allowed, but I managed to squeeze in three more witnesses, neighbors from down in the lake region who had known Eustis all his life and could testify to his peculiarities. By then the clock was pushing five; Judge Holiman called it a day. That left Eustis and the closing arguments.

After supper I played *Don Giovanni*, all three albums, and got to bed by midnight. Next morning, Saturday, Eustis took the stand. I hadnt warned him. When his name was called he didnt understand. He sat with his hands in his lap, the same as always, and when I touched his shoulder he looked up vacantly. "Take a seat up there," I said. The courtroom buzzed behind us. He looked at me for another few seconds, then rose and walked to the dais. Turning, he gazed out over the raft of faces, blinking like a man emerging from darkness. Ben Rand stood with the Bible extended, ready to swear him in. He rattled off the oath, but Eustis just stood there. They looked at each other and it seemed to me that Rand was a bit afraid. Back in the crowd, a woman giggled nervously. Suddenly, as if this were some sort of signal, Eustis bent forward and kissed the Bible. He probably thought that was what they were waiting for. The woman giggled again. A drawn-out sigh went up, a release of pressure, and then a babble of voices:

"See what he did?"

"Kissed it."

"I'll be dog."

I glanced at the jurors. Some were perfectly round-eyed. Others were shaking their heads, turning to look at one another. Seeing them, I knew I had done right not to warn him, though doubtless there were some who were thinking I had coached him, told him where and when to plant the kiss. It wouldnt have been half as effective if I had.

The questioning was short. I asked him nothing of any real importance; all I wanted was a chance for the jury to see him under pressure. Besides, I knew Tolliver would show him to better effect. "Your witness," I said. The courtroom was completely silent.

Tolliver rose with a sheaf of papers in his hand. He stood in front of the witness chair and I saw on top of the papers the photograph Lonzo had taken on the morning the girl was found, bloated and naked except for the wire and tetrahedrons and a tatter of rag theyd laid along her crotch. Tolliver held it so that both Eustis and the jury could see it. He looked from Eustis to the photograph and back, and began to cross-examine.

Q. We've heard the testimony, seen the exhibits. We've read your confession. Now I want you to tell us the considered truth. *(Pause.)* Why did you kill this girl?

A. She was wicked, evil.

Pause.

Q. And you set yourself up as her judge?

A. No sir: God told me to do it—I thought it was God.

Q. Ah. And was it?

A. No sir. *(Pause.)* It was the devil.

Pause: followed by a nervous laugh from that same woman somewhere out in the courtroom. Tolliver turned, walked off a ways, and then came back, standing in front of Eustis, hands on hips, giving him an up-from-under look.

Q. And yourself: were you also evil?

A. Yes sir, I was. I was evil too.

Q. Then why didnt you destroy yourself?

A. The voice never told me to.

Then came that nervous laugh again, loud against the silence. Judge Holiman rapped with the gavel. "That laughing has got to stop," he said, leaning forward, narrowing his eyes above the swoop of bulldog pipe. He held the pose for another moment, then turned to Tolliver. "All right, Mr District Attorney. Continue."

Tolliver went on with it, getting exactly nowhere. He and Eustis were like two characters in a scene from an Elizabethan comedy: they believe they are discussing the same subject, yet each has a different subject in mind. And theres the humor of it, as Corporal Nym says. Finally Tolliver gave it up and turned him back to me.

I rose and bowed to the bench. Eustis still sat high on the dais, blinking behind his glasses. The crowd leaned forward, eager for some more. I turned from the judge to the jury, bowed again, then turned back to the bench. "Defense rests," I said. A sigh went up, collective, then a babble, mounting quickly to a roar. The clock on the front of the balcony said a little after ten.

There were no rebuttal witnesses. Judge Holiman granted a twenty-minute recess for submission of instructions and final preparation. When this was over, Tolliver launched his closing argument. I sat with my back to him, sketching Mozart themes on a scratchpad while he talked. I listened, however, and I must say he was learning.

One statement I remember in particular. He stood with both hands on the jury rail, leaned forward. "Defense has offered testimony in an attempt to show that Eustis isnt 'normal.' Well—I'll frankly admit I dont think he's 'normal' either." He placed a sarcastic emphasis on Normal every time it came around. " 'Normal' people dont drown their eighteen-year-old paramours in lakes. The point is, gentlemen, he not only knew exactly what he was doing; he did everything a sane and cunning man could contrive to cover his tracks, even to the extent of visiting a barber shop to get himself slicked-up to face his family. Now counsel for defense"—a rearward gesture of the hand—"is going to tell you such things are 'abnormal,' even insane. But, gentlemen, I submit that it was not only normal; it was logical. He did what any runaway husband does before facing his wife when he comes in off a bender. I dont want to get personal and I wont ask any embarrassing questions—God forbid—but I think it's likely that some of you gentlemen here in the jury box have probably done the same."

Two or three of them grinned, looking at once sheepish and proud of themselves. He had them going, all right, and he kept at them.

"And, gentlemen, the same thing follows in almost every action. Thats only one small example. No matter how illogical, how 'abnormal' his actions seem at any given step along the way, examine them closely, as a whole, and youll see how well he planned his crime, how skillfully he covered his tracks. The ironical thing is, he was caught—as criminals such as this are usually caught—by one small point he overlooked because it lay in a direction that seemed least likely. He was caught because a deaf-mute boy saw his true name on the flyleaf of a Bible. Ironical—yes. All through this case we've heard testimony about how God talked to him: he had Him on a direct wire, you might say. Well, here's a point where the Hand of God really levels a finger and says, There: Luther Dade Eustis, Solitaire Plantation. It was a Bible that betrayed him. Theres the Hand of God for them, gentlemen, since theyre determined to drag Him into the case."

This was mostly double-talk. One minute Eustis wasnt normal, the next he was. But it was the kind of talk that counts with a jury. Finally, however, Tolliver's inexperience began to tell. He didnt know when to stop: he talked and talked, until finally the jurors had almost forgotten the really good points he had made at the start. He stood, chin raised, addressing the ceiling, listening to the sound of his voice. If I had been his partner on the case, I'd have grabbed him by the coat tail and pulled him back into his chair. As it was, I kept hoping he'd keep on and on, hammering cold iron.

And he did. The clock was crowding twelve when he finally stopped. I rose as soon as he began thanking them for their kind attention (as if they could help themselves—) and when he stepped back I crossed to the rail where he had stood, leaned where he had leaned—my palms were in his palm-prints—and began to speak before he'd gotten seated.

"Gentlemen, I know youre tired and I wont keep you long." I gave it to them straight, sonata-form: Exposition, Development, Recapitulation. "The facts are in," I said. "Theres no use mouthing over them." I gave it to them the old army way: 1) Tell them what youre going to tell them; 2) Tell them; —then 3) Tell them what youve told them. "However," I said—

So much for the Introduction, the tuning up. I unstrapped my watch and laid it face-up on the rail between my hands. Afterwards, when I bent forward, pausing between sections, I heard it ticking: the busy little symphony of Time, like the breaking of so many straws. I had made myself a careful allotment and I stayed on schedule.

—Exposition: 10 minutes. Dr Goodnight (degrees and experience such and such: "the State's own witness, mind you") had testified that any man who did such and such would surely be judged insane. Eustis did such and such, as we have learned from the testimony, and therefore could not be held morally responsible for the crime with which he was charged.

—Development: 15 minutes. (A rehash of the above, a bit fuller, a bit higher-flown, with some enlargement on particular acts included in the such-and-such.) Actually no psychiatrist was needed: we ourselves could judge the mental condition of such a man as Eustis had been shown to be. However, we had been relieved of the need for making any such judgment; a qualified expert, called by the State, had done the judging for us.

—Recapitulation: 10 minutes. (Back to the start, almost *da capo*, leading up to a final flourish:) "Gentlemen, they have no case against this man. They never had a case. The whole unfortunate occurrence never belonged in a court of law. It comes within the province of medicine, treatment of the unbalanced, the insane. I thank you."

It was twelve-thirty. I strapped my watch back on, returned to the table, and sat down. That last was a little thick but it seemed to go. I didnt look at the jury. Eustis sat with his hands in his lap, head hung forward. All through the trial, his conduct could not have been better.

We sat thus, side by side, as we had sat these past four days, while the judge gave his final instructions to the jury. It took some time, the way he drew it out, but at last it was over. They rose and filed for the door. Tonight, most likely, theyd be at home with their wives, catching up. I watched them go. Then I turned and looked at Eustis. Tolliver wanted his death. I wanted something less. The jury—what did they want? As for myself, I knew I had done my best, sonata-form closing argument and all. Whether it had taken effect was another matter. After all, there are those to whom even the molto adagio from the *Heiliger Dankgesang:*

would be no more than noise; theyd squirm to hear it.

9. Turnkey

I wasnt there for the verdict and here is why. Soon as Nowell got launched into the wind-up of his closing speech to the jury, the sheriff went up to the bench and spoke to the judge. Judge nodded, still watching Nowell, and the sheriff turned and crooked a finger at me. I swear youd think he owned me body and soul, for a hundred and twenty a month plus food and lodging, such as it is. "Bring the prisoners up for sentencing," he says.—"Aint the judge going to knock off first for dinner?" "Just go get them," he says, acting weary, outdone. He's always saying to me, You talk too much. My trouble is I get lonesome in that jail.

Anyhow, I went and got them. Roebuck helped. We marched them in a group out the front door of the jail and across the back yard of the courthouse, up the stairs. Old man Lundy was in the lead because he was the top of the list. Thats the way it's always done: first the white folks, then the niggers, Truman and Mrs Roosevelt notwithstanding. When we came through the door into the courtroom, the first juror was filing out and Eustis and Nowell were sitting side by side at the table, one looking about as unconcerned as the other. That Nowell. Punch him with something sharp, and what would run out? Ice water. "Step up in front of the bench," I hollered at old man Lundy. He looked different without his bottom plate. His jaw didnt fit his face. Somehow all the pride had been drained out. Judge Holiman looked down at him, then struck a match, made a show of lighting his pipe, and flicked the match back over his shoulder toward the slopjar. All this time old Lundy was standing there, looking up at the judge while the judge looked down at him. The judge was ten years older, pretty near.

Finally, when he'd gotten his fill of looking, Judge cleared his throat with a sound somewhere between Hock and Hark: says, "You got anything to say before sentence is pronounced?" "Hey?" Lundy was partly deaf. He raised one hand and cupped it round his ear.—"You want to make a statement before being sentenced?" "What good would it do me if I did?" "No good, Sir, no good at all. It's merely formal, a thing I ask for the sake of the books." "Then I reckon not"— he mumbled; you had to be used to the sound of it before you could understand him "—except the whole by-God thing is a by-God shame and a outrage."

He was a caution: I swear. Four days ago, when I took him back to the jail after the jury brought in the verdict, he was laughing and wanting to caper, jerking his head around and up and down. "When do they turn me aloose?" he wanted to know. He had said all along theyd never convict him, and being half deaf he thought the circuit clerk had said Not Guilty.—"What the hell, old man," I said: "Theyre going to hang you." "Hey?" he says. "Whats that?" I had to shout it in his ear: "Theyre going to *hang* you!"

I'd forgotten the legislature adopted the electric chair a few years back. But, chair or rope, there wasnt any doubt about it now, standing in front of the bench and looking up to where the judge was fixing to read the sentence. "Then, Mr Lundy—" Judge Holiman leaned forward to get as close as possible, inching ever closer on his elbows and watching him over the ledge of the bench as he said it—"I sentence you to be committed to a felon's cell and there to be safely kept until the tenth day of October, in the year of our Lord nineteen hundred and forty-nine, at which time you shall suffer death by electrocution." He was clean to the ledge by now, peering almost straight down. "And may God Almighty have mercy on your soul." "I hope so," old man Lundy says, and turned and took a seat in front of the rail.

I watched Eustis all through this and he didnt so much as blink an eye, though I knew for sure he must be thinking how strong a chance there was that he'd be standing where old man Lundy stood, listening to those same words with the judge inching forward to watch him over the ledge, after the jury came back and said its say. Up till then I thought it was all an act put on for the jury's sake, something Nowell put him up to. But now the jury was gone and he still didnt care. I swear I almost had to respect him: unless of course it's like Nowell says, he's crazy.

That done, Judge Holiman sent one of the bailiffs out for sandwiches and coffee, then swung back around and went on sentencing. There were twenty-eight of them all told, four more white men and twenty-three niggers. It took him less than forty minutes. Then he lifted a sandwich out of the sack, opened the coffee carton, and rared back. He had sixty miles to ride to Lefever County and another court convening Monday morning. Whenever the jury was ready *he* was. He didnt intend to delay them.

Roebuck came along when I marched the prisoners back to jail. He'd been sidling up to one of the jury bailiffs, getting the lowdown. Theyd sent out for cokes and potato chips and were sitting around discussing the evidence. "How does it look?" I asked him, meantime keeping an eye on the prisoners. —"Didnt say." "How long you reckon theyll be?" "No telling," he says. That Roebuck.

So anyhow, in the light of what little he told me, when I got the white ones locked in their cells, the niggers in the bull pen, I went downstairs and told Martha to put dinner on the table. It was near one-thirty and I was truly ready. "Put it on yourself," she says, tight-mouthed. Refused to so much as turn her head in my direction. "It's in the oven, warming. Ive already ate." She wouldnt even look at me, backbone stiff as a ramrod. She was acting the way she always acts when something has her riled, which is most of the time. Thats because of the goiter. And like a fool I tried to explain: "Why, Martha, I was only doing my job." "Job," she says. She sniffed. "Call that a job? Spending the livelong morning standing around the courtroom so every snooping brazen hussy in Jordan County can see the big pearl-handled gun on your hip and think youre Somebody? You think I dont know them, them and their rumps and their tits?"—And mind you, the sheriff says *I* talk too much. It's like being lonesome, only more so. Coop him in here with Martha for a spell, then turn him loose and see if he dont talk a mile to the minute, just from pure relief at having a chance to get a word in edgeways.

The kitchen is up front, with a table by the window facing the courthouse. I took the plates out of the oven, set them on the table (greens, cornbread, potatoes boiled in their skins, and a slab of fatback: I'll say one thing for her—she can cook) and sat with my back to the window, eating. Theres no telling how long it was: I was mighty busy there for a while, filling my emptiness, for when a man my size gets hunger pangs it takes more than a sop to suage the growling. But something out of a clear blue sky caused me to turn half round in my chair and face the window, looking through it toward the back steps of the courthouse. It was like a hand had nudged me: 'Look at there!' And I looked and the steps were empty, not even a loafer cooling his scalp in the shade. All there was was a flock of sparrows hopping around, pecking among the peanut hulls in the dust, dodging amongst the empty coke and pepsi bottles. I was about to turn back to my plate when: whoosh! the sparrows swirled up like a whirlwind funnel had grabbed them. Flap: the door slammed open, and here came Eustis walking down the steps, Buck and the sheriff on each side and the crowd pressed close behind. I'd missed the verdict.

Here I'd been thinking the jury would be all day and maybe part of the night bringing in a verdict, but here theyd done it already, before I could finish my dinner and get back

to the courtroom to see them come in, see Eustis stand and
face them, and hear Ben Rand read it off. Whatever it was,
it was quick. I wondered whether that was bad or good. For
Eustis, I mean. The judge had given them five possible verdicts;
they could have brought in any one of the five.

1. *Guilty as charged in the indictment.* (The chair.)
2. *Guilty as charged but disagree on the sentence.* (Life.)
3. *Guilty as charged, recommend life.* (Life.)
4. *Guilty of manslaughter.* (One to twenty years.)
5. *Not guilty.* (Turn him loose.)

All I knew for sure, seeing him coming down the back steps
under guard, was it hadnt been Number 5. But I thought to
myself, It's the chair, as sure as shooting; it's going to be a
double-header, him and old man Lundy, like they said.

I made it to the door before they got there, had it open
waiting for them when they came up the steps. There wasnt
a thing in his face to give me a hint. When they got through
the door I swung it shut, full in the face of the crowd, and
dropped the bar. "What did they give him?" I asked Roebuck.
—"Come on, Roscoe," the sheriff says, standing at the staircase door. "Unlock this thing and lets get him back to the cell."
I unlocked it, swung it back, and they went up ahead: first
the sheriff, then Eustis, then Roebuck. I brought up the rear.
"What did they give him?" I asked Roebuck, toiling up the
steps behind him, panting onto the back of his neck. He made
like he didnt hear me, close as I was. That Roebuck.

By then we'd reached the top. We went on down the
corridor, Indian-file between the cells with prisoners hanging
onto the bars to watch. Old man Lundy was face down on
his cot. When we came past he raised his head, eyes like a
blind man's eyes, milky white as if the salt-water tears had
bleached them, and a face shaped like a wedge, narrowing
down to the sunk-in bottom jaw. I passed them, first Roebuck,
then Eustis, then the sheriff, and unlocked and swung back
the door of the cell. Eustis went in. I clicked it shut behind

him, turned the key, and shook the door to test the lock and hinges. He went straight to his cot and sat down sideways. I couldnt tell a thing from watching him. He sat the same as always, with his elbows on his knees. When I turned back, Roebuck and the sheriff were walking down the corridor toward the staircase. I hurried and caught up with them as they were starting down. "What was it?" I said. "Whats all the mystery? What did they give him?" "Life," Roebuck says, talking back over his shoulder, going down. "They gave him life."

That Nowell. That Parker Nowell. You cant beat him. He'll do it every time. All youve got to do is make it mean and messy enough: Parker Nowell will take your case. If there was enough of him to go around, the State could have saved the money it invested in that portable electric chair. Howsomever, there will always be the ones like old man Lundy, the simple ones. Got to brooding one night in a cafe down in Glenmora, tanked on beer because the marshal had caught his youngest boy breaking into the back of a grocery store and sent him up to Parchman for a spell (where God knows he belongs) until finally, drinking more 3.2 all the time and mumbling more about what-all he was going to do, he got himself worked into a regular lather and walked home, took a pistol out of a dresser drawer, and went back downtown and shot him, once standing and twice on the sidewalk, all the while with the marshal begging him, "Dont shoot again. God's sake, dont shoot again! I'm killed aready," and then got brought to Bristol, tried and sentenced, and now was waiting for the day when my cousin Luke, State High Executioner Luke Jeffcoat, would bring the truck and hook up the circuits and ride him off the earth in the old shocking chair. All he was really guilty of was too much beer and brooding, too much pride; the shooting itself was incidental, you might say. And Parker Nowell wouldnt take his case.

Then on the other hand, just look at Eustis. Got cunt-struck, tricked a girl off on an island, then played out on her and put her in the lake with a dozen yards of rusty wire and a pair of concrete slabs, then went home to his wife down at the south end of the county, and sat there till the Law came, ready to make a full signed sealed confession. And Parker Nowell took his case. Now all he had to do was bide his time at Parchman, following a plow or swinging a hoe, the same as he'd been doing since he was big enough to hang onto one and lift the other, until the day some governor celebrates his final week of office with a stack of pardons a yard high on his desk, and Eustis can come back home and do it all over again, for all *I* know, except you can bet your bottom dollar that the next time he wont be toting a Bible with his name writ big in the front for a dummy to read.

It dont seem fair. One gets the chair, another gets life—all because Nowell's wife ten years ago (I never saw her, understand, but Ive heard; they say she was a looker, one of those slicked-up society twats, as smooth as cream) picked up her skirts and skipped off with a so-called friend of his, soured him on the world and all it had to offer, and now he hits back this way. No wonder they say Justice is blind. No wonder they put a bandage round her eyes.

By now we were at the bottom. I went past them again in the lower hall and lifted the bar and opened the door. Russell Stevenson and Lonzo Mercer were standing on the stoop, about to knock; Steve's arm and fist were already in the air. Lonzo had his camera under his arm. He's a window dresser by trade, but he picks up an extra piece of change every once in a while taking pictures for Doc McVey because the real photographers, professionals, dont want to be bothered with coming to court to testify. People say things about him I wont repeat. So far as I'm concerned, thats *his* affair. It's his mouth. Far as I'm concerned, he can use it to haul coal in if he wants. Still, it does seem strange. It really does.

A good many people were standing around in the yard, the extra curious, lounging in front of the jail to breathe the air Eustis and old man Lundy had walked through. Captain

Billy Lillard was nearest the steps. He had on all his ribbons, all his medals, and was flicking his eyes around, not missing a trick. Steve and Lonzo stood aside for the sheriff and Roebuck coming out. When the sheriff saw Lonzo with the camera under his arm, he stopped and turned and spoke to me (he's had trouble with the *Clarion* from the start; theyve been riding him about slot machines and whiskey in the county, as if that wasnt every sheriff's right): "The reporter can talk to Eustis after a while, if he's willing. But keep that kodak out. I dont want my jail turned into a peep show for the benefit of every loafer with a nickel to buy a paper."

Lonzo's face fell a mile. I found out later he'd been expecting to shoot one through the bars from out in the corridor. *Fruits of Sin* he'd call it, something like that, thinking maybe the wireservice people would buy it. Steve's face didnt change at all. It couldnt very well, not for the worse. It sure couldnt get any longer than it had been ever since the day he got that letter from the editor of *Real Detective* saying they couldnt use his story on the Eustis case because theyd already bought one from "your fellow townsman Benjamin Peets." That was a month ago. At first he planned to wait till Eustis got the chair (he was sure he'd get the chair and that would make a better start and finish for the story) but he got jumpy, worried for fear somebody up the country would beat him to it. He had a premonition, as they say. So he went ahead and wrote it, sent it in. And sure enough, somebody had: old Benny Peets— "Your fellow townsman," the editor said, rubbing it in—and Steve's been soured on things in general ever since.

So anyhow I shut the door and went back to the kitchen to draw myself a cup of coffee. I figured I had earned it. Martha was standing at the sink, giving the dishes a second wash. She'd been that way about everything since her goiter started bulging; it made her think of germs and things like that. It made her jealous, too, thinking I didnt want her because of the swelling in her throat. I had to be careful not to let her catch me looking at it. I had to act like a criminal, shifty-eyed, whenever we were together with the light on, and in the dark I had to be careful not to touch it. She stood at the sink, backbone stiff as ever, and I came past her, took a cup down off the shelf and poured it full. "Are they still standing round out there?" she says. I stirred in milk and sugar, not saying anything. She could see them through the window if she'd look. "What makes folks so mean?" she says. Her backbone sort of wilted. She was getting over being mad.—"It's the way they are," I said, and took a sip.—"What do they want? his blood?" she says. "Is that what they want?" All she asked was questions. I didnt answer, and she went on. "They ought to thank him's what they ought to do, for taking that floozy out of circulation before she got around to one of them." And she went on with it until finally, sure enough, she was yelling about rumps and tits again. She's been excitable ever since the goiter first started to bulge.

Still, I dont know but what she's right—anyhow partly right. Maybe we ought to be thankful. Maybe the world is in a balance: so much sin and evil, so much good. Maybe we ought to be thankful to the ones that get in trouble. Maybe they draw the evil like a billy goat in a barnlot draws the fleas. Yet here they were wanting his blood, as if the fleas that were eating him werent enough.

That was as far as I got with that, because here came another knocking at the door. I figured it would be Steve, wanting to know was Eustis ready to talk. It was getting close to deadline. But when I got to the door and opened it, there was Eustis' wife (she had been crying) and Brother Jimson the preacher (the ugly face on him had caused me to waste a night back in early July, hunting through my WANTED circulars) and the daughter called Rosaleen (a right good-looking girl, in a countrified way) with her husband, one of old Uncle Denny Poteat's boys from down on the lake—I couldnt remember his first name. They stood on the steps, looking up, the three of them sort of huddled behind the preacher. The crowd was still pretty thick behind and beside them, nudging one another and talking out of the corners of their mouths, just barely loud enough for her to hear what they said. "It's the wife." "Not much to look at, is she?" "Thats a fact." "Looks like she could be drug through a keyhole without scraping." "Have to shake the sheets to find her, hey?" "Thats a fact." "I'd a run off on a island myself, I reckon."

The sheriff hadnt said what to do, so I took it on myself to let them in—the preacher too—and led the way upstairs, back to his cell. He was sitting where I'd left him, no different from always, sideways on the cot, with his elbows on his knees and his chin on the heels of his hands. We could see him from a distance, through the bars. This time, though, he turned and watched us coming. That was something he'd never done before. His glasses flashed once, turning, and he got up and came to the door, standing with his hands curled round the bars. I stepped aside and leaned against the wall at the end of the corridor, watching for hacksaws.

Brother Jimson was in front. The others followed his lead. "Brother Eustis," he says. Eustis put one hand through and they shook—that sudden, once-up, once-down handshake country people use, awkward at it because they do it so seldom. The wife was sort of hanging back. Eustis turned loose of the preacher's hand, took hold of the bars again. All this time he'd been watching his wife across the preacher's shoulder and she was sort of hanging back. Not that she was scared. She wasnt scared. It was more like she had gone back to her girlhood and was shy. Her eyes were red around the rims from crying and the daughter had one arm around her waist. They stood like that, in a group, sort of huddled. Then Uncle Denny's boy came around from behind. Eustis put out his hand again. They shook, in that same stiff-armed once-up once-down way, and Uncle Denny's boy stepped back. Thats the rule with these country people: first the men and then the women, no matter where. I know, for I'm a country boy myself. Or used to be, at any rate, before I married Martha and moved to town.

All this time Eustis never stopped watching his wife. She stood with her hands clasped waist-high over her stomach, eyes rimmed red. That was why theyd been so long getting back to the jail when the trial was over. Theyd been in the washroom at the courthouse, trying to comfort her after the verdict was read and Judge Holiman passed sentence. You cant tell about women: I swear you cant. Here he'd got the best they could hope for, life—had been saved from the chair, which four days ago everybody *knew* he'd get, Nowell or no Nowell—and she broke down and cried. What would she have done if he got the chair like old man Lundy? Sat there dry-eyed, maybe. You cant tell about women, no way in the world. It could be she just cried from pure relief, like sometimes a man wont start to tremble till whatever danger he's faced is over and past.

Now that the preacher and the son-in-law were out of the way, she went up to the cell door where he was standing, watching her and holding onto the bars. She reached out and covered one of his hands with both of hers, then bent and kissed the back of the other hand. The knuckles were white, he was gripping the bar so hard. She made a little choky sound between kisses, sort of moaning, and he stood looking down at the back of her head, at the knot of hair screwed tight and hard as a golfball. Theyd been married thirty years yet I could see she'd never done a thing like this before. I turned my head—it didnt seem right to watch; it seemed somehow sort of unreligious. But just as I did, I caught a glimpse of his glasses misting over. It takes real trouble, something worse than a goiter anyhow, to make people know how much they mean to each other.

The others looked away too, the preacher and daughter and son-in-law. We wouldnt even look at each other while this was going on. Finally, though, the daughter got her quieted. "Now, ma," she says: "Now, ma," over and over again: "You promised you wouldnt. You promised." It didnt take long. Pretty soon they were standing there and talking. Except for the bars, it was like he'd been under the knife and this was afterwards, with the family gathered in the hospital room where he'd come back to them, bleached and pale but out of danger. They talked about home, what-all was happening. Luty Pearl was fine, they said—that was the youngest daughter, the natural. So was Myrtle. Rosaleen and Cary (—that was his name, Cary: one of Uncle Denny Poteat's boys; I hadnt been able to call his name till then) were going to move in with the wife and the girls. Theyd help to keep the place up, make the crop. "So dont you fret," they told him; theyd be waiting when he got out. Some wait, I thought. Still, you cant tell. Mississippi has had her share of peculiar governors, and there would be more to come.

When they began to run out of words about home, they shifted to the weather. This was one wet year, the wettest on record maybe, barring floods. They talked about that for a while, Eustis putting in a word every now and again. It was getting on for train-time; they began to sneak sidelong glances at the preacher. So finally he went closer to the cell door. "Brothers and sisters," he says. "It's time for prayer." His voice boomed out. They all knelt down—Eustis inside the cell, up close to the door, the rest of us out in the corridor (I knelt too, finally; it didnt seem right not to)—and Brother Jimson prayed out loud and strong. All down the line, and in the bull pen too, prisoners came to the bars and watched. Except old man Lundy: he was face-down on his cot, asleep I think, though I couldnt say for sure. Brother Jimson mentioned paths of righteousness, the tempered wind for the shorn lamb, the ninety-nine and the one, and so on and so on. It was a good strong prison prayer—though, truth to tell, I thought it ran a trifle long.

Soon after that I took them back downstairs and stood in the doorway watching them follow the path that led around the courthouse, past the monument, toward the depot where theyd catch the train for home. They went two by two, the preacher and the Poteat boy in front. The Confederate, high on his pillar, watched them too. And he wasnt all. Captain

Billy Lillard and a sprinkling of others more or less like him were still there. Maybe theyd leave now. Maybe. But not Captain Billy: he'd be here till nightfall most likely, unless something else came up. My daddy was one of the boys of '98: Company A, First Mississippi. They spent the war in Florida, waiting on a boat to take them where the insurrectos were. He told me about old Billy Lillard once. They started calling him Captain as a joke, and it stuck and he was honored. There are young folks nowadays really think he was a captain in that war, but I can remember my daddy saying in confidence that old Billy never so much as got off KP. He couldnt learn the drill.

It wasnt until I turned from closing the door that I remembered Eustis hadnt eaten since this morning. I'd been so busy going in and out and up and down and around, I hadnt had time to think. So I went back to the kitchen and looked in the oven. The fatback was all gone but there was plenty of greens and cornbread and potatoes left. I peeped through the crack of the bedroom door and Martha was taking her nap, sleeping as usual with a face-towel over her throat so I wouldnt look at her goiter unawares. Moving careful not to wake her, half on tiptoes, I loaded a plate and poured a glass of buttermilk from the crock, then started up the stairs. I'd been up and down them so often now, I was beginning to feel like an ant trapped on a corkscrew.

He wasnt sitting this time. He was standing with his hands on the bars, watching me come down the corridor toward him. "Evening," he says, of his own free will and accord— the first time I ever knew him to speak without being spoken to. I usually had to speak twice before he would so much as turn his head. I unlocked the door to give him the plate without spilling the food. Then I locked it again and gave it a shake to test it. While he sat on the cot, wolfing the greens and taking fast deep sucks of buttermilk that gave him a white mustache on his upper lip, I stood and watched. He wasnt long. When he had finished he wiped at the mustache with the back of his

hand and passed me the plate tipped sideways through the bars
and then the glass. I was turning to go, when: "Er . . ." I heard
him say, clearing his throat and saying Ah, both at once. I
stopped. "Whats it like up there?" he says, holding onto the
bars.

He meant Parchman, the penitentiary. They always ask—
except of course the two-time losers; they dont need to ask.
And I always tell them. I figure it's better for them, knowing
what to expect. I stood holding the empty plate and glass. The
others had come to the bars to listen, all but old man Lundy
who was face-down on the cot, the same as before, asleep or
not. Nothing about Parchman applied to him. *He* didnt care.

"I'll tell you true," I said. "It aint so bad, considering." Then
I told him. "They dont have cells like this, for one thing. No
walls, no bob wire. Nothing like that. They have camps: two
for whites and eight or nine for the niggers. You sleep in a
big long room like a barracks and you have your own buddies
for card games, such as that. Once you begin to sort of get
used to it, you might even like it. Lots of them do. Theyve
had people to hang back when their time was up.

"It's a farm," I told him, "a plantation like back in Slavery
days—eighteen thousand acres, mostly cotton. They give you
your own mule and everything. You go out in the morning, eat
in the field, and come back in at sundown. Thats during the
season. Off-season, Sundays, rainy days, you sit around the
bunk house, reading, talking. It aint bad. Stay in line, youll
be all right. Otherwise the sergeant's got a strap—Black Annie,
the niggers call it. It's better than solitary. (They dont have
solitary like most prisons. Solitary's inhuman, the warden says.)
And the first Sunday in every month is visiting day. Thats
when the women come."

"Women?" he says. You should have seen his face. Down
the line, the other prisoners were hugging the bars and listening, heads turned sideways.

"Women," I said, and I explained it to him. "In the olden
days, before automobiles, they came on a train called the Mid-

night Special. It dont run any more; they come by car. But the convicts still have a song they sing about it. All that morning youll see them in the bunk house, taking showers, patting on Aqua Velva, chewing Sen-Sen, and the niggers off in the other camps will be singing:

> *Oo-woo! Oo-wee!* (going like a train whistle)
> *I'm bound to be satisfied, I'm bound to be free:*
> *Let the Midnight Special shine its light on me!*

And if youve walked the chalk and the sergeant likes you, he'll turn his head in the other direction while you and your visitor wander off a ways . . ."

"How long will it be?" he says, breaking in.—"Will what be?" I said, thinking maybe he meant how long would he be up there.—"Before I leave this place?" he says. I swear I believe to my soul he was anxious to get started. The others were leaning against the bars, white folks down at this end, niggers up in the bull pen. So I told him about that too.

"The long-chain man will be here a week from Monday," I said. He just stood there, looking blank. So I explained. "It's a name from the olden days, like the Midnight Special, when everything went by rail. The traveling sergeant took prisoners up to Parchman on the coaches—ran a long chain down the aisle, with shackles for their ankles. Thats where he got the name. Nowdays he comes in a bus, painted yellow like a school-bus, with a lock on the door and cage wire on the windows, but they still call him the long-chain man the same as always. He's coming a week from Monday and he'll park outside the door. When he calls your name off the list, youll step inside."

I left him then, still standing at the bars. As I came down the corridor, the others were turning back to their cots, the ones that had been tried and sentenced and the ones awaiting trial next term, in March six months from now. I went down the stairs again, winding round and round the center pole—four times up, four times down, within the past two hours, sixteen times around that pole; I swear my feet were killing me—and just as I got to the bottom, heading for the kitchen with the empty plate and glass, there came another tapping at the door. Theres never any rest for the weary on such a job as this. I said to myself it must be Steve, finally come for the interview. But then, coming back from the kitchen, I remembered it was past his deadline. This couldn't be Steve—he must have let the interview go till tomorrow, intending to use it for what he calls a follow-up.

So anyhow I reached for the bar and the rapping came again, right in my face. Hold your horses, I thought: Just hold your horses, and opened the door and who should I see standing on the first step off the stoop? Miz Pitts—mustache and all. She had something in her hands but the sun was in my eyes. A little ways behind her, clear of the steps, the dummy stood with his bushy hair and little round ears that hugged in close to his head, as if they knew themselves how useless they were, and a croaker sack bulging one shoulder. Theyd come to town with vegetables out of the garden. Nobody else was in sight, not a living soul. Even Captain Billy Lillard had given it up.

She didnt say 'How is he?' or anything such as that. "Here," she says, shoving forward with both hands, and I looked down and it was the same as before: a round tin plate with a freshly laundered square of cloth on top, sugar-sack material bleached white, the creases still sharp where she'd ironed it on the island.—"I'll give it to him," I said, and took it from her. It was a sweet potato pie, and that made five: one every other Saturday since he came. Dummy scowled. He didnt like it. Sunlight was on his cheeks like the fuzz on peaches. They turned, one after another, and walked away in single file, following the path on past the monument toward town, going to peddle the vegetables, swap them for groceries and row back home to the island.

I barred the door and went back to the kitchen with the pie. Martha was snoring in the bedroom, asleep with the towel across her throat. While I was cutting myself a wedge of pie—

testing for files and hacksaws—I wondered: What is it about him that draws the women, mustached or no? I couldn't understand it. But no matter: No matter, I thought; all that will be far behind him where he's going, and anyhow what does *he* care? All he's got to do now is sit up there in that nice cool cell with me to fetch and carry while he waits for the long-chain man.

THE CIVIL WAR: A NARRATIVE

Volume I: Fort Sumter to Perryville
Volume II: Fredericksburg to Meridian
Volume III: Red River to Appomattox

"Here, for a certainty, is one of the great historical narratives of our century, a unique and brilliant achievement, one that must be firmly placed in the ranks of the masters...a stirring and stupendous synthesis of history."

—Chicago Daily News

"This, then, is narrative history—a kind of history that goes back to an older literary tradition.... [It] is one of the historical and literary achievements of our time."

—Washington Post Book World

Civil War History
Volume I: 0-394-74623-6/$24.00
Volume II: 0-394-74621-X/$24.00
Volume III: 0-394-74622-8/$24.00
3-volume boxed set: 0-394-74913-8/$72.00

JORDAN COUNTY

A fictional chronicle of seven generations in Jordan County, Mississippi, a place where the traumas of slavery, war, and Reconstruction are as tangible as geological formations.

"Mr. Foote's writing is marvelously exact and positive. His attitude toward his people is respectful and human, as though he had thought about them a great deal and knew too much about them to take them for granted."

—The New Yorker

Fiction/0-679-73616-6/$10.00

LOVE IN A DRY SEASON

Two wealthy Depression-era Mississippi families are joined by a ruthless fortune hunter from the North, forming an erotic and economic triangle that renders the clash between North and South with a violence all the more shocking for its intimacy.

"A fascinating drama...the atmosphere is superbly managed; and on every score, this is a first-rate job of story-telling."
—*Philadelphia Inquirer*

Fiction/0-679-73618-2/$10.00

SEPTEMBER SEPTEMBER

In September 1957 the South is mesmerized by the racial confrontation on the steps of the University of Arkansas. So mesmerized that the three white protagonists of this novel believe that no one will notice the kidnapping of a small black boy—whose grandfather happens to be one of the wealthiest entrepreneurs in Memphis.

Fiction/0-679-73543-7/$9.00

SHILOH

A fictional re-creation of the battle of Shiloh in April 1862 conveys both the bloody choreography of two armies and the movements of the combatants' hearts and minds.

"Imaginative, powerful, filled with precise visual details...a brilliant book."
—*The New York Times*

Fiction/0-679-73542-9/$10.00